Goddess of Nazareth

GODDESS OF NAZARETH

The intimate conflicts of Israel's
most famous couple—*in their own words*

Starke & Hartmann, Inc

Goddess of Nazareth
© 2022 by Martin Zender

Published by Starke & Hartmann
P.O. Box 6473
Canton, OH 44706
www.starkehartmann.com
330-454-1061

Printed in the United States of America

All rights reserved. No part of this publication may be reproduced, stored in a retrieval system, or transmitted in any form by any means, electronic, mechanical, photocopy, recording, or otherwise, without prior permission of the author, except as provided by USA copyright law.

Publisher's Cataloging-In-Publication Data
(Prepared by The Donohue Group, Inc.)

Names: Zender, Martin, author.
Title: Goddess of Nazareth : the intimate conflicts of Israel's most famous couple -- in their own words / [Martin Zender].
Description: Canton, OH : Starke & Hartmann, Inc., [2021]
Identifiers: ISBN 9781956293043 (paperback) | ISBN 9781956293050 (digital)
Subjects: LCSH: Mary, Blessed Virgin, Saint--Marriage--Fiction. | Joseph, Saint--Marriage--Fiction. | Marital conflict--Fiction. | Man-woman relationships--Fiction. | Christian life--21st century--Fiction. | LCGFT: Christian fiction.
Classification: LCC PS3626.E444 G64 2021 (print) | LCC PS3626.E444 (ebook) | DDC 813/.6--dc23

BOOK ONE

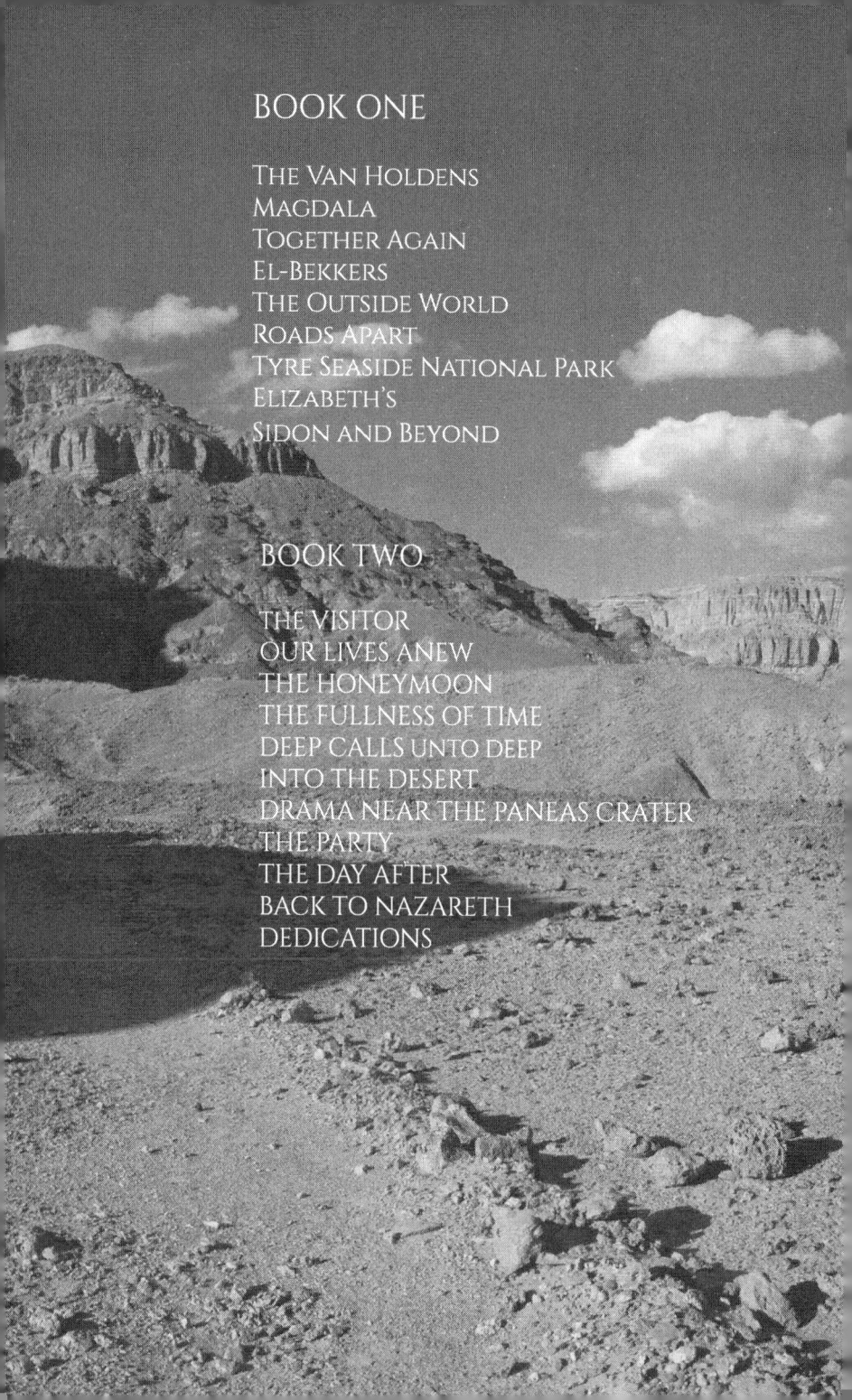

The Van Holdens
Magdala
Together Again
El-Bekkers
The Outside World
Roads Apart
Tyre Seaside National Park
Elizabeth's
Sidon and Beyond

BOOK TWO

The Visitor
Our Lives Anew
The Honeymoon
The Fullness of Time
Deep Calls unto Deep
Into the Desert
Drama near the Paneas Crater
The Party
The Day After
Back to Nazareth
Dedications

"Therefore a man shall forsake his father and his mother; he will cling to his wife and both of them shall be one flesh."

—Genesis 2:24

BOOK 1

CHAPTER 1

THE VAN HOLDENS

This is our first book, and sales are proving that reviewers don't know everything—hallelujah. Still, it is humbling to read in published periodicals that one's carefully-selected words pretty much roll downhill and crack apart like rotten coconuts. I am "melodramatic" (*Bethel Gazette*), and the record of my two fainting spells and "hormonal fits" (*Mid-East Contemporary Reader*) give my writing "an undesirable neurasthenic touch" (*Bethel Gazette*). Besides this, I "move in and out of diction" that makes me sound like I "jumped out of a Tiberian romance novel" (*Yarmuk Book Reviews*). But I rejoice today, because my voice "does become more natural in Book Two" (*Yarmuk Book Reviews*).

If you think that's bad, feel sorry for my husband: "The story on the whole lacks human pathos, especially from Joseph. He refers to other people as stupid way too often ('stupid as bath tile' in one place). And even more disturbing, Mary's parents are frequently described as foolish and unenlightened. These points in the story reflect especially badly upon Joseph. And where such compassion lacks with human beings, it is lavished upon dogs and cats!" (Jer ben Edrie, *Sidon Times*).

And this awful surprise—my husband possesses the romantic intuition of granite: "When Mary tells him that she is pregnant by an act of God, he doesn't believe her. The logical conclusion is that he suspects her of unfaithfulness. It is his reason for leaving Nazareth and running (literally running) to Antioch. For all the passion Joseph feels toward Mary, his reaction is too quickly diffused. For all his hopes and fantasies of seeing Mary in the fabled leather *gara*, he should be just that tormented by the visions of Mary giving up this pleasure to another man. Jealousy ought to at least equal the pitch of the man's passion and love. Any normal human being would be tormented and crushed by the perceived betrayal" (*Sidon Times*).

It drives me to hormonal fits that my husband has so carelessly forgotten to portray himself as a normal human being.

But now, the sin of sins: "Does Gabriel really say the word 'singular?' This sort of Phrygian rhythm plays well for Rabbi Shaufun in chapter twelve because he is an obvious caricature, but celestial magistrates must distinguish themselves in substantial ways" (*Gaza Sun Weekly*).

It's a shame that Gabriel, the Phrygian plagiarist, was not apprised beforehand concerning which words would disservice him. As for Shaufun, anyone wishing to experience an "obvious caricature" may do so at 33 Heleni Lane, Caesarea, ISR 09.

My husband and I intended to write a manual for married people, and have. That you are one of many, many people reading it (in this, its third printing) tells us that we have not labored in vain. This book will help men and women deal with their intimate conflicts, conflicts that we believe to be universal. The "problem" is that we have chosen to tell our life story in the process, which we apparently stink at—God be praised. And so the deeper, unintended purpose of this book—the higher purpose—may be to immediately accomplish what I had always thought my diaries would accomplish in the end. If this is so, then I truly am the handmaiden of the Lord. And Joseph is the butler.

If you want well-rounded characters, I suggest you read something out of the Yehiam Yad series.

I rumbled down the dusty hill that morning, something I never did. I'd heard of rumbling, yes, but it was something reserved for earthquakes and volcanoes, not people. It involved cataclysms of earth. Large mammals rumbled also, I suppose, in their stampedes (a rumbling herd of elephants, for instance), but not delicate women carrying jugs of water atop their heads.

Every day before this I trudged up the hill outside Nazareth, then meandered to the well, then trundled back down. Trudging, meandering, trundling—these I did. So why, suddenly, was I rumbling? Why did my legs now swing free down the hill, with the other girls laughing and trundling through my dust? Where did the strength come from? The imperviousness to danger? I have often marveled, when thinking back to that morning, at how the largest and most consequential things in life begin so inconspicuously. And yet, when one looks back, one does see the difference.

"It's about time," Mother scolded when I got back to the house. "Did you fall in?"

I set the jug down just inside our doorjamb, bending with my knees and not with my back. I strove for such ladylike mechanics that anyone watching would have guessed the jug to be empty. Yet some of the water sloshed and beaded on the packed dirt floor of our entranceway.

I stood tall and smiled. "It has a lot to do with the weight of the water, Mother, and the fact that it's inside the jug."

I wasn't trying to be smart; this is just the way my mother and I joked with one another.

My mother, whose name is Marney, threw back her long, graying hair and assumed the stance of an oriental fighting master. "You're not getting Roman with me, are you?"

I knew she was only being funny, so I said, "No. But I do find myself becoming more straightforward and logical with age. And Aunt Mimi tells me I'm developing Father's sense of humor."

Mother popped out of her stance. "Ho! You must be needing an aspirin, then."

The hot sun charged through our doorway. A particular beam broke past our wood and limestone defenses, striking a small potted cactus next to our newspaper rack. I noticed how beautiful the beam was. The beam reminded me again of my father's sense of humor, and this brought to mind an anecdote.

"Do you remember what Father told his supervisor when he delivered the Binge district for the first time in his life?"

Mother snorted—a bad habit of hers. "Why bring *that* up?" she said. "Thank God for the Slag Brothers, is all I can say. You want to hear something? Ben stopped cursing the day he quit the postal service and started hanging doors for Dathan and Dan. It's a good thing your Joseph doesn't work for the Evil Institution."

"Oh, Father never cursed too badly I suppose."

"Missy." This was my mother's nickname for me. Her hands now rested where her hips should have been, and she forced sweet motherhood to her face. "What does any of this have to do with your father's sense of humor?"

"Remember that one terrible supervisor? Didn't Daddy call him 'the bug,' or something?"

Mother snorted again, and nearly drew in a fly. "May God have mercy upon The Roach!"

"Daddy was carrying the Binge district for the first time in his life," I continued, "and when he arrived back to the office three hours late, The Roach asked him why he had taken so long. Remember? And Daddy said…" (I craned back my neck, forced down my brows, and lowered my voice to imitate Father's), "'I would not have been so late, sir, except that I kept having to stop to deliver the mail.'"

Mother began to laugh. She attempted to fashion a sentence beginning with, "And that dear man will be—" but she never could finish that sentence, because of her laughter.

All I could do was stand and watch. Mother tried to finish her sentence three or four times. Instead, she strained out her wheezing hilarity in such progressively tighter wheezes that it seemed she would choke. Anyone but Father and me would have called a doctor. Mother always did recover from these outbursts, but now, as always, her opening stabs at recovery only fueled new explosions of whatever was ailing her. The tears now ran down her cheeks and into her mouth, which looked like the entrance to a wine cave, if wine caves should ever come to be ringed by teeth and dissected by a uvula.

The last time she'd enjoyed an outburst like this, the neighbor man had told her that he thought the dog next door wanted to buy her property. When Mother had asked why he thought so, the man said, "Because he just left a very large deposit."

I thought to otherwise occupy myself—even starting toward the kitchen—when Mother waved a hand as if to say, *No, wait. Please. I'm better now.* But she was not better, and nowhere near it. Her hands were on top of her knees now, and she was sobbing. I knew what Mother was going to say, anyway. She was going to say, *And that dear man will be home in fifteen minutes, so would you please go and ready the pitas?*

So I just went and readied the pitas.

"Forgive me, Mary, but I've never heard of writing that just kicks down the stall door and runs for Jericho. No fancy introductions, you say?"

This was my father. I was hauling the burned pita shells to the table as he said this, at the same time admiring the great man's eyes. So deep and blue were they, but also somehow small atop his gigantic mustache and whiskerless chin. The eyes could be fiery and politely demanding, as they were now, and yet still scan the table for goat's milk.

"It's a new kind of book, Daddy," I said. "A diary, actually. Real-life things. No fancy scrollwork like they panned *The Porcus of Dan* for; it's just the facts."

"Ah," said Father. "None of the pseudo-sacred literary shams we're used to reading."

"Exactly."

He smiled. "So now, I am curious."

"Take these burned pitas," I said. "I somehow manage to burn them every afternoon. Correct?"

"Not at all," Father protested. "Last Wednesday, for instance."

"Your father is right," said Mother. "No fires *that* day."

I smiled politely. I was not sensitive about my cooking

because it was not something I took pride in or tried to be good at. "I appreciate that," I said. "But the point is that these things ought to be recorded. For posterity. When they dig up Egypt some day, they'll find the rotting pharaohs, and the boats—"

"Yes!" Father said. "The boats that were supposed to have taken 'the great kings' across 'the almighty Nile' toward 'the eternal sun.' What camel dung!"

"You and I know that, Daddy. But the world won't know until they dig it up. Everybody will laugh—then. Egyptian religion will finally get its due. Bad for them, good for the world."

Mother certainly couldn't leave that alone. "Either *that*," she interjected—already beginning to shake at the mere contemplation of what she would say—"or people will be so hypnotized by the pyramids that 'mystery merchants' will package the whole rotting commodity in wicker baskets and sell it to the masses on amulets and pottery shards as some 'better way!'"

She had barely ejected the sentence before convulsing into another fit of hysteria. In fact, Mother was so pleased with her ridiculous idea—that human pride could somehow swell rather than bow with the finding of the pharaohs—that she expelled a pepper ring.

I thought that Father would restore us to order, and he did. He lowered his milk glass to the table, licked his mustache, and appeared pensive. "Let me see if I follow you, Mary. You believe that writing down these, er, common things…will someday…keep the world humble?"

I really thought so. "It may seem like a strange leap to you now, but think about it. The prophets have been silent for such a long time. I think it's the nothing before the something that's about to shake the world, maybe even the universe. I just feel it. And I feel that it revolves around us."

I was not exaggerating or trying to sound large. Ever since I was a child, I had a sense of destiny. It would come at different times, always unannounced. I would be sitting in my bed, or reading a book, or feeding the chickens, and it would come—a euphoric rush of purpose. You think it's boastful, what I've written. I cringe myself, reading it. But it wasn't boastful, just a fact. You had to know our family. It wasn't this way with me only, or my parents, but with all the Van Holdens, including my uncles, aunts, and cousins. We had a history.

"Funny you should mention it," Father said. "I've been feeling the very same thing."

Mother also agreed that something big seemed primed to occur. "I could have sworn I was being watched yesterday," she said, retrieving the pepper ring and eating it in one gulp.

I wanted to move the subject away from our destiny and back to my writing project, so I said, "These pitas will be long gone by the time they dig *us* up."

"Oh, I'm not so sure of *that*," Father said, giving the platter a sideways glance.

I ignored Father's ill-timed joke and continued with my point. "How else will people know how we lived? How will they know about my cooking? About our foot races and family jokes? They'll think that the niche where our card table sits was some kind of sacrificing place. No one will think that we played *wadi-tot** at the central crisis of the universe."

I was doing it again, and I could have hated myself. For as many times as I strove for humility, I mounted my horse of oratory and betrayed all things meek. Sometimes it seemed that even my explanations of humility would trigger torrents of wanting to sound smart. Where this hypocrisy

---
* A popular card game. Literally, *small dry river.*

came from, I didn't know. But once it started, it was hard to stop.

The table quieted now as my family considered this latest outburst. It took but a moment.

"They'll have sacred writings," Father reasoned. "God will preserve what is true through a modern-day prophet."

I agreed. "But the facts will be amended," I said. "People will put in what they want. They'll see and hear things that weren't there. Who's content with an invisible God these days? It will only get worse. People will glorify the seen. When we were quiet, there will be music. Where we sang, quiet will come. They'll worship all the wrong things. They'll put light for darkness, darkness for light. They'll build churches in our name—"

"Stop right there, please," Father mercifully interrupted. "They may very well build churches to honor us, Child. It has happened before; I'm thinking of Abraham, and our forefather Jacob. But there will always be indiscreet young ladies who will giggle and paint their fingernails in such sanctuaries. They'll ruin everything, believe me. I've seen it in Bethel. No matter what holy thing one tries to preserve today, the young people squash it. This is good and bad. The soul-worship is ruined, yes, but also the true."

"He's right," Mother said. "Elizabeth tells of a synagogue in Samaria where half-naked *mecholah naar*† play timbrels and conga drums—on the altars. I kid you not. It's come to that today. They're doing that now. It crazes me."

"Someday, even—ziggophones in the choir pit!" Father joked.

"Ben, don't exaggerate. What we're saying, Missy, is that God will not allow any of us to become *gaba orah*."‡

---

† Hebrew. Literally, *chorus boys*.

‡ Literally, *exalted light*. Idiomatically, *superstars*.

I listened patiently, but a torrent of wanting to be right pushed me past the brink of propriety. "You just don't understand," I said. "You don't understand how people are. Will you listen? The day will come—I'm not sure how or why—but the day will come when people will pay money just to touch the ground where this old oaken table once stood."

Spirituality and family destiny were one thing, but this—this was too much even for Father. In a burst of righteous indignation, he reached out a hand to cuff my head. (He would never have slapped me, ever.) With a corresponding burst of maternal strength, Mother caught Father's coming arm and pushed it away hard, sending the head of our home backward in his chair, onto the floor. This was not the first time such a thing had happened, but how could one ever get used to seeing one's Father's sandals thrust up above the table that way? I was afraid that, this time, it was all my fault.

A moment of meditative silence followed, during which we could hear Father quietly chewing. Mother stared at the far wall, chewing as well, and breathing heavily through her nose. We heard father clearing his throat, then humming a short song. He asked for a napkin, which I placed into his upstretched hand. He would not be denied, ever, of his pride.

Slowly and deliberately—as though he'd planned the whole thing—Father righted himself. He dusted his mustache with the napkin, then once again scanned the table for goat's milk. An awkward minute ensued at our home. By the commencement of the minute following, each of us was either fondling or trying to chew something made of wheat paste. Supposing that this would erase the scene from memory, we, each of us, erred grievously. I wanted to get away, though Father was the first to cough.

"I'm very tired," he said, "and I'm getting a cough. But I do thank you, Marney and Mary, for lunch. I need a nap.

Will you all excuse me? I've a door this afternoon over in Brexhall."

Neither Mother nor I said anything. As for me, I was ashamed of myself. But if this was truly so, why did I suddenly feel so happy? It was as if I could sense by the way Father's sandals flapped as he walked from the table that the greatest Van Holden in all Israel was sorry about what had happened at the table, and that he had come to see the wisdom of my writing.

"Hum-diddle-dee-ding, the prophets sing. Hum-diddle-dee-do, the kings all stew."

I was singing my favorite ditty later that evening, in darkness. I'm skipping ahead to evening for time's sake because nothing much happened between lunch and bedtime except that Mother and I killed nearly a hundred flies with Father's papyrus rolls. We swept the little black carcasses into the yard with our brooms, ate quail and bread for supper, then shared sections of *The Qumran News*.

I walked down the hallway in darkness toward the family bathroom. I had already put out the lamp in the kitchen. It was ten in the evening, the twenty-fifth of Tammuz. Why I did not carry the lamp with me into the bathroom that night, as I always did, I didn't know. But I was soon to find out.

Mother and Father both retired around nine. Because they were in their fifties and never drank coffee past two in the afternoon, as I did, they retired an hour before me.

I walked quickly past their bedroom, aware of the dry ends of my hair trailing behind me in a self-made breezelet. The hallway was so quiet that I could hear myself walk. Everything was soundless except for the tiny crunch of my walk and my little song, which I was now humming.

I had to reach to feel the jambs at the entrance to the bathroom. That's when I heard the voice.

"Come in now, but please don't say anything."

I reached down and pulled off my right sandal, holding it as a weapon. I was afraid to run. There was no way I was going to turn my back. There was someone in my bathroom, a man, and I couldn't see him. I knew it wasn't my father because it was not his voice. So I said, "Who are you? I have a sandal and I'll kill you. I'll kill you with it, I swear." I was certain that if I ran I would die, that the strange man in the bathroom would run after me and push a knife into my back and leave me to die.

"You'll kill me with a sandal? I'll have to think about that one," the voice said. "It's *singular*."

It was strange how much calmer I became when the voice said this. The voice didn't sound at all threatening. "Who are you?" I asked again. "What do you want?"

The voice cleared its throat. "I'm the angel Gabriel," it said, "and I want to talk to you. Now please, put your sandal back on and come into the bathroom. The last thing I would ever do is hurt you."

The angel Gabriel. It couldn't be. It was impossible. Gabriel was the most important celestial messenger in Israel. It was Gabriel who had visited our great prophet Daniel to grant him understanding of his vision in the days of Belshazzar. Gabriel? In these modern days? It simply could not be. And yet something else in me said, *Why couldn't it be Gabriel?* This was the Van Holden in me.

"Come in here, and I'll assure you that it is me," he said.

He was reading my thoughts. Only an emissary from God could do that. I was still afraid, but I felt myself moving slowly toward the edge of belief. "I need a light," I said. "I want to see you."

"There is a lamp here in the wall," said the voice. "Come and light it."

"I have no matches."

I heard a fumbling of clothing, then something falling to the ground. There was the slightest muffle of complaint, then more fumbling. Suddenly, a match flared in the darkness. A hand and an arm, these only, became a dull orange entity floating through blackness toward the lamp. The wick got touched then and the room, too soon, began glowing. I stared at the lamp, afraid to turn toward what it illuminated. Fighting the urge to scream, I moved my eyes slowly toward the entity.

"Do I look like someone you know?" he asked.

The odd thing was, he did. He looked like our milkman, Ak Ein Karem. And yet it wasn't Ak. "You look like Ak Ein Karem," I said. "It's remarkable."

"It isn't *so* remarkable. I can look like anyone. I take that back. I can look like anyone in the context of The Plan. Believe me, Mary, I would have done this differently."

I walked into the bathroom, unafraid. "You know my name."

"We all do."

"Who? Who knows my name?"

"All of us in this house. You sensed our arrival earlier."

I quickly thought back through the day. "After lunch?"

"Yes."

"I thought I was just happy that my father felt bad about trying to cuff me. I thought he had finally understood my writing."

"No, I'm afraid not. Your father still has no clue about that. That was us filing into the living room."

"How many are you?"

"We are five hundred thousand tonight."

"I didn't hear anything."

"I will ask you a question, Mary, and you will answer with your instincts. If five hundred thousand celestial beings proceed abreast simultaneously through a single wall, even with two people asleep in the next room and one singing in the hallway, will the two people wake up or the third suspend even a snippet of her song?"

I looked around the dimly-lit room, seeing nothing but feeling everything. "No," I answered.

Gabriel didn't do anything then, except to look down at his fingernails.

I said, "They are here now?"

"Oh, yes. Many more outside the house. All the heads of kingdoms. This is a big event, Mary. Very big. You have no idea how big. In fact, you will not in your lifetime comprehend even the fringes of it. Some of these sovereignties have waited over thirty thousand years for this night. Massa, for instance."

"Massa? Who is Massa?"

"He's the one your mother felt watching her. He was watching her, all right. He stood between her and the kitchen window yesterday while you were at the well. He stood *this close* to her and stared into her eyes."

"Why?"

"Massa has never recovered from the creation of humanity. The race bewitches him, more so than the others even."

"Massa scares me. Is he here now?"

"No. His is the only realm not represented. His presence was forbidden."

"Thank God. Please, let's stop talking about him." I shook an involuntary chill off my neck. I felt glad now that Gabriel was with me, and that he was friendly.

I cannot explain how a person can suddenly ignore the gaze of half a million celestial sovereignties and pipe up with a question, except that curiosity conquers all. And so the question came, "Why are you here? Why are you here to see *me?*"

Gabriel took a deep breath. It seemed an awkward thing for him, because the air came in little spurts. I stared at him and thought of asking, *What's wrong?* Thank God I did not ask. Gabriel stiffened. Everything in the room became different then. The casual mood of the last minute's conversation was gone. Something serious and heavy had come. I could not look at Gabriel's eyes anymore. I stared down at his feet; he was barefoot. A dog barked somewhere outside, from far away. Somewhere in another world, my parents breathed. Maybe a minute passed. A tear began rolling down my cheek. Then another.

"You have found favor with God," Gabriel began. "You are favored, Mary. You cannot know how much. But this I tell you: You shall be conceiving and be pregnant and be bringing forth a Son. And you shall be calling His name Jesus. He shall be great, and Son of the Most High shall He be called. And the Lord God shall be giving Him the throne of David, His father, and He shall reign over the house of Jacob for the eons. And of His Kingdom there shall be no consummation. I say to you, the Lord is with you. You cannot know. You cannot know, dear Mary—my child—how blessed you are among women."

I could not move. The tears were now streaming down my face onto the floor. I could not even move my hands to my eyes, to help myself. Then I began sobbing. My shoulders thrust up and down in heaves. I could not stop it. It hurt. I could not help myself.

"You are espoused to a man."

He allowed me to compose myself. Then, finally, "Yes, Lord," I stammered. "But…we haven't…"

"I know that. And you won't. There will be no sexual relationship. Not yet."

"But…"

"That is correct. No *shamat.*"

"Then…"

"Holy spirit shall be coming on you, and the power of the Most High shall be overshadowing you; this is why the holy One Who is being generated shall be called the Son of God."

"Then…"

"Tonight, while you sleep."

"Sleep? I cannot sleep."

"You will. It will happen very early in the morning, at three-thirty. You will not awaken. You will not feel anything. Take comfort in knowing this, that Elizabeth, your relative, has also conceived a son in her infirmity, and that this is the sixth month for the one they called barren. Nothing is impossible with God. He will fulfill His every declaration."

"Then I am the handmaiden of the Lord. I want this. Let it happen as you say."

Suddenly, the lamp blew out and the laundry chute snapped shut. I said, "God!" Gabriel was gone. They were all gone, all of them. I knew they were. I was covered in darkness now, alone.

It was the twenty-fifth of Tammuz. I knew that I would walk to my bedroom when my legs decided that they could move. What did I think as I stood there feeling so alone in the big world? I could think of only one thing, and it was: *Joseph! Joseph, come to me!*

CHAPTER 2

MAGDALA

"Throw me the ball!" said Rent Hassler—loud enough to irritate dead people—at the same time waving his arms from across the court. "I'm open!"

I ignored Rent's rantings and gave my man a leg feint. Good-bye, friend! It was true that I lacked several vital ringball skills, but I made up for this with insane anaerobic extravagances that elicited gasps. I wish I could have stopped and listened to the gasps, but the cost in concentration was too exorbitant. Now that I'd left my nemesis guarding a whiff of my aftershave, I "raced" toward the ring.

There was only one man separating me from *baqa yanach*.[*] Or was that a sycamore tree? The fate of the Welldiggers depended on what happened next.

I am smelling something strange now, and it is not me. It's the smell of an unwashed and very hairy man. It proves

---

[*] Hebrew. Literally, *success-lay*. Idiomatically, *winning lay-up*.

to be the same figure separating me from *baqa yanach*, except now I know that it is Dante Grimm. This man separating me from four critical points and victory, the man sprouting leaves, hair, and bird's nests, is Dante Grimm.

When he is not murdering people on ringball courts, Dante Grimm runs an insurance office. He insures all my carts because he has no competition. He has a monopoly-hold on cart insurance in Nazareth and in many other towns. No one can do anything about it because the cousin's son of Grimm's grandfather's niece runs part of the town. Grimm appears civil when he's insuring my carts, but it's all because of money. I know this man, that he fakes civility to earn a living. But on the court he is a murderer—his true self. Besides being large and overcome by mutant follicles, Dante Grimm is nuts. Life holds neither care nor fear for Grimm and his clan. But allow me now to return you to the office.

At the office, Grimm smiles at you because of your cash. He appears to be looking at you, but he is admiring his feats of robbery reflected back to him off your glassy eyeballs. As touching constitution, Dante resembles the tree previously mentioned. As touching intelligence, his skull is a hollow prison house containing only one thing: a very lonely bee.

Note this: the man also smokes Carthaginian cigars. He wants to pass you one, but you must refuse. If you smoke one, you will die. It has always been this way with anything Carthaginian, including their versions of Job. After lighting his cigar with a small campfire at the brimstone end of a stick, Grimm passes you something, very gently, to sign. You must sign it because it is illegal to run carts anywhere in Israel without insurance; that's the whole thing.

After you sign your life over to Grimm, his papers, his smoke, his rotten toenails, and the birds in his hair, he will want to pet your corpse, that is, to invite you to keep the pen with his name on it: *Dante Grimm*. He actually tells you this: "Keep da pin." While you are recovering from the forced charity, Dante calls for someone to bring your ass around front. By all these tricks, the man appears civil. On the court, however, Grimm and his cranial-bound bee bisect your carcass and step between the torn halves for *baqa yanach*. Scoring is the only Grimm-courtesy in the world of the ring; no "pin" for you, friend, and not one donkey waiting where you want it. Other than his inherited nuthood (his mother's name is Bork, if you can believe that), Grimm consists of beard sweat and a useless push-shot. Defensively, he is a right forearm and two *very* hard elbows.

I decide to drive the lane. Perhaps I should defer from saying that because of how much of an exaggeration it is. Let me just say that I decide to explore the lane, to look into the possibility of continuing my journey and winning the game. My excursion probably would have been a pleasant one, aside from Grimm thrusting his hairy arm again and again and again at me. Grimm punctuates each of his rude arm invasions with, "Ung!" I'm not spelling that correctly because Grimm noises cannot be spelled. I knew that if I had looked into Grimm's eyes, I would have seen pupils the size of urn bottoms. Grimm's pupils were large and mean enough to scare his evil grandmother, Belshazzette, seated behind the green ropes of the old people's section, chewing on her burlap overshirt and picking ticks from the backs of her hands.

I see you in that corner, Rent. I want to render you the ball, truly I do. You are so much better than me, friend. But I hear the voice of my father instructing me from the grave: "Go the distance! Challenge Dante Grimm as David challenged Goliath!" But I realize, of course, that this is just me talking to myself; nobody can talk from the grave, not even my father. Besides, I am such a selfless man. I want Hassler to have the glory. I promise you that this has nothing to do with distrust of my shooting skills, the questionable integrity of my jawbone, or my dubious likeness to David.

I stop dribbling, compliments of Grimm. Now it's either pass to Hassler or attempt a jumper over the primate. A large stone pot bangs three times from the corner, signifying, of course, ten seconds remaining in the game.

I bend my knees and lift the ball for *raqad*.† All my fans think I'm taking *raqad*, but he is wrong. Dante Grimm also thinks the ball is ring-bound, to similar result. For at the last moment, I snap a bounce pass to Hassler. By my standards, this is a daring move. By the standards of the world, it's llama poop. The move is not so daring as to keep Grimm's ape-boned arm from my chin (the bone an enchantress will someday employ to stir cauldrons of her beans), but it is sufficiently bold to give Hassler a clear shot at the basket and the win.

Delivered now of all responsibility for winning the game, I can thankfully watch Rent.

Rent Hassler bends into his own version of *raqad*. Hassler is stylistically perfect; think of Abu Knesset before his knee injury. And Hassler perfected Formidable Concentration in Sports years before Adler Cardo (of Canaan Camel fame) had ever worked himself into anything even remotely resembling a fit of staring.

Rent's shot falls short, and the Llamas win the game. Game, Llamas. For the seventeenth time in a row this season, the Llamas win. How wonderful, I thought, to be a Llama.

Rent Hassler stiff-armed three reporters on his way to the bench, then damned the Llamas.

---

† Hebrew: *jump-up*.

"Damn the Llamas!"

I tried to put my hand on his shoulder to offer a comforting word, but he shrugged both things away.

"Why did you throw me the ball, Jabrecki?"

"Um—you were waving for it?"

Rent spit. "Do you do everything I say?"

"I try to. Grimm was blocking the lane, see, and—" I directed Rent's attention to my chin. "Look here. This is why I'm rubbing my chin and talking funny. I'm injured."

"*Dodo*.‡ Why didn't you just drive the lane?"

We called each other *dodo* all the time. Except for me. I never called anyone *dodo*. None of us even knew what it meant. Nevertheless, we were all, somehow, *dodo*. "Grimm would have killed me. Thank God he only injured me for life."

"Then you go to the line. God, you're *dodo*."

That was a nice thought, but I'd have only gotten three shots and we needed four to win. (I have never made three shots in a row—to my knowledge.) Rent knew all this, but he wasn't thinking clearly. He was all flushed and red. His bald head shone terribly. I acquainted him with the particulars of shots and points.

"So we rebound and somebody goes *baqa yanach*," he said. "Or you throw one off the bark and Bondo puts it in. Is that so hard to believe? Moses and Abraham, we did that against the Lions."

Now he was irritating me. I told him that I had wanted to win the game as much as he had, which may have been a lie. I was no Rent Hassler. I paused to watch our fans and their disenchanted fannies exiting the arena. I re-thought everything. Maybe I should have driven the lane. Maybe I was *dodo*. I said all this out loud.

---

‡ Origins unknown.

"Maybe you should have and maybe you shouldn't have," Rent said. "I missed the shot and I'll have to live with it." Rent sat down on a bleacher and stared at the floor. "So what happened to your chin?"

"Moses and Abraham. I told you. I drew Grimm to pass to you." I had not told him that, specifically. "I blew it," I said. I felt bad now.

"Don't be hard on yourself. It's only a game."

"Does that line work for you?" I snapped.

"No," said Rent.

"Then shut the devil up."

I stomped off to the showers.

Don't lead her to the door. Instead, walk next to her. Join hands but make sure the hands don't sweat. Intertwine the fingers but not so that they jam or sweat. Let the hands be light so that night air gets through and dries whatever of your wetness wants to trickle down past the ends of her fingernails.

Bring her from the sidewalk to the porch with the purpose and pace of the moon. Slowness is everything now. Rent said it. Amman said it. They all said it. It's the hardest thing—*they* said. You mustn't be a race horse— even though your heart is beating like a horse's heart. Master your emotions; *they* said that. But the moon above knows how it is with me. And so he smirks and winks. Her back is to the moon, so the wink and the smirk is man to celestial orb. A man is mastered, everyone knows that. Woman is *Gebereth*,§ the trainer of all beasts. I want only to keep my weakness from showing, at least until I face her on the porch. There,

---

§ Hebrew: *Mistress*, Mighty one.

I will grasp her and bring her near. It is my plan. But the moon is laughing now, and I may as well join him. But this was Amman's instruction, word for word.

I linger at the porch now through my own heartbeat and breathing. I will do it. *Shut up, moon, and watch now.*

Ah. Why is it so hard to look into her eyes? I know. It is because I will drown in them; it is because I will drown in the blackness of the oils of her inner eye.

The *Gebereth Shotet*¶ paints the eyes black and blackens each lash. My *Gebereth* sits naked astride a bench on the eve of our union, attended by women. The women surround her, bend about her, paint her, powder her, tie her skins and instruct her how to use them. Hair is always loose and long here, tossed everywhere in terrible ringlets and the laughter of the *Gebereth* who fathom the skin of reptiles and how to tie it.

The *Gebereth Saphah*** is fifteen years old and glistens with oil. She, too, is naked save for a gold Egyptian choker and a gold chain belt enthroned above her sacrum. The belt sits high atop her hips, then plunges in front at the belly into nine thin chains hanging between her legs when she faces the bride to squat with her brushes until the lips are large and dripping.

Her chains lay floored in the squat where the hair lays drawn where she squats to paint the pout of *Gebereth*. Boy-slaves unpinned the mane in the loosening gown belt, falling to the paving stones with the gown and tresses in a fear to gaze at *Gebereth Saphah* and her ringlets. Slave-girls oiled and bejeweled her. Boy-slaves bore her sedan chair through Caesarea.

Behind the bride, in blacksnake, another *Gebereth* rubs snake oil down the bridal backlick rubbing up the oil through the back nails rubbing up scratching the rubbing and...

¶ *Mistress of Lash.*

** *Mistress of Lips.*

"…up. Joseph. Come on. Wake up."

"What?"

"Wake up, for God's sake."

"Where is she?"

"Where is *who?*"

"Where is Mary?"

"In bed, I'm guessing. Get a grip. You wanted to get up at five-thirty, so come on. I've got the coffee going. You're supposed to be at Mary's at noon."

I rolled onto my stomach. Where were my covers? Father Abraham, it was another dream.

I drove my face into my pillow and breathed its air. The air smelled like Mary. Everything did. The morning was still dark blue, but the inside folds of my laying place brought light to my open eyes. I listened to bits of my escaping air. I wished for the covers, to hide me. I needed a cocoon so as to bring back the dream and stay warm in it. But the spell would break, I knew. Here it came already. The trailing edges remained, thankfully, where I balled up onto my side and warmed myself. And yet the dream frightened me because it exposed what manner of man I was.

Rent appeared in the doorway, outlined by a small kitchen lamp, his right arm resting high against the jamb. His armpits were the hairiest in Israel. "Are you going to lay there all morning, or are you going to get up so we can argue some more about the game?"

The game. Breathe. Got to relax. You're at Rent's house, in Magdala. You lost the ringball game. You should have driven the lane, but you are dodo. *You went to the bar but you didn't drink because you don't do that. But you wanted to. It's Tuesday, the twenty-sixth of Tammuz. You're supposed to be at Mary's at noon, for lunch. But you need coffee now, and lots of it.*

"Look at this stuff, Joey. Black as sin, and yet it's God's gift to man. Do you know how many people had to suffer so that we could just sip this and say, 'Ahhh'"?

I had finally rolled off my mat and gone to the hole—a shot in the dark, as it were. I deposited wide left, but Rent's bathroom forgives such indiscretions. I dipped a hand into the wash bucket to ease myself into the day, but the water only beaded like dew on a spider web. I shook the web, accomplishing nothing. Not one spider relocated. My jaw felt like the '06 war with Midian.

"What are you talking about?"

"This coffee," Rent said. "It came from Arabia. How did it get here? I'll tell you. People had to pick it. Laborers, and lots of them. Millions. And they probably had flies buzzing all around them, driving them nuts. Kids, too. And do you know how hot it is in Arabia? I went there for a tournament with the Whirlwinds. It's about a hundred and twenty in the shade. But coffee beans don't grow in the shade! So they pick the beans, sack 'em, and load 'em up on the backs of mules and tromp up the Asir mountains, then across the desert about two hundred miles to Jidda. Once they get there, about a million and a half people beat 'em with stones. Bang, bang, bang! They just beat the *sheetzi* out of those beans day and night until they turn 'em to powder. Then they pour the coffee into burlap bags by the homer and load it onto barges and float it up the Red Sea. Then up through the Aqaba, and into Ezion-Geber. That's where they load it onto camels and donkeys and slaves. Then somebody whips the slaves, of course, and up she goes, up the King's Highway, across the Jordan, over to Reed's Market, and into this beautiful brown mug. God *damn*."

Rent Hassler was a morning person.

"Sure," I said. "Can I have some?"

Rent filled my mug, but I only laid its lip against my own bottom one. I sat cross-legged on the floor against the west wall of Rent's living room, my knees drawn up nearly to my chin. I breathed in and out of my paradise, cradling the mug close, my elbows sideways atop my knees, my breath sending concentric semi-circles across the surface of the paradise—not that I could see any of this. I had just read in a book somewhere that this is what generally happens.

"Stop being so upset about the game, Joey. I told you I blew it, and I meant it. Forget about what those guys at Akeem's said last night."

"I guess it's just that way when your team wins."

"It'll be different next year. We're drafting Ark Dotson."

I opened one eye. "The guy from Gaza U?"

"Five foot eleven. He'll have Grimm over a pig hock."

"Mm."

Hassler went on and on about Ark Dotson, about his parents and his grandparents and his hook shot. I stopped listening midway through and started thinking about Mary. My spirits lifted at this and I started on my coffee. Rent thought it was his speech that was stirring me, so he climbed out onto new branches of Ark Dotson's family tree, finding new species of nuts there at the ends of the branches. He cracked these nuts, removed the fruit, and processed the fruit into butter.

I looked out the window. Faint morning light lit the Sea of Galilee. In an hour, I would leave. It would be a pleasant eighteen mile jog home to Nazareth. A little warm later on, but not too bad. The Magdalan Way was one of the few lined with trees. No towns to speak of between Magdala and Nazareth, but some Galileans had built beautiful homes and they'd be pulling water about then and would give me some.

"...lucky that the Hippos didn't get him because of what I just said. Right, Joey?"

"Huh?"

Rent wrist-shot the last of his first coffee onto the floor (*into* it, actually) and laughed. "Unless, of course, they draft Mary. Then young Joseph will go man-to-man, or man-to-woman, I should say. Then we'll see who will have who over what."

"I'll drive the lane then," I said.

"And hope to be fouled."

In my resuscitation, I asked Rent why he'd never married.

"Who'd have me?"

"There's some name from your hoary past."

"Madelene Spenkker. And she *was* a whore."

"The girl with the lips."

"The pout. You remember her? How can somebody caress a vowel like Hassenaah DeLore just taking your pancake order? Can you tell me that?"

I couldn't even venture a guess, but I doubted that Madelene's lips were the first thing Rent noticed. I should have left it alone. "So her lips were the first thing you noticed, huh?" This was the exact opposite of leaving it alone.

"No, not really."

"Then?"

"I shouldn't tell you."

"Oh, but you should."

Rent set down his mug. "It was her ass."

Dodo! I'd done it now; I'd stirred the sleeping Deity. I cowered in my private corner, awaiting the divine strike. It was a woman's backside; that's what it was, and nothing else. *Nothing else.*

I scanned the room beneath my lids. Nothing came or moved, but even so, escape seemed unlikely. The subject was broached now. I waited a little, breathing. Why was I still alive? Of course: *I hadn't said it, Rent had*. But I had baited him; it was I who'd asked. Why had I asked? I knew why, and it was over the edge of this precipice that I now gazed. I considered the consequences of jumping. That done, it was all over for me.

"How could you see it?"

"She wore a belt. All the waitresses wore belts."

"What kinds?"

"Chain belts. The kind with rings."

After swallowing a *very* hard and dry ball of panicked intrigue, I inquired into a local law forbidding a woman to display her form in public.

"The gal who owned Birdie's had a couple friends on the council who looked the other way. But they didn't look the other way at the waitresses, I can tell you that." Rent paused, but not for effect. It was more like reminiscing. "Madelene. *God.* Narrow waist, then nothing but hips. And that ass. A deadly combination, Joseph. Whenever she went back to the kitchen—swing time." He had me in a trance. Then, "More wake-up?"

Rent retrieved the pot from the kitchen—a welcomed break. I extended my mug, which shook like a palm frond. "Hold still," Rent said. I stared at the coming black liquid, gleaning peripherally from the window that it was quarter after six. I'd be four hours jogging to Mary's, longer if I walked. Thirty more minutes was all I had. A basket of figs sat in Rent's kitchen; I'd get some soon. Somewhere in the bedroom lay my backpack; Rent would lend me a canteen. The important—and startling—thing was that I was still alive. I cleared my throat, feigned an air of unconcern, and posed the following, sophisticated query:

"So what happened?"

"At Birdie's?"

"With Madelene."

"Oh, she was a real Jezebel. Everybody wanted her. I saw her a lot, but there was never a commitment there. It was never anything like what you and Mary have. (The name "Mary" thrilled me every time I heard it.) Madelene always had headaches," Rent continued. "Her head was a goddamn civil war. I'd take her up to The Ramban on weekends, but those long fingers would wander up to that gorgeous forehead, and the evening was shot. I found out later that she was going out with another guy, that insurance bastard from Madaba. *Garnard*. But she never broke it off with me. I'm a decent-looking guy, right? Nice arms, right? Well, I'm stupid is what."

"It's not your fault."

"Thanks, Joey. Look, I've never told this to anybody, but you're a sport. Remember I used to play for the Whirlwinds?"

The whole civilized world knew that Rent Hassler used to play for the Whirlwinds.

"Well, there was this big weekend tournament up in Tyre. Between games the team went to town to get meals. There was a market there that had great sandwiches: Hasdas. The sandwiches were stupendous. Me and another guy were the only ones who'd found it, so we kept it to ourselves. There was a girl working the counter there—Anna. Don't think I had the guts to ask her name; I overheard it. She was interested in ringball and asked about the games. I couldn't believe that. Madelene only cared about games on payday, and I was All-Palestine three times when I was seeing her. Are you following me? The only time Madelene cared was when the *Jerusalem Post* did. Seriously, Joseph. *Are* you following me?"

I nodded and nodded.

"Anna wasn't on-your-knees beautiful like Madelene, but she was saucy. I couldn't see much of her body, but she was fit, I could see that. Fifteen on the sauce scale. She bunned up her hair so that it stood on top her head like the Tower of Goddamn Babel. I could tell by the way she waited on people that she was halfway off the camel, like me. You know—nuts. But serious, too. You know the kind. She joked about me wanting extra peppers on my sandwich. She said I was warm enough already."

That got to him. It put Rent under, as it would any man. They socialized after hours. The bonus, he said, was that she never had a headache. "Not once the whole weekend, Joseph. I was like, 'Are you sure you don't need an aspirin? I've, like, got this gigantic bottle of five-hundred aspirin. Here, why don't you just swallow a half dozen. Are you sure you don't want to go home?'"

I laughed a little, then tried not to cry. Rent shifted in his chair, and I could sense that something big was about to happen.

"The third time me and the other guy went there, Anna asked where we were staying. 'We're camped out in a little room off the gymnasium,' I said. She couldn't believe that ringball stars didn't have some fancy hotel in town."

"She didn't know how the league worked," I said.

"Mother of Abraham, Joseph. That's not the point at all."

I knew it hadn't been.

"Did you hear me? '*Ringball stars.*' She asked if we wanted to stay at her house. And she'd just met us. But she could tell that we were decent guys. Besides, she said she lived with her parents, and that they were big ringball fans. She said they'd be thrilled to have us."

"But Deke was your coach then. Deke wouldn't ever have let you stay at a girl's house."

"Deke wouldn't have let us stay at Abraham's house."

"So what did you do?"

"I snuck out. The other guy—Al Sorganta—he was in it for the sandwiches. Fine with me. *Perfecto!* So on Friday night, I snuck out. Right out the window."

"Crock!"

"Oh, Phineas. You haven't heard anything yet."

I stared at this bulk of revelation named Rent Hassler who was resting now against the inside east wall of his house. Rent had a habit of pulling on the little tuft of hair beneath his bottom lip when he was nervous, and he was doing that.

"So I get to Anna's about ten o'clock," he continued. "There's lights on in there, which I'm glad to see. I probably knocked like a woodpecker because nobody answered. My teeth are chattering, Joesph. I'm wrecked. Then I get brave and really knock. I can hardly stand how loud the knock sounds. Then Anna answers the door, and—Lord have mercy on every damned one of us."

It was already all over for me, so I leaned toward Rent, into the revelation. "How much mercy? Tell me how much mercy the Lord needs to have on us."

"She's wearing a purple *chaphet*†† kid, if you follow me. And it's not even falling to her knee."

I stood at the door behind Rent, for that's where I fell when he spoke the word *chaphet*. The form of a woman *can* be seen through so gauzy a garment if the woman is backlit, and "the back of Anna's living room contained lamps," said Rent.

I pushed Hassler aside hard and stared at Anna's feet. Rent's voice lost strength when describing what encased these feet: "She wore those strappy sandals with the pointed toe that not many girls have the nerve to wear. The kind Josie Dolan wears."

Before I could stop myself, I fell to my knees to kiss Anna's sandaled feet. I kissed them fifteen times each without so much as a breath. Then, looking up but still so far away, I asked, "Where were her parents?"

---

†† Hebrew, literally: *delightful wish*. Idiomatically, a brief, feminine sleeping robe.

"Therein lay the thing. They were visiting her dad's other business up in Sidon."

I kissed Anna's feet again, as fast as I could, thirty times again, then said casually to Rent. "Oh, my. So she set the whole thing up."

"Like a carnival tent with a vestibule for the pachyderms."

"So where was Al Sorganta?"

"Al-the-fuck *who?*"

I forgot about my coffee then, my backpack, the figs, the dawn, noon, and why I had once cared about such things. I pushed hard at Rent's broad and stupid back now, sending us both deeper into that infamous living room.

"She told me to sit on the sofa. I tried to look at her eyes and not those parts of her tearing apart that *chaphet*, if you follow me. But I'm a decent guy, right? But the girl's wearing a purple *chaphet*, for God's sake. But anyway, we talked. Can you believe that? We talked about ringball, and about her family. I asked about her mom and dad."

"Good play," I said.

"For God's sake, Joseph. Concentrate. That's what I used to do with Madelene. Keep her attention, make something happen, wait for the head to explode. But with Anna, I wanted to ask. I was *interested*. Here's this gorgeous woman sitting in front of me in this purple *chaphet*, and I'm like, 'So what does your dad do in Sidon? Rents condos? That's super.'"

This ridiculous comment relieved me. I bit my lip because of the pleasure of it, kept biting because of the pain. It was just like Rent to fall into Anna. Something like that would have never happened to me. Ever.

"And then she says, 'Do you want to see my poems?'"

That was the oldest line in the book. "It's the oldest line

in the book," I said. Or maybe the thing about paintings was the oldest line. I wasn't sure which was the oldest line. "It *may* be the oldest line in the book," I said. *Something* was the oldest line in that infamous book, and it had to do with either art or literature concealing a human's basic instincts.

Rent smiled. "Not this time, Joey." He walked over and touched my knee. Then he reached to his own table and demonstrated how Anna had reached over to hers, next to her couch, and pulled out a large notebook. Rent opened this imaginary book. "And Joseph. It's filled with poetry. And it's wild stuff like you used to write in school. One was called, 'Wade Through the Cactus Dung.'"

Rent stood and extended one arm toward the ceiling in the manner of a stage player, the hand of the opposite arm tucked behind his back. He turned stoic now—a player of tragedy. "'*Wade through the cactus dung, at the end of a dark day. Step in it and around it, as the dromedaries play. Flick it, stick it, choke it with a rag. Douse the flaming metaphors, inflate a blubber bag.*'"

I rubbed my forehead, needing to weep. Breathing, the tears passed. Rent sat back down and stared at me. I stared back.

Rent pretended with the rubbing of his hands to muse about the future, then feigned with the scratching of his neck to have forgotten the past. He then rubbed the flat of his hand against his three-day stubble to enhance this pair of deceptions.

"The unimaginable followed," he finally said. "And I mean it."

This was it, then. I checked the room again for celestial assassins. Seeing nothing, I panicked; angels were ever invisible moments before they killed you. Everything was my fault. If Rent continued, my death would ensue. *But if I'm going to die*, I thought, *I may as well live.* This thought amazed me; I was amazed that a person like me could have entertained it. But that's how badly I needed to know.

"Understand, Joseph, that everything I'm about to tell you was respectable."

I repeated that word, like a parrot.

"I didn't feel raunchy. I still don't. This was science."

"Science," I said.

"Anna was a scientist, with some kind of degree in it."

"Degree. Got it."

"I was feeling restraint, like I was part of a grand experiment that I, myself, had to watch."

"Thank you. An experiment. Now say it."

Rent cleared his throat and looked around the room. "Maybe I've said enough. Got a cigarette?"

"*Dodo!* Why would I?"

"Sometimes I wish I smoked, is all. And you. Anyway, it's light out. You've got to be leaving soon."

That was just like God, wasn't it? *You've got to be leaving soon.* Thank You, Lord of Every Disappointment I've Ever Lived Through. I weighed the consequence of these words against those I was hearing, then against those I wanted to hear. A small period of suspense ensued, when the scale went up, then down. But then I knew.

"Please," I said. "We're friends."

Rent raised his eyebrows, then stood to stretch. He walked to the window to peruse the world. I rose to kill him, but then relaxed. *Of course. He played lead in all the school plays.*

When Rent had turned back, he pretended to fish a cigarette out from under his clothes. He stuck it in his mouth and went to light it from a dead lamp on a wall sconce. He jutted his chin and stuck out his rear end as though it had been pulled there by a rope attached to the opposite wall.

With the "cigarette" lit, Rent sucked it hard and made his cheeks sallower than cheeks trained in such arts. Then he pinched the prop close to his mouth with a thumb and forefinger, drew back more poison from the tip, then moved the cigarette straight down to just above his knee. He bounced a little then, at his knees. Then he craned his neck to the ceiling and blew the invisible equivalent of a storm cloud, a harbinger of the Second Flood.

"Mack Ackner," I guessed.

"Exactly. How did you know?"

"I've seen almost all his plays."

"Did you see *Harney Barney*?"

"Four times, including the re-make."

"That's where I got that."

"I know. Where's your rattlesnake?"

"I don't have one."

"So, before I kill you—what happened?"

"You ready now?"

"About a minute before Ackner showed up."

"Such confidence. And you, but a boy. What do leather *garas*‡‡ do for you, brother?"

I have only shown you, in this writing, the opening curtains of my dreams; you cannot know the rest, you cannot. This word *gara*, uttered by my boyhood friend, was an eel piercing my soul with a hundred sharpened teeth, injecting me with a thousand thrilling poisons. Rent had gone too deep now, far too deep. The stage was lit and here I was. He had found too much of me, and there I was—innocent boy Joseph—with nowhere to run. Why had everything changed? Was it the dark of that early morning? The coming sun? The coffee? The disappointment of the previous night's game? The

---

‡‡ Hebrew, *diminished;* a small, stringed womens' undergarment.

bar? Was it the suspense and excitement of seeing Mary? It was everything; it was the way everything smelled and the way the coming light now reddened the room.

If I answered Rent's question, then time would mark my change. The answer would be out forever in a world too big to protect me. But this was Rent Hassler, and my life was over anyway—or at least half over should the grace of God spare me. Perhaps it was God's plan to kill me on the way to Mary's. I thought of how good it would feel to die. But then I thought of how good it would feel to utter my truth. This impending release brought a sea-wave of happiness. I decided, then, to roll with the happiness. I would roll in the direction of the release of truth. My struggles left the building then with Rent's fake smoke. There was no tomorrow, no oblique rectangle of window. And so:

"A lot, Rent. Very much."

"Yeah. You and about a million other guys. So I'm sitting there, we're done reading poetry, and we're looking at each other again and talking. Nothing is awkward. We're talking about her kittens and her brother's snake, and how the snake got out once and tried to eat the kitten.

"So she's laughing about that, and then she suddenly reaches back and starts taking that stick-thing out of her hair. You know what I'm talking about? You know those stick things? She's having trouble with it, so she says, 'Can you help me with this?' and she turns a little bit and I start wrestling with it. But God, my fingers are shaking and I'm just about worthless."

Rent's fingers are shaking. He's right; they're shaking badly—and worthless. I try to stabilize them with the power of my mind. I go to that room with Rent and grab each of his fingers, mentally stabilizing each one, conforming each finger to the vital task. But the whole hand is shaking now.

I roll my eyes. It is unbelievable to me that Rent could be so helpless in this, our hour of need. His ineptness reaches supernatural lengths. I could push his hand through the motions of some desperate hair-stick language, and I do. He finally manages to get the stick halfway out.

"Halfway out, for God's sake. Can you believe that, Joseph? I'm absolutely terrible." Anna makes it less awkward by setting fire to another corner of our camp: "'You've probably been wondering how long my hair is,'" she said. "'Hasdas makes me keep it up.'"

I'd been wondering about that so hard, myself, that I dove now toward the base of Anna's neck, to inhale her coming glory from the bottom up.

"I told her that, well, it had crossed my mind."

Then the idiot asks how long she'd been working at Hasdas. I threw him to the floor and kicked him for that. No one man could be so stupid. Anna breathed steadily in the midst of Rent's panting—praise her. She knew she had snapped away his rug with her thin, lithe wrists.

"She knew everything, believe me. I didn't tell her I had been fantasizing about her hair for, like, every hour since I'd met her. She probably already knew it, anyway."

Anna stood up and unfolded her body then "like a Phoenix. Then she takes out the rest of the stick." The stick is now a part of our past, thank God. "Then she starts shaking out that hair with her hands, caressing it and pulling it, groaning for it to come out for her. And it does come, so that it just keeps falling and coming out, and God knows where it's all coming from, this dark brown and very chocolate and very sweet-smelling mound of glory. And I could hear it come out, I swear to you, Joseph. And it's framing her face, like sunbeams or something. And then she starts running her hands through it again, to bring more of it out."

I look up again, agape at the coming glory.

"Then she bunches it way up on her head, and does this little thing with her voice while looking straight at me—then she lets it go."

Isaac and Jacob!

"The hair had a sound to it, like—"

A waterfall of wheat stalks?

"—like I don't know what. Then she started swinging her neck…and making her hair come together in back…and pushing and pushing it, not literally pushing it, but making it move with sharp little flicks…these very sharp little flicks of the neck…"

"She had it all back then, and it just framed her. The hair against those shoulders and those bare arms—it just begged scrutiny—what could I do? But then she puts her hands behind her ears and she pushes her hair way out at the sides, way out with her fingers so that it stands out like a mane."

My kneecaps buckle again and I sink to the floor, pulling myself across that floor like a flipped jellyfish, spine to the earth's core so as to see the coming glory in brighter, more splendid hues.

"But then, when she gets her hair where she wants it, she just stands there with her hands on her hips."

We fellowshipped around the word "hips" until a God-breathed moment of silence came; an interval of holy quietude during which Rent took the opportunity to seat himself. But then, "she starts asking me these questions, like, 'Why do you think men like a woman's hair so much?' and 'What does it do to you when I do this?,' and she does some new thing that—I swear to you, Joseph—no woman has ever thought of."

Rent's leg now bounced involuntarily up and down. Here it came, then.

"Then she grabbed part of her hair and arranged it, strategically, in front of her. Now follow me. Then she reached over and started pushing the *chaphet* down at one shoulder. Then she pushed down the other side. Nothing happened, so she started tugging at it from beneath, at the *chaphet* around her waist, straining to pass it over…her…you know. Then—God and Abraham—the laws of physics had their lovely way, and holy Moses and Abraham, and David and Isaac—and throw in Joshua and Caleb, if you want to. She's wearing a *gara*, Joseph. A black leather *gara*. I had seen some drawings, but nothing can prepare a man—"

"Stop!" I said it too loudly. Rent stopped; he knew me. I blinked, as if finally awake. I said then, "I can't do this." I said, "It's a sin." I said, "It's a woman's body. You're not supposed to see it."

"We didn't do anything," said Rent.

"It doesn't matter. It's sacred."

"Everything in Israel is sacred."

"But some things are more sacred than others."

"But even the sacred things, we can sometimes see. Like the holy of holies."

"Have you ever been *there?*"

"But it's allowed," said Rent. "At certain times. By certain men."

"At certain times."

"But this was a time."

"It was *a* time. But it wasn't *the* time. You're trying to justify it."

Rent pulled at the softness beneath his lip. "It's not like I'm okay with it. It's not like I didn't feel guilty."

"Did you?"

"I don't know. Maybe I didn't." Rent paused. "No. There was none of that." This was not a revelation to Rent. The revelation, I think, was that he could say it out loud to another man.

"So why did you say you did?"

"I'm trained to. You're supposed to feel guilty after something like that. But this was different. Is it wrong to look at drawings?"

I stroked my lack of facial hair. "Yes."

"Drawings of the mind?"

He threw me with that. I knew the answer, though.

"Well?" he said. "Can you control those?"

I knew the answer, but I protected my weakness, even from Rent. But Rent knew the weakness, the universal debility, so I had answered Rent's question by refusing it.

"All these other things are natural progressions," Rent said. "From the mind, to the paper…"

"To Tyre."

"Okay. To Tyre. But not to the bedroom."

"Are you sure?"

"I swear, Joseph. Wouldn't I know? Was I that gone? It wasn't like that. I used to think your way, before that weekend. But this was different. It was art. I can tell you what happened next, if you want. I think you'll feel better."

"I'm not sure I can hear it."

"Pretend you're not listening."

At last, I smiled.

"You're my friend, and it's a duty. I'm a pervert, you're normal. You're strictly a professional, right? It's not like you want to hear it." Rent laid his back against the wall now; he had amused himself.

This was an astonishing game, and it was over. I had spun and lost. I did want to hear it, with pictures and pomegranates. What if I didn't hear it? I would still, for the rest of my life, want to. So which was worse, to want to hear it for the rest of one's life, or to just go ahead and hear it—imbibe from the bottle—and try to go on? After all, I hadn't done it. It was Rent.

"Black, huh?"

Rent leaned forward again and clapped his hands hard. "It's the black against the flesh tones that does the trick. Anna said it's the contrast of good and evil. The good is the flesh and the tone of the skin. The evil is that some poor old cow had to die, and the skin had to get beat and soaked and tanned and delimed and God-knows-what-else to make it black."

"The contrast..."

"That's what does you in. Anna said it's what attracts man to woman in the first place. All the opposites. All the things she has that men don't. Attitudes, too. Women are—what? Aloof? Why is that? God made them that way. Men are desperate. Well? Do women chase us? Hell, no. It's us, panting like dogs, chasing them all over blast-ass Israel. At least in our minds. Why is it? Well, it's God, if you can dare believe that. Women don't need it like we do—at least that's how they come off. It's all in the programming. Anna explained it. I think she's onto it. I honest to God think she has it figured out."

Right down to the deliming agents. Had the Death Angel been wandering the corridors of my brain, he'd have heard the quiet noise of completion, the soft clicks of puzzle pieces coming softly together, irregular shapes forming year after year that had only recently sought their mates, the rounded nub to the receiving half-moon, the yellows to the yellows, the reds to the reds, the fern leaves to the fern leaves. Yet even this would have succumbed to a greater noise, to the appearance of the bigger picture, the landscape I had longed to see.

"I've often thought about that," I said.

"About what?"

"About what makes men and women different. About why it's so...intense."

Rent clapped his hands together again and whistled.

"Huh?" I looked up, startled. What had I said? I was getting in too far. I needed to retreat. "I mean, I don't think about it all the time."

"Look at this," said Rent. "I'm sitting here, disrobing a woman before our very eyes, and we're discussing some point of philosophy."

"But it's there."

God, was it ever. This was the thing about Anna, and why Rent refused the guilt. It was like an experiment, he said, full of passion, but not passion-*ate*. It could have been that; the door can be opened if two people agree to it. But they can also keep it shut. It's within the power of the will. Rent didn't think he could do it, but he did. He credited it to Anna. And there were other doors, the door of the intellect; the soul; the dream-life. It was stunning to Rent how thrilling it was with so many of these doors closed. Could I imagine—could I?—a world with most of these doors open?

Yes.

Not only was I not dead, I was more alive than I had ever been.

It all made sense. I had often thought about it, had even sought the Scriptures. I had mentioned some of it, indirectly, to Mary. But she never grasped my direction. It wasn't her fault, probably. I was too timid. All my references were overly dim. I would point to the Sea of Galilee, or to a kernel of wheat, or to the sun and the mud and the flowers, especially the flowers (explosions of fertilization), and the bees that would be rushing with their pockets of pollen to the feet of the queen. But it was all too allegorical. Mary's mind would be on something else. I would never press it; it was too fragile of a petal. Mary saw in the sun the love of God. I saw that, too. But the sun was also on fire.

That morning with Rent Hassler changed my life. Everything. I did not feel so alone now. There was at least one other man in the world who shared this part of me. It was impossible that Rent could have all my thoughts, and I could never tell him everything. Never. Not even if Rent spilled his cup and my own dreams came forth. Not even then. But who could know? Anything seemed possible now. The forbidden room had been entered; at least the door was ajar. I felt exhilarated. I even felt God smiling down on me; amazing! Maybe my thoughts and dreams were not so evil after all. And Anna! One more soul. Yet it did unnerve me that Anna lived in Tyre, that she inhabited planet earth, that she knew the secrets. I wanted to talk to her, to ask some questions of my own. I wanted to ask about the sun and the pollen and the queen, to see what she thought.

But what if she untied and re-tied her *gara*, as she did with Rent? What if she pulled it high on her hips and asked if I liked it there? What if she stalked like a panther in front of me, instructing me to study that smooth valley between waist and hips, to see how the string-ends behaved there? Rent had been able to take it. Would I?

He said it was possible. He said he had passed from lust to a more distant but enjoyable watching, at the snap of her finger. Could a woman have such power? Could I be as controlled as that? Anna knew every checkpoint on that highway, like the milestones on the Magdalan Way I would soon walk. The stones were her possession, as well as the perfection of their placing. She knew when to stop, when to go on, when to construct, when to tear it all down. The wise man said that there was a time for everything, a time to laugh, to cry, to live, a time to die. There was a time to build…and a time to tear it all down.

I thought I could have survived the rest of the weekend. I could have gone to the market and thrown the cherry tomatoes into the air, then run beneath them and caught them in my open mouth. I could roll in the grass with her in the sun and write poetry. I could say one line, she could say the next, I could say the next. I could do that, and she could write it all down. I would have done it better than Rent, though. Rent would have rhymed rose with nose. I would rhyme bone with nose, while Anna would find folds beneath the lips of ibexes.

With Anna and me there would be cucumbers and carriages, creams that did not exist, and "minstrel tarts on the waves of paper ducklings." I knew I could do that. And the grass. And the pushing each other in the wagon, in the marketplace. And maybe—maybe—I could have shopped for *qum*.§§ How exciting! But too dangerous. No. I would probably have said, *No, I can't do that*. I could not have gone back to her house, I don't think, and watched her walk in the *qum*—no. She had too many walks. There were too many straps. The straps were too thin. There were too many ways.

He had not seen her breasts—she had purposely put her hair there. Anna did not want to hurt Rent. She believed in marriage, in the sanctity of the vows, the cleanliness of the bed. She was a virgin. Why didn't Rent marry her? He still could, he said. He was working up the nerve to ask her again. He had seen her twice since, but never like that. They wrote letters. They kissed. Rent *had* asked for her hand, but she had another friend up in Caesarea. That figured, Rent said. But it wasn't like that, she said. It was special with Rent, and he believed her. She just wasn't ready. What bothered him was that he had not heard from her in over four months. His most recent communications had been returned unopened. Not even the post knew her address. That bothered him.

---

§§ Hebrew, *to cause to rise*; elegant, tall shoes for women.

She was thinking of opening a business. "An underground thing," Rent said. He said that Anna was enterprising. Her parents were wealthy and she never had to work, but she thought she could help people with her knowledge.

"What kind of business?" I asked.

"Education," Rent said. "She wants to educate people about…you know…*shamat*.¶¶ Maybe have some products. Things. Hell, I don't know. An information store. And what things, I really don't know. But it sounds great. Get people into all those nooks and crannies—the secret rooms."

There. Rent had said it. "Who built these rooms?" That always pricked me. I knew the answer, but asked anyway.

"Where does everything come from?" Rent said.

"From God. But leather *gara?*"

"Why not? Go back to Proverbs." Rent quoted from memory: "'Yahweh has made everything for its own purpose.'"

Stupendous verse—I liked it—but I had to lay out my fleece. "Leather *gara?* Come on. They're probably just a product of these immoral times."

"Immoral—?" Rent leaped from his wall as if pushed from it. "Okay. I've got one for you. Every generation thinks it invented *shamat*, right? So listen to this. Anna says that about two years ago some Egyptian archaeologists dug up a leather *gara* in a peat bog near Lisht. Says it was about two thousand years old."

"They're sure that's what it was?"

"C'mon, Joey. What else? Anna actually saw a drawing of it in a book."

Rent fell back against his wall again, delivered. My mind wandered on a wave of comfort and great joy across the

---

¶¶ Hebrew, *release, let go*; euphemism for sexual relations.

deserts to Egypt, to a long-ago bedroom in Lisht. Or was it a living room? Or maybe a patio on a roof with a parapet ringed with torch lights, dry and hot. Or a cellar with candles and drips from inside the walls. I allowed myself a sudden rush of camaraderie with the woman so long ago decorated, a connection, from my anonymous squat in a Magdalan mud house, to some ancient Egyptian adventuress in the sun of my gaze who was yet, this minute, salted to a pulp in three hundred cubits of linen. I shook my head to dislodge the reverie.

The one other thing I could not dislodge—as Rent helped me with my backpack and sent me with a handshake and some figs down the Magdalan Way—was, *I have got to talk to Mary about this. Today.*

CHAPTER 3

TOGETHER AGAIN

I sat on our front steps with our cat Pharaoh. Father had named him. It was a funny name, because Pharaoh was so friendly. He was very small and light, as if he had hollow bones and was missing most his organs. He was a short-haired, very light-colored gray, full of black stripes. God had given Pharaoh nice, white feet. His eyes were his most remarkable aspect, green and large like big cut slices of kiwi. He was so light that you barely knew you had him on your lap. His tail stuck straight up in the air almost all the time. It stuck straight up this morning, and he purred like mad as I stroked him.

"Do you see Joseph yet, Pharaoh? He's late."

Purr.

I had been sitting on the steps since eleven-thirty; it was now one o'clock. Joseph was supposed to have been here at noon. Every fifteen minutes I would get up and walk to the road, to look East. This was the Magdalan Way. It was a new road, not paved, running from Nazareth to Magdala and the Sea of Galilee.

I looked and hoped to see Joseph approaching through the heat shimmers. I shielded my eyes to look. Sometimes I thought I was seeing him, a black form coming through the heat. But it wouldn't be him. It was never anything, maybe only a large bird or a dog. The road I could see was barren of humanity. But Joseph was somewhere on it, getting closer to Nazareth, I knew.

I wanted to walk west and meet him anywhere. We would walk back to the house together and talk. It would be good for us to be alone with God, even briefly. We could join spirits with the great men and women of faith who had walked here before us. And I would tell him. It would be our world, alone under heaven.

But my parents would not let me travel alone, I knew.

The sun was really beating down now, and it was hot. I went inside.

"Is Joseph spiritual enough for this?" Father sat in the living room in his favorite chair, slouched down into it, his bare feet pointing straight out. And coffee, always coffee. He could drink it no matter what the weather.

"He loves God, I know that."

"This would be too much for any man," said Father, "whether he loved God or not."

"But Joseph isn't 'any man.' He's a God-fearing man."

"Ah, but what happens to the 'God-fearing man' when he begins to hate God?"

"What do you mean by that?"

"He will not trust God after this. He has trusted God to give him a wife. Now God has given him a prostitute? And now—what?"

"How can you say that?"

"Think about it."

"But you believe me."

"Ah. But I'm a Van Holden. I'm used to such things. Joseph is a Jabrecki. I believe they're famous for—what?—making donkey carts?"

"But you hang doors for the Slag Brothers."

"Hm. Well, we shall see. It would be a miracle is all I'm saying. A Jabrecki!" And he humphed.

I asked where Mother was.

"Down the hall, preening. The news you gave us this morning has done much for her hairdo. I don't know what's happening, precisely. I went by the bathroom earlier and noticed a beehive forming on top of her head; there may be honey by this time. Maybe you should go and check. I am afraid to see what may be happening next."

I found Mother as Father described, standing in the bathroom and straining at the mirror.

"Mother, what are you doing?"

"Missy! Welcome to the groomery, also now known as the Chamber of Visitation. I have the creeps in here, I can tell you. *Very* good creeps. It's all so wonderful. Do you like my new hairstyle? I think it's becoming."

"But *what* is it becoming? Mother, what are you doing to yourself?"

"Don't you know? I'm primping for the angels. Who knows which celestial magistrate will be flitting about me today. Michael, perhaps. Why, the one you call Massa could be back, and I'm his favorite toy. He may be peering into my eyes this very minute. Oh. Could you please pass me my eye pencil?"

"I will not."

"Missy!"

"Mother, you're missing the whole point of this. God has given us a special task in His kingdom. It has nothing to do with trying to look good, for heaven's sake. You attracted Massa well enough when you still looked like—"

"Careful, Daughter."

"When you still looked like good old Mother. Now please."

"Mary!" It was Father calling from the living room. I was sure he'd be telling me that Joseph was here. "Have you completed your barn chores?"

"I haven't even started them."

"Then please do so. Some of the chickens seem ready to claw the house down and—*arrrf!* One of them has just jumped through the window!"

I ran down to the living room to find Pharaoh chasing a chicken across the floor. Father was howling over it, fully entertained, coffee everywhere but still in his mug. "What need have we of dancing girls and the minstrels of Egypt? For we have Pharaoh and the renegade chicken! Get him, Pharaoh Boy!"

Pharaoh and the chicken made harebrained paths through the room, cutting around furniture, making sunbeams show up in the dust. Pharaoh couldn't leave the ground like his nemesis, but ran faster than the chicken and its desperate attempts at flight. When Pharaoh had the chicken cornered by the yucca plant, I stepped in. As I stepped toward them, the animals relaxed. One could see it. They gave way to me, especially the chicken. I grabbed the chicken and he relaxed in my arms. It was odd. Father noticed it.

"Even the chicken senses," Father said. I wanted to deny it, but I couldn't. "A chicken has more sense than a Jabrecki, it is said."

"Said by whom?"

"It will become the saying," Father insisted.

"Please don't say that." With the chicken under my arm, I escaped outdoors.

The chicken relaxed in the crook of my arm. It was a clean bird, I knew that, but it seemed even more so now. Something inside the chicken pushed up and out into its feathers, making all things right. Some strange inner substance crept into its feet as well, but God called the substance "good." I nevertheless held the chicken tightly into the outdoors. Its feet started moving (in a running motion) even moments before I chose to deposit it to upon the earth. And so it knew.

Gabriel was right, I knew. It had happened. I laid awake in bed through half a candle after the visitation. I willed myself to stay conscious, but eventually surrendered to sleep. The next thing I knew, light was on the walls. A triangle of sunlight crossed the wall of my room. It appeared to be crossing, anyway. I stared at it forever and watched it crawl. I decided to watch it overtake my favorite crack in the wall, the one that looked like the western shore of Galilee on the maps.

Sometimes when I would dream it would be a minute after waking before I was sure it was a dream. This thing was different. The instant I awoke and saw the triangle of light, I knew it wasn't a dream; the light carried the history of what had happened. But it wasn't really light I was seeing; it was something that had been light in the recent past. This is what carried the history. Anyway, there were footprints, also, in the bathroom, where Gabriel had stood.

I knew I was pregnant. I looked at my hands; they were different. I felt my hair. I stroked the ends of my hair and stared at the dry ends. The ends were drier now, because things had left there to go to the baby. I rubbed my forehead and there was less blood beneath the skin. I looked down at my feet; they were different. The air I breathed was the same, but now I could feel particles in the air that went to deep parts of my body. I felt my neck. I ran my fingers along the bump in front, then along the sides in the smooth parts of my neck. It was different, especially in the smooth parts. It was not the skin that was different, or the bump, or the smooth valleys on either side of the bump where my fingers ran. Everything underneath that was making me what I was, that's what was different. It was like candle and flame, the candle being the body and the flame the invisible power underneath. Our science is wrong. It's not the body that's the product of our internal energies; it *is* the internal energy. There is no difference, is what I'm saying, between inside and out. The only difference is that the candle, the body, is the same—at least in the moment—but the flame is always different and changing.

I walked differently. I was more careful, more aware of every step. Where before I would walk while thinking where to go, now I was aware of how each step was making me where I was. My steps were not passing, because everything had shifted to the present. Walking down the hallway to the bathroom, for instance, I knew that what separated me from the bathroom was time. Were it not for time, I could be in the bathroom and in the hallway simultaneously. I felt frustrated, then, at my slavery to time.

My house wasn't the same. It was the same in its substance and in the things that occupied it, but there was material in the substance that made everything different. It was moving. Worlds of things moved in the materials. Energy subsisted in the spaces between the worlds. I couldn't see the movement, but I could sense it. The chair in my bedroom, for instance, looked still. Yet it was moving, deep down. It looked solid, but it wasn't. I thought I could put my hand through it, but I couldn't. It was frustrating to be unable to push through into the ethereal.

I knew that the sovereignties were everywhere now, not at once, but at different times and in different places. Sometimes in the kitchen, sometimes in my bedroom. I did not want to disappoint Mother, so I never told her, but they weren't with her, they were with me. They were more interested in Father than in her. I didn't tell Father, either. Massa was an aberration; he had been banished for the eon. And yet Mother talked frequently to him. Again, I didn't tell her. Father's puns amused one and all. His organs of reproduction were things of renown to the celestial dignitaries; I could never have told him that. He will read this, and will know it for the first time. He scratched his manhood often, thinking it was the heat.

I went to the barns, trying to keep the animals from touching me. It didn't matter with Pharaoh, because he was clean. And I don't mean he was clean in not being dirty. I don't even mean it in the sense of Moses. He was clean spiritually. I realized that morning why he was so light. I knew why his eyes were green and why I could look at them and feel comforted. Pharaoh knew what had happened. He talked to me with his tail and his eyes and his voice. I'm not suggesting that I knew what he said; I didn't. But I could sense that he was communicating and that I was feeling better because of it. So who's to say that I didn't know? Pharaoh was my companion, more so than my parents.

I walked in-between the goats to feed them. Ordinarily, they would nudge me and shove their heads into me and try to jump like dogs because of the food. But this morning, they just stood and watched me walk with it. I walked right through their midst and had an easy time placing food in their mangers. Pharaoh went with me. The other animals paid close attention to him. This was probably nothing new, but something I was just then noticing.

It was the same with the chickens and the cows, both with me and with Pharaoh. The cows never fought me. They didn't fight this morning, either, but they lowed oddly. The lows were longer and lower. Pharaoh walked ahead of me, and the tone of the lows changed as he passed; it went up. The tails of the cows twitched in odd directions, some of them making the figure of ten. It was all numbers. There were sounds among the chickens, many times the usual. I'm not talking now about the sounds I heard, but the in-between sounds that I never did hear. These were numbers also. The chickens were doing something with their heads that was wonderful, and new. At least I thought it was new. But now that I'm writing this, I'm thinking that it wasn't new at all, but that I was just then seeing it.

I was surprised to see stars out in the middle of the day. When I finished my chores, I looked down the Magdalan Way.

※

I had come around the curve, and there was the good old straightaway. I strained to see Mary. I knew I was way late. I had lolly-gagged and walked almost half the distance. I didn't start thinking about things until I'd run past the Horns of Hattin. I told myself: *Don't start thinking until you turn southwest from Kuneitra Street onto the Magdalan Way. Wait until you pass the Horns of Hattin before you sink the thinker and think like a sinker! The Horns of Hattin are baffles of cotton, not rotten, the cotton, and so slain is the mutton!* I was taking a little advice from the wise man—albeit spackled with my own ecstatic vocabulary—about deferred pleasures. I knew that the conversation at Rent's would do more even than running to annihilate time. Bye-bye, shadows on the sundial! Each sentence of that conversation was a nub of pulp in a grapefruit of happiness that I could suck the daylights from. And there were ten thousand more nubs. It was such a great world now. A world full of pulpy, sunny nubs. Mary was going to flip—in a good way, I hoped.

I pictured her in the *chaphet* and *gara*. Now *there* was nubby pulp, spraying enough sourness to make any man's mouth squinch. Before, it was only a dream. But now I had New Bravery Bordering on Honesty (I should write a book with that title.) The kosmos twinkled for me now. Road grass blew toward my feet, and the kernels in the wind, rubbing, had a language I could hear. All this spoke to me of the *shamat* of Mary, and of our untapped glories.

Distance rolled by and by. I wasn't moving—the world was. I was not yet in the presence of Mary—*my Princess, my Goddess!*—and I had to talk to somebody, so a raven resting in a scraggly jujube squawked and he regrets it—I suppose—to this day. "Porter of the jujube, where leaves fall free. Speak! Disgorge your mysteries to a man with blisteries!"

Squawk!

"Oh, funny you should mention it. I've just been thinking about that, my charcoal wonderbird. We shall go directly into the sanctuary for the hanky *pank*tuary. Pretty Little Priestess in the Cubicle of Our Weaknesses, eh? The Holy Place, face-to-taste—oops, did I say *taste?* Surely the God Who invented it all shall glory in the *vent* of it all. Yes! Is He really so rabidly out of touch? Oh, I think not, Winged Tot! A fun place to 'go at it,' eh? Smack on the Sabbath! In the face of David—that's where we mated! Oh, loveliness! Thy concubines! Thy table wines!—enclosed where the sun does *not* shine. Who is the high priest this month? Hannais? Hannais, old boy, sorry about that, your Magistrat! Did I expose my little *pubicle* in the middle of this *cubicle*. Did I break something? Some *law? Oh, pshaw!* Do I now atone for licking her throne? *Too late!* Wham bam, kill a lamb!

Kiss her feet, bye-bye sheep! (I was laughing hysterically by this time.)

Squawk!

"Oh, no. Lud and Put and God and Abraham, no, no, I've never seen it. Never beheld Her Holiness—if you know what I mean, Black Bean. But forgive my scattered amulets that I *want* to. Forgive my beryl and onyx and agate and sardius *desires*. Forgive me, Winged Emissary, my carbuncles and cow cuds, and do overlook, speedily, this gold-embroidered filigree from my Mistress' table."

Squawk!

I was thinking about how thirsty I was—that's when I saw her.

We walked a hundred fathoms after the first hand wave. We met in the middle of the road. Here, finally, she was! I gave her my hand, for that is all we knew. We both just smiled at each other. Her presence was as the sunshine.

We hadn't seen one another for two and a half months. I had stayed with her family the previous Nisan, when we had all gone to Jerusalem for the Passover. It was in Jerusalem, in the house of her Uncle Alexander on Tyropeon Street, where we'd been betrothed. There was a big party after the Passover, and we were as good as married. Almost as good. I still didn't get to kiss her; we were lucky to be holding hands. We spent our last night together in our favorite restaurant in Jerusalem, The Jaffa. And now, here she was. My God. *Mary*. I looked at her with new eyes from the sky—and from beneath that glorious peat bog near Lisht.

"Mary. I missed you like crazy. Sorry I'm late."

"Two hours, Joseph. What happened?"

"I stayed at Rent's longer than I should have. Sorry about that. The time got away."

"Rent Hassler? You'd have been better off with robbers."

"Oh, Rent's all right. He said to tell you hello. Everybody on the team says hi."

"I forgot that you had a game. Last night?"

"Yesterday afternoon."

"Did you win?"

"We lost by three points to the Llamas."

"Sorry about that. When do you play next?"

"Thursday. It's the last game, against the Leopards. Then the playoffs. But I don't think we'll advance. Nobody thinks so—especially not the *Enterprise Review*. Or so I hear."

"They don't know everything." Hand-in-hand, we walked toward her house. "I've been thinking about our wedding," Mary said.

This was my opening, and I walked through it with New Bravery Bordering on Honesty. "I'm glad to hear that, Sweetness. As for me, I've been thinking quite a bit about our wedding *night*."

My poor statement died without a friend in the middle of the air. I thought it had *merely* perished, but no. It fell like a chunk of dead pigeon meat to the road, landing with a splat. Then the day quick-baked its body. We stepped over its corpse and left it behind for vultures—poor vultures; they probably regurgitated it. I looked straight down at the brown road rolling beneath our sandaled feet. I at least thought that Mary would squeeze my hand, or say some little thing.

"Mother re-arranged the living room again."

"Again? Imagine. So…where is the sofa now?"

"In the corner closest to the hallway. Near the yucca plant."

"Imagine."

Ben was the first to squawk from the front porch. "Joseph! Good to see you again." He extended his hand. "How are things on the Magdalan Way?"

"Warm," I said.

"I'll bet."

I took Marney's shoulders, kissing her lightly on her turned-out cheek. "Hello, Mum."

"And the same to you. Do you need water?"

"A hin, if you have it."

"Ha! Such a funny boy. I'll put you out at the cow trough."

Mary and I plopped down on the sofa closest to the hallway. Pharaoh jumped up to purr and nuzzle me. We had a thing, Pharaoh and I. I needed him now. "Good kitty," I kept saying. Pharaoh was "a good cat," a "fine kitty" and "quite the cat." Ben waited for the girls to step into the kitchen before launching into his regularly-scheduled interrogation.

"What time did you leave, Joseph? How is the Sea today?"

"I left around eight. The sea is lovely. A lot of boats out today."

"Pleasure-craft?"

"Oh, some fishing boats. Pleasure-craft also, yes. Some of those rower people doing their rowing."

I knew something bad was about to happen. *Where was Mary?*

"Pleasure, pleasure, pleasure," Ben said. "It seems that pleasure is all people care about these days. Especially young people. What do you think about all that?"

I didn't think anything about it, and I said so.

"How spiritual are you, Joseph?"

Mary was back now and saw what was happening. She gave her father a mean eye in secret, trying to compose herself in time, but was late in getting it away. Ben didn't care. I asked him why he wanted to know how spiritual I was. I asked him why he *always* wanted to know.

"Think about it, son. You're marrying my daughter. It's important to both Marney and me that our daughter be cherished by a man who seeks God and understands His ways."

I told him that I was that man, that I did seek God, and that we had already talked about this forty-nine times. I returned to Pharaoh and then without looking up said, "There's more to God than the rituals and the feasts. We can't contain God. There is more to God than slaying lambs and building tabernacles. We need a tabernacle relationship with Him every day. Not just three times a year."

Mary scratched at non-existent tics on the back of her hand. Ben looked oddly defeated. *Good,* I thought. I suddenly hoped he would rebound and pursue me. Marney interrupted us with water.

"Hydrate, everyone! Hydrate! It's another hot one. No fun! In fact, Joseph, I should send you and Mary out to the well. I should get you to draw us a double load."

"Give the kids a break, Marney," said Ben. "They haven't seen each other in a while."

"You're right, Ben. I can't believe myself. Grab a broom then, you kids, and sweep out the barns."

Good old Marney. I silently thanked God for her. She asked about the game. Mary's mother was a big fan of the Welldiggers—of Rent Hassler in particular. I told her we had lost, but that it had been close. She asked how Rent had played and I told her, although I purposely left out the part about Rent missing the winning shot. "Sometimes it's better to get clobbered than to barely get beat," Marney said. "It's just so *frustrating*"—and she stomped her foot.

I had been staring at Marney and finally decided to ask if the Living Organism overtaking her head—the Colossus that everyone struggled to ignore—was the latest style in

Nazareth. "I have been away nearly three months," I said, "and I did not realize how quickly the hair fashions change." I pointed directly at the Colossus. "Are we now taking the lead from Gaza?"

Marney blushed and delicately pat-patted the pile with her fingertips. "This old thing? Oh, it's only to impress the—"

"Mother!" Mary interrupted.

"That is, well, it's simply to impress the big old donkey sitting over there in the easy chair."

"Hello," Ben waved at us. "I hate it, whatever it is."

"Maybe we should all eat some *cheeses*," Marney said. "Or pepper hash, perhaps?"

I asked aloud if I was missing something.

Mary jumped up so fast that her kneecaps popped. "I think it would be easier if Joseph and I just lunched at El-Bekkers."

Marney wouldn't have it. "Oh, Mary. No. Moses. God. To send you two off when Joseph has just arrived, I just don't think that—"

"It's fine, Mum," I said. Something bad was happening and I needed to get out. "I really have to talk to Mary," I said. I looked at my bride-to-be. "About the wedding and all." Mary stared blankly at me.

"Dinner, then. Fried cod and potatoes, I insist," Marney said. No one said anything in return. "Now, you two lovebirds scoot over to El-Bekkers. We'll expect you back around six."

Ben had gotten up to shake my hand again. "Get the mushroom soup," he said. "It's great."

I said, "Okay, Ben. I think I remember that about the mushroom soup. I think I might have gotten that once. I'll probably get it again. The soup, I mean."

I pushed out the door. I almost forgot to take Mary's hand. I almost forgot her completely. Everyone waved—or something. When we turned at the end of the sidewalk to see if Ben and Marney were still watching us, Ben looked weird. I know what it was now—it was the look of an owl, but not an ordinary owl. No, it was the Nubian Nightjar that sits at the Dead Sea with cookie-sized eyes and a beak from hades, gazing down its great Nubian nose at the soon-to-be-doomed. The owl seemed to be saying directly to me—to squawk, rather: *It's been nice knowing you, Jabrecki—sort of.*

CHAPTER 4

EL-BEKKERS

I couldn't get out of the house fast enough. There was no way I wanted to eat lunch with my parents. I wanted to be the one to tell Joseph, not Father. I knew Father would keep up with his little hints, not that Joseph could ever have guessed. But it did seem better just to leave.

We had good memories from El-Bekkers, which is why Joseph wanted to go there. This is where we came when we first met.

Mother was the first to meet Joseph. It was at a Viper's game in Ramah, while she was visiting my cousin Elizabeth. It was Mother's birthday, and Elizabeth surprised her with tickets to a game. Mother had never been to a professional match. It was no coincidence that the Vipers were playing the Welldiggers of Nazareth; God controls even the movements of ringball teams. Mother was a big fan of Rent Hassler. In fact, she only met Joseph trying to meet Rent.

Elizabeth had a brother on the arena janitorial staff, and he arranged for her and Mother to meet the Welldiggers after the game. But by the time they found Hadrian, Elizabeth's brother, only Joseph and a few others were still in the arena. Mother had rushed up to Joseph and asked, "Where's Rent Hassler? Has he left yet?" This became a joke between them.

While talking to Joseph, Mother discovered that he lived year-round in Nazareth, just a short walk downhill from our house—another divine arrangement. "And he's quite handsome," Mother told me later, "and I think he's third on the team in point average." That was a lie. He was second-to-last, and Mother knew it. It surprised me that she thought I cared. It didn't surprise me that she had lied. I'd never even been to a ringball game before meeting Joseph; I didn't care much for sports.

It was three weeks later when my parents escorted me to Joseph's and introduced us. Mother was right about Joseph being handsome. But what I liked most about him were his eyes. Ordinarily, if a man looked at me the way Joseph did that day, I would have turned away. But Joseph's gaze made me want to return it. His was a good gaze. Joseph had very compassionate eyes. I could tell from his eyes that he was a gentle person.

We went into his house; Joseph was living on his own. His mother and father had both died, and he had one younger sister living in Azotus, and a wonderful dog, Mandy, the old family pet now in Jeshra's care. It was clear that Joseph loved animals. He lived with a cat named Reuben. It was funny and sweet the way Joseph talked to Reuben throughout our visit that day. Joseph was rummaging through his kitchen trying to find us a snack, and we heard him say, more than once, "Now Rubie, where did I put those crackers?"

We ended up going to El-Bekkers that evening, with Joseph and me sitting across from one another. Whenever our eyes met, I would smile and look away. That was just me. But then I would almost instantly look back up again, and

I could tell that Joseph had never taken his eyes from me. I would look down again and smile, then would look back up. Joseph would be smiling, and I would smile back. It was so exciting, but it also made me nervous. I had never looked at a man that way before. My parents kept talking about things that night, but who knows what things? Neither Joseph nor I had any idea. We just nodded occasionally and made affirmative little grunts.

It was dark when we left El-Bekkers that amazing evening. My parents tried to wedge in-between us, but Joseph managed it so that he and I walked next to each other all the way home. We walked about ten fathoms ahead of my parents.

I'll never forget what happened next. Just as we reached the door to my house, Joseph said, "I won't be able to even open this door until we touch hands. That's the secret thing to opening this door, to touch hands." So we reached out and did it. It was very quick, because Mother and Father were coming up from behind. But it was so exciting. And it was more than just touching; Joseph squeezed my fingers. I couldn't help but squeeze his back. It was a small thing, but thrilling, because I had never done that before with a man.

We were able to get together several more times after that, in-between Joseph traveling with the Welldiggers. And we would always come here, to El-Bekkers. It was *our* place.

We knew that we wanted to marry, and we talked to my parents about it. They approved of our marriage from the start, though Father did have reservations. He did not trust the name Jabrecki. It didn't sound spiritual to him, he said. It was not "an old Israelite name." This was the wrong way to judge a man, and Father knew it. He could never justify his superstition with any fact. In the end, Father admitted that

Joseph was a good man. And so Joseph and I were betrothed in Jerusalem only three months after we met, during the Feast of the Passover.

※

The corner booths at El-Bekkers were ill-designed, and still are. That's the only thing I hated about the place, those ill-designed booths, not that it was ever a problem again once I befriended the waiters. The booths were designed by a craftless maniac. The booths are really two booths made of one table. The seats are at ninety degree angles, and the table is cut with only about a palm's width in-between. We made the mistake of getting seated here once with a family—a couple and their kid—already seated across the gap. It was so awkward. The other couple stopped talking as soon as we sat down. The kid just stared at us. Who could blame them? We invaded their dinner like the Midianites invaded Shechem. I wanted to apologize for bothering them. *Sorry for the invasion*, I wanted to say. *Aren't these booths a joke?*

The waiter that evening was too stupid to appreciate what was happening—stupid as bath tile. He talked all hushy, as though he were seating us for an intimate, romantic dinner, when really he was casting us into the maw of a family picnic, in progress. He was handing us our menus that time and I wanted to say, *I wish you were smart just long enough to realize how stupid you are.* It wasn't his fault, I was just mad. Mary kept giving me her "please behave" look, so I finally gave up and crossed the border. I asked the family their name. Why not? It was Shearim. "As long as we're sharing this evening repast," I said, "I thought we might just go ahead and get to know one another. So, how's that lamb, Homer?" Mary kicked me under the table. She thought I was being smart. I wasn't. Our evening was ruined. We ended up talking about Dot's asparagus garden. I decided then that we'd never get the corner booths again. And we never did.

Joseph seemed very uptight, not himself. We didn't talk much all the way to the restaurant. I thought it could have been that he was tired from his walk. Or maybe he was bothered about my father questioning his spirituality again. In any case, this was the first time I was dreading a meal at El-Bekkers with Joseph. Dreading is too strong a word. I was just not sure now how I'd break my news to him. It was all so simple before Father had said, "Now God has given him a prostitute." Before that, I was just going to tell him. I was even excited about it. It was amazing news. It had not even occurred to me that Joseph might not believe me. It was unthinkable, really. I had just assumed that he would believe me, that he would see the fulfillment of scripture, and that he would rise to the call together with me. But now I thought that I had to tell him in just the right way. That's what was making me nervous. What was the right way? I would have to trust God to put the words in my mouth. The waiter led us to our booth, and I prayed: *Please help me say this the right way. Please make Joseph believe me.*

Our favorite waiter, Huram ben Huram, led us to a booth along the wall. I had slipped ben Huram a shekel at the door, so he knew where to go—good boy. These were the booths underneath the cedar lattice, with all the plants hanging down, the best seats at El-Bekkers. For romance, this was where you wanted to be, beneath the green tendrils of the love gods dripping over your head. We had sat here when we first met, when we came here with Mary's parents. We got lucky then. Now it was all skill—and the occasional chunk of currency.

I leaned back in my booth to let El-Bekkers dig its familiar fingers into my psyche. The restaurant was cool and dark in the middle of a hot, bright world.

Plates and more plates, heavy with food, sat gorgeously upon the upturned palms of waiters, who hurried. The hurrying waiters—*more coffee, please!*—turned my inertia to decadence. I hadn't eaten since breakfast, so the smell of steak was sexual. My mouth glands disgorged juices that said: *Bring us meat!* Empty wine glasses, upside-down, clinked in bunches between the fingers of our white-dressed men. I shuddered to think that the wind, somewhere, blew. Knives and forks inside our palace struck plates that had found homes. The hum of talking filled El-Bekkers, but no one said a discernible word. The smoke above plates and mugs still traveling spoke of meat, hot bread, and the many kinds of coffees from green, inaccessible mountains. You'll want to hear something about the aromas of these drinks, and so: the aromas wafted from aqua, yellow and brown-red mugs matching the plates on which the waiters served us bread. There we were, sitting motionless like pyramid bricks in our latticed kosmos. I loved everyone in El-Bekkers that day, I remember that. We were, all of us, escapees from reality in our civilized cave, with so many *other* people so far away, battling storms and foodlessness. That's just what it felt like, and I loved celebrating life with fellow livers in a *den* of life.

"Look at those arches, Mary." I pointed behind her at the architecture. "Look how they overlap between the rooms. Room, shadow, room, shadow. Ever notice how deep this place is?"

Mary turned to look. "I guess not."

She must not have known how happy I was just to look across the table and see her, so I did four things, in this order: 1) I reached over the table, 2) I took her hand, 3) I brought her hand to my lips, and 4) I kissed her hand.

"Joseph. Not here."

She tried to take her hand back, but not too convincingly. So I hung onto it firmly and kissed it again. I smelled it as well. I breathed it in deeply.

"What in the world are you doing?"

Huram ben Huram came for our orders. He had quit asking long ago if we wanted wine; we always refused. So he was just as surprised as Mary when I said, "Ben Huram, what's the finest product in that wicked cabinet of yours?"

Ben Huram clapped his hands. "Ah! Thank you for asking, Mr. Joseph. Let's see. We have wonderful red wines just in from the vineyards of upper Galilee. But allow me to suggest a Tishbi Muscat from the vineyards of Gaza. Very white, very light—as we say."

"Permission granted. And yes, we *do* say that. What goes with mushroom soup and a T-bone?"

"Red."

"Ha! So much for the muskrats from Gaza, then." I looked at Mary—it was a bad idea—then back at Ben Huram. "What do you think, Dr. Huram?" It was a show-question, because neither Mary nor I knew anything about wine.

"We don't even drink wine," Mary said.

"Wait! I forgot!" said ben Huram excitedly, "We have bottlings now, just in this week from the experimental vineyards of the Negev—if you're feeling sporty, that is."

"Funny you should mention that," I said. "No, really. I'm serious. You can't believe how sporty I'm feeling right now. Red or white?"

"Red."

"Full-bodied?"

"Oh, yes. And fruity. And very smooth."

"Full-bodied, fruity, *and* smooth?"

"*Very* smooth, said ben Huram."

"This is such a good day. Can anyone believe this day? Somebody help me here."

"Can I bring you and Mary a bottle?"

"Just two glasses, thank you."

"You'll never regret this."

"*I'll* say."

Off ran ben Huram, and Mary was just staring at me.

It wasn't going well. Joseph was acting crazy. First, he kissed my hand. I can't say I didn't like it. I did. I just didn't like him doing it at the restaurant. But then he smelled it. I might not have thought that was so strange, except for *how* he did it. He practically inhaled it up into his nose. I felt that people were looking at us because of it.

What really shocked me was when he ordered wine. Everyone in Israel drank wine—everyone except us. It was one of the things of being Joseph and Mary. We just didn't drink it, or any other alcohol. We would even make fun of people who did, including my parents. We considered ourselves too practical for it. Too above it, or something.

But now Joseph ordered us some strange concoction from somewhere in the desert. It sounded awful. I didn't want to drink it, but neither did I want to disappoint Joseph. So when the waiter came with our glasses, I tried it. Joseph "proposed a toast." I'd never heard of such a thing. I didn't know what to do. "We just clink our glasses together and make a wish for ourselves," Joseph said. "We make a wish for happiness," he said. No one in Israel ever did such a thing. Ceremonial sippings, yes, but not this. I didn't know where Joseph got the idea. *Probably from Rent Hassler*, I thought. We did it anyway. We made a toast "to us." I felt so foolish.

I tasted the wine, and it tasted like poison. From the look on Joseph's face, it was the worst thing he had ever drank. But he tried to disguise it and pretend that he liked it. He said, "Ah, now *that* is a full-bodied wine," as if he knew. His voice sounded so artificial when he said that. I had no idea why he was pretending this way. "You don't even know what a full-bodied wine *is*," I said. "Why are you even saying that?" And then he became a little irritated, I think, and said, "That's true, Mary, I don't know what it is, but if there is such a thing *as* a full-bodied wine, then *this* is most certainly *it*." It was a ridiculous conversation, and I couldn't believe we were having it.

Our glasses just sat there on the table then. Our food came, and Joseph ate like a Philistine. He would pause long enough to sip from his wine glass, although I couldn't touch mine again. How would I tell Joseph now? I kept praying silently to myself, asking God for an opportunity.

Joseph kept talking about "new and different" things. He spoke of our future, and kept saying the words "new and different." He never mentioned specifics, it was just "new and different." He also said we needed "fun and excitement" in our lives. He kept using these phrases again and again, without ever saying what precisely would usher us into this magical state of being. I decided that God was building a bridge for me. I did have something to share that was new and different, and very exciting, though I could not contribute much to Joseph's "fun."

Then God rolled out the red carpet when Joseph asked about my writing. He was talking with his mouth full, as usual.

"It's been weeks since I've worked on my diaries," I said. I placed my fork down on the table without a sound. "I'm ashamed of myself, really, for not keeping up with them. I'm ashamed at my lack of discipline."

"You're trying to put everyday things down on paper, right?"

"Yes," I answered.

"Tell me why again? I've forgotten."

Ordinarily, Joseph's memory lapse would have upset me, but this brought me my chance.

"You know about the Van Holdens," I said, "and how we feel about destiny."

"Your Father has mentioned it a few times."

"I believe God has set us apart for spiritual activities, to accomplish a great purpose in His plan of the eons. I'm recording the details of our lives so that people will know how human we were. I want God to get the glory for whatever happens with us."

"Sounds like a worthwhile project. You're related to the prophet Isaiah, right?"

I could hardly believe my ears. "*Hello?* I'm a descendant of David."

"That's who I meant. I think he's related to Isaiah, though—right?"

"Not even close."

"Hm. I could have sworn he was related to Isaiah. Too bad. Have you ever tried this mushroom soup?"

"Have you read him lately?"

"Who?"

"Isaiah."

"Isaiah the prophet?"

"No, Isaiah the pickle-barrel salesman."

"C'mon, Mary."

"Can I quote you a passage?"

"Sure."

"'The virgin shall be pregnant, and shall be bringing forth a Son, and they shall be calling his name Emmanuel, which is being translated, 'God with us.'"

"Line one-hundred."

"Two-hundred and six."

"Well, how about that. A virgin giving birth. More bread?"

"Do you believe that Messiah's coming?"

He was mutilating the bread now. "Of course," he said. "Why do you ask?"

"You know that the Messiah will be born."

"Is that really true? I thought He was going to ride in on a white horse or whatever."

Now Joseph was buttering his mutilations. I grabbed his knife and made him look at me. "What scriptures are you reading, man? I just quoted you the passage. Who do you think the prophet is talking about? His name shall be 'Emmanuel,' which is 'God with us.' Who else could this be but Messiah?"

"Okay. I'll agree that it must be the Messiah, but—." He reached for the bread again.

"Can you stop it for a second? Hear the rest of it. 'The virgin shall be pregnant, and shall be bearing a Son.' It's this Son, born of the virgin, who shall be called 'Emmanuel.'"

"All right. So what? Why are you bringing this up right now? I was hoping we could talk about our wedding night." Now he reached for his water.

"Because the Messiah will be born in nine months."

He stopped in the middle of his sip, and his glass moved slowly back toward the table. At last, he'd heard me.

"Nine months? How do you know the Messiah will be born in nine months?"

"Because I'm carrying Him."

"What?"

"I'm carrying Him."

"Carrying *who?*"

"The Messiah."

I set myself like flint to look at my betrothed. I wonder now what I expected him to do. But I do know. I expected him to throw his hands into the air, to cry, to look amazedly at me. I expected him to jump up from the table and whisk us to the Nazareth gardens where we always went to watch the peacocks and talk about God. I expected him to take me there so we could feel amazed together. I know what I did not expect. I did not expect him to laugh.

He put his water down, and that horrible smile came to his face; I can see it still. At first I thought it was a smile of happiness. It wasn't. "You're carrying the *Messiah?*" He said it so condescendingly. There was butter on his lips. Then he started to laugh. But he didn't just laugh, he laughed like my mother laughed. Each of his explosions severed bonds holding us together. I didn't think I knew what hate was, but I hated Joseph then. I hated him. He finally wiped away enough of his tears to see mine.

"Mary. What is it?"

"I told you what it is!"

"But you were joking."

"Oh, no. I'm pregnant, Joseph. The angel Gabriel came to me last night. I talked with him. Do you understand that? Gabriel, Joseph! He told me that I was the chosen one, that the spirit would come on me. And it did. I'm carrying the son of God!"

"Hold it, hold it. Slow down, please. You're telling me you actually think this happened?"

"Yes, it happened!"

"Are you feeling all right? Seriously, because—"

"*Damn* you."

"What?"

I strained to keep it together. "Damn you to hades, Joseph Jabrecki! You don't believe I'm pregnant!"

"You're...*pregnant?*"

"God, Joseph. Have you even been listening?"

"You're going to have a baby..."

"We're going to have a son."

"A son. Wow. Moses. So...who was it?"

I didn't know what he meant. "What?"

"Who put it to you? I mean, you're pregnant. You're pregnant, right? Whoa. Whew! Sorry it took me so long. I'm kinda stupid. So—do I know him? This is *really* big news. I mean, congratulations. Forgive me. Which game was I at?"

I wasn't sure who I was talking to then. It couldn't have been Joseph. I was so confused. I was so alert. "Didn't you hear the prophecy? The *virgin* shall give birth."

"Yes, well, here's the thing. People like me don't study that much. You say you're still a virgin?"

"Yes!"

"But you're pregnant."

"Yes!"

"Well, damn. That's amazing. Seriously! I really do need to study more. Did your parents put you up to this? It goes so well with the whole...Van Holden mission shit."

I heard it, but I didn't. I could not hear it; I could never have heard it. "I'm pregnant by holy spirit!" I said. My voice was breaking now, and shrill. Everyone was looking at us.

"Holy spirit has a dick. Wow."

"Shut up, Joseph!"

"Oh. Okay. Good idea, Mary. I think I will. I'll shut up now. Can you finish my soup, then? For some reason, I'm just not that goddamn hungry anymore."

Then he threw down his napkin and left.

That was El-Bekkers, the fullness of it, the brevity, the terror. Ben Huram came and said something; he took my arm. This waiter and I exited into a world where the wind blew, and where the brightness blinded me. Somewhere in time, I left the restaurant alone on the arm of a man in a clean, white apron. The man was in an apron, I remember that; an apron without spot or blemish.

CHAPTER 5

THE OUTSIDE WORLD

It was a great day, up until when my world fell apart. Other than that, yes, it was a fine afternoon. Glad to see you again, Joseph. Please come in. Don't forget to hydrate. Let's go to El-Bekkers. Get the soup. Stop kissing me, I hate the wine. Looked into Isaiah lately? Oh, by the way, I'm pregnant. But don't worry, it wasn't a man. Ha! I'm a Van Holden, and we're above such soilings. The holy spirit did it to me, Sweets. Don't you believe that? It happens every day. God wanted to save you the trouble—isn't that thoughtful of Him? God always has the best in mind for us. By the way, our baby is the Messiah. You're the Daddy of your own Redeemer! You and I can change his little diapies. We can teach him to peepee in the outhouse. But maybe he won't need to peepee. Ha! He'll be a Van Holden.

When I thought back, I realized how little I really knew Mary. We had only known each other six months, and most of that time I was out playing ringball. How much can you learn of someone from five or six meals? From three trips to the park? What had tricked me? Possibly her eyes. Yes, those were it. It was a stone-hard thing, realizing I could never trust again, ever. I felt like I lost my naivety that day—that's what killed me. I liked trusting people. I liked the world. I just didn't know until then how the world regarded me. I knew about adultery; I wasn't that naïve. I just never thought it would happen to me.

It was immature to just leave, but how can you philosophize over a hurricane in progress? I ran home outside my body, watching myself run. But then the stabs would return me to my wall, which was Jericho. And Mary had blown the trumpet.

I broke only one thing, against a real stone wall in my kitchen. It made me sick, all the people who knew about us. I said terrible things to God before I threw, while throwing, and later, while kicking the fragments of my favorite coffee mug. But God decided to let me live. It was the worse punishment. It would be public scandal, and I would be the brunt of it.

If you lay spread-eagled on the floor on your back and look up at your ceiling, imagine what would happen if an earthquake struck and your ceiling fell on top of you; it's a joyous thing. But the ceiling stays put and you hear yourself breathe, so you realize you're thirsty and so you pour some old well water onto your face from the canteen of a bachelor.

And you think.

It was Mary who was in trouble, not me. She had committed a capital offense. If I wanted to accuse her, Mary and Whoever would die by stoning. They would. The following is from *These Are the Words* ("Leviticus"—*Ed.*), an excerpt from the law of Moses:

In case there should be a maiden, a virgin, who is betrothed to a man, and another man finds her in the city, and he lies with her, then you must bring forth both of them to the gate of that city and stone them with stones so that they die, the maiden on the score that she did not cry for help in the city, and the man on the score that he humiliated the wife of his associate. Thus you will eradicate the evil from among you.

Ever seen a stoning? Lucky you. They tie the people up and carry them to the pit. Two people do the carrying, three if there's a struggle. The condemned are still human until the ring of the pit, where they graduate in tears to victimhood. The rocks come so hard because the killers are afraid to kill—isn't that strange? If a witness stands at the edge of the crowd behind a man who is fat, that witness can hear bones break. If the witness cranes his neck to look out from behind this man, he eventually discovers that bones are white. The skin turns black, they say, but the witness (yours truly) doesn't get that far.

I did not hate Mary. I didn't even hate the man. I might have been able to kill him in his sleep, with my fists, in the dark, if I'd thought hard enough about what he'd done. But I couldn't bring anyone to the pit. He'd brought it on himself, I knew, but Mary would go with him, and there was no way, not a way in the world I could let that happen.

I kicked more pieces and swept the floor. I swept and swept it. If only we hadn't been betrothed. But it was official. In Israel, betrothal is the same as marriage. The only alternative to stoning was—

Divorce.

I swept more, wept more. I would divorce Mary—that was it. I'd do it quietly. If I did it right, betrothal would disappear and would never have been. Mary would be free, and I'd never have to say "adultery." Did I really want to be married anyway? There were more reasons besides adultery to dismiss a wife. Seriously. I could say she changed religions. I could say I was moving and she refused to go. I could say she'd contracted leprosy (ridiculous, of course). An obscure law (I looked it up and found it) said I could dismiss a wife for insulting me.

I sat down on the floor and stared through the dust. I breathed it in. That was it, then. She had insulted me; no, she had damned me. I'd been en route to hades for nearly an hour now, and felt like it. There were witnesses. There must have been a dozen people, at least, who had heard her.

That would be it, then. I didn't have to say it, the witnesses were my back-up. If anyone asked, I'd say, "I have my reasons." Mary couldn't deny it, not with witnesses. The alternative would preclude her from denying anything. The only person who had to know about it was the lawyer. I didn't know one, but Rent did. Maybe.

I would return to the restaurant at nightfall. Where was ben Huram when Mary had said it? Others must have heard her; I needed two witnesses. I started feeling brutal, but better. What was the date? I repeated it in my mind. I'd return in a few hours to get names. Or else I'd curl up in a ball and get swallowed by Earth, like the sons of Korah.

"Missy. What happened?" I fell in tears into Mother's arms. "Where is Joseph?"

"You're puzzled," Father said. "But why? It is this: Joseph has not believed her."

Mother thrust me out at arm's length so that my neck whiplashed back, then forth. "Is that true?"

"Yes!" I sobbed. "Now please, let me go."

But instead of letting me go, she damned Joseph, tied him to things, beat him, compared him to animals and left him to die. None of this comforted me.

Father finally hushed her. "It is not the fruit of a venturesome heart, such disbelief. Boldness doesn't enter into this, Marney, as if the man had it. He's a Jabrecki, thus, he cannot help himself. The goat eats garbage, the chicken eats corn, and the Jabrecki turns from God. Are you amazed, my family, when the palmer worm burrows away from the sun? Then why all this fuss when a Jabrecki rejects the spirit?"

The one thing that the dying do not need is speeches.

"Go to your room now," Mother said, "And Ben and I will discuss this."

"You can't discuss this without me," I said, wiping my face with my sleeve. "I'm of age."

"She's the one who was called," said Father. "It's different now, Marney. Let her wash, then we'll have a meeting. But for now, coffee. I like that new Grecian blend, with a sprinkle of cinnamon. Is there any left?"

I washed my face and walked across the road to Wallace Khawalida's. Wallace said he could watch Reuben indefinitely.

I loaded up my backpack, stuffing as much dried meat into it as I had stored. Dried meat, walnuts, pistachios, and parched corn. I could stock up again in Ptolemais. Then, an extra set of clothes and a washing-towel. I would not tie up my bedroll until morning. My plan was to run. And run.

"This meeting has come to order." Father pounded his fist on the coffee table. "Let us all take a sip of the Grecian bean." I hated that my father could be so practical at such a time. Nothing was bothering him yet. We did what he said and sipped. "Now, family, we have a problem. Mary, our dear daughter and the recipient of God's favor, is betrothed to a man who will not have her."

"We don't know that yet," I said.

"Ah, then. May I ask, Child, how it came about that you ventured home today alone from the restaurant?"

I had been looking into my lap, but not anymore. In my anger at Joseph, I mocked Father. "Ah, then. He threw down his napkin and left. He told me I could finish his soup."

Mother rubbed her forehead. "It's not exactly grounds for divorce." She was much calmer now, and was fussing with her hair.

"But it is," Father said. "I wasn't there, but I presume to know something of what happened. Joseph accused you of indecency. Correct?"

"In a manner."

"In a manner?"

"In so many words."

"There you have it, then. It's a false accusation. You're entitled to be loosed from betrothal to a man who, by defaming you in this way, has become odious to you."

"A stench in your nostrils," Mother said.

"Thank you for the elucidation, Wife. Now, we need only prove before the priests that Joseph has done this."

"But I don't *want* to prove it," I said. "I don't want the priests to know about it. Why can't we just leave it alone? Why does it have to be so complicated?"

"I think we're forgetting Joseph's end of this," said Mother. "None of us are thinking what Joseph might do."

The only thing that moved then was the tip end of Pharaoh's tail, sticking out from underneath him as he lay on the back of Father's chair. Father was smoothing his mustache. "Perhaps, indeed perhaps," he finally said, "we must lower ourselves to consider this from the Jabrecki viewpoint. I had not done that before. It's difficult and distasteful, but a necessary evil. Consider what the man might be thinking. I fear, just now, that Joseph may be capable of bringing charges against *you*, Mary." He paused. "You know what that means."

"But she's innocent!" This was Mother.

"We all know that," Father said. "But what will the priests say? Of a truth, you are pregnant, Child."

The impossibility of it fell upon us like a millstone then. The silence of the previous minute was nothing compared with this. Who would believe my story? The priests? They did not even believe their own prophets. For the first time since my visitation, I rehearsed my testimony through the ears of others. Sitting cross-legged on the floor, I spoke it to myself, then listened. I felt the disbelief. I saw the looks on the faces of the priests. Father was right. It was so hard not to think like a Van Holden. Forcing myself to do it brought the worst kind of light. Most of the world were not Van Holdens. Joseph was not, the priests were not, and the executioners were certainly not. I pushed my face into my hands and shut my eyes. The harder I pushed, the more lights appeared, little sparkles of blue and green. I was dizzy and crowded. My eyes were hot. *Joseph, what have I done to you?*

"You're at the mercy of Joseph."

I looked up. "What?"

"It's all up to him," Father said. "The law is on his side."

"How do you know?"

"Child. There is no recourse known to me, in all of Moses, for a betrothed woman whose impregnation comes by holy spirit." Father was deflated. He would never in his life, under any other circumstance, have uttered the word "impregnation." He fell back hard into his chair, dislodging Pharaoh. Again he said, "You're at the mercy of Joseph."

Mother fussed with her wedding band. "That dear man…"

"Then I'll go see him," I said. "I'll go tonight. Let's all go to his house. He'll listen to all three of us."

Father dismissed the plan. "It's too soon. It will hurt our case to go now. We'll appear too anxious. The wound is too fresh in his mind. I think morning will be soon enough. Early morning." He looked up at Mother.

"I think we should go *now*, Ben," she said.

"It's settled then. We go in the morning."

El-Bekkers was busy, but God was with me because ben Huram stood at the door receiving diners. "The owner paid your bill," was the first thing he said. The bill. It would never have occurred to me to the day of my death—another humiliation. I gave ben Huram a silver piece, then took him aside. Did he have a minute? "No, not really." I slipped him a shekel. "Only a minute," he said.

Had he heard Mary damn me? "Yes, I'm afraid." Would he say so in the courts? "I really don't want to get involved, Joseph." I tried to explain how important it was. No one's life was at stake. It was a simple matter of divorce. I could tell he was in a hurry. "I guess I could do it, if nobody got hurt." I promised him no one would. Had anyone else heard it? "Only half the restaurant. You made quite a scene." I only needed one more witness. Could he give me specifics? "I talked about it with Al Soroff and his girlfriend. They heard the whole thing." Was that the same Al Soroff who was divorced himself? "That's the one. They were in the next section over." Then for sure he'd help me. "*Probably* he will." Could ben Huram ask him? "I guess so." I needed a promise. "Okay. I'll ask him." I had to know when. "He comes in every Thursday for the men's supper." I was sure that Soroff would help. I thanked ben Huram, slipped him another shekel, asked him to keep it all quiet. "I will. Good luck. I mean, it's terrible."

Back home through the night. Few lights. Looking up the road, I can almost see Mary's house, up on the hill. Must turn away from that. Slip into my door, into anonymity. Tomorrow, very early, I will be gone. And now, pen and parchment. But first, tea. I'm going to enjoy this, as much as I'm able.

Start a fire behind the house, stir it, boil water. So alone now. Something perversely wonderful about that. Spearmint leaves, three, into the mug. Water into it, releasing the life. Now honey, the food of the gods. All dark and quiet outside. My father used to say I was never so happy as when planning a running trip. The spoon clinks. He did not know the fear that mixed with the joy to make it bittersweet. *Clink, clink.* The spearmint smells so good. There is much of it in the roadbeds between here and Sepphoris. I will chew it. Between there and Ptolemais? I didn't know. That was the thrill of it.

My table is empty, such simplicity. Parchment, pen, table, mug. It's all I need. The room is bare except for my bedroll, bag, tarp, tent, and backpack, all against the wall, organized in minutes. There is joy in simplicity. Why did I ever want to be married? The bedroll, the floor, the earth, slip into sleep. But first a sip of tea. Perfect. Steam up my nose, clearing my head. I smile inwardly, sit and think. A fly lands on my mug, right were I'm drinking. Always, always, back to reality. Flick him away and wipe where he was with a finger. All clean. Pick up the pen and begin to write:

Dear Rent,

Tomorrow morning I'm leaving for Ptolemais. I'm finally going to do it, to run from Ptolemais to Antioch, three-hundred miles up the coast of the Great Sea, the length of Syria. I've always wanted to do this, up the coast, from Mt. Carmel to Mt. Silpius, across the river and into the great city. I've always wanted to see Antioch, not from the back of a donkey, or with a gaggle of strangers in a caravan, but under my own power, solo, by the sweat of my brow. To run over the aqueduct, over the Orontos River, alone, and see it. Over the bridge, the hump of the aqueduct, then Antioch spread before me. Just to write the name of it excites me. Antioch! I'm actually going there. This moment, as I sit writing to you, Antioch exists. Way up there somewhere, where I've never been. I will see it. I'm scared and excited, but I have to do it. You know me. The road calls.

I love the road. It takes me back to when I was younger, to the runs around the Sea of Galilee, the races to Lake Semechonitis, the run to Damascus. You know about the run to Damascus I made with Banias in '93. How many times have I told you where we slept in Caesarea Philippi? That run was a watershed event in my life. That's when I knew I could be self-sufficient, that I could endure, and that I could live a life of bare simplicity, forever if I had to. If you can do it for four days, you can do it for a hundred. Banias and I used to say that. And if you can do it for a hundred, you can do it forever. That run was a passage of manhood for me. This will be the same, I think.

I figure to run the marathon distance every day, plus about seven miles. About twenty-five miles a day. At that pace, excluding Sabbaths, I should make Antioch in two weeks. It will be a test of my endurance. I'm in pretty good shape, but not that good. That's the appeal of it, Rent, of not knowing for sure how it will feel. Every mile after a hundred is unexplored territory. Who knows? I may get a job in Antioch, do some carpentry, and keep going. I've never seen Greece. Can you imagine? Running all the way to Greece.

The more absurd, the more it excites me. As I sit here tonight at my kitchen table (you can picture where I am), it's not out of the question. I think I could really do something like that. The bigger it is, the easier for me to swallow. Why is that? I don't understand it myself. It's all or nothing. That's how I think these days. I'm headed more and more in that direction in my life. The older I get, the more it takes to get me out of bed. I should be depressed to even be writing this, considering how young I am. Oh, well. People have died younger than me. Of old age, even.

Something happened between Mary and me, something bad. That's what this is all about. I can't write about it in detail now. I'm too tired. I haven't even figured it all out yet myself. I might be extremely angry right now, for all I know. I refuse to feel. I'm putting it out of my mind. I will write you more from somewhere along the way, when I sort it all out myself. But things are not good. I have to leave Nazareth. I don't have to, but I want to. It's for the best. God is ordering my circumstance, just as we discussed.

This is the perfect time to do the run. Maybe it's escapism, I don't know. I try not to analyze my motives. What good does that do? Motives don't matter, only the work and the doing. I want to run. All I want to do is run and keep running. I can think about anything on the road, or I can think about nothing at all. Both are the same, on the road. I'm serious about Greece. I think that could happen. The spur of the moment of this is what excites me. If I had sat down and thought about it, planned it for a year, I don't think I'd be doing it. I'd be thinking too much, and you know how thinking ruins everything. The excitement of just leaving and not telling anybody—that's the thrill of it. It's going to keep me awake tonight, I know. I feel pretty good right now. I'm drinking spearmint tea. This is where I want to be, on the edge of the cliff. Is this more exciting than ringball? You tell me.

Speaking of ringball, you know what this means. I'll be missing the last game. I'm sorry. My heart isn't in it. I hope you understand. Just tell everyone I got sick. Tell them I got

Job's boils, the plague, a carbuncle—I don't care. Use your imagination. That reminds me: Don't say anything about Mary to anyone. I'm thanking you in advance for this. It would not be good for people to find out. I'll explain more to you later. I would be there for the last game under any other circumstance. But you don't need me anyway. You can admit it; I won't feel bad. If the season was at stake, I would play. You know I would. But you don't need me. Give Af some playing time. He can do a lot for the team. Go Welldiggers. I ask you this favor: Please mail my last paycheck to Sidon. It's Monday now. I should be in Sidon by Thursday. I'll take a day off and spend the Sabbath there. Send it to the main mail station, general delivery. Seal it with your regular seal, so I can identify it to the clerk. Thank you for doing this. I'll write you from Sidon, to let you know I got the check. I'll stay in Sidon until it comes.

One more thing. Do you know any cheap lawyers in Nazareth? Anywhere? Please let me know when you write.

Thank you again. May the God of Abraham, Isaac, and Jacob bless you. Thank you for the hospitality you recently showed me. It was a memorable visit, to say the least. You are a good friend. I remain yours in grace and in peace,

Joseph

P.S. Go Welldiggers. Leopards = Losers

I thought I should also write a note to my sister Jeshra, in Azotus, and give her my itinerary in case something happened. I scribbled off the note, not explaining much. It was only a list of the cities I'd be in. I would post it in the morning, along with my letter to Rent.

Very sleepy now. Maybe I will sleep after all. I try not to think about anything. I roll out my mat and stick the backpack beneath my head for a pillow. That reminds me that I have food there; I'm hungry. I take out two figs and lay back down. I forget about the lamp, so I get up and put it out, then go back to bed. Maybe it will be cool tonight. I reach over and find my sleeping bag, then lay it over top of me. I try not to think about anything. There is no moon out, not one piece of light in my lonely room. The aqueduct over the Orontos River, people say, is whiter than pearls. I try not to think about it. One more fig? No. It's the last thing I remember, saying "no" to the fig.

CHAPTER 6

ROADS APART

"Pffft. Mary, wake up. Mary? *Pffffffft!*"

"Daddy?"

"Come quickly and eat. Your mother has eggs and dates. We're going to Joseph's."

"What time is it?"

"Six o'clock. I hardly slept last night, and neither did your mother. Hurry, please. There's coffee on."

I washed, dressed, and went to the kitchen. "Good morning, Mother."

"'Morning, Missy. Eggs are coming. Where's your cup?"

We heard a thunking in the hallway. Father appeared, hopping on one foot and trying to fit a sandal onto the other. "Leave the eggs. Everyone."

"Ben? What is it?"

"We must go. Now. Get your light coats. Follow me and do not speak."

We filed out the door like a war drill, then eased down the hill in the darkness toward Joseph's house.

"Stop walking so loud!" Father ordered. He was talking in a coarse whisper to Mother.

"But there are so many tiny stones and dried mud balls in the road, Ben. And my sandals don't fit right."

"Why are we sneaking, Father?"

"We are not sneaking."

"Then what do we call this?"

"A fair question, Missy."

"Quiet, Wife! We are simply walking softly."

"We're sneaking, Ben."

"We are not."

"*I* know. It's that book you're reading, *Salt Sea Intrigue*."

"That's got nothing to do with anything, Marney. Now please, will you concentrate?"

"I know where you are in that book," Mother said. "I look, you know. You're on chapter fourteen. There's a lot of sneaking in that chapter, I know. I know what you read, it's my business. Admit that the book has had an effect on you. It's no shame."

"I'll tell you what *is* a shame…*God help me*."

We arrived at Joseph's and Father rapped on the door.

"He's still sleeping," Mother said. "Rap harder."

"I know what to do," Father said. He rapped harder. Still, no answer.

"Let's go in," Mother said.

"We can't," I said. "It's his house."

"Knock louder," Mother insisted.

Father pounded.

I said, "You'll wake the neighbors."

"Look in the window, Ben."

"We can't, Mother. It's eavesdropping."

"Mary is right, Marney. It *is* eavesdropping. We'll *crawl* in."

"Father!"

The east window was nothing but a light wooden shutter. Father easily breached it with a stiff push, and he was now bent over the sill, at his waist, half in and half out, when a loud voice said, "Ho, there! What are you doing?"

The voice made Mother and me jump. Someone was standing in the darkness, under Joseph's tree. Mother had her hands up, as if it were a hold-up at the treasury. "Joseph?"

"Wallace Khawalida. Who are you?"

"Wallace! Thank goodness it's you."

"Marney Van Holden?"

"Yes, yes, it's only us. Well now. What do you know."

Wallace stepped out from the shadows. "What are you doing here? Is that Ben sticking out of Joseph's window?"

"Oh, yes, that's Ben, just him. Oh, he's kicking. I wonder if he's lost something. Do you think he's stuck? Ben, what is your status? Are you stuck?"

An agitated voice came from halfway in the house. "No, Marney, I'm doing my morning exercises. Now, if your conversation with Wallace is finished—and I do hope that it is—perhaps you and Mary could pull me from the middle of this domicile."

The three of us removed Father from the sill. "It's a good thing I had a light breakfast," Father said. He was brushing himself off in such an artificial way, however, that I could not look at him.

"Joseph isn't home," said Wallace.

Mother craned her neck and her hairdo tilted. "Not home? Where could he be at this hour?"

"I don't know, Ma'am. He said last night that he had business out of town."

"What business?"

"He didn't say."

"Did he say where he was going?"

"No, Ma'am."

"When will he be back?"

"I don't know. But he said it might be a while."

My heart sank.

"Well," said Father, smoothing his mustache until I thought it would catch fire, "I guess this ruins Joseph's birthday surprise."

"It certainly does," Mother said. Here they went.

"Cancel our order at the bakery," said Father.

"Done, Ben. And the party hats from Dag's Hattery…"

"Canceled, likewise. The mind of man plans his way, but God directs his steps."

"So true, Ben. The plans from men's minds get snuffed out like lit candlesticks, smothered by the divine tsunami."

"So much for the roll of streamer paper I dropped in Joseph's window."

"He can decorate it himself, when he gets back. I hope he likes red."

"It's his favorite color, Marney. He told me so."

"Well, we'll be seeing you, Wallace," said Mother. "Don't tell Joseph anything about this."

"I won't, Mrs. Van Holden."

"Thank you, Wallace," Father said. "We haven't even eaten yet."

"Is that right?"

"No one likes cold eggs," said Mother. "Peace be with you, Wallace. And with your chickens."

Then up we went, flat-footed, up the hill toward home.

"A showpiece!" Father sat at the kitchen table throwing raw popcorn kernels at our trash basket. Most of them pinged off the basket and skittered across the kitchen floor.

"What a work of art we have just brought into the world," he said, referring to our embarrassing caper at Joseph's. "Gray and flat like the stupidly-celebrated Bordenkhan prints at Carmel. Fiddleblitz!"

"I'm sick about Joseph," I said. "I must talk to him."

"To hades with him, Mary," Father said. "It's you I'm concerned about."

There was no sense protesting to Father. If only he knew Joseph's heart. And yet where was my betrothed? I was heartsick. I'd been thinking back over and over again about what I'd said to him at El-Bekkers. I had been so impatient, so self-righteous. It's true that Joseph had mocked me, but it was only because of how coldly I'd broken my news to him. I had mocked him and made him feel foolish. His laughter was self-defensive. I practically dared him to believe me. Father questioned his spirituality overtly. I did it more subtly—but still I did it.

Other things bothered me as well. I had asked God to show me the way, and He hadn't. Worse, God had led me down the wrong path.

There is no God beside the God of Israel, and He has made everything for its own pertinent end, even the things we consider distasteful. I always thought I knew God's ends. I thought I knew what to pray for. But now? I prayed, and everything turned out wrong. I had sincerely asked for God's help, and this is what He answered: He drove Joseph away by my own hand—to where?

God hears prayer, I know. I only doubted my prayer. Did I want His will? No. I wanted my own. The contrasts brought this to light; the holiness of the call, my failure with Joseph—all in one day. I started to doubt everything then. Everything. Even the visitation. I don't mean that I doubted I had spoken with Gabriel. I doubted the purpose of it. Was God deceiving me to teach me something? It seemed possible now, and that scared me. It scared me that God could fashion His plans without me.

What a terrible sentence I have just written! That you are seeing it means I've let honesty have its say. Here I am, for all to see. I write a sentence without thinking, and it becomes a window into my heart. I can't take it away, or I lie to you. The sentence, too, fashions its plans without me.

My only consolation was that God was God. This had to be part of His plan. If it wasn't, unworthy was He of His name. El-Bekkers, every detail, was destined beforehand.

Isaiah writes, "For I am the El, and there is no further Elohim, and the limit is as Me. Telling from the beginning, the hereafter, and from aforetime, what has not yet been done." Even my clash with Joseph, then. If not, then Isaiah lied, as well as He Who sent him. Who becomes judge as to what God tells, and what He doesn't? Everything that happens, does so "from the beginning." Does anyone claim to predate that? I don't.

This was an answer. I didn't like it, but it was something.

I don't like El, sometimes. Hear me on this. The alternative is worse: a God outside circumstance. His title, El, means Subjector. It says what God does: He subjects. The Supreme of Israel subjects creation—the earth and all in it—to His fiat.

Consider the heathen king Nebuchadnezzar of Babylon. God drove him from his palace to the fields, to live among beasts. This is what it took for him to acknowledge God: to grow claws, to eat grass, to lick the dew like an animal. Was I to become a Nebuchadnezzar? My family?

While I wrestled with these theologies, Mother and Father fretted. For all the trouble, I had to smile. Not at my situation, but at them. I had never seen them so stumped. They were a picture of bewilderment. A funny thing came into my mind then. I imagined my parents inside a picture frame, with a little gold plaque at the bottom of the frame. The plaque said: BEWILDERMENT. I tried to keep from laughing, but then I pictured Father in a frame of his own, bent over Joseph's windowsill. The plaque beneath this picture said: MORNING EXERCISE ROUTINE IN DOWNTOWN NAZARETH, TO TRIM THE WAIST.

I laughed out loud.

"I wish you'd share the punch line of whatever exquisite joke Beelzebub is whispering to you right now," Father said.

I told myself, *stop laughing*. When that didn't work, I said, *thou shalt stop laughing*. The "shalt" failed also, so I gave up and said, "Beelzebub says Joseph's favorite streamer paper color is blue, not red."

Father was exasperated. "What's the use?" he said. "What is the use, O God, of trying to talk to a family such as this?"

Without warning, Mother practically shouted, "Elizabeth! She and Mary are in similar circumstances."

Father reacted as if a two-headed mule had just leaped through the window. "What has that got to do with anything, Marney? Elizabeth isn't pregnant by holy spirit, is she?"

"Gabriel didn't say, specifically," I interjected. "But he did say that she had conceived. He said, 'Elizabeth, your relative, has also conceived...' That sounds to me like it was *she* who did it. It was different with me. With me, Gabriel said, "Holy *spirit* shall be coming on you."

Father was satisfied. "There. You see? It's different. I don't see what Elizabeth has to do with any of this."

"A miracle is a miracle," Mother said. "Elizabeth has been trying for twenty years to have children. She and Zechariah have tried the banana cure, the upside-down cure, the cure with the purple—"

"Thank you, Wife. We're informed."

"Wait, Daddy. Gabriel did say, 'Take comfort in knowing this, that Elizabeth, your relative, has also conceived a son.' I wonder why he said it would be a comfort to me? It hasn't been that yet."

Mother spoke. "He really said that? Then rejoice! If that's true, I know what he meant. He meant that Elizabeth would be your comfort *now*."

"How?" I asked.

"You must go to Elizabeth's. I believe that God will give you your answer there. Miracles are happening, miracles by the day. I don't see why God should withhold one more and solve this problem with Joseph. The answer, I believe, is at Elizabeth's."

Father opened his mouth to object. Then he closed it. Then he opened it again, only to slam it shut. He shifted in his chair. He was seeking fault with Mother's idea, I knew. He shifted again, each new position an objection confounded. Mother looked pleased. As for me, I knew it was right. I needed to go. If Joseph could be gone, then so could I. I dreaded the thought of sitting home crying, waiting for him. I was nearly certain he'd return. It was the anguish of "nearly" that made me want to leave Nazareth. My doubts would be drowned on the road. At Elizabeth's, I could be a little girl again. Elizabeth would be strong for me, and I wouldn't have to wonder if I was in Joseph's dreams.

In deference to Father, I tried to keep from running to my room to pack. Finally, and without crediting the source of inspiration, Father said, "It's the Van Holden solution. Mary, prepare your bag. You're going to Ramah."

"Yes, Father!"

Mother went to the kitchen to bake konafa bars while Father sat with Pharaoh, pondering the logistics.

Elizabeth lived south of us in the Judean Hills, a three-day's journey. Only five or six caravans a year moved south on the Jerusalem Road, and the next caravan, Father said, would not be moving until Tishri, the upcoming holy season. There was possibly another coming through in a week, he said, for a large wedding in Herodium, but it wasn't for sure; he had only heard the rumor. My parents considered accompanying me to Ramah, but they wanted me to have time alone with Elizabeth, as much as I needed. Traveling alone on the Jerusalem Road was out of the question, so Father decided I should travel with the mail run. Before I could protest, he was out the door and headed to the mail station, to inquire. I thought it was a terrible idea.

Mail ran each day up and down the Jerusalem Road, two groups of three men on donkeys, running twenty miles a day each week between Jotapata in the north and Hebron in the South. I knew two of the men in the group known by Father: Irbed Gev and Jen Afula. While pleasant enough for a five-minute chat, they were not my idea of travel mates. I'm not saying they were killers, or rapists, or thieves. I'm saying they were—men. For some reason, Father liked them. He had subcontracted them two years before for the Slag Brothers, and the four of them gathered once a month at Irbed's in Sepphoris for all-night games of *wadi-tot*.

The third man, Stewart Salkhad, had worked with Father at the Evil Institution. Rumors had it that Salkhad at least bathed every holiday.

Father returned from the mail station, singing. He had arranged everything, he said, down to the time I would arrive in Ramah. "But you can't leave today. The boys won't be in Nazareth until Thursday. Two days. I consider that a stroke of luck." I was willing to wait a week for the wedding party. "Nonsense. This is a sure thing. Believe me, Mary, I would not send you with these men unless I knew them, and knew them well. I would trust them with my life. Now, in a game of *wadi-tot*, no. I would not trust them any farther than I could throw a camel across the Great Sea. But with you? Yes."

Father had rented a fourth donkey for me, "a beautiful she-ass, round-rumped, vibrant, gray, and ready for action."

Irbed, Jen, and Stewart pulled up at precisely seven in the morning. Each of the men carried large mail sacks and traveling panniers for their personal goods. My gray donkey tagged behind Stewart's by a rope. "Her name's Jezebel," said Jen.

"What are those pink things hanging off Jezebel?" Mother asked.

"Them's Mary's panniers," said Stewart. "Pink panniers for Mary. We dyed 'em ourselves with aspalathus juice. Different from our brown'ns. What you think, Mary?"

"They're lovely," I lied.

Mother gave me her woodpecker kisses. "I love you, I love you, I love you. Be careful. Elizabeth has some explaining to do. We should have known of this. Find out what happened, and why we didn't know. A full report. Write next week, or—"

"Thank you, Wife. I'm sure Mary will inquire. Godspeed, Daughter." Father hugged me. "Give our best to the Van Holdens in Ramah. Miracles await us there."

"I will. Write me as soon as Joseph gets home."

Father turned to the mailman with the gator-skinned turban. "Irbed, you old muskrat. Get down here and help Mary tie her load."

"Your wish is my reprimand," said Irbed. "Ha!"

We managed to stuff everything into the panniers; I didn't need my traveling bag after all. A final good-bye to my parents, and we were away.

I didn't want to talk, just ride. But this was an impossible dream. To Irbed, Jen, and Stewart, talking came as naturally as wiping the brown juices seeping at intervals down their chins. For the first five miles, no one said much. As we entered the wilderness of Esdraelon, however, the dam broke.

"You can call me Stew," Stewart said. "Stew's what they call me, pretty much everybody."

"True enough," said Jen. "And Foggy, and Cocklenuts, and Swiper, and Bone. But mostly Stew."

"That's nice," I said. "I'll call you Stew."

"What's happening in Ramah?" Irbed asked. "Family?"

"I have a cousin there."

"I got family," offered Jen.

Irbed turned so sharply at this that a neck bone cracked, and a ghastly brown blob of *whatever* splashed between Jezebel's ears. "Yeah! And every summer Jen's family come out o' their trees for a *re*-union."

Everyone laughed. I said, "How nice."

Then Jen said, "Strange, but it seems to me that a man what lives in a thatched hut made o' *monkey* turds, such a man oughtn't not be throwin' millstones at other folks' turd domiciles, through the walls o' *his*'n. Fact is, ain't nobody seen the likes o' the Gev clan."

Stewart let out a low whistle. "Tell 'er, Jen."

Irbed turned around again, and I ducked. "*Dang* now. Say *one* thing 'bout that, Jen, and the undertaker's comin'."

"Oh, don't worry, Irb. I ain't makin' nuthin' of it. I don't tell your mama, of how she wrestled a hippopotamus up at the Yarmuk River Games—"

"Close the trap, Afula!"

"I doubt you know 'bout that one, Mary. Irbed here, he come from a long line o' hippo wrestlers. Fine folk, and I mean it. Just seems a tad strange that Irbed's mama be the only—"

"Shut the barn door, Jenny!"

"... she be the only *mama* what competes there, let 'lone takes the cup."

"*That's* it!"

Irbed jumped from his donkey and made for Jen. But Jen was already dismounted and running into the Esdraelon countryside.

Stewart and I sat and watched. Stewart cheered for Irbed. Stewart asked me who I was taking. I didn't know what he meant.

"Which you want t' win? Say 'Irbed.'"

"Yes. Irbed. That was a terrible thing Jen said about his mother."

"I know it. His mama ain't that fat." Stewart turned thoughtful. "Still, I wouldn't want t' be the hippo."

The boys returned, dustier than when they'd left.

"Who won?" Stewart asked.

Irbed said, "Nobody, you muddler. We decided we wasn't actin' godly in front of Mary. It was a civil dispute, and we ought to be civil. We promised Ben to deliver Mary safe to Ramah, not kill and maim each other. *Say?*"

It sounded good to me, nearly. And so we were on our way again. We made the mail drop in Ginaea, this being a matter of withdrawing the smaller bag from the bigger one on the back of Irbed's donkey—the "piggy-bag"—and picking up the outgoing Ginaea mail. This, we put into a blue sack flung across Stewart's donkey. Yes, I said "we." By nightfall I was one of the boys, a part-time employee of the Evil Institution.

We found our lodgings toward dusk, three miles past Ginaea on the east side of the road. These were cabin-type lodgings, clean and safe, though expensive. Father was paying for the cabins; one for me, another for the boys. The boys were happy. Were it not for me, they'd be in their tents. They still carried gear, as they would continue their journey without me from Ramah, but as long as I was with them, there was no need for tent pegs and tarps. "Bunks and pillows," Jen sighed when we had disembarked that first night and transferred our gear. "The kingdom done come."

We continued the next day through Samaria and Sychar, delivering mail and picking it up in each of the towns. Outside Sychar came the hard climb up Mount Gerizim. "Mount Grizzly Bear, we call it," said Jen. Up we went, and down the other side toward Bethel. Again, we lodged between towns.

We were careful to get in by sundown the second night, for it was the Sabbath. I had enough food and water to stay in my cabin. I read Scripture through the morning and early afternoon, then wrote Mother and Father in the evening. I don't know what the boys did, or how strictly they observed the Sabbath, if at all. I had my doubts. Irbed knocked on my door in the afternoon and asked if I wanted to "lay for gator" on the Antipatris. As I said, I had doubts.

Finally, my last day was underway. Now that we were off Mount Gerizim, it was hot.

A terrible thing happened around noon: I fell off my donkey. It was so hot, and I was poorly hydrated. I felt myself swoon. The next thing I knew, I was leaned up against Jen's chaps, and Irbed and Stewart were splashing water on my face and asking ridiculous questions. The only question I remember was, "Who's the premier o' Egypt?" I couldn't remember falling.

"We heard a big thump," said Jen, "and next we know, Jezzie's coming down the road without you. You all right? There's a nasty bump back your head."

My pride was hurt, mainly. I asked how far to Ramah.

"Only ten more miles," said Stewart. "We'll have you there by five."

"Then let's sail," I said, quoting the mariner Aaron from *Salt Sea Intrigue*.

My mood was growing dark. I was aswirl again in theologies, doubting God, doubting my call, wondering why things had gone so sour with Joseph. *You just made me fall of my donkey, Lord.* It was a small thing, but large to my mind. It was an insult, and I took it personally. The God of Daniel, Who with outstretched hand moves nations and men, takes time from His celestial duties to push Mary from her ass, the ass with the pink saddlebags. I was feeling dizzy again. I said, "I need to stop."

"There's a big willow up a ways," said Irbed.

We stopped and I drank. I stuffed down three of Mother's konafa bars. Stewart asked if I thought I could make it. I could, I thought. We remounted, and the miles waded by.

"Look!" said Jen at last. "Ramah! Mary, you got directions?"

Within a quarter hour, I was deposited at 16 Dan Street. Stewart said, "Now, Mary, we're going to wait here until we see who's retrieving you."

The men had been wonderful companions, and I told them so. I blessed them in the name of God, giving them each the postal salute they had taught me back in Sychem. I patted Jezebel as the boys readied for departure.

The front door opened and a woman stepped out.

"That yours?" asked Irbed.

"It is."

"God bless your visit."

"Pleasure having you."

"Be seeing you, Mary."

And then they were away.

And there stood Elizabeth. It had been so long. I knew she wasn't expecting me, and it must have been a shock for her to see me standing there. She squinted, shielding her eyes from the midday sun. Did she even know it was me?

"Elizabeth! Peace, in the name of God!"

"Mary?"

Strangely, Elizabeth did not step toward me. What she did do I will never forget. She raised her arms and shouted in a loud voice, "Mary! Blessed are you among women, and blessed is the fruit of your womb! And whence is this to me, that the mother of my Lord may be coming to me? For lo! Even as the sound of your salutation came into my ears, my baby jumps with exultation in my womb. And happy is she who believes, seeing that there shall be a maturing of that which has been spoken to her by the Lord!"

At these words, I felt a power surging up through my feet, through my legs, and into my chest. It was a heat. My chest was heaving in the heat, and through it. My face flushed and God's spirit moved through me, consuming me, more so than I'd ever felt. I didn't think of how to answer Elizabeth. I did not even think to marvel that she knew I was the mother of her Lord. I did not have to think, because God's spirit supplied my words as fast as I could say them.

"My soul is *magnifying* the Lord, Elizabeth. And my spirit exalts in God, my Savior. For He looks on the humiliation of His slave. For lo! From now on all generations will count me blessed, for the Powerful One does great things for me, and holy is His name, and His mercy is for generations and generations to those fearing Him. He does mightily with His arm, He scatters the proud in the comprehension of their hearts, He pulls down potentates from thrones, and exalts the humble. The hungry He fills with good things, and the rich He sends away empty. He supported Israel, His offspring, to be reminded of mercy according as He speaks to our fathers, to Abraham and to his seed, for the eon."

Having said all this, I passed out.

CHAPTER 7

TYRE SEASIDE NATIONAL PARK

The dilemma was where to eat lunch. Two places appeared next to one another in Jotapata: an El-Bekkers-looking restaurant called Saladins, and a funky-looking pile with red and white striped awnings over the windows, Kerack's Kitchen. In the spirit of adventure, Kerack's won. The wacky potpourri of styles suited me. Not only had strange awnings arrived here, but an octagon-shaped roof with a weather vane came to call, the weather vane being a three-humped camel. Just under the roof, along the perimeter, Egyptian figures sauntered in their bent-armed way toward some unknown destination—possibly Saladins.

The place hummed except for one little table for two in the corner. This was obviously a workingman's diner, ringing with coarse talk, smoke, constantly-cleared throats and the pushing of heavy chairs away and toward tables. Clerks, carpenters, coppersmiths, fullers and farmers, soldiers, doctors of law, together frequenting this afternoon meeting place, made me happy. In less than five minutes I realized why I'd found a seat; the washroom door immediately to my left swung ceaselessly with patrons, closing each time with a dead-raising slap. Several diners pointed and laughed. I didn't care. I loved these people. I was a stranger in the world of Kerack's, and it was fine.

"Hi. My name's Dora. What can I get you?"

"Hi, Dora. I'm Joseph. How's the tuna salad?"

"Questionable as ever."

"I'll take it. Could you stuff it into two pitas for me? Also, a bowl of chickpeas, please. And watermelon. And an order of baklava, if you have it—with honey. And a cucumber for the road."

"Hungry today?"

"Now and forever."

"Is that your backpack?" She pointed to the pack I'd slipped beneath my chair.

"Yes, I'm traveling. Running, actually."

"Where to?"

"Antioch."

"Running to Antioch!"

"Yes, ma'am."

"The owner will just love to hear about this. How about two orders of baklava, one on the house?"

"That is very gracious."

"I want to do it."

"God bless you, then."

This meal at Kerack's Kitchen has nothing to do with anything. I probably would never see Dora again for the rest of my life, or the man who apologized for the washroom door, or the weaver named Ochran who heard about me from the owner and came back to say, "There's a wonderful restaurant in Antioch, Jezzines, that you simply *must* try, and get the swordfish but don't get the vegetables, and tell Kell Jordan that Ochran sent you and don't forget to visit the Maritime Museum on Tulk Street." I mention Kerack's Kitchen because it represents all of the places I visited on my trip, the humble dens of cooking providing humanity more than mere calories, but fellowship and caring besides. The common goodwill of man toward man is what I found at this establishment at half past noon on the twenty-seventh of Tammuz in a city called Jotapata, an experience to be repeated many times, in many places.

So now that you've heard the voices and the chairs and the washroom door—even if you haven't felt even one of the backslaps I received there—you'll keep all this in your mind now and forever and I'll mention such eateries no more. Only know this further thing, that when I went to pay my bill, Dora said, "That man who left a short while ago, Ochran, he paid your bill. He told me to tell you that God was with you." So now you know why the tears came. And you can understand, now, why I asked Dora for two more tuna pitas and an order of baklava to go.

※

Who had ever seen Ptolemais? I hadn't. Since the time I had slipped from my door before six, I'd been thinking of the Great Sea, looking forward to the hour when man and water would meet. I imagined coming over a rise and seeing her stretched out green to infinity. Of course I'd seen her before, but not at Ptolemais, and not in such a manner. In the meantime, Mount Carmel appeased my appetite for scenery; once I'd crossed the Kishon River, the western face of it danced ahead. As far away as it appeared to be, I knew I was near the foothills. Even so, the road to Ptolemais was long, flat, and hot.

My body felt so fresh. The biggest temptation early in these things is to do too much, too fast. The excitement attacks your common sense, and off you go like a horse. I'd done that before and paid the price. So I decided, on this first day, to mix in a little walking. It's the best way to travel, anyway. The brief walks—five minutes out of every twenty—give the running muscles time to recuperate. When you start running again, the running muscles say, "Thanks for the sit-down. We're back in business." To them, it's a sit-down. This combination of forward motion, combined with food and drink and short naps under various trees, can keep one going forever, it seems. The incomparable Jason Pagiel of Megiddo is a prime example of that.

Playing ringball for the Whirlwinds had given me muscles I'd never had. Once in a while I'd allow myself to look down while running—just to see how my body fared, understand. New landscapes rose along the sides of my arms, merging into the great frontal muscles of work. New veins sat atop my shoulders, and long-buried striations quivered along the humps of the round muscles. I liked watching my legs, and seeing how tanned they were. I admired how the muscles, sinews and joints worked together toward the goal of motion, without my conscious thought. Sometimes I felt removed from my body, a spectator gazing down at a miraculous organism: It was as though I were a human variety of equestrian; a fine and brown beast of motion, running tall through the sun against the wheat fields of Galilee. All is vanity, that's true. But all is of God as well. So we glory in our youth, while we have it.

About halfway to Ptolemais, a bell rang. This was the famous Barquq monastery. I caught up to the deep dong of sound as the last peal evaporated.

The monastery sat far back from the road to the north in a cluster of palms, its massive tholoi (the weird plural of tholos) clinging to Earth like giant suction cups. Above one of the tholos, resting atop a capital, was what looked like an immense stone urn, *probably crammed with the ashes of the dead*, I thought. It was all very bizarre. Weird architecture. I considered approaching the place for a cup of water (my fill-up from Kerack's was already gone), but I thought twice. I thought I would be disturbing some sad, waterless reverie.

As I passed the monastery, another, lighter bell rang out. I thought it was probably the call to prayer. I converted this to my advantage, making ten paces between peals. This was faster than I wanted to run, but it made the distance fly by. I laughed at the impiety of my game. I pictured the somber white souls of the monastery, draped in burlap, tied in ropes, shuffling off to the chapel to chant and pray, or whip themselves into mango mush. And here was I, a man of pure air and exercise, practically sprinting up the Ptolemais Road, singing songs to the peals from *Harney Barney*, the bawdy play that Rent and I had talked about in Magdala.

I pictured the slow procession of the monks through the hallways. *Come on, Shuffleheads*, I thought. *Where are your strides? Get a tan. Digger-dee dig, with a nibble of nigh!* (That was from *Harney Barney*). I felt quite uncharitable toward the monks. I was feeling charitable toward God, however, thanking Him continuously for sparing me the traumas of monkhood.

What exactly do they drone on about in there, I wondered. I thought for a moment about running back and checking. I would sneak up to see if I could detect any drones. Perhaps the drones would be careening about. But then I thought, *Come on, Joseph. Drones do not careen, especially not in monasteries. Careening is too happy a thing for the standard monasterian drone. Songs careen and laughter careens and shouts careen off the mountains, but drones in monasteries hit the walls like bumblebees (the suicidal variety) and die on contact.* So I started running again, putting a bent knuckle to my nostril and blowing a wad of snot onto the Ptolemais road. It came out clean and perfect, that wad. What a wad it was, exiting without hesitancy or regret—no wiping on the forearm required for it. So it was a great day filled with the simplest pleasures.

Now four o'clock, tired as I'd ever been, but here was Ptolemais. My first thoughts were for a meal and a room. As badly as I wanted to see the Great Sea, I decided that morning would be soon enough. I loathed running the extra mile to the coast. If I didn't find restaurants or an inn there, it would mean a mile run back. Then, in the morning, I'd see the same mile again en route to the coastal road. Had I been mounted, the choice would have been easy. But the foot-traveler becomes a conservator of strides, begrudging any fathom that does not reduce distance to the goal.

I found a good-looking seafood place in town, El-Fauron, and my momentum took me right into the place. Fiscal caution to the wind! How quick I am to abandon moderation when the soul clamors for celebration. I had made it to Ptolemais, after all. I almost ran out of El-Fauron, however, when I saw the price tags. But pride rescued me again and I succumbed to the flesh—to the flying fish specifically— which smacked of pepper and rue. I tipped like a crazy man, and I wish to explain that.

The harder against the financial bricks I find myself, the harder I throw money at the bricks. There's logic to this, warped as it is, and I'm sure you want to hear it. When you see clearly that the situation has bettered you, you dare the situation. It's your way of laughing at it, which is your way of preserving your sanity. What are you laughing at but your own helplessness? Laugh or die. When a situation is manageable, it's a test of management skill, nothing more. Being skilled, you manage. It's nothing. But when the situation is lost, it's an opportunity for God to work a miracle and for you to rest. I do always like it when that happens. For me, helplessness is a thrill, like taking the Jerusalem taxis. Once you're on those things, you're on, and you can't get off until you either arrive at your address or crash. Jerusalem taxi drivers can ruin your day, it's well known. Before you step into their carts, the control is yours. After—it's theirs. So you give in. You hang on for your life and think, *Well, hell, this is relaxing—in a perverse sort of way—because for a blessed while I will not be the captain of my fate.* This especially appeals to businessmen, who are *always* captains of their fates.

So when I heave my money against a bad financial cramp I'm thinking, *I'll hurry this thing along, deepen it, get God going on His miracle.* Away go the remaining mites, into the wind or a waiter's apron. I'm a happy man. One last bit of advice: It's best to spend one's last mites on fleshly extravagance, such as flying fish, kiwi juice, or a bad waiter's apron. It enhances the giddiness. Repeat: Do nothing practical at this time.

I had always thought of sex the same way. This brings me back to Mary. I know I've avoided even the mention of her, but that's how it was all the way to Ptolemais. I'd shoved Mary into a subconscious cranny and just ran down the road. I refused to feel pain. The only acceptable pain then was the blister on the little toe of my right foot; *that* I could manage with a lance and some aloe.

They say that the ultimate humiliation is death. I'll admit that death is pretty embarrassing. I have always felt a pang of embarrassment for the deceased. There they lay, not caring what they look like, refusing even to greet family members or the mortuary staff. Death is humbling, not for the dead, but for those ambling by to sniff it.

We live, breathe, work, and try to do our best in life. What do we get? Old Uncle Dahne laid out cold on the straw, some brown fluid trickling from his nose, his legs white stones and nothing to look at before lunch, believe me. The morticians rush about, chatting, planning, pushing plants and flowers and people. Uncle Dahne must be wrapped and caved by nightfall, before he emits poor advertising for the shop owners. Uncle Dahne, who built good carts all his life, who would give you a discount on your birthday, who let his children play in the shop when he was supposed to be concentrating on a cart for the mayor, whose wife saved dinner for him, kissed him when he came home, made sure of the quality of his vegetables, embraced him later beneath the sheets—this *same* Uncle Dahne, again sheeted, who must now or never be wrapped, whisked, and stuffed into a cave before he sends us home pinching our noses—this is the man lying before us. *Get him out and in before he stinks*, is what the morticians are thinking. They would never say that, however. What they say is, "Let us hurry along now, Filice. Let us say our last good-byes, all you dear Jabreckis and Kieslers." But now you know what they're thinking: *We've got to get this meat cured and caved before the flies take over.*

I was talking about sex. The only matter under the sun able to compete with death, is sex. I speak from the male point of view, the only point of view I own. Man is master of his race—that's what we're told, anyway. They tell us that we're the stronger of the opposing sexes. It's a fine theory, when you can finally stop laughing long enough to consider it. For your edification, I print a saying I wrote while contemplating this very brand of comedy: *The weaker sex is the stronger sex because of the weakness of the stronger sex for the weaker sex.* It's really not confusing. If you're a male at least three weeks past puberty, you'll grasp it immediately.

I have much more to say about this, but it's not the time. Even so, here's another of my proverbs: *Men discard decorum and thinking along with their tunics.*

I would much rather talk about the Great Sea now, that beautiful body I encountered the next morning as the sun crept onto the earth behind me. I arose early and ran to greet the great sea. Except for the squawking gulls, God granted me solitude. I stood on the beach to see the coming surf, which bowed at the feet of the newest human curiosity. I waded into the surf to my knees. The waves liked me better outside their realm, for they thought to forcibly eject me. But the sand sucked me fast, and between the sand and the waves I was in danger of a soaking. So I sucked myself out and hopped to the edge, to watch.

A wave would come as far as it could. When the water exhausted itself, the foam took over. Foam cannot overtake anything, however, and so the foam became bubbles that the sand swallowed whole. The luckier bubbles popped themselves. Then a new wave would come and repeat the mistakes of its forefathers. It reminded me of a verse from Job:

> Who enclosed the sea with doors, when, bursting forth, it went out from the womb; when I made a cloud its garment, and thick darkness its swaddling band, and I placed boundaries on it, and I set a bolt and doors, and I said, 'Thus far you shall come, but no farther; and here shall your proud waves stop?'

A pelican at sea dove for fish. I saw the pelican, but did not hear it slice water. The splash was too far away to hear. *Good-bye, fish, recently of the sea, now of the pelican's great beak!* I could smell the pelican, I swear to you. There was another smell also, a very old smell. I couldn't place it. It fit nothing I had ever smelled before. It may have been the death of the fish.

I closed my eyes to listen to the sea. On and on it went. And so. I had only imagined the genuflecting waves. I had only imagined that they raced around me. I opened my eyes and watched the pelican again. Down it went for a niblet, with me or without me. No bubble of foam cared that I mourned its demise. The surf pounded in the night, under the moon, under the stars, under a cosmic cataclysm. It had a God to obey. The sea obeyed a thousand laws it was ignorant of. How stupid I was to have imagined myself a curiosity.

It was time to leave.

A sun halfway up the sky loses its mystery. And so does the sea, at about ten thirty. Ten-thirty is the enemy of all contemplation, thank God. The sun and the sea merely cast sparkles at that hour, dazzling the eyes of anyone happening to be running up the Tagibah Highway. By the time I reached the tiny town of Mamshar just before lunch, I was a tradesman again, bartering sweat for distance in the office called Earth.

The shore at Mamshar was rimmed here and there with thatched hut roofs sitting atop sticks. Hundreds of palms thrived along the shore in bunches. Beyond this pleasant little fringe were fishing boats, and some sailboats; pleasure-craft (as Ben called them) moving placidly through the sparkles. Many young boys fished from shore. *Catch yourselves a whale*, I thought happily.

I was feeling better because tomorrow I would be in Sidon. I'd take a little holiday through the Sabbath. Sidon was where I'd receive the letter from Rent, God willing, and the check from the Welldiggers. My plans for that check included stuffed crab (God forgive me) and a seaside inn.

Intervening was Tyre, and my second night on the road. The maps said there was a national park on the water three miles past town. I thought about looking up Hasdas before leaving the city proper; Hasdas, remember, being the sandwich place where Rent had met Anna. But I was afraid that Anna still worked there. I was not feeling sociable. All I wanted was to eat and sleep. If I met Anna, I'd have to be clever and funny and comb my hair—three things I was unwilling to do. Besides, Anna was not at all what I needed right then. I didn't even know if she was still in Tyre. I think Rent had said that they had met two years before. Nobody works at a sandwich joint for two years, do they? But why take the chance? Besides, I didn't know where Hasdas was. *Better just leave it alone*, I thought. So I did.

I found the park well before dusk. Still, I was tired and grousey.

The man at the gate said, "Welcome to the Tyre Seaside National Park. Are you alone today?"

"Unfortunately."

"Will you be needing a shower?"

"Besides food, it's my primary need."

"That will be eight dram, sir."

I coughed. "Sir. I wish merely to lie on the ground, not purchase the real estate."

"Sorry sir, but our rates are eight dram a night, five without a shower."

"So what do my taxes pay for?"

"The maintenance of the park."

"So why do I have to pay to sleep in it? Other parks are free."

"We have *showers*."

"Do you." I pointed behind his desk. "You have a bucket. I know about these things."

"It's a *nice* bucket. Teak, I think."

I handed over the drams and asked if there was a commissary.

"You can't be serious."

"Nothing in the way of food?"

"This is a national park, sir, not the Athens agora. I'll give you Spot 2."

"This is a privilege?"

"It's right under a walnut tree."

"I hope you have a well."

"You insult me, sir. Fifty paces to the right of your site."

"Is this park quiet?"

"As long as you don't snore. Oh. Here's your bucket. And a map. Enjoy your shower."

I was the only camper in the entire park. Spot 2 (out of three, I think) required the clearing of millions of fallen walnuts. I bent over and hurled them backwards between my legs. A spectator would have said, "Behold, a dog digging its own grave." With my chore concluded, I barked. I swear to you I did. I barked like anyone's dog. Then I undid my ground cloth and draped it upon the earth. Spot 2, eh? Die of envy, sheol, for this was death to my happiness. How could my mood swing so dramatically? Everything felt crummy and dark.

I set up my tube tent. A tube tent is as dumb as it sounds, and twice as humble. It's a glorified tarp sewn into a circle with two pieces of leather cord sewn on and sticking out each end. I attached the cords to trees on either side of my tube tent and behold—a tube tent. I threw my sleeping bag into the tent, grabbed my bucket, and headed for the well and a shower.

I filled my bucket at the well. Now—where was the shower? I consulted my map. The shower was a half-mile walk, on the opposite side of the park. A half-mile walk for an upright tube tent (this is the "shower") with an iron pole and a hook. It may as well have been twenty miles distant. I drew down a curse upon the head of the gatesman, a curse that would leave him dead at his post within the hour. When I came to myself and realized that the shower location was not the man's fault, I quickly withdrew the curse, so sure was I of its potency. I hoped it wasn't too late.

I finally arrived at the shower, hung my bucket, ducked inside, stripped, and threw my clothes out the top. Then I tipped the bucket.

I don't know if you believe in the Ice Age, but it came to the Tyre Seaside National Park that evening from the bowels of a teak bucket. The water was so cold that I screamed. I hardly ever scream, preferring to save such extravagances for imminent death.

All I needed now was my towel. *My towel*. My towel was at camp, in my backpack. I had forgotten my backpack, and thus my towel. I'd have to put on my dirty tunic and defeat the purpose of the shower.

I take back what I said about animals not living at the Tyre Seaside National Park. One animal lived there, a badger. I knew it was a badger because I recognized the prints where my tunic should have been. The tracks led to a hole and then disappeared.

"Hello, Adam, my forefather." This is what I said, out loud, as I walked naked the half-mile back to Spot 2. I thought about running, but something about it seemed so undignified. It was dusky now, for which I was thankful. I told myself to keep breathing, to take easy strides, to pretend it was the Garden of Eden and that I was Adam returning from a surveying expedition of my kingdom. The only difference I could appreciate between Adam and myself was the cooperativeness of his badgers and the higher overall temperature of the water. At least I had my sandals, which I'm sure would have comforted me had I encountered another soul—Methuselah, say—on the way back to camp.

The only worse thing that could have happened at the Tyre Seaside National Park was a storm in the night. This arrived, by my reckoning, at about three in the morning. I considered walking naked to the gatesman's post—in memory of my earlier expedition—and requesting a site on higher ground. Spot 3 had seemed a finger taller, and would have delayed my drowning by nineteen seconds. I reconsidered that plan, forgetting that the gatesman was likely dead courtesy of my earlier curse. So I dog-paddled out of my tent and climbed one of the trees I'd tied it to. It was in this tree, wrapped in my remaining clothes, that I shivered and cried and recited several of the sadder psalms concerning lightning, water, and my additional curse of darkness:

> He clothed himself with malediction as his coat, which entered him like water, and like oil into his bones. Yahweh is collecting the waters of the sea together as a waterspout, restoring the abyss in treasure vaults. Let all the earth fear Yahweh (okay!); He sent off His arrows, with which He scattered them, and He multiplied bolts of lightning, with which he discomfited them. So the channels of water were made to appear.

A month later, at the first sign of dawn, I attempted to let go of my tree-branch home. Unfortunately for me, I succeeded brilliantly. My turn of luck delighted me—until the forces of nature (the main force being gravity) ruined my mood somewhere between the tree branch and the surface of the water, which blessedly broke my fall. To save time and celebrate my good fortune, I groped for my backpack before resurfacing. It was a short swim, then, to the gatesman's kingdom. He asked if I'd enjoyed my stay.

"Quite a storm we had last night," he said. "Who can predict *those* kinds? I hope I didn't give you—

"Spot 2?"

"Whoa. God Almighty, how were the walnuts?"

I was neither warm nor dry until Sarepta. My backpack remained damp for three days. The only good to come from my memorable stay at the Tyre Seaside National Park was the lightening of my load (I left my tube tent with the sleeping bag still in it tied to the trees at the park, where it probably remains to this day) and a resolution to never, ever camp again the entire trip. I'd get a job selling walnuts if I had to.

I lunched at a roadside table in Sarepta, in view of the sea. A mere twelve miles then separated me from Sidon. With nearly seventy-five miles logged, I *needed* two days of not moving. The running was harder than I expected. The walking occupied more of me than I'd planned, not enough to call my adventure a walk, but enough so that a twinge of guilt flared whenever I told people I was running to Antioch. It was pride again. Sometimes it helped me, sometimes it hurt. Still, I mostly ran. I didn't feel like explaining, so I just told people I was running to Antioch. If they saw me walking, so be it. Let *them* try it.

Antioch was a far-off dream. My world was Sidon and nothing beyond. It appeared in my sights just before supper; low white buildings huddled close; tall and curvy palm trees overlooking the kingdom that was this particular city. A Welldigger game brought me to Sidon the year before. I knew exactly where I wanted to stay—the Habima, a moderately priced inn just off the sea, clean with a good restaurant. But first, the mail station.

I ran up the steps, only to wait for an eon behind an elderly woman mailing a souvenir turtle shell to Tarsus. "It'll be there in six weeks," said the clerk. "Guaranteed." Guaranteed in six weeks? I could run it there in four. The shell's previous owner could have made it in six.

I then inquired after my letter. "Sorry," said the clerk. "No Hassler letter. Nothing for you today."

"When will the mail be up in the morning?"

"Nine. First come, first unnerved."

This was bad news, but then good. I'd have two days off without the guilt. Tomorrow was Friday, then the Sabbath. Three days running, two days off. At this rate, Antioch was far off, indeed. But who cared about Antioch? I navigated now for the Habima of Sidon.

Room 10 lay down the hall from where I'd stayed with the team when we came here to play the Tigers. It was so different, being with the team then, and being alone now. The contrast pained me. I thought about the game with the Leopards. Was it tonight? Why even remember? I'd abandoned the team—or so it felt. I stood outside my door at the Habima and looked up the hall, imagining Rent running down it dribbling a ringball, or Af in his underwear, or Amman waving a deck of cards, looking for a game of *wadi-tot*. I thought about starting up a conversation with the desk clerk. I liked his spirit. He said I could have a free newspaper in the morning. But going down to chat sounded too hard for me. Crawling outside myself was more trouble than I wanted. Was it fatigue or buried thoughts of Mary keeping my usually-happy self from society? I hadn't the energy to crack the code.

I ordered the stuffed crab I'd been dreaming about, and a salad that tasted like the Exodus (not a good thing). Dessert was mango pastry and a dipping bowl of bright orange syrup. Why not get fat? Why care? Full but empty, I returned to my room. The best remedy for such a condition, I have found, is unconsciousness. I entered that state around eight-thirty, not surrendering it until eight-thirty the following morning.

A leisurely breakfast, a newspaper, an overcast day, no running, a new attitude, and off to the mail station. Life was good again. And this time—a letter from Rent! At a bench outside the station, I tore it open. The first thing I saw was the check. Mother of Zeus, Rent had some explaining to do, not that I was complaining; there was an additional week's wage on board. I hoped it wasn't a mistake.

> Joseph! I trust this letter will get to you on Thursday, Friday at the latest. You old badger! I envy you. If you are sitting on the white bench outside the mail station right now, next to the statue of the flamingo, then you are the luckiest man alive to have so-far survived this adventure. I can't believe the news about Mary. Listen to me, and listen good: it's a glitch, a flip, a farndoggle of fleeting chronology. In other words, it won't last. I don't care what happened, this is only an ostrich egg on the highway of happiness. You and Mary were meant for each other. You just need a break, that's all. Let your lungs collapse in relief. Don't give up on that woman, or you're the biggest dodo in Israel. There is no other woman in the world like Mary. Having said that, I might tell you what a dodo you are anyway.
>
> You should have rested in Tyre! You could have looked up Anna. I have been wondering what happened to her. You could have gotten free room and board (and possibly more, ha-ha). She has not written in four months, as I told you. Is it my breath? My underpants? I've sent letters, but they might as well have been boomerangs. Maybe she has relocated, who

knows? You could have asked around and found her. I should kill you for this. Someone could have told you something. The wind may have spoken of it, or butterfly wings. Tree bark perhaps. If you had written me sooner, I'd have begged you to stay in Tyre. Oh, well. God's will be done. (I hate it when this happens.) You know you are not a dodo at all, you're a brave man. You have the sperm-holders of a rhinoceros in heat on the Feast of Tabernacles. Don't let anyone tell you you're dodo. *We* know you're dodo, but not for this. I read your letter and thought, *What a lucky dodo*. I envy you, Joseph. You will never regret this run. How are the legs? Mine feel just fine!

I hope this check gets you to Antioch. Don't be surprised at the amount. This is your pay, plus a little extra from me. If I can't run to Antioch, then I can live the dream through you. What do I need money for? The concubines of Magdala are on strike. Take some time and rest. Eat well, and often. I can't imagine running twenty-five miles a day. You must be going through food like a menstruating Philistine.

Don't worry about the game. But you're wrong—we do need you, and if we lose it will be all your fault. It won't be the same without you. You're better than Af. Even Af knows that. Even his grandmother has said so. Who is going to pass the ball to me so that I can lose the game? Af drives the lane and misses the lay-up himself. We may hire his grandmother. I will write you again in two weeks in Antioch, and report to you that this is just what happened. Then you will see that I have been a prophet all this time. Oh, for a prophet's wage!

Again I say, don't give up on Mary. Have you given her any reason to give up on you? Moses and Abraham, if you ever did anything to lose that girl, I would have to curse your favorite reproductive organ with a cactus-like curse. Don't blow it with Mary, Joseph. She's a rare one. This run will be good for both of you, you'll see. It is all a matter of notches on the sundial.

I don't know any lawyers in Nazareth. I only know one lawyer, and he lives down in Tiberias. He's also a crook—sorry for the redundancy. You won't need one of these gasbags anyway. Cease troubling yourself, son.

To other business! Do you remember I said that Anna's parents had a business in Sidon? Well guess what? *You're in Sidon!* Do me a favor, Joey. Look for the business. I beg you. These people rent condos. I forget the name of the business, except I know that the word "condo" is in the title. Their last name is Corbin. Ask around, can you? Check at the mail station. I'd like to know where Anna is. You know why!

What else? Who knows. Certainly not me. What's this about maybe running all the way to Greece?! If you run to Athens, I will think you've stripped your brain bark. So send me a postcard from the Acropolis. Just kidding. Listen. No Israelite woman is going to wait for a guy who's out throwing the discus with nude philosophers and eating weird sandwiches. Keep your head. I hope Antioch is enough for you. If it's not, do what you must. God is in control, we both know that. God's control is the absolute. The relative is: hop a freighter from Antioch and get your dodo derriere back to Mary!

God bless you, Joseph. Yes, the evening and morning you spent here were special. I will never forget it.

Now, may the God of Abraham, Isaac and Jacob bless your way and keep you safe. If you meet any good-looking women who happen to be gushy about meeting a ringball star with gorgeous arms, write me!

Sincerely yours,

Rent

P.S. Check General Delivery when you get to Ancyra, the town before Antioch. I don't trust anything in Antioch, especially not the mail service. Who knows, I may have more money for you. Knowing you, you'll spend all this and not have anything left for passage home. Write me if you learn anything about Anna, or about life in general. Remember: Check the station at Ancyra!

What gorgeous literature. The day disappeared as I read and re-read Rent's letter. Three days, and already I pined so hard for human companionship. Good old Rent. Always true. But aloneness is why I started this. Rent was right about Greece; it was a madcap plan. I wasn't so sure he was right about Mary, though. He didn't know what had happened. I could not tell him in a letter. I would have to do it face-to-face. Forget boats, I could travel overland to Magdala and plot my sequel. Rent would have me. I could talk to him then.

The money—thank God. I could now lodge comfortably all the way to Antioch. God's ways astounded me. He sent the storm, soured me on camping, made me so crazy as to abandon my gear in Tyre, then loaded me with enough money for inns all the way to Antioch. I knew God blessed worthies like Abraham and David. But me? The grace store operates on overtime, apparently.

Stuffing the letter into my pocket, I felt light. Asking the mail clerk about—who was it?—the Corbins?—sounded too hard. What I needed now was a bank.

Down Jebel Street, left on Taba, right on Neweiba Lane, then three blocks past the yellow mosque—*it'll be on your right*, said the clerk. And I shouldn't have any trouble, he said, cashing a check drawn on the Ambassador Bank of Magdala.

Short walk down Jebel Street, turn left onto Taba, right onto Neweiba Lane, then look for the mosque. But now, forget dull monuments of religion. Because if a purple and green condor had alighted on the sidewalk, I could not have been more shocked at what appeared on the first block of Neweiba, mosques be damned. There, next to a bakery, sat a tiny stone shop with a modest sign nailed atop the door that said: SHAGAH.

CHAPTER 8

ELIZABETH'S

I woke up on a sofa with a full moon rising. No, wait. It was Elizabeth's face, hovering over me. At the other end of the sofa, a large man had my bare feet propped on his thighs and was digging his thumbs into the soft parts of my underfoot, grunting. It was Zechariah. I tried to sit up on the sofa, but a strong hand pushed my forehead back to the pillow. "Not yet, Mary. Just rest. You must rest now. What an awful trip you must have had."

"No, it was—Elizabeth?"

"Shh. Try not to talk. We're taking good care of you, taking care of everything. I have chicken noodle soup warming on the fire."

"What happened?"

"You fainted, dear."

"When?"

"As soon as you got here. About fifteen minutes ago. You mentioned something in the driveway about the mercies of God speaking for the eon, and then down you went like a bag of beets. It was terrible. Zechariah carried you in and deposited you here. How are you feeling?"

"Fine, but…I can't believe it happened. It's the second time today."

"What is?"

"Fainting. I fell off my donkey in Bethel. At least I *think* that was today."

"How awful!"

"It was embarrassing, and—oh! My head hurts."

"Yes, we found the bump, and a nasty one. Zechariah is taking care of it now. The pain should be gone in no time. Zechariah is an expert at this, you know. He helps me all the time with my menstrual cramps, but of course now that I'm with child and the child is filled with spirit and—"

Zechariah bounced violently up and down on the couch, stopping Elizabeth in mid-sentence. I tried to sit up again, to get a better look at the large man at my feet. I started to say something, but Elizabeth pushed me back down. "Rest," she said. "You must rest." Zechariah, meanwhile, transferred his ministrations to the thick parts of my feet beneath the great toes.

"He can't speak, Mary. Gabriel took his speech away. It happened in the temple, you see, when—"

Again the big man bounced on the sofa, two large bounces.

"He doesn't want me to tell you. He wants to save it for tonight. Isn't that right, Zechariah? You want to save it." Zechariah nodded. "He wants to do it for you like he did it for me."

"Do what?"

"When Zechariah came out of the temple that day, that now famous day, he couldn't speak. No one knew what had happened, but he was acting crazy. He had been in the temple longer than anyone on record—it was a record, I might add—and when he came out—" There were two more big bounces on the couch. "Oh, yes, I'm saying too much already. Anyway, when we got home, Zechariah acted out what had happened in the temple. It was really quite fun."

"Like the charades game."

"Precisely that."

"Why didn't he just write it down?"

"Oh, you know Zechariah. He couldn't sit still. No chair could have held him that night. Pencils would have snapped like reeds in his big fat hand. He threw himself all over the room, like Jan Kiddleman. You'll love the performance, you really will. Zechariah should win a Bakhan for it. Anyway, speaking of amazing stories…" She was looking down at me, very close to my face now, and staring.

"Me? Oh, yes. Maybe not as exciting as your story but… How did you know? How were you sure? Your words thrilled me, when you said what you did about the fruit of my womb. You did say that, didn't you? I wasn't dreaming it?"

"You were not dreaming."

"I've been doubting my call. But…how did you know?"

Elizabeth moved her hand and placed it slowly and carefully on my stomach. Her face was now only inches from mine. It was disconcerting. "Holy spirit, Mary. Holy spirit told me it was you. I knew."

"On Sunday?"

"Early Monday morning. I woke up in the middle of the night."

Elizabeth began moving to her knees.

"What are you doing?"

"…the mother of my Lord."

"Elizabeth. Get up."

Elizabeth was on her knees now and had placed her head on my belly. I could hear her chanting softly, "Lord, be merciful, forgive me my sins. Lord, be merciful, forgive me my sins..." She said that over and over. Then, much louder, "Oh, God of compassions and mercies, see Thy humble servant and hear her humble prayer!"

"Elizabeth, please. You're making me uncomfortable. You shouldn't be doing this." I tried to turn on my side, but she pressed her face harder into my stomach so that I couldn't move.

"...save Thy people Israel, and Thy humble servant Elizabeth, of the daughters of Aaron, who tries every day to please Thee and to do what is right, and whose husband, of the tribe of Levi, of Thy servant-nation Israel, while in the temple ministering unto Thee, hath spoken to Gabriel—" There were two big bounces from the end of the couch. "...anyway, Lord of mercies, hear Thou these humble supplications, we beseech Thee, and amen." Elizabeth got up quickly from the floor and returned to my head. She was looking at me again from a comfortable distance as if nothing had happened.

"That wasn't right," I said.

"He's the Messiah of Israel."

"He's not that yet."

"Then what is He? A mass of rapidly multiplying cells in a wall of blood clinging to the lining of your uterus?"

"In fact..."

"I know things. You can't stop me."

The conversation was headed in an unpleasant direction. "Tell me more about when you knew," I said. "That fascinates me. Was it—?"

"Three-thirty."

"Yes! Did you see how strange the light looked that morning?"

"Calm, Child. I saw it all. There will be plenty of time to talk...well, for some of us." I wanted to see Zechariah's reaction to that. "Stop trying to look up," Elizabeth said, and she pushed me back down. "Zechariah is not going away. You must keep resting, and I must stir the soup. Zechariah has many more cures inside those paws, many more." I snuck a glance at Zechariah, and he was smiling. My headache was already beginning to fade.

"Why didn't you tell us this had happened?" I asked.

"Holy spirit forbade us. It's all I've been able to do to keep quiet. I wanted to climb to the roof and tell all Ramah. We were not to speak to anyone outside the home. But the ban has been lifted."

"How do you know?"

"It lifted at your conception. Three-thirty, Monday morning. I just knew it. Holy spirit again."

"Did you know I was coming?"

"Holy spirit did not tell me that. In fact, I was composing a letter to you when I heard the voices outside."

"Did you tell me that your child leapt when I greeted you?"

"That's what I said, and there's good reason why. There's plenty of time later for details. I'll stir the soup now, and you—you must rest."

Zechariah and Elizabeth cared for me like a daughter. Elizabeth was the daughter of my father's oldest brother, since deceased; she was twenty years my elder. Whenever anything troubled me, I could tell Elizabeth. She always understood. I could go to Mother also, and I did, but Elizabeth and I enjoyed the greater spiritual connection. It was exciting—and significant, I felt—that we had been called together.

I felt much better after two bowls of soup. I was still very tired, but the dizziness was gone. Zechariah's foot massage had removed my headache, though I was surprised to feel the size of the bump on the back of my head. It was sore to the touch.

After a warm chamomile tea for dessert, I became sleepy. Elizabeth escorted me to the guestroom. Considering that she had not been expecting me, the room was beautiful. It was sparse, with only a bed, chair, nightstand, and washbowl. But it was clean. That was Elizabeth; neat and very organized.

The day had turned overcast, and a light breeze blew in through the window. The breeze smelled of aloe flowers, from Elizabeth's garden. Elizabeth's drapes were off-white and undecorated except for scalloped edges all around. The drapes blew in toward me, then back out again. I watched them. In and out with the breeze, the curtains breathed. The room was warm, but not hot. The drapes breathed with my breathing. I closed my eyes as I lay on the bed.

I awoke groggy and disoriented, God knows when. It took a moment to remember that I was in Elizabeth's guestroom in Ramah. My thoughts were out of focus. I thought about Irbed, Stewart, and Jen, and wondered where they were. I wondered if the mail was getting delivered on time. I said a silent prayer for them while staring upward at all the cracks on Elizabeth's ceiling. My mouth was chalky and tasted like the smell of the goat feed back home. I turned my head to look at the drapes again, and they lay limp. There was a circle of wetness on my pillowcase, where I'd been sleeping. I laid my cheek on the circle and it was cold. I did not feel like getting up. I heard the door creak, and Elizabeth peeked in.

"Are you awake?"

"Yes." My voice sounded like a frog's voice. I had to clear my throat three times to make Elizabeth understand me. "How long have I been asleep?"

"Three hours. You must have needed it."

"Three hours! Ugh. My mouth tastes like goat feed."

"Lord God of mercies, how rude can your cousin be? I have not even filled your bowl."

"I haven't cared. I would have taken care of it myself, but…" I willed myself to sit up. My hair hung all over my face, so I pushed it up and over my head. "I can't imagine what my hair must look like."

"It looks wonderful."

"For the birds, maybe."

"Your hair is so auburn and shiny and long. I've always envied it."

"I have split ends."

"Who doesn't?"

"Samantha Omayyad."

Elizabeth smiled. "Besides her."

I put my head in my hands and rubbed my forehead. I hated waking up, and still do. I'm a terrible riser. My body is so slow. When I sleep, I sleep deeply. Mother and Father say that I sleep like a hibernating bear. They also say that I snore. I believe them.

I started rubbing my eyes. I suppose that if I had a secret passion, this was it. My eyes always seemed to itch, especially in the morning, or after a nap. It always felt so good to rub them. There was always some deep itch way down in my eyes. Sometimes I would rub them so hard that I worried I'd turn them inside out. I was always glad, after a long and satisfying rub, that I could still see. I didn't really enjoy this particular rub as much as I could, because I knew Elizabeth was still at the doorway. Being self-conscious, I couldn't let loose.

"Elizabeth?"

"Speak, mother of God."

"No, no. Where did you get that? I'm not the mother of God, I'm the mother of His Son."

"What's the difference?" Elizabeth was now in the room and had come over to sit on the bed with me.

"My baby is to be the Son of the Most High. Gabriel said that."

"Gabriel? Goodness. I didn't know it was Gabriel. Oooo! I just got goose bumps. I'm sorry. Go on."

"I'm not even the mother of the Son, really. I'm only carrying Him. Did the spirit tell you how I conceived?"

"By spirit."

"Yes. And so I'm not the mother, specifically."

"Oh, come on, Mary. You will suckle the Child, and raise Him."

"Yes, but—"

"Then you're the mother, and I'll hear no more about it."

"I can live with that. But not the mother of God. God can't have a mother, can He? Before all, He is."

"All right. Perhaps I meant to say that you were the mother of my Lord. I'm sorry. Mother of my Lord is indeed what I meant. I don't know why I said the other. I didn't mean to offend you, or the Child."

"I haven't reckoned it as offense. As for the Child, I don't see how you could have offended *him*."

The room was getting hotter, and I wanted to change the subject. For the first time, I studied Elizabeth's belly. Elizabeth with child! I had not really paused to consider the miracle of it. "Holy God. I have just for the first time appreciated the miracle in front of me. That wonderful belly." I smiled. "Six months. By God Who lives, it's a miracle."

Elizabeth looked down and gently rested a hand on her bulging midsection. "God has chosen us."

"I can't deny that."

"Have you wondered why?"

"I've done nothing but wonder—for a week now. It can't be that we are worthier than anyone else."

"Why would you say that?"

"Just this past week, I know myself better. God has shown me things. He has humbled me and made me doubt things I've never doubted before."

"This is a good thing?"

"Two weeks ago, I would have said no, never. Now I'm more open to it—to the purpose of doubt, that is. I told you I've been writing about my life. I thought my life was humble. But I'm thinking now that it's all been theory. What is humility? Is it only what appears humble on the outside? What if one is still prideful on the inside? I'm not saying I'm convinced about anything yet. But God made me fall off my donkey, for heaven's sake."

Elizabeth laughed a small, uncomfortable laugh. "God does not make people fall off donkeys."

"I believe He does."

"Why would the Almighty take the trouble to do such a poor, mean thing?"

"That's exactly what I was wondering. It angered me, at first."

"You wasted your emotion."

"Can I be honest? It did anger me. But I'm beginning to see purpose in it."

"And what might that be? To make you appreciate how hard God's earth is?"

"Maybe the call is so high that I would become proud because of it."

"And so being flung from your ass has solved this?"

"Not everything. But why not? I'm just saying that Yahweh is in everything. Anyway, Gabriel said that I had found favor with God, that's all. I'm not sure that favor has anything to do with worthiness."

"Favor presumes it," said Elizabeth.

"Not necessarily. He also showed favor to Jacob."

"But he was not Jacob, he was the Israel of God. God changed his name to Israel and he became father of our people."

"But when was he called? It was while he was still Jacob. God called him before Peniel. Way before that, even. Think about it. He chose him while still in the loins of Abraham, before he could do anything good or evil."

"I think you're wrong. I say it respectfully."

"How could it be otherwise?"

"Listen to me," Elizabeth said. "God saw what he would be, that he would become Israel. God saw him in his worthiness and called him out, seeing what he would become."

"There's no doubt that God knew. But he was separated unto God before that. I ask you this: Who made Israel the way he was? Who made him Jacob?"

"But—"

"I don't wish to argue, Elizabeth. Not in your house. But the very name Jacob means *supplanter*. I know you know this. Our forefather Jacob used trickery to supplant God's ways for his own. Are we any better? Is it enough to say that Yahweh called him before he did good? Indeed, He called him while his deeds were evil."

"Mary!"

"Jacob himself said, 'I am not worthy of the least of all the mercies, and of all the truth, which You have shown to Your servant.'"

"Again I say, this was before God named him Israel."

"You don't think he sinned after?"

"There's no record."

"Do you want to hear it?"

Elizabeth began to fuss. She had been looking me in the eye until now, but now she looked away. "You don't have any examples besides Jacob."

"I have a dozen. There's Abraham."

"Oh, please."

"'Oh, please?' Who was it, then, who went into Sarah's

handmaiden when he doubted God's promise? He didn't even believe the messenger of the Lord. But it was worse than that. He didn't believe Yahweh Himself."

Elizabeth blanched at this. At the time, I didn't know why. It was a relief when she said, "Tea. I have given you the sleepy kind, now we'll have something brisk. The weather is too good for us to be in here. The wind is lighter. We'll talk about other things in the new chairs Zechariah made for our anniversary. I've put them out in our favorite spot near the garden. Zechariah is napping, so the ladies will have their hour."

I smiled. "After I brush my teeth," I said.

Elizabeth's backyard was larger than any in Nazareth. Three large date palms provided shade, with many smaller laurel and juniper trees pushing their way heavenward. "The best time to plant a tree is twenty years ago," Elizabeth said. "The next best time is today."

We walked out to the garden. "I'm growing cereals this year," Elizabeth said, and she showed me where she'd planted millet. "And we should have all the lentils we can eat, as you can see from this corner." Elizabeth pointed to a yellow-stringed area containing her lentils. "I've got sixty plants this year." Then she pointed out the usual garden things: cucumber, endive, garlic, leek, and onion.

"I smelled aloe earlier."

"It's right underneath the guestroom window."

"I thought it was in your garden."

"Not this year."

"Where are your flowers?"

"I planted them around the house this year. No room in the garden, with the beans and millet. You'll be surprised to know I'm growing henna. Has your mother ever grown it?"

"No."

"They're the tall plants next to the window, with the red flowers."

"There's so many," I said.

"I want to make cosmetics from the leaves. They're famous for that, you know."

"Cosmetics?"

"I've got a book on it," said Elizabeth. "The cosmetics aren't for me. Some of the young women here use them. I see an opportunity to make a little money. Why should these women buy their cosmetics at the market for retail price when I can offer them the same thing, and fresher, for a discount? I've got a book on how to make three different cosmetics. I can't remember their names right now; they're long. Anyway, I have this idea of getting other women to help sell them for me. I figure I can get a commission on whatever they sell. If I get enough women to sell it, I can stay home and tend to the plants, take care of my baby, and still make money."

"Good idea."

"Oh, I don't know. Zechariah thinks it's crazy, but what does he know? I just wish I had planted the henna three weeks sooner, and three times as many plants. I can't do anything about it now. Only three months to the baby. I'll show you my lilies."

We looked at the lilies, then settled into the chairs on the edge of the garden. Elizabeth had fetched our tea from the boiling-pot on the back porch, and now we relaxed and looked at the clouds in-between the date palms.

"There's a cloud that looks like a horse, a big white horse," Elizabeth said. "I always thought that Messiah would ride into Israel on a horse like that."

"That's interesting," I said. "Joseph said the same thing."

"That's the man you're betrothed to?"

"Yes."

"I'm sorry I haven't asked about him. How are things?"

"No good."

"Did you tell him about the visitation?"

"Of course."

"And?"

"He didn't believe me."

"Don't say it!"

"I wish I didn't have to. It's partly my fault."

"What's his family again?"

"Jabrecki."

"I've never heard of it. It's not an old Israelite name."

"Yes, I know. Father says the same thing."

"Ben is a wise man."

"Sometimes."

"Now, Mary…"

"What difference does it make what a person's name is? Joseph's an Israelite. If he were a Jebusite or an Amalakite, I could see it."

"Esau was also of Abraham."

"Joseph is not an Esau!"

"Calm yourself. I didn't say he was."

We both looked at the clouds and said not a word for a long while. I didn't want to tell Elizabeth that Joseph had fled Nazareth and that I had no idea where he was.

"What do you think our children will become?" I posed the question while still perusing the sky.

I could tell that Elizabeth had been waiting for the conversation to take this turn. As soon as I asked, she raised both arms slowly to the sky and shook them, so that her bracelets jangled. "They will become great men, Mary. Great men!" Elizabeth kept her arms raised and looked into the sky for the longest time. "Great men!" she said again. She said it three times, shaking her bracelets each time. I wondered when she would tire. I noticed from looking at Elizabeth's arms that she was aging and not taking very good care of herself; I will say no more. She finally lowered her arms—much faster than she had raised them—and turned to me, fighting for breath. "It goes without saying in your case, of course….The greatness, I mean…But my son, too, shall be great. But you, Mary…You are bearing the Messiah of Israel. The Promised One. The Coming One. The Branch of David. The Christ. The Ancient of Days. The Redeemer. The Son of God. The Prince of Peace…the mother of my Lord." She was moving again to her knees.

"Stop!" I shouted. The volume of my voice surprised me. I looked away. Elizabeth sat back down quickly and began smoothing the wrinkles in her lap. "Tell me of your child," I said quietly. "Who is he to be?"

Elizabeth was still tending to her wrinkles. "I can't say too much. I don't want to ruin Zechariah's grand performance. My son is to be great, I will say that. Not as great as yours, but he will ride together with Him. Our sons are to change the world. Has it sunk into you? I've had six months now to consider it. It may take you that long, or longer. The white horses. They will come. The white horses will come."

I didn't care for such grand talk. "What makes you so sure?"

"Your son will deliver our people from our enemies. This is the promise of the fathers. Israel is destined to rule the earth, and Messiah is destined to deliver Israel. God promised Abraham that his seed would rule over all the families of the ground."

"That's true."

"Your Son, Mary. But what do we see today? Does Israel rule the families of the ground? Ha! Israel *licks* the ground. We grovel at the feet of Rome. I know you're not much into politics, Child, but have you heard that the Romans have taken over the country?"

"Very funny."

"I'm sick to death of it, myself. The novelty has played out for me. So many taxes. They bother you in the marketplace. They bother you at the well. They bother you in the streets. They walk through the neighborhood and look at your house. They come by and pick your onions. Do they ask? Oh, no. They don't have to ask; they're Romans. And what are we but Jews? I imagine they chop up my onions and use them on their pork roast sandwiches. Animals!"

"They leave us free to worship."

"They do. Yes, you're right. The planets align for us this day. Lucky us."

"We're blessed. I've never heard you talk this way."

"It's high time. Our sons will assume power from on high. Under God, they'll expel Rome from Israel. After that, Greece. And that will be just the beginning. Every nation on earth will be forced to bow to Israel. It's coming. The stage is being set. Haven't you looked forward to this day? Finally, we will dwell in safety. No more war. No more famine. No more death. And to think that we have a part in it."

"I do hate death."

"Gone. Abolished. It can't come too soon for me. I just pray that God does it soon. I hope your Messiah isn't ninety years old when he ousts Caesar."

This statement of Elizabeth's shocked me. "He's not my Messiah, he's the world's. Most of all, he's God's Son. God will dictate what He does, not us. We don't know God's timing. Besides that, God always does just what we do not expect Him to do. Think of Joseph. And Abraham. Abraham didn't father Isaac until—"

"I know, I know. There you go again. Always with the bad news. Always with the wheelbarrow rolling downhill."

"I'm just trying to be sane and practical about it. It's not bad news. It's good news. But it will be according to God's design, not ours."

"I'm certainly glad *you're* trying to be sane."

"Oh, Elizabeth. I didn't mean it that way."

"What is said, is said. It's all right, Mary. You have trusted my spiritual senses before, but you've forgotten now. It's not too hard to figure out, this business. Think about it. What is meant by 'Redeemer?' Have you thought about that? The Messiah will redeem Israel. And how do you redeem Israel? You start by ousting Rome. We are going to rule the earth. And how do you do that? By establishing Zion as the capital of the world. That's where our white horses come in. It's in all the literature. All conquerors come on the white horse." Elizabeth looked to the sky again and breathed heavily. She finally collapsed all the way back into her chair and sighed loudly. "But now I see that our horses have become ducks. Lord, grant me patience."

"It's a glorious picture."

"The ducks?"

"Redemption. The abolition of death."

Elizabeth looked over at me. "Yes, and you haven't even touched your tea."

"I'm just sitting here, taking it all in. It's so peaceful here. This is the best place in the world to just sit and think. These are such good days—except that I don't have a husband."

"God has given us much. He will take care of that, too."

"I wish I could be sure."

"We have reason to be proud," said Elizabeth.

"Isn't that what comes before the fall?"

"I didn't mean to say proud. I meant that we rise above the grind of life, you and I. We rise above the problems of everyday living. We have a mission."

"I know that God has chosen us. I know we have a mission. But I told you before that God has been humbling me."

"I said I didn't mean to say proud. I wish I hadn't said it now."

"I think we already had this conversation."

"Maybe once is enough."

"This is so strange," I said. "We've never disagreed before."

"I can't say that I like it now."

"Is it getting chilly out here, or is it just me?"

"It could be that a storm is coming. Zechariah better be getting off that roof. It's time for me to get supper ready. Don't forget, you're in for the performance of a lifetime."

"I'm looking forward to it. I'll help you in the kitchen."

"Nothing of the kind. You are going to relax. I have a wonderful book for you to read. Did you see it in the living room?"

"No. What is it?"

"Zechariah and I have been reading it. It's another in the Yehiam Yad series. It's very good. It's called *Salt Sea Intrigue*."

The storm didn't come, but a delicious mussakhan did—chicken roasted with almonds and onions on round pita bread—and bourekas for dessert. Elizabeth and Zechariah cleared the table. I offered to help, but they wouldn't hear of it. "Audience members at the Taraffila Dinner Theater do not clear their own tables," Elizabeth said grandly, "but we do invite them to leave a tip." I fished in my pocket for a shekel. "Good Lord, Mary, I was just kidding."

Elizabeth disappeared into the kitchen and returned with two huge bowls of popcorn, "Fresh-popped this morning at Zeeber's Market. I'd have popped it myself, but I can't find the spices they use." Elizabeth handed me the bowls, then ran around the living room extinguishing all the lamps, save three. These, she put on the floor. Footlights," she explained. "Just like on Botta Street." A foot stamped three times behind the archway between the living room and the kitchen. "Just a minute, Zechariah! I'm positioning the footlights! All right." Elizabeth cleared her throat and held out her jangling arms. "And now, ladies and gentlemen—and Savior-Mothers from Nazareth—we present to you, lately of Damascus and Antioch, for one night only at the famous Taraffila Dinner Theater in downtown Ramah: The Amazing Temple Drama!—*with* exclamation point—a rare performance performed by our own Zechariah Taraffila. Take it away, Zechariah!" Elizabeth ran to the couch and we applauded furiously as Zechariah began his pantomime. Immediately, he began making a huge square with his arms.

"The temple!" Elizabeth cried. Zechariah stood with his hands on his hips and rolled his eyes. "Oops!" Elizabeth said, "I'm not allowed to guess." Then she turned to me and whispered, "Anyway, that's the temple."

"I knew it was. Very good, Zechariah!"

Zechariah swung his arm back and forth.

"Painting! You're painting the temple!"

"Good guess, Mary. But wrong."

Zechariah sniffed the air where he had just swung his arm.

"Incense! You're burning incense in the temple!"

Zechariah quickly pointed at me and nodded yes. Then he flapped his arms like a bird.

"A bird flew into the sanctuary?"

Zechariah nodded no. He flapped his arms more gently and began walking in a circle.

"A *bat* flew into the sanctuary."

"Good grief, Mary," Elizabeth said, "How could a bat get into the sanctuary? Concentrate."

"Um…"

Zechariah got to his knees and looked up, as if imploring.

"A messenger of the Lord. An angel!"

"Good!" said Elizabeth.

Zechariah then got on all fours and began pawing the air. He opened and closed his mouth like a wild animal. He stalked the room furiously, pretending to roar.

"Oh, my goodness," I said. "The angel rode in on a lion?"

"Think," said Elizabeth. "Think *history*."

Zechariah gave Elizabeth a mean look and swiped a paw at her.

"Oh, I'm not supposed to help you," Elizabeth said.

"Wait. I know. The angel in the days of Daniel. The angel who closed the mouths of the lions. Gabriel! You saw Gabriel!"

Zechariah jumped up and pointed yes.

"I saw Gabriel, too," I said. "He spoke with me."

"Yes, we know Mary. Now please, watch what happens next."

Zechariah bit his fingernails and started shaking.

"You're frightened. Filled with fear."

Yes again. Zechariah flapped his arms again, then wagged his finger.

"Shame on you."

No.

"Naughty."

No.

"No-no?"

Sort of.

"Don't be afraid!"

Yes!

"Gabriel told you not to be afraid."

Precisely. Now watch, they said. Zechariah pointed to Elizabeth, then pointed to his own belly, then began rubbing his eyes as if he were crying, then put his hands together and looked to heaven, as if praying.

"You have prayed for Elizabeth to have children, but she has not borne. That's what Gabriel said to you. He knew about that."

Precisely. Zechariah pointed to Elizabeth again, put his hands together at the top of his stomach, and made his hands go out in a great arc.

"But Elizabeth would be with child."

Right. Now, jumping up and down with a gleeful face.

"Joy and exultation."

Correct. Swimming like a fish now.

"I have no idea."

Cheeks blown out.

"A big fish."

Stuffing hand inside mouth.

"A man-eating fish."

"This is a hard one," Elizabeth said.

"Jonah!"

Yes! But shaking head no now.

"Jonah, but not Jonah."

"Greek Jonah," Elizabeth whispered.

"John! His name is to be John!"

You've got it, Mary," Elizabeth said.

Fingers coming down now from the sky onto the belly.

"I have no idea. It's raining? Your stomach is getting wet."

No, no. Fingers coming down from the sky, into belly, smile on face.

"Happy that your stomach is getting wet."

"Think, Mary. Forget the rain. What else comes from above?"

"Holy spirit!"

Yes! Another sour look for Elizabeth. Hands coming out again in arc from the belly.

"The child will be filled with the spirit while still in Elizabeth's belly."

"That's why he jumped when he heard your voice," Elizabeth said.

"Oh, my goodness. That is wonderful."

"Isn't it?"

If you don't mind. Riding a big horse now.

"The white horse!"

No. Jumping in air.

"A jumping horse?"

Flapping arms again.

"A flying horse."

Yes.

"John will ride on a flying horse?"

Fanning face. Rubbing hands. Warming hands by fire.

"Flames."

Yes.

"Okay…what happened to the horse?"

"Still the horse," said Elizabeth. "Pay attention here. This is the good part."

Snapping reigns. Riding in a chariot.

"Think of a man," Elizabeth whispered. "Come on—this is the good part."

"Um, a man in a chariot, flaming horses…Elijah!"

Yes!

Hands coming out of belly again.

"The baby is Elijah?"

"Oh, for heaven's sake," said Elizabeth.

Fingers coming down from the sky again.

"That's the holy spirit again."

"Yes. Now concentrate. Put it all together."

"Elijah…spirit…John will have the *spirit* of Elijah!"
Yes! Yes!
"Oh, my goodness. That is wonderful."
"I told you it was the best part," Elizabeth said.
Fingers coming out of mouth now.
"You're speaking."
Flapping arms.
"Speaking to Gabriel."
Quizzical look. Pointing to Elizabeth. Pointing to his own belly. Crying.
"Still no baby."
Quizzical look again. Shrugging.
"How can this be? My wife can't have a baby."
You've got it.
"I asked the same thing of Gabriel. I asked him how it could be."
"Well," said Elizabeth. "Zechariah asked him, too. But apparently Gabriel has more patience with doubters of the female persuasion." Zechariah shot another glance at Elizabeth. "Sorry," Elizabeth said. "Please go on."
Shaking finger again.
"Shame on you."
Yes.
"Shame on you for not believing me."
Yes.
"Oh, my. How terrible."
Hand clamped over mouth.
"You can't speak because of it. Gabriel took away your voice because you did not believe him."
Precisely. Walking now. Walking, walking, walking.
"You came out of the temple."
Gesturing wildly.
"You tried to tell everyone what had happened."

Shocked look.

"Everyone is surprised."

A shrug, then arms sweeping at feet and looking all around.

"So you came home."

"And here we are today," Elizabeth said.

Zechariah bounded down off the "stage" to sit with us in his favorite chair, panting in his own sweat.

We sat quietly for the longest time. The oil lamps sent long, bizarre shadows all around the room, on the ceiling, on our faces. It was mostly dark. Everything was quiet. Zechariah's breathing was the only sound. Finally, Elizabeth spoke, almost in a whisper. "He doesn't mind that he can't speak. He is to have a son. The joy has overwhelmed him. I have never seen him happier. He flits around here like an angel himself. He works in his shop, helps me around the house, even cooks meals with me. He has never done that before. And in the bedroom?" Elizabeth paused and looked over at her husband. Zechariah was breathing deeply and regularly now; he was asleep. "In the bedroom…well…" Elizabeth looked down at the floor and a faint smile crept up the corners of her mouth. "Things have been good."

"I can tell you're very happy," I said.

"And now you. These are the best days of our lives. All of us."

I knew these were wonderful days, but my joy was incomplete. I longed for Joseph more than ever. Being at Zechariah and Elizabeth's was a rich time for me, and I was very happy for them. But their joy, their togetherness, made me more aware than ever that I was without a man.

So how was the trip a comfort? I didn't know. Elizabeth was supposed to have comforted me, which is why I had come in the first place. Mother and Father both believed it. Gabriel himself had said it. I thought and thought about it. I thought about it while walking in Elizabeth's back yard. I thought about it in bed at night. We seemed so different now, Elizabeth and I. Was this a comfort? I didn't see how.

I did not like what I saw happening to my cousin. In some ways her pregnancy had made her harder. More pragmatic. She rejoiced in the miracle, yes. But her miracle was different for her. It was different than mine was for me. We had both seen the sunlight; we were both filled with spirit. What of the sunlight? It does a different thing to wax than it does to clay. Thus also with the spirit. It was the same spirit, I knew. Only the vessels differed. Maybe that was the key. I prayed to God for understanding.

I thought about Joseph. I had felt so superior to him. Looking back on that day, I remembered. Even when I met him on the road, I felt superior. There was something about him that day; he seemed so worldly. There was a gulf between us, I sensed; a vast chasm. I had shamed him at El-Bekkers. Why? Was I becoming my father? It was a troubling thought. The only thing that comforted me was thinking of seeing Joseph again. The chasm didn't seem to matter any more.

It would be different now. Joseph served God, I knew. I knew he possessed the spirit of God. What had I been looking for, then? I had been looking for the spirit as I had always known it. And so I was limiting God. That was the end of the matter: *I was limiting God*. I was telling God how to manifest His spirit in Joseph. This was another humbling realization, and yet it brought me a measure of peace. It did not bring Joseph to me, or his hand into mine, or his eyes to my eyes, but the love in my heart for him flared like the corona of the sun. *Oh, God, Joseph! How I love you!*

I thought of staying in Ramah until John was born. But I couldn't do it. The longer I stayed, the sadder I became. I knew this was selfish. I tried not to let Zechariah and Elizabeth see my feelings. But I think they knew.

Elizabeth and I spoke more about God. We spoke of what the future held for us. But these conversations happened more and more infrequently. Eventually all I did was more housework. Elizabeth was full of energy, but it was harder for her to get around. Zechariah helped, but he was spending more time in his shop, building a cradle and a swing for the baby, and a new chest of drawers for Elizabeth.

Elizabeth obtained a midwife in her seventh month, a skilled and confident woman named Zophai. Before long, Elizabeth and Zophai seemed closer than Elizabeth and I. I felt my usefulness expiring. I longed for home.

I told Zechariah and Elizabeth one evening after supper that I was leaving. They said they understood. Still, they asked why I would leave so close to the birth. "Stay and celebrate with us," they said. I was tempted. But another month in Ramah seemed unbearable. I wanted to go home.

Zechariah checked the mail run. It would be a week before my friends would be through Ramah again, headed north. I would wait. And so, a week later, Irbed Gev, Jen Afula, and Stewart Salkhad loaded my worldly belongings onto a new donkey, Alice, and we set off on the three-day journey home. It was not as happy a time, heading north toward home. The boys did all they could to lighten my mood. Sometimes, during the day, I would laugh. But at night I cried.

Appropriately, it was raining when the boys dropped me off at 19 Hen Street. It was supposed to feel good, to be home. But no matter where I was, I took my life with me. It was that life that brought the tears, even as I touched the doorknob of my house.

CHAPTER 9

SIDON AND BEYOND

The door looked bronze and gleamed beneath the ungleaming day. The sign above it said: SHAGAH. It couldn't be what I thought it might be. To know for sure, I only had to walk across the street, to open the door and go in.

Dozens of people walked around me. I reviewed, to myself, what I already knew of the word *shagah**. I'd studied it intensely. A wine store? It did fit. It was only a wine store, then; just deadly alcohol. (*But something told me that it wasn't that at all.*)

No one knew me, so what harm to cross the street and check? The shop had a window; it was a simple matter of walking past that window, then. Probably a bunch of wine bottles is all I'd see.

I needed fried potatoes, however, and a little wooden stick to skewer them with. The potato place on my side of the street, catty-corner from SHAGAH, made this my stalling tactic of choice. Had it been a licorice store, then licorice would have been the tactic. Carrot soup, then that. Candles, then candles; I could sit and sniff a vanilla tea light for hours.

---

* Hebrew. Literally, *to wander; reel; stray; lose control; be intoxicated*

From my potato station, nothing appeared through the window of SHAGAH. *Just get up from your table and walk on over. You can't see anything from here.* There was traffic and more traffic, so I skewered potato after fried potato. This worked for a while, but then there was such a dearth of roadlife that God Himself must have stopped it as far north as Berytus and south as far as Tyre. I was running out of excuses.

I left my container on the table and crossed the street.

It was a fine door, real bronze, cool to the touch. I analyzed the craftsmanship. "What a door," I said out loud. "I wonder who made it?"

I was within my rights as a citizen of Israel to look into any window I pleased. *Challon atsar*, they called it. *Window shopping.* So I walked past.

Well, no wine bottles. Not much of anything; it was too dark inside to see. I walked past again in another thwarted quest for life. That was my answer, then: the place was closed. *It's closed on Fridays*, I said to myself. Odd, but not crazy. There was no risk then, in turning the doorknob.

The doorknob turned easily in my hand, and noiselessly besides.

I would just let go of the doorknob, then, and walk away. But some people were coming down the sidewalk. My hand was still on the turned knob. If I left now, I would look silly. The people got closer, so I pushed on the door. My surprise at the weight of the door made me push harder, and that's precisely how I was tricked into entering SHAGAH—by the coming people and the weight of that door.

Chimes tinkled above me, betraying my presence by means of a stone and six iron pipes. I let go of the door and it closed into its own wake, like a boulder behind Ramases II in the pyramid at Cheops. The pipes and the stone had their last little say, their final tink.

I had been announced. But to whom?

The room was dim and my eyes still reeled from the street. With nothing to see and the street so gone, other senses blazed ahead of me. I thought I smelled cinnamon. There was another scent, the unmistakable one of myrrh.

There was movement in the back, coming closer. A person was walking out from another room. There was some light now coming from that room, illuminating a tall arch. Acropolis-like pillars flanked the arch between the rooms.

"May I help you?" It was the voice of a woman, from the middle of the arch.

"I'm not sure. Is this a wine store?"

"No, I'm sorry. The wine store is on Jehu Street. Would you like directions there?"

"Oh, no thank you. I don't drink." *Brilliant, Joseph.*

The woman walked closer, and her clothing rustled. This was something that ordinary clothing did not do. And neither did ordinary clothing shine. Light was slowly returning to my eyes.

"Are you traveling?"

"Running, actually. I'm from Nazareth. I'm running to Antioch."

"Who is chasing you?"

I laughed a little. "I'm an adventurer. It's a sport for me. I'm in Sidon for the Sabbath."

"Nazareth. *Lah Chatser*."[†]

"You know about that? We have a terrible reputation."

"And yet you are doing a great thing. I love that incongruence. You *should* be from Nazareth. It suits the greatness of your task. Where do you find yourself?"

"Pardon?"

"Where are you staying here in Sidon?"

[†] Hebrew: *Nothing-village.*

"The Habima."

"I love the Habima. It's the best inn on the coast, I think."

"It's beautiful, yes. They give you a free newspaper."

"I love the restaurant there."

"That's my favorite thing, too."

My mouth was dry and I was dying for water, but I could not make myself ask for it.

The room was coming into view now, as well as the proprietress.

The woman in front of me was stunningly attired. She wore a dress that, from somewhere below her hips and all the way to the floor, flared out farther than any dress I had ever seen. The bodice, which itself shone, gripped her hips and extended farther down her body than any bodice in the history of the world. These details came by periphery, the gift given man by God allowing him to see without looking. Silk—or something—with overlaid lacery covered her neck, shoulders, and arms, clear to her hands.

I needed to say something intelligent, and soon. It seemed appropriate to comment upon what was now beginning to appear on shelves, and to be hanging from hooks, and to be leaning against walls. The most inappropriate thing would have been for me, a stranger, to compliment the proprietress on her dress. And so I attribute the following to the overpowering aroma of myrrh:

"Your dress is beautiful."

"Thank you. Do you like the color?"

"I do."

"It's the most basic of colors."

"I didn't know that."

"But who wears it except at funerals? What a waste of the perfect color."

"I see. Do you have any water?"

"Please wait here. And do look around."

I thanked God for water, extolled Yahweh for the gift of thirst. The woman turned, but not without noise or sight. Her dress swept and gleamed as she walked, until she disappeared around a pillar. My eyes followed her, even after she had vanished. It was only when standing alone in her wake that I said to myself, *I have never seen red hair so beautiful.* It fell about her shoulders in ringlets.

I meandered about the place. The things I saw, I pretended not to. You'll recall what I said earlier about the deferment of pleasure. It was enough to know that golden shelves held wonderful things, and that gleaming hooklets let things of wonder hang dangerously adrift.

The walls were dark red. Touching one, I was surprised to feel softness. Fillium? No. The tiny fibers moved too easily. I walked down the wall with my fingers on it—a remarkable feeling. Then I saw it, a dark plaque of asherah wood and a sheet-leaf of beaten gold upon which a craftsman had carved two columns of verse. I looked closer. *Oh, my God.*

For in the window of my house,
Through my lattice I looked out;
And saw among the simple ones,
Discerned among the youths,
A young man lacking sense;
Passing through the street near her corner,
And on the way to her house
he sauntered along;
In the twilight, in the evening of the day,
In the midst of the night and the gloom;
And lo! a woman came
to meet him,

Attired as one unchaste, a wily heart.
Boisterous is she, and rebellious,
In her house abide not her feet;
Now outside, now in the broad ways,
And near every corner
she lieth in wait:
So she caught him and kissed him,
And emboldening her face she said to him:
Peace offerings are by me,
Today have I paid my vows;
For this cause came I forth to meet thee
To seek diligently thy face
and I have found thee:
Coverlets have I spread on my couch of pleasure,
Dark-hued stuffs of the yarn of Egypt;
I have sprinkled my bed,
With myrrh, aloes, and cinnamon:
Come! let us take our fill of endearments
until morning,
Let us delight ourselves
with caresses;
For the husband is not in his house,
He hath gone on a journey afar;
A bag of silver hath he taken in his hand.
On the day of the full moon will he enter his house.
She turneth him aside with her great persuasiveness.
With the flattery of her lips
she compelleth him:
Going after her instantly
As an ox to the slaughter
he entereth,
And as in fetters, unto the correction of a fool.
Until an arrow cleaveth his liver

*As a bird hasteneth into a snare
And knoweth not that for his life it is!*

"It doesn't have to be that way."

"*What?*" I turned quickly; she was standing directly behind me. She had come noiselessly.

"It doesn't have to be that way," she said again. "A man can avoid it."

I was at a crossroads. But the route I would take had already been chosen. By others. By things. By the passage of time. Had I not spent that night with Rent, or been heading now on foot to Antioch; had the room been filled with anything but myrrh; had the light been a single candle stronger, the walls a lesser red, the pillars a grain coarser; had the bodice of the proprietress not extended farther down her body than any other in history; had I not been so recently betrayed by Mary; had the hair of the proprietress been a calmer color, I would not, for the world, have said:

"Miss?"

"I am."

"How can he? She turns him aside."

She moved closer. "I did not say that man can avoid woman. If she's as persuasive as *this*," she gestured to the plaque, "man is powerless. Solomon compares it to fetters. It's that and more."

I swallowed hard. She passed me my cup. I sipped and then returned it to her, for my hand could not steady it. "But you said it doesn't have to be."

"Not with *this* woman."

"With the wife?"

"Precisely."

"And that's where shagah comes in."

I had astonished her. She unhanded the cup. "How did you know that? I thought I was the only one who had found this."

"I thought *I* was the only one. I stopped in the middle of the street when I saw your sign."

She reached over and took me by my wrist. A hotness entered my arm where she clutched me. "Come and look at this. Read what I have on the wall here."

She led me to the wall beside one of the pillars, and here was another plaque, similar to the first:

My son, do attend to my wisdom;
To my comprehension, stretch out your ear,
In order to guard foresight,
That your lips may preserve knowledge.
For the lips of an alien woman drip with honeycomb,
And the words of her palate are slicker than oil.
Yet the after-effect from her is bitter as wormwood,
Sharp as a two-edged sword.
Her feet are descending to death;
To the unseen her steps hold firm.
Keep your way far from her;
Do not go near to the portal of her house,
Lest you should give your splendor to others
And your years to the cruel one.
Drink water from your own cistern,
And the flowings from the midst of your own well;
Should your springs scatter forth in the streets,
Your rillets of water in the public squares?
Let them be yours, for you alone,
And not for aliens along with you.
May your fountain become blessed;
Rejoice in the wife of your youth,
A loving hind and a graceful ibex;
May her affections satiate you in every season;
May you be intoxicated by her love continually.

*Why should you be intoxicated, my son, by an alien woman
And embrace the bosom of a foreigner?*

I wanted to impress her, so I said. "That word 'intoxicated'; in both places, it's the Hebrew word *shagah*. It means to stray off the path, to lose control of yourself and do things you would not ordinarily do."

"Even wrong things," she said

"Yes. Like with drinking. That's why I thought this might be a wine store. I was half hoping that it was."

She stifled a smile. "You're the first one who has thought that. No one else knows the meaning."

"Isaiah used it to describe the effects of wine."

She quoted scripture now: "'And moreover, these by wine do stray, and by strong drink they go aside.' The word 'stray' there is *shagah*. There's always something strong causing it. And there's always a victim. And helplessness. Without helplessness, there's no shagah. Do you see it that way?"

"Yes. You almost have to be taken out of your mind."

"The drunkard becomes a victim through wine," she said. "Man does through woman."

"You see man as a victim, then?"

"Of course. Don't you?"

"I always have."

I looked into her eyes now. They were large, dark, drawing. My mouth came undone; my jaw slackened with new and exotic oils. A new warmth possessed my body. I was free, it was indescribable. I could say anything, do anything, be anything. My thinking was clear as transparent glass.

"What did you think when you first saw it in Solomon?" she asked.

"The same word used for a harlot and a wife? It gave me hope. But I wondered…how?"

"As in, 'how can men lose themselves with harlots, but not with wives?'"

I nodded.

"Tell me what you think."

It took me a moment. But then, "With the harlot, it's illicit. The man lets everything go."

"But not with the wife."

"There are borders there."

"He can show the harlot everything. He would give her anything. Why can't this happen with the wife?"

"Familiarity breeds contempt," I said.

"May I suggest something to you?"

She turned and walked five paces, the precise number I would need to grasp her perfections. She faced me again. It was then that the cosmos shifted. Once again, she spoke.

"The alien woman beguiles. She knows how to seduce a man. She is aware of his weaknesses and presses them. She knows what will bring him to shagah. Once he enters that portal, he's lost. He yields himself totally to her. She is goddess, and he must worship her. He has become her slave. She can make him *do* anything, *be* anything, *say* anything."

Warmth and pleasure fell over me—another wave. My body moved beneath it and I shuddered involuntarily before the black-dressed woman. I knew she saw it; I wanted her to.

"That still doesn't answer why the wife can't do it." I said it too softly. I was disappearing.

"That's the revolution. She *can*."

I ran my hand through my hair and looked down. "I'm sorry. I'm standing here and…I can't believe we're having this conversation. Where did this come from? I'm so sorry."

"Why apologize? We are having it, aren't we? And it's wonderful. It's happening, isn't it? This conversation? We're having this conversation just as I am wearing this dress. I *am* wearing this dress, aren't I? Please look and tell me if I am wearing this dress."

I looked up at her. The warmth came now in rivers. I looked at her dress, knowing she was watching me. Her bodice gripped her tightly with leather laces that began just below her breasts and extended halfway down her thighs. The explosion of dress followed. I gazed up and down her womanhood; I could not get enough of her. I absorbed her, consumed her. I could not stop staring at her form through the bodice. I stared at her waist and her hips, and at the smoothness of her tight, black belly. I could not stop seeing her curve. A small whine came from my lips. "Please don't let this happen to me," I said.

"*I* will decide what happens to you. You're not ashamed, are you?"

"No."

"Tell me, then."

"I am not ashamed."

"I am a beautiful woman. God made you to appreciate me. You can't help yourself. You *know* I'm beautiful. You're too much of a man to deny what you see. I think you should hear yourself say it. Tell me what you're feeling."

Lights and alarms coursed through my musculature. "You are so beautiful."

"Keep looking at me. Don't take your eyes off how God made me. See what He has done with my body. See what the bodice does. These decisions are mine, not yours."

"Oh, God."

"Stop moving your hands. Leave them at your sides. Let it happen. *There.* You like being a man, don't you? It feels so good to be a man in front of a woman. Doesn't it? Tell me."

"Yes. Oh, God!"

"There now. It's all right. Stay still! You are obeying your nature; it's beautiful. You can't help what is happening, and that pleases me. Don't move or try to hide it; you honor me with it. It can't help it. Never be ashamed of it. God made you how you are, and I know you like it. You love how it feels. Tell me you're not ashamed."

A tear crawled down my face and I heard a voice say: "I am not ashamed."

"*There*. This is what I adore in you. Tears make a man. Never fear your passion. Never deny your weakness. You must never be ashamed. Will you ever?"

"I will never be ashamed."

Suddenly, she pushed her hips into a wide circle and cried, "*Worship!*"

I lost my breath then, and my hands balled into fists. An incredible shaking boiled inside of me. "Father God!" I cried. And still I stared at her belly and hips.

"Look at me!" she commanded.

My eyes shot upwards from her body like buoys released from the sea.

She was smiling. "Have we even introduced ourselves?"

"God…!" This was my gasp but then, barely expelled, it became my laughter; the laughter came, but it wept. It started quietly, the weeping, then somersaulted downhill. Tears ran into my open mouth. She stood in front of me with hands on her hips, unruffled. I laughed and I cried. My hands were on my knees now, which trembled. Something powerful had broken within me. I stood up and ran both hands through my hair, then closed my eyes. "Dear God and Abraham. We have not even introduced ourselves. Imagine." And the tears stayed wet.

She tendered a handkerchief. "You are a beautiful man. Here. You are a *very* strong man—and you're not married."

"No," I said. "And tell me, Lady Shagah. How do you know that?"

"Look at your hands. They cannot rest."
"What just happened?"
"I can tell you, but I will not. Not yet."
"May I sit?"

She touched a finger to my shoulder. "Honestly. You're fine. Shall we?" She gestured toward two small tables against a railing. "Some tea, now. Since you're an expert on shagah, I will show you things that you will *greatly* appreciate."

I'd never dreamed of being on the stage, myself, yet here I was, an actor in a play: the table prop, the prop of the chair, the script that said "sit," that said, "look shocked," that said, "feel exuberant." A woman had just seen me—albeit beneath my clothes—but there was no shame. She told me not to be ashamed, and I wasn't; it happened at her word. She said that I was a man. If this was so obvious of a thing, then why was it so large of a revelation to me? She used what I was and pulled me with a power I'd never felt. *Shagah?* This was textbook. What else could happen? The pressure of the script closed in on me. For a moment I considered leaving—before she could lure me into the second act. It surprised me that I'd even thought that. Wasn't I in control of myself? How useless were my decisions? I knew how I would have answered that before, but the world was different now. *Completely* so. At least I was a man; she had said that. And she acknowledged God.

She returned with two cups of tea. I stood strongly, but with noticeable weakness.

"Cinnamon," she said, "with a touch of kava to soothe the passions."

I extended my hand. "My name is Joseph."

"I'm Anna." Seeing the look on my face, she said, "Is something wrong?"

I repeated her name, then asked for her surname.

"Corbin. Anna Corbin."

"My God," I said. "This is your store. You're not in Tyre."

"Not that I know of."

"Your hair's not brown."

"How did you know that I used to have brown hair?"

"We have a mutual friend, I think. Rent Hassler?"

She touched her cheek. "*God*. How do you know Rent?"

"I play ringball with him."

"Bless David. I can't believe it."

"I thought your parents were in Sidon."

"They are. They rent condominiums on Tab Street."

"Rent is dying to know where you are."

"This is unbelievable."

"He's sent you letters."

"Recently?"

"I think so."

"I haven't been home. He told you about me?"

"I know that you used to have brown hair."

She shook it. "Into every woman's life, changes come."

"Your hair is wonderful."

"Have you seen what's hanging on the hooks?" She pointed to the garas. I nodded. "Just checking," she said.

The door opened and the chimes announced a customer. A man and a woman entered. "Please excuse me," she said.

The couple bought some lotions, talked to Anna, then left. Anna returned to our table.

"You didn't shagah him," I said.

She laughed. "He's married. Do you think I just shagah everyone who walks into the door?"

"It's strange that no one came in while we were… talking."

"Give God credit for that."

"You believe in God."

"I'm of Asher."

"I'm sorry; I wasn't sure. I mean, the dress and all."

"Why do you think my shop is in Phoenicia?"

"Ah!" I watched Anna's delicate hand raise her teacup toward the sparkle of white face powder, appreciating now why her eyes and lips had struck me so. "Anna, how can I look at you now, and not be...completely ashamed?"

"You were supposed to fall apart back there. You're a man. Did we disrobe?"

"No."

"Did I touch you?"

"No."

"The power was invisible. Are you ashamed when you sleep?"

"No."

"When you eat?"

"Of course not."

"Then why this? Do you enjoy these other things?"

"Of course."

"Aren't they weaknesses?"

And so this was the dawning; weaknesses, all of them. Was it really this simple?

She said, "I have weaknesses too, you know." I asked what they could possibly be. A smile nearly came as she played a fingernail around the lip of her cup. "Sometimes I don't know when to stop."

I inhaled and then let the air out hard. "You said you had something to show me."

She led me to the wall where qum sat on shelves. I was dust in her whirlwind, the most attentive dust ever to blow.

"Why do you think men want to see women in these?" she asked.

I ran my fingers over the fantastic creations, studded along the sides and on the straps with tiny gems. "Men like how women look in them. They like how they walk." That was the effect, not the cause, and I knew it. I was lost; it was evident. She looked past my dishevelment and fondled the straps. Then she lit the wick of my universe with four sentences.

"Men *shachah*‡ in the presence of womanhood. It is instinctive. They wish to pedastalize woman, that they might humble themselves before her." She gestured to qum. "Behold, the mobile throne."

You've just turned the key to my cosmos, Anna, but I will pretend that you haven't. God! I will pose as the answerless person of a minute ago and stupidly stay the enlightenment, like this:

"Shachah belongs to God, and Him alone. Please. I know, I'm sorry, but there's always something stopping me. Because it's God alone to Whom we owe shachah, and none before Him. The first commandment. What about that?" Ignore me, please, like you did before. Look beyond me and strike another wick with your heat.

"This isn't about God, it's about woman."

"But the alien women is a goddess. You said that."

"Small 'g,' Joseph. The psalmist calls the judges of Israel, 'gods.' It's in the literature. A god is a subjector, relative or absolute. It's strong, yes, but generic."

"But shachah…"

"Nebuchadnezzar fell on his face and worshipped Daniel," she said. "The word is there. 'Then king Nebuchadnezzar falls on his face and worships Daniel, and he says an approach present and incense of attainment are to be libated to him.' Daniel did not object. Did he pretend to be

---

‡ Hebrew, *to bow down the self; worship*

God? No. He was a great man, *under* God. He interpreted the king's dream, and even told him what it was. Only the Almighty had that wisdom, but it flowed by His choice through the veins and breath of a man."

Why hadn't I seen it? God was invisible, but Daniel was seen, yes, and the king could only see. So the king disassembled before the pitcher God poured with, in awe, his face toward earth. He, a man, received shachah. I saw it then. I had known it forever, but the light had just come. There is too much power sometimes, in this world, when standing is revoked for creatures with blood—whenever this power appears.

"That is shagah, Joseph. It leads to shechah. Shagah leads to shechah. What divine wordplay. Don't you think so?"

"So I was worshipping you."

"Quite so. The world was gone. You'd have been on your knees if I'd wanted you there."

"I can still worship God."

She smiled. "I'm not the Almighty."

"Not yet."

Anna tilted a hand toward where God had experimented with me. "You obviously need a goddess, Joseph."

She understood it. No, more: she admired it. All men needed a goddess, she said; only the strong admitted it. The brave, alone, came forward. The rest hid behind doors and beneath coverlets. They quaked in their nightsweats and wondered what lived in them—what *thing*.

God sculpted woman to make man give her everything. The curves are no accident. The hollows of the cheeks and that smooth something near the tendons of the neck; this happened on purpose just after God made the waterfall. The men tumble over the precipice in bubbles; the wives think the men are idolaters. Do droplets of water regard with blind adoration the powers that press them in obedience to a stronger Fiat? The answer is yes, but the water doesn't sin. Men are slaves of a woman's form; women are slaves of a man's strength—that part of him able to please her. In ignorant women the power lies latent, like lava beneath the curtain of skin that will melt every earth, if loosed. But it stays caved in these women, and mankind walks safely by; most men are depressed. The street women unveil this by nature, by boiling, so that men flow along and don't return home, but come blistered and bubbling in it, skin crackling but screaming red and laughing besides. The woman gets anything; everything.

Shagah leads to shechah. I could write a song about it now.

"The knowledge of her body is the wife's key to happiness," Anna said. "But the wives say to me, 'We're objects. Oh God, they objectify us,' and yet it's God Who made them how they are, both the men and the women. 'It's too late for complaining,' I say, 'God is resting now. So use your body. Decorate it. Only half the world's humans can be as suns in their own cosmos; the rest are men. Let a body align for you. He will rotate for you, revolve around you. Your flesh is but the conduit. It leads to the soul—to you. *Eventually* to you. 'But it starts with the form, sorry,' I tell them." She stood up. "Along that line, I will show you my latest project."

She withdrew to the back room again and returned with a leather pouch the size of a bank bag. "You said you like qum." I nodded. She slipped her hand into the bag and withdrew two thick strips of the blackest leather. But they were not strips, they were—

"*Qum-aqeb shaq-kasah.*§ I call them *shaqasah* for short. They go clear up a woman's thigh, Joseph. Like qum, only no straps. Look. Solid leather, all the way up, with laces to tighten. But see the bottom. See what I've done."

---

§ Hebrew, literally: *raised heel leg cover.*

I know. I see it, Anna. I am beholding a miracle, I know that. Let me recover from this. You did something here, a few weeks back at a cobblery in Sidon, that will enchant humanity for a thousand years hence.

"I understood the purpose of qum," said Anna, "but I never liked the look. Not very *womanish*."

Does it escape you, Anna, that the process is nothing now? Does it escape you that the creation is bigger than whatever made it? But because it sits upside-down in your hand, it's safe. You captured it, and it's caged now. If your words could ruin it, I'd leave them be. But they can't and I'm a writer, so I feel responsible to record this for the world to come:

"See what I've done. I've taken out as much of the platform as possible. This heel is just as tall as the platform was, but it's down to this narrow post now. There's nothing in the middle; it didn't always look like this. After removing most of the platform, I still didn't like it. It looked like stilts. Picture it."

Her flat hand made a line from the top of the heel to where the front of the platform used to be.

"Everything was the same height, but it looked like stilts. That's when it occurred to me to lower the toe."

She ran her hand along the bottom of shaqasah.

"Look. The toe is below the top of the heel now. The toe is lower than the platform was, but the heel is the same height. I lowered the toe while keeping the heel high. That was the key to how this looks now."

She turned it right-side-up, running a finger down the curve of shaqasah, from the start of the heel and then down to the toe.

"I never thought I'd get this. I just wanted something feminine that would shagah a man and drive him to shachah. It was man's natural bend, but I could hurry him there; I wanted it on demand. So I worked with one of the cobblers here in Sidon, and with a tanner. I supervised everything. When I first got the heel separated from the platform, the post was too thick. I liked it at first, but something wasn't right. It was too thickish. I had this wonderful curve beneath shaqasa, but the heel looked clunky then. *The heel should be as narrow as possible*, I thought. So I went back to Tubal. He's the cobbler.

"I told him to keep sanding around the heel. 'Keep narrowing it down,' I told him. I felt like a mad enchantress. Tubal is an old man, and kind, but I tested his patience. He thought I was mad. He would say, 'This? Have we got it now, Miss Anna?' I kept trying it on, and the heel kept holding. Every time it held, I told him to make it thinner. 'Keep sanding,' I said. 'This time,' he'd say, 'it will break.' And I said, 'More, Tubal.' I wanted the extremity. The heel finally broke and I said, 'Make it again, but like we just had it.' I thought it was the ultimate, but only for a day. The heel was narrow, but not pretty like the curve."

She stroked the curve.

"I had this wonderful curve, and a straight heel. I wondered what would happen if the heel was also curved. I thought, why not taper it? The top should be square, substantial enough to bear the foot; we had that. But why did the bottom have to be as thick? I thought it didn't, so I went back to Tubal. 'Get out the sanding paper again,' I said. He tapered it like a crazy person, from top to bottom. I kept trying it on, and the heel kept holding. 'Keep going,' I said. Each time he sanded, I tried it, just like before. Each time the heel supported me, I put him to work. Every time the heel worked, I wanted more. 'More!' I kept saying. The heel would support me, and again I'd say, 'Keep sanding.' He really thought I was mad. But we got it down to this. I love how this looks. It's a weapon. Evil, but good. Man with woman is so good, Joseph." She smiled. "As long as man is kneeling."

She shook her hair and a ringlet fell over her face. She pushed it away. "After all, they go with *these*," and she pulled another length of leather from the glorious bag.

"Look at this, Joseph. *Yad kasah*.¶ Kidskin, same as shaqasah. Feel it. I made it to go clear up a woman's arm."

I felt along the length of yad kasah, and my fingers had enough heat, it seemed, to threaten its constitution.

"'A second skin,' I said to the tanner, and he gave it to me. The tanner said, 'They'll tear,' but I think he thought I'd be gardening with them. Anyway, it all goes with *this*," Anna said, and with a thumb and forefinger, she withdrew a gara. She handed me the bag and held both ends of the gara by the ends of the strings. She stared at it admiringly, putting the two of us in a common boat.

"What is it about it, Joseph? Do you know?"

I did not, but I was so educable.

"It's the lines, meeting the lines where the hips fan around a woman's stomach. Not all men see it this way, but you do, I can tell. In voluptuous women, where the ridges of the hips extend from the waist-parts down both sides of the stomach to the temple—that's where gara works." She held it to herself. "When a woman pulls it taut," she said, "to the hip-shelves, the strings parallel this wonderful line, this gorgeous line, from the narrowest waist-parts to the temple. Everything points to the temple."

Reverently, we both simply stood there.

"This has never been modeled for a man," she said, "none of it. Can you imagine what this would do to a man? How quickly it would reduce him?"

¶ Hebrew, *hand covering*.

I had a feeling about it.

"Do you know why these things are black?"

I lied and said no.

"It's the contrast of a black thing," she said, "and the death of the black thing against the living flesh tones. It's evil and good. Like the heel of shaqasah." This brought her to her best description yet of the heel: "Ferocious, yet a delicate women rides atop of it."

God created good and evil, she was right. Isaiah, line three-hundred. Without evil, good cannot be known. Not one snowflake can ignite itself upon the lily. Extreme opposites make for extreme depths. Force apart the poles, and the world collapses. Harlots know it, and so they paint their nails red and do alarming things with their hair.

"I'm teaching it to the wives," Anna said.

"But why death?" I said.

"Something had to die to clothe her."

I looked at her. "So it's the power of life and death."

"Not literal life and death, but the power, yes. Women. Queens. Goddesses. God's most beautiful creatures. It will cost man to be with her. To see her is a gift. To touch her, man must sacrifice at the temple. He must offer something. It must cost the man, just as it cost the animal that died to sheathe the woman."

"I've seen parallels in the temple," I said. "The procession of priests, the laver, the altar, the incense. All the preparations. All the initiations that the high priest endures before arriving at the holy place."

"The laver, the altar of sacrifice, the blood," she said. "My God. How far have you taken this?"

"The ark of the covenant. The cherubim. As I'm standing here thinking about it, the cherubim may be the hips flanking the holy of holies."

"Fantastic. You may be right."

"I think it's significant that the first couple, in Eden, wore skins. I wanted to hear your take on death."

"We're only at the surface," she said. "Where did it all start?"

"There's something still missing," I said, "and I think it goes back to Eden."

"It *has* to start there," Anna agreed.

I looked at her. "Maybe you'll find it."

"Maybe *you* will."

We stood there.

"Is there a special woman in your life?" Her voice was mellower now. Softer. Not as sure.

"There was."

"What happened?"

"We separated."

"I'm sorry. Recently?"

"Very much so."

I wanted to bury all that. I wanted, instead, to speak of the ensemble. I wanted to speak of gara and shaqasah. I wanted to speak of shagah, shechah, shamat. I wanted to stay dust in the everlasting whirlwind.

"Do you sell that ensemble?" I asked.

"It's still in the production stages. I may be putting laces on the hand and arm coverings, like you saw on shaqasa. I don't know. I haven't unveiled anything yet. You're only the second patron to see it. This is the only set I have, but I suppose I could sell it. Why? Would you be interested?"

I stared down at the floor now, becoming depressed; most men are. "I think it would be a good thing to have—I mean, if I ever got married."

"I'm afraid that it would be very expensive. A hundred silver pieces, at least."

"Oh."

"And I wouldn't even be making a profit, at that."

"It was just a thought."

The chime above the door interrupted us. "It's Omri," she said. "I'll be spending some time with him."

"Shagah? Shechah?"

Anna lowered her voice. "I swear to you, I don't go around shagahing and shechahing everybody. He wants something for his goddess's birthday." I stared, not comprehending. "Karin, his wife. Married twenty years. A month ago, they were near divorce. Someone told them about my store. I spent the week before last with Karin, two hours a day, counseling her. They have a new life now. That's what I'm in this for." Anna looked so steadily at me that I could not hold her gaze.

"You're special, Joseph."

"I appreciate that."

"Is Rent still at the same address?"

"Still in Magdala, yes."

"I'll have to write him."

"He'd like that." I looked around the room. "I should be going."

"I'm glad you came."

"I wish we could have talked more about Mary…I mean, about wives. That's the whole thing with shagah. The wives."

"It's the knowing. I only saw you on the outside. The wife sees your heart and mind. Those are two more doors. Combined with the form, it's the deepest level of shagah there is. I've never experienced it. I pray that you will. *Someday.*"

"Maybe I'll see you again."

"You know where I am. But here. Take my card. I just made these." She retrieved an advertisement from a desk near the door. "'Goddess of Sidon' is what I've been calling myself, but I'm not liking it. Now that I've been speaking with you, I wish I was 'Goddess of Nazareth.' I would love the incongruity of that—the great and the humble, side by side."

"Then change it," I said. "It's not too late. No one will know you're not from Nothing-Town."

"'Goddess of Nazareth,'" she mused. "It has an exotic ring."

"It's dangerous-sounding. Do it, Anna. It will make you famous."

"God bless you," Joseph.

"And you also."

I excused myself past Omri, the happy Omri. The chimes rang out, but this time the final tink died without me.

The run went on and on. Berytus. Tripolis. Aradus. Laodicea. All the same towns, just different places to buy a banana. The Great Sea was oftentimes bright, distancing itself from me. I was so lonely. Someone once said that it's not good for a man to be alone. A man said that, I think. A man without a woman.

I drew nearer to my goal, or what I thought was my goal.

On the morning of my last day, in the still-dark of Seleucia Pieria, I hauled my carcass onto the soft-packed road from a small beachside inn. The ocean came invisible except for the ghost-whiteness of the caps and the noise of water. The waves pushed me.

The fish smell was there again. Always. Different, but the same. Whether the fish were dead, I still didn't know. It may just have been the smell of the coastline. Or of Seleucia Pieria. Or of surf where seagulls bobbed and dipped. But the smell was a constant presence. I felt it had always been there, like Mount Silpius, even before men came to be on the earth.

I had never been there.

The first of the sun was orange and hazy. The sun made the morning orange. The haze was from the faraway mountains. The sun lay to my right and was easy to look at because it was pastel orange and not bright behind the haze. It was small, far away, but endeared the hills of Syria to me and didn't make me sweat. I would always remember it that way.

The Pieria Highway was vacant, so I sang hymns. I will never forget that morning. There was a quality to it. It was both vibrant and dull. The road was flat because the continent was at its edge. I could talk easily to myself, to the gulls, to God, because of the quietness of the continent.

I stopped for brief, sweet rests. I toyed with the day. It was thirty miles to Antioch, a distance that would have intimidated me two weeks earlier. But the distance, this day, was a child's toy. It wasn't distance at all, but rather thirty miles as one studies a map at his kitchen table with spearmint tea, and traces a finger easily along the map lines, over their folds, their colors, their great fathoms, and hums to himself. It was that easy; it was nothing. So I toyed with it, lifted it gently, sipped it like a great hot thing, placed it gently back, then sipped it again.

The map never did show the wheat brittle brown, or my legs brown, or my chest heaving naked beneath me. That was a harder thing to find, but I found it. And I found the seagulls over and over again, and the golden fields of wheat, and the sky that was now Syrian blue, and the sun that once again looked like the sun I'd known.

All the while, I wondered how I'd come so far. When I thought that it was merely from the gait of my legs, I was amazed. I hadn't tried to do it, nor had I borne down on it. I had not overly pushed. Yet somehow I'd come three hundred miles. It did not seem like something I could have done. I had simply lived, was living, and would continue to live.

Ten miles out of Seleucia Pieria, I turned inland on the Antioch Road, the last road of the run. I would head northeast along the Orontos River, through the forests flanking it. Crossing Foothill Road beneath Mount Silpius, all that would remain would be a right turn onto the aqueduct, the aqueduct itself, then a downhill stroll into the city.

The sky became bluer still, the running easier.

I reached Ancyra at 3:30. I had to check the mail station for a letter from Rent.

I unlatched my chest strap, wiped my face with a handkerchief, pushed back my hair with four fingers, and dropped my pack against a wall—again.

Mail stations are dark and hot, they always are. The floors and counters are dirty. You lean your shoulder into the door; they are always hard to open. The door never closes, so you push it shut. But there are rocks on the floor and the door doesn't shut well. The floor is stony and your sandals scuff it. The hair of the clerk curls strangely, it always does. Many addresses are scrawled on the walls of the station.

There is no letter from Rent, but a letter from my sister Jeshra. I take it outside and sit on the ground next to my pack. I lean my back against the wall. It's hot.

She is happy for me, happy that I've almost reached Antioch. She loves me. I love her, too. "I love you, Jeshra," I say out loud to no one. Then this: *I hate to tell you, Joseph, but our Mandy is dead.*

No. What?

Our Mandy is dead. I had to have her put to sleep. She was not eating and could not stand anymore. It was something in her joints, and something else. Joseph, she was miserable.

Oh no.

I did everything.

I know you did, Jesh.

It was the hardest thing I ever had to do. I took her there myself.

Mandy.

I will miss her so much, Joseph. Think how long we had her.

I walked to a restaurant in Ancyra and sat at a window table and ordered iced tea and a sandwich.

"Are you all right?" the waitress asked.

"My dog just died."

"I'm sorry."

"It was the best thing; Jeshra said it was the best thing. She did everything."

"I'm so sorry."

"Thank you."

I unfolded my map of Syria and spread it on the table. I wondered about the aqueduct over the Orontos River, about how it would be. The aqueduct separated Antioch from the jagged edge of earth called Silpius. There would be the aqueduct, the Orontos River beneath, then Antioch itself.

I left the restaurant.

There was nothing wrong with the sun. There was not one thing wrong with the pebbles at the mail station, or the iced tea, or the road, or the woods that now flanked both sides of the road. The price of the meal had been fine, the running was fine, it was a fine day, cloudless, perfect, as I'd dreamed it would be.

My body was doing what it always did, slowly at first, then finding itself beneath the pack and hitting the line. But the road did what it always does to me.

Mandy, little dog. Little dog at the animal shelter, big feet jumping at the fence. Little dog, first day of summer, I was ten years old, my family went together, we fell in love with her.

She barked, was alive, played games among the boxes beneath our work table. She got dusty and hid toys. She was so pettable beneath the fig tree when I went there to lay as she laid, wondering how a dog could lay like that. We looked at the sky together; she rolled over and I petted her. Bedraggled Mandy, the nothing-dog, so nothing except to us and to God. Nothing but hair, eyes, a happy tongue. No pretensions or pride, just silly love, foolish devotion, tired sighs before bed—so close to me.

Now, gone. Gone to the earth, or to where fire goes. Never to be, never to lay again, never to be seen or felt, or to wonder again upon this vale of soil.

"I need to stop, God." I said. "Almighty, I need to be somewhere else now."

He did not ask a question.

The world looked away as I walked alone into the thickness of woods. All the inhabitants of heaven knew, because my tears were already coming.

I went into the woods where no one could see me, and I fell to my knees near a stream and a rock. I cried, and oh, how I cried. "Mandy. Mandy, I loved you, you know how much I loved you." I cried hard and unashamedly for everything our family was then. I made myself so sad because I wanted to feel everything. It cut me that I was greater than them; that life was superior to death; that death had claimed them all and they were no more, but that I yet knelt in this woods. How that cut me. But I, too, would die—they had only gone first. Then I fellowshipped with them and looked up from some roots where I knelt.

A thorn bush was there, and the sun came through trees and lit it. It was terrible. I was so tired. I curled up on my side on the floor of the woods, where death could find me. My tears came again because I was just so part of the soil. I needed the sanctity of the woods.

The earth was dying beneath me.

BOOK 2

CHAPTER 10

THE VISITOR

I fell asleep. When I awoke, I was in Mary's back yard near the latticework, sitting on the big rock by the roses. Gabriel crawled through the laundry chute.

"Mother of Zeus. Why did you use the chute?"

I must have surprised him because he stopped. There was no moon and the air was dark pitch, but I felt him stop and I knew he was on his hands and knees.

"Joseph?"

"No. Elijah. Why did you use the chute?"

"Sport, I guess. Did you hear anything?" He had stood up and was brushing whatever he was wearing.

"Just her threatening to kill you."

"With her sandal, no less. I'd never heard that one before. It was—"

"Singular."

"Did you hear anything after that?"

"I quit listening after the match ordeal. I knew it was going to get holy in there."

"Good boy. I questioned the whole procedure, believe me. But I can't say I disagree with the choice."

"Mary is a nice girl."

Gabriel blew a little air out his mouth in a silent whistle. I imagined he was smoking a cigarette and had just released a fine stream of smoke. But I knew that angels didn't smoke.

"Nice? Hm. She's the rainbow. She's every color in this spectrum of yours. Funny and jolly and happy and weepy; and bouncy like a ball."

"She took the news like a ball?"

"I'm talking about the overall picture."

I slid down the rock so that my back worked into a post-glacial recess. Gabriel's patellae popped as he lowered his too-big frame to the manure pack. "Sorry about that," he said, "I'm not used to these."

"The cosmos moved tonight," I said.

"Yes, well, just another link in the life of zephyr final allemum." My silence amused him, and he laughed. "Don't worry. If you'd understood what I just said, you'd be traveling faster than a comet right now toward the right hand of God."

"I'd like that."

"Indeed."

I squinted hard to see The Famous Being. But I couldn't see anything in front of the dark outline of the house, so I gave up and went after what I wanted as a playwright, which is how I secretly saw myself.

"Tell me everything that happened. Can you? What did she say? How did she look when she saw you? She had to have just about fainted. Did she marvel that God had chosen her out of the millions? Tell me how much she marveled."

"Well, I must say that this is a change of pace, Joseph Jabrecki. And the whole time you didn't even wonder why she admitted so easily to being pregnant? Don't you think she knew the law? Did that ever occur to you? Didn't you think it a bit strange?"

"You know how that is. Forget all that. This is the night and I'm here. C'mon. Can't you give me something?"

"Nothing beyond what's written."

"It's written?"

"It might as well be."

"And you can't even give me one little thing?"

I knew by the length of the pause that Gabriel was reconsidering. "I will just say this, that it always amazes me—and all of us, really—how God works truly great things among people who act so—goofy, is it?—and fall back in their chairs and scream at flies?"

"Who was screaming at flies?"

"Oh, Mary and Marney. They slaughtered dozens of them. It was a big to-do for all of us. Thing was, they were using 1QIsa. I covertly rescued it later, but my goodness." I sat blankly. "The Qumran scrolls," said Gabriel. I still didn't answer. "*Isaiah*." I still didn't answer. "Joseph, someday people will put that flyswatter in a museum in Jerusalem and people will pay many, many shekels to see it."

"*That's* weird. What was Ben up to?"

"Nothing but puns. I stood at his elbow at supper for the longest time, trying to understand them. I kicked myself later for wasting so much time, especially as I had to make so many last-minute adjustments. I never did get the puns, so I classified them as soulish human stupidity."

"Perfect. What's Mary doing now?"

Gabriel paused, as if to listen. But he wasn't listening, he was looking. "She's just gone back to her bedroom and is lying on the bed. It will take her about two hours to fall asleep. She's pretty worked up right now. Would you rather see her or look at her thoughts?"

"I'd rather see her. But I'd ruin something, I think."

"You're right."

"What am *I* doing?"

"You're asleep at Hassler's. Otherwise, you couldn't be here."

"How do you become a man?"

"What?"

"How do you become a man?"

"Asking for yourself, or a friend?"

"No. I mean, how do you—Gabriel—fashion yourself into a man?"

"Oh. I don't know. I just do it."

"It's not hard?"

"No, not really. I can do it anytime. Correct that. I can do it anytime *He* wants."

"There's got to be more to it."

"Persistent, aren't you? I did it when Mary was putting out the lamp in the kitchen. As she was walking down the hallway, I was already in the bathroom. I made myself look like Ak Ein Karem."

"The milkman?"

"The milkman."

"Do you still look like him?" It was so dark that I couldn't clearly see him.

"Unfortunately, yes."

"Why Ak?"

"She'd seen him before. Think about it, Joseph. I didn't want to kill the girl. It was bad enough already. And I guess I can tell you what I told her. I would have done this differently."

"Like how?"

"In the light of day, for one thing. I would have done it as a young man, a suitor perhaps, who had wandered into this very garden, looking at the roses. My second choice would have been at the well outside Nazareth. I would have become a traveler looking for Donkey Street. Or the nut shop. But God's ways aren't man's." He paused to sigh. "And they certainly aren't mine. Oh, by the way. You're supposed to tell me about the scroll-spinning incident."

"What's that?"

"You tell me. Think back. Something about you poking your finger at some scrolls one time."

"Oh, *that*. Why do I have to tell you about it? Don't you know?"

"I don't know everything. You're going to write about this some day and He wants it included."

"*Who* wants it included?"

"God does."

"You're kidding."

"Look. Joseph. You're an important part of all this."

"By default."

"Stop that. We want a little more information about you in print. There's more to you than meets the eye, even yours. Did you know that you are descended from David?"

"That's a good one. Did you hear that as a joke from Ben?"

"I'm serious. The Van Holdens make a big fuss over their genealogy—as well they should—but they've got nothing on you. In fact, you're more in tune with the spirit of God than they are."

"I'm waiting for the punch line."

"It's not a joke."

"More than *they* are? You don't mean Mary, too. You just mean Ben and Marney."

"I mean Mary, too. All of them. God has chosen you as much as He's chosen them."

I had to reflect upon that. "You're talking about *King* David—right?"

"I could give you your line all the way down, if you want it."

"Fire away."

"Your father was Jacob."

"That's easy enough."

"Your grandfather was Matthan."

"Right again."

"Do you know your great-grandfather?"

"Eleazar."

"Correct. How about before that?"

"My great-great grandfather was Eliud."

"Before him?"

I had to think about that one. "Achim. I think."

"Yes, Achim. Before that?"

"I don't know. I don't know anything before that."

"Achim's father was Zadok."

"The priest. Yes, I guess I do remember my father talking about Zadok. But that's as far as I know."

"You didn't know that Zadok's father was Azor?"

"Hm. Maybe. But he's the limit."

"Azor was of Eliakim."

"No clue."

"Eliakim was of Abihud. Abihud's father was Zerubbabel."

"No kidding? The temple-building guy? Are you sure about that?"

"Get a hold of yourself. Zerubbabel's father was Shalthiel, and his grandfather was Jeconiah. That takes us up to the Babylonian exile. Now it gets scary."

"How scary?"

"Jeconiah's father was Josiah."

"The famous king of Judah. He sat on David's throne."

"So did the rest of these men. Josiah was of Amos,

who was of Manasseh, who was of Hezekiah, who was of Ahaz, who was of Jotham, who was of Uzziah, who was of Hehoram, who was of Joshaphat, who was of Asaph, who was of Abiah, who was of Rehoboam."

"All these kings. Your sure about all this?"

"Listen. I've been waiting years to tell you this. I've been following you and Mary since you were babies. You two have been my assignment for a long time. And Zechariah and Elizabeth as well. Everything having to do with Messiah, I've attended to. All the practical things, like telling you people. As I told Mary, you don't realize how big this is. I put in for this job more than a hundred thousand years ago. You don't know what I went through to get this gig. Believe me, you're related to all these kings. It's not that hard. I watched you kids from the womb. I knew you even before that."

"All this has been planned?"

Gabriel laughed. "If you knew what an understatement you just uttered, you'd be amused at yourself, you really would. But back to this genealogy business. Do you have any idea whose Rehoboam's father was?"

"I should know this."

"King Solomon."

"Mother of Zeus! I'm related to Solomon!"

"Calm down, man. If you're related to David, then you're related to Solomon. King Solomon is your great-grandfather."

"It is unbelievable how many *wives* that man had."

"Honestly, I find it fascinating what things you consider important. He's the son of David. Now, do you need me to go back to Abraham?"

"Refresh my memory."

"Jesse, Obed, Boaz, Salmon, Nashon, Amminadab, Aram, Hesron, Pharez, Judah, Jacob…"

"Isaac and Abraham. Unbelievable. Why didn't I ever know this?" I looked down now, scratching at the dirt. "What a waste."

"It's not. You weren't supposed to know until now."

"Why? You have no idea how this would have helped me growing up. I'd be a totally different person right now."

"I know. That's the point. It wouldn't have helped you. Had you known it, you'd have ended up like…look…we had your character development in mind the whole time. Everything is proceeding perfectly. But now that I've told you all this, we're going to need the 'Me No Torture' piece, whatever that might be. He wants it tagged onto the end without a single comment. Not one. And you can't edit it. However it is now, that's how it's going in. This is firm. Got that?"

"Sorry, but I don't even know what you're talking about. The 'Me No Torture' piece? What's that?"

"I have no idea. Something you wrote."

"I never wrote anything like that."

"Yes you did. Think."

I thought hard. I couldn't come up with anything.

"Go way back, then," Gabriel said. "It must have been a long time ago. You wrote it, don't worry."

I thought back through high school. Nothing. Then:

"Okay. Yes. It was in my religion class; way back. I must have been nine or ten years old. They almost kicked me out of school because of that, how could I forget? I got a whipping over it. It's not a great piece. I couldn't even write back then. I'm not even sure I still have it."

"Oh, you still have it. He wants it tagged onto the end without a single comment."

"Who wants it tagged onto the end of what?"

"*God* wants it. On the end of the chapter. When you write about this."

"I'm going to write about this?"

"Twelve years from now."

"Seriously. I have no idea where that paper is."

"You'll find it."

"You've got to let me edit it, then. It must need it."

"That's nice. Don't edit it."

"Please. As I recall—"

"Finished! It's finished, Joseph. Now, tell me about the scroll-spinning incident. We're going to need that in here, too."

"I'm surprised you don't already know about it. You're an angel. Don't you sit at the right hand of God?"

"Now and then. Anyway, I don't know everything. We're all specialists."

It unnerved me that I should be informing The Great Being. How much did he know about humanity? Would I shock him? How much detail could he stand from the likes of me? Would he think less of me if I were honest?

The darkness between us made me bold. Besides, he seemed so charming. I didn't realize until later how stupid I was to think this. Gabriel possessed unfathomable powers. He could destroy me in a moment, if he wished. But he was a good Being, I knew that. He was effectively disarming. Whenever I read scripture, I used to think, *how stupid for anyone to question an angel.* But I hadn't realized how unassuming they come across. I had no idea that they could look like milkmen. I understood now why people questioned them. This is probably why I razzed him as soon as he emerged from the laundry chute; it was my first reaction. Anyway, I decided to relax and be honest.

"I was feeling very crappy then," I said. "Everything was getting me down. We have a saying here that goes, 'Life's a shitshack, then you die.' Sorry about that. It's a terrible saying."

"I've heard worse."

"But I was living it. Everything I did was wrong. Everything was screwed up. I remember asking my mother at that time why she put up with me, and she said, 'I don't actually know.' I worked up a smile for her because I was sure she was joking. But the smile was fake. Besides, when I smiled, my mother said, 'There's a piece of broccoli between your teeth.'"

Gabriel seemed to hang in the air for a second, as if unsure what to do with what I'd just said. But then he did it: he started laughing. And when it would have been proper for him to stop, he kept on. I wouldn't have believed that an angel could forget someone's feelings like that and laugh right over them, but he kept on and it got more raucous. It was scary, really. But it cut me down at the same time. Was my sorry state so funny that it could debilitate Pure Holiness?

I let him go a while, then said, "Gabriel, you wanted to hear this. I don't see what's so funny about it anyway. It hurt my feelings."

He was sniffling. "Elohim! I had no idea people cried when they laughed. Look! Oh, Elohim and Michael. I'm sorry, Joseph. This is so new to me. Please go on. I'll try not to let it happen again."

"Well, during a trip to the market right after that, I found myself accidentally glancing at a beautiful woman nine or ten times."

I was laying for him that time, I admit it. About five seconds elapsed while Gabriel processed the information;

the humor was a bit complex for him. But as soon as it hit him he laughed so loud that I was afraid he would wake the Van Holdens. He must have known that nobody could hear him because he wasn't being careful.

"Acci...acci-*dentally*...Oh!" And this went on for a good half minute.

I continued my story, only louder, because I wanted Gabriel to feel bad about laughing at me—and I was laying for him again.

"I ended up standing behind this woman in a line to buy pistachios." I said. "And I kept staring at her even when she made for the door. And she actually had the nerve, on her way out, to ask me why I couldn't take my eyes off her."

Gabriel had composed himself briefly. "Really? And... and you said...?"

"And I said, 'Well, it's mainly because I have lust in my heart, and you look so great in that little tunic.'"

Angels can bend over and gasp, I now report. So much time elapsed between some of Gabriel's inhalations that I started to worry that I would kill him. Then I thought, *no, he's immortal*. So then I started to chuckle in spite of myself.

In-between his hackings, Gabriel said that he had not known a pathetic thing could be funny. As I already said, it never occurred to me that an angel might not know everything. He wanted to know where "funny-sad" had been all this time, and if it had always been here. I told him it had been here for a while.

"You have shown me a new wrinkle, Joseph," he said. "I thank you for this."

"Happy to help."

But I felt like he wanted more. So when he asked, "Tell me, what did *she* say?" I really stretched the trip line. I paused for as long as I could, using everything I had learned from

Aldo Aqsa. I really wanted to level him this time. I waited for the perfect silence, then said in a sing-songy way, "Well, *she* said, 'Do you know that you have a piece of broccoli between your teeth?'"

I was pleased with the results of my effort, but as this was so experimental, I had no idea when Gabriel would be himself again. So I figured I might as well go inside and make a pot of coffee, since apparently no one could see or hear me.

I could not resist glancing into Mary's bedroom. All I saw was a dark form on the bed. *Dear Mary.* She turned over, and I quickly walked away. I could not bring myself to intrude upon her. So I went into the kitchen and started some coffee, read bits from the *News*, poured two cups of the brew, then returned to the garden—using the door. I suppose it was ten minutes. I did make out Gabriel's form then, stretched out flat. He appeared to be on his back. He was breathing heavily.

"Are you on your back, Ak-wanna-be?"

"I seem to be."

"Better now?"

"I'm over the top. I'm good now, Joseph. I think it's over. Oh, how I needed this."

He was soon sitting up, and I extended his coffee into the darkness.

"I was thinking about what you said," I told him. "It *is* all about weakness then, isn't it?"

"Weakness is freedom, yes. Did you put cream in this?"

"No."

"Thank God."

We both settled back to where we had been.

"You were very weak then," Gabriel said.

"It was worse than that. I was a sinning piece of shit.

What bothered me so much was that, all this time, God was rolling revelations down at my feet. He was playing like I was this bride and His revelations were this perfect silk runner rolling at my feet. And He was just rolling these revelations down from His throne. My scripture times were so fruitful."

"And you thought, 'this can't be.'"

"Exactly. I couldn't believe He'd do this for me, that He would be showing these things to me, of all people. I knew what kind of person I was."

"What did you say to Him?"

"I said, 'This just isn't right. This runner you're rolling ought to be black, not white. And it ought to flatten me.'"

"And kill you."

"Exactly."

"What did God say?"

"He said, 'The runner is always white and it comes to bless you. Don't worry about it.'"

"God said, 'Don't worry about it?'"

"Yes. But I told Him that I still felt ridiculous."

"What did your feelings have to do with anything? I don't understand that."

"That's exactly what He said. He said, 'What do your feelings have to do with this?' Then He said, 'Do you think I chose you because you're a wonderful person?' I already knew the answer to that, but it hit me like a cubit of marble when He asked it."

"How did you react?"

"I didn't. The answer was so totally obvious that I didn't need to say anything. He read my silence and said, 'I chose you because it pleases Me to favor you.'"

"That's beautiful."

"More marble to the head. But I resisted it. I actually resisted marble, if you can believe that."

"Why did you resist?"

"I could hardly stand to think that His love could be that unconditional. It actually pained me."

"And He said, 'If you don't understand this, then you don't understand Me.'"

"That's exactly what He said. But I wanted to understand Him. So I said, 'I want to understand You.' Then He said, 'So quit moping.'"

"Yes, that makes total sense."

"That's when the weird thing happened. He told me to get my scrolls out and spread them all over the floor."

"Ah! Now we're getting to it. But this is new to me. Spread your scrolls?"

"Oh, I'd heard of it. But I still said something like, 'Do what with them now?' I didn't want to embarrass myself in front of the entire universe. And He said, 'Spread your scrolls, put rocks on the ends to hold them down, close your eyes, then spin the scrolls around. Keep your eyes closed, then put your finger down anywhere. Once in a while I make this work for somebody.'"

"So you did it?"

"Like a champ. I said, 'Like this?' And He said 'Spin them more.' I said, 'Like this?' And He said, 'Yes, but you're being too careful.' So I went wild on them. Some of the rocks flew off and some scrolls rolled shut. I thought, *Oh, well.* I was crawling all over them. Finally He said, 'That's enough. Now keep your eyes closed and put your finger down anywhere.' I said, 'Where?' and He said, 'Anywhere.'"

"And?"

"Line three of the forty-fourth Psalm."

"Oh!"

"Yeah."

"Say it."

"'For by their own sword they did not possess the land; and their own arm did not save them; but Thy right hand, and Thine arm, and the light of Thy presence, for Thou didst favor them.'"

"That's what it's all about, Joseph."

"Then God said, 'I love you, Joseph.'"

"And you did what you're doing now."

"...how could I help it?"

Me No Torture
by
Joseph Jabrecki

Some day they may again torture and kill people who believe in God. Too bad for them, because they won't get far with me. It's not because they couldn't crack me, but because I would tell them whatever they wanted to hear.

"Do you believe in God?"

"No, Sir."

"Would you bow down before any idol we put before you?"

"Yes, Sir."

"What would you do if we told you this slab of granite was God?"

"I would say, 'Hello, God!'"

"Do you like and respect us?"

"Oh, yes. I both like and respect you."

Then they would let me go, and I would have tricked them. Because really, I do believe in God. Really, I know that God is not a slab of granite. And God knows that. He also knows that I do not want to be tortured by crazy people. He understands this sort of thing.

```
    But I will tell you that, should God's
spirit somehow move me to confess Him and
suffer for His sake, I will do it. Otherwise,
I will lie like a crazy-assed son of a bitch.
```

I awoke to see thorns against the sun. I could have sworn I heard God ask if I was all right.

"Better," I said.

I left the woods.

Turning right from Foothill Road beneath Mount Silpus, I found the aqueduct over the Orontos River to be smooth and white.

CHAPTER 11

OUR LIVES ANEW

My knife demolished a pepper in the kitchen. "Everything's the same, Mother. Nothing changes. The sun doesn't care, the moon doesn't care—tell me what cares!"

Mother stood clear of the carnage. "These are the best days of our lives."

"Really? Then where is Joseph? Every day we say, 'Today he'll be back.' And every day is the same. I walk past his house every morning, and he's not there. He may be dead for all we know. And it's all my fault."

Chop!

"Missy!"

"I go to Elizabeth's, the wonderful thing that was supposed to comfort me. What happens? Only seeing that Elizabeth and Zechariah are so happy. Ecstatic. Me? Always the same. This is comfort?" Chop! "I'm not even showing yet."

"What are you saying?"

"How do I know I'm pregnant?"

"Gabriel himself told you. Then it was confirmed through Elizabeth. What more do you want?"

"Oh, but look, Mother." I put down the knife and ran my hands frantically over my belly. "Where's the baby? Do you see anything?"

"It hasn't even been two months."

"I should be showing by now. Where's the baby? *I* don't see him. Do *you?* Is he moving? I bet he's dead!" I was shaking now.

"Calm down. Have you menstruated?"

I screamed. "Don't even *say* that word!"

"What is wrong with you?"

"I've skipped a month before. I've miscarried!"

"You're not making sense. You haven't been the same since you got back from Elizabeth's. I think we should call Doctor Han."

"It's a trick! God is humbling me, don't you see that? I've been a wicked person and I'm being punished now. It's a big trick, don't you see? It's so much fun for the celestials. Don't you see how they're using us?"

"Stop talking that way." She gave me a small shake. "I won't have it."

"And neither will I! I won't have this baby!"

So much for the kitchen, then.

The darkness was descending again, only harder. My pillow was the perfect snuffer of light. Maybe it could stop whatever terrible thing was destined to occur. Yet whose fingers were these—thin, bony, and old—that gripped themselves beneath my pillow? I screamed, and the little lights came again, the greens and the blues.

For the first few days after returning from Elizabeth's, Father had tried to read to me from the psalms. "Read the *other* psalms," I said, "the ones about blood. David lusted after it, so let's hear about it. Read it. Tell me!"

David, King of Israel. When he wasn't running from those wanting to kill him, he pursued the people he wanted dead. That was his living, his occupation. And God was behind it all. Father said, "No, but see David's prayers. See how he offers thanksgiving to God in spite of everything. Even in the trouble." But I could not see past the empty, white bodies. "I'm not David," I said. "Sorry, now read about the blood." But he refused, and he walked away from these sessions shaking his head, admitting, at last, that I was better left alone.

We saw a freshly-killed mule on the way home from Ramah, is how this started. The blood of the mule lay in a big fresh pool in the road. "Don't look, Mary," the boys said, but I did, and I felt myself leaving my body. In the weakness of the mule, I saw my own weakness. I said to myself: *That's you*. My blood could be spilled, just like the mule's. I was a storehouse of veins and arteries, kept alive by a thick, red liquid that a prick to my neck could send onto the road. All the way home from Ramah I tried to stop thinking about it. "Talk to me about something," I'd say to the boys. They would ask what, and I would scream, "Anything!" They were patient, but they knew I wasn't well.

Even after I got home, the blood in my own body tortured me. I started hating even the sacrifices that supposedly averted Yahweh's anger. I flailed away at heaven: "You kill innocent animals to appease yourself. Why don't you just kill us all and get it over with!"

Here in my bed with the greens and the blues, I did not even want to believe anymore. At least the heathen were ignorant, I thought. Their highest god was the sun, and that warmed them. They cried for the dead, yet bloodletting was Israel's chief amusement. And God's. But the heathen, they basked in the sun all day and tried to please it. They gave to it *shechah*, that is, worship. To them, the sun warmed them. They lived happy lives in its light; no prophets, no prophecies, no altars of sacrifice. Their sun was not waiting to rise on the day He had predestined them to die. They did not know that God Himself had designated a day when the sun would turn to blood.

Where were my visions now? In this very room where I now feared my hands, I had slept in the arms of God. Isn't that poetic? Even the wall was full of glory then, when the first sunbeam moved across it and lit the crack that looked like the Sea of Galilee. In the morning, everything was new. But now? The glory was faded like the glory on the face of Moses. *Nothing* was new.

So all I could do was will myself to breathe, and to keep breathing.

Then, I felt a presence. And I kept feeling it. Finally, I had to look. It was Pharaoh, lying on my bed next to me.

"Oh, God, Pharaoh. Please help me." I was so glad it was him. I reached out to touch him, and he turned the side of his face to me, so I could rub him. I rubbed him and he purred. He closed his eyes and breathed in and out. The sides of his stomach went in and out with his breathing, and I thanked God for that. "Breathe in and out, Pharaoh. That's it, Boy," I kept encouraging him. *Pharaoh's whole world is my hand rubbing the side of his face*, I thought. *I wish I was Pharaoh. I wish I was a cat.*

I wanted Pharaoh's eyes to hypnotize me. So why did he suddenly look away and, in a little jump, leave the bed? He stood at the door and I thought I would open it for him. It surprised me that I could even get up.

Pharaoh walked down the hallway, and I followed. Mother and Father were nowhere in sight. There was not one sound at all in the house, not even lunch. Pharaoh walked into the washroom, and again I followed. He stood calmly at the laundry chute. "Do you want to go out, Pharaoh?" This was his access to the garden. He pushed at one side of the swinging door and went out. I pushed on the regular door and went out with him, into the garden.

It was a warm day, but so overcast and dirty that the clouds sat copper-bottomed. I didn't even care where the sun was, or if it existed at all. I said, "It can go to hell"—speaking of the sun—and that didn't even bother me. "Pharaoh. Where are you, Boy?" Then I saw him on top of the large rock by the roses. "You've found a warm place, my little cat," I said. And then it was as though Pharaoh said, *And you have, too.*

I saw a smooth, hollowed-out place in the rock that I hadn't noticed before. So I sat down on the soft ground and leaned my back into the recess. It felt so good. It was so solid, and it fit my back perfectly. "This is comfortable, Pharaoh. Where did you find this?" I looked up to see him, but he wasn't looking at me. He was looking behind us, toward the gate. I could not see the gate from where I was.

"Personally, I, too, would have done it in the light of day. I would have done it as a young man, a suitor perhaps, who had wandered into this very garden, looking at the roses."

That voice. Dear God.

"Or at least at the well outside Nazareth."

That gate! Where is the gate? Who's coming?

"I see his point, really. Become a traveler looking for Donkey Street. Or the nut shop. But God's ways aren't man's. And they sure aren't mine."

Where my body had been folded against the recess in the rock, there was now only a scuffle of desperate hurrying. That, and a curious cat sitting on top the rock cleaning himself, bending his paw to his tongue, looking up occasionally at a man and a woman embraced near a still-swinging portal, the woman in tears, the man saying the name "Mary" over and over again. And the hollow of that man's shoulder was, for the moment, that woman's God.

"Well, Holy Abraham. Look who it is."

"Good to see you again, Ben." Joseph held out his hand, but Father wouldn't take it.

"It's not good to see you, Jabrecki. Where have you been? What makes you think you can just walk into my home? You're no longer welcome here. You abandoned my daughter, you bastard. I want you to leave. *Now.*"

"Father. Please don't. Listen to him. He's had a dream."

Mother came into the living room from the kitchen. Then she looked as if she'd just seen a spirit. "Joseph!"

"It's me, Mum. God brought me back."

"She is not your Mum!" Father shouted, and he lunged at Joseph with the energy of a schoolboy. Joseph ducked beneath the flailing arms and grabbed Father by the waist. "She is not your Mum!" Father shouted again, and he hammered Joseph's back with his fists. It was as if I was watching a play. Joseph stood up beneath the blows, with Father now folded over his shoulder. "I'll kill you, you bastard! You ruined my daughter! Let me go!"

Mother was hollering for Ben to "Stop it! Stop it!" but he couldn't and didn't until Joseph had stood so calmly for so long that the humiliation finally drained the life from Father. Joseph said, "I was wrong, can we talk now?" and he walked across the living room and lowered Father into his favorite chair with a compassion reserved for the wounded.

Joseph sat my mother down with a word, and called me to his right hand. "Everything is different now," he said. "I thought the worst, it's true. I couldn't hear the spirit then. You're right, Ben, I am a bastard. But I'm here to ask your forgiveness. Things have changed." I still believed I was the one who had driven Joseph away, and I started to say it, but Joseph held up his hand and said four words: "I had a dream."

He had told me breathlessly, by the gate, about the encounter with Gabriel. And about how he'd ended up in Ancyra by running. He kept the running from my parents, but told them of his grieving for his dog in the woods near Ancyra, of falling asleep and of coming, in a dream (or being transferred in spirit, awake, he was not certain which) to our garden on the night of my visitation. He had looked into my room and saw me, and he believed. "I always *did* believe," Joseph said, and Father grunted without looking up from the floor. "No, Ben. It's true. Gabriel showed me that. But it was too deep for me, can you understand that? Belief that deep has to come from God. *Ben?*" Father would not look up. "I love your daughter, and I want to raise our son. I swear to you, I want this."

When he got to Antioch, he wanted to come home. He tried to find a caravan, but none were moving. He tried for a ship, but it was beyond his means. God blocked all these things, so Joseph bought a donkey in Antioch, and an inexpensive tent, and headed back along the Orontos River. He had taken the coastal road to Antioch, but it had been too busy and he wanted to be alone, so he took the mountain road back. I would have been afraid of robbers, but these were nothing to him, and I didn't realize why until he said, to all of us:

"I swear that what I'm about to tell you is truth. On the seventh night, I was ready to make camp at Emesa. I knew I shouldn't make a fire, so I rummaged through my pack for dry foods. That's when I saw a light, like a fire, burning fifty fathoms away in the woods. I went to see what it was, and as I walked, the wind started blowing. *Hard.* Branches swayed and I worried that they would break off and fall on me. But as soon as I worried, the wind stopped. Like that, it was gone. Even stranger, the fire had disappeared. It was there one minute, then gone. So I went to where the fire was, and there was a large boulder. I touched it, and it was warm. No, it was hot. It was as if it had been heating up in the fire. I didn't know what was going on, but after what had happened in Ancyra, I knew it was God. So I prayed out loud. I hardly ever do that, but I said, 'Lord, what is this? What are you saying to me?' Then I looked down and saw the scrolls."

"*What* scrolls?" Mother and I said together.

"An armful of the scriptures. But I didn't know it then. I grabbed them and walked back to my camp to see what they were. It felt safe to start a fire now. It was scripture, the law and the prophets. And some of the psalms. Not a complete set of the psalms, but everything else was there. They had been stacked next to the rock."

Mother said, "Someone just left them there?"

"I don't think so," Joseph said. "It looked that way, but I doubt it now. The spirit of God was at that place. The wind, the fire, the rock. How else do you explain it? Too many things happened. Wind does not do what this wind did. And where had the fire gone? Who leaves scrolls like that sitting outside? No. God Himself moved through those trees, and I believe He gave me the scrolls."

Father groaned again, but Mother said, "You were not even in Israel."

"I know," Joseph said. "Not even in Israel…" and his voice trailed off.

He read and he read. God gave him understanding concerning His plans for us, for our son, for humanity itself. At times, in the woods, Joseph laughed and praised God—and he danced! At other times, he wept. Not all the news was happy, he said. God took him from light to darkness to light again in a display of spirit that, in my mind, rivaled my own call. But the most important thing God told him was that he was to be a husband and a father, "and a son-in-law to you," he said to my parents. "We're going to need each other. You're my family now. I would have been home sooner, I swear it, but that's what happened. It wasn't my plan."

It was the plan of God, the subjection of El. "I wouldn't have been home, anyway," I said to him. "I would have been at Elizabeth's." Then to my parents I said, "Do you see God's timing in all this?"

Father was the one who had to say something now. It was he who had to bless our union. He would have stood to speak, I know, but he looked so tired. I wanted to help him, but I couldn't. I flexed and unflexed my hands, trying to wish God's will into his mouth. Mother, too, looked desperate for him to bless us. Father took several deep breaths.

"It's unfortunate," Father began, "the manner in which I spoke to you, Joseph Jabrecki. I will pray this evening, and offer a sacrifice to God for my sin. And maybe, perhaps, the God of mercies will forgive me. And yet…" Here it came. "I do not see how He could forgive me were I to give my daughter's hand to a man I do not really know, to a man who wanders outside Israel to escape his troubles. I rejoice, Joseph Jabrecki, that you have found your peace with God. I rejoice that you study His sayings and take them to your heart. But I do not know in what manner you keep God's holy law, if at all. What does that matter? I cannot give my blessing when God, inside me, shows no blessing to give." And so. "I am tired and old. I long to see the God of Israel, to meet Him. Have I met Him? Have I met Him, Joseph Jabrecki? I have been to Jerusalem three times a year, each year since childhood, in accordance with the law. And yet, still, I am an old and tired man. The glory of Israel comes to my daughter, yes. She has spoken with Gabriel, even. But what have I seen?" He waved one arm limply, then replaced it alongside his chair. "And now, outside Israel, a man, Joseph Jabrecki, says that God moves in the trees for him. And gives him dreams, like the dreams of our forefathers."

"Ben…" Joseph began.

"Please. I cannot hear it. It is too much for me. I am afraid that I cannot give a blessing when God, inside me, does not give it." Father closed his eyes. Mother bowed her head. I was ready to run to my room. But God, even still, had subjections to play.

Before I knew he was doing it, Joseph had taken both my hands and raised them over our heads. I looked at him, to question what he was doing. Our eyes found one another, as they did on that day we'd first met. I said, "*What?*" and Joseph said, "Twirl, Love." So I twirled beneath our upraised arms. "Twirl again," he said, and I laughed a little bit, but I felt light. I twirled. The wind did come then, a secret tempest, and we swayed across that living room in a dance that, from the beginning of time, had not been seen. It was a dance of no recognizable step or rhythm, having no anchor in the history of our people.

The invisible wind blew harder, and Joseph scooped me up into his arms, and the wind turned me in circles so vast that I squealed and said, "Joseph! You'll let go of me!" But he didn't, and he couldn't. So I relaxed into the cradle of my lover's arms and let my head fall back. My hair swirled around and around, out the door it seemed, into the sky, then out into the vast universe. I was a child again, full of joy before the gaze of God. The spirit seemed to lift me past the ceiling, holding me out to an unseen celestial host that shouted, "Mary! Let go!" And let go I did, falling free and full of trusting into the arms of my betrothed.

When Joseph had set me upright and I'd rejoined the world, an unusual sound came. It was a quiet, very secret kind of laughter, like a brook barely trickling beneath melting spring ice. And when I looked to the chair where the hands still hung limp, I saw a man thought to be old in his own eyes, a man heaving in his shoulders now to a rhythm he did not know, to an unaccountable mirth that, perhaps, had been welling up within him for years.

"The slimmer the dress, the slimmer the veil, Mary. The poofier the dress, the shorter the veil. We have a slim dress here, I just didn't realize it was *this* slim. So the veil is too thick, I realize that now."

"Do we have time to fix it?"

"We *have* to fix it," Mother said. "Here. Put these orange blossom clusters around your neck."

"On a sheer, fitted jacket?"

"It's all the rage in Gaza."

"Which is proof that we shouldn't do it. I thought we were doing the white lace rosettes thing."

"Well, at least now I know that you never listen to me. That's on your grandmother's honeymoon gown, dear."

"Sorry. I forgot."

"You're so beautiful, Missy, that it doesn't matter. I just wish that Zechariah and Elizabeth could be here. But they're having celebrations of their own, with young John. Now. Spin for me, Daughter." I spun.

"Who is spinning in here?" It was Father, who had sneaked into the room.

"Mother told me to spin."

"Good! Spin again. Spin until you're dizzy. It's a wonderful day. My only daughter is getting married. I can hardly believe it."

"Are you happy, Father?"

"Of course not." He winked at Mother. "But I'm making the best of it. Now, where is that forty talent bag of salted nuts, Marney? I've appointed myself official food taster."

Where was Hassler? He was running late, as usual. I paced the living room, and this was a mistake. It was hitting me again. I lay down on the floor and squinted at the ceiling. Again, the room spun like a millstone. I couldn't stand it, so I closed my eyes. Why today? I tried to get off the floor, but I fell over. *Just great.* I tried to open my eyes, but even when I only peeked I felt as though my insides would spill out.

There was a bang at the door. "Joseph?"

"Who's there?"

"I'm not sure, but I think it's Rent Hassler."

"Rent! Come in. Don't step on me."

Rent tepidly entered the living room, then feigned shock. "A corpse! A corpse that dresses itself for its own funeral!"

"Thanks for coming."

"Yes, well, you're looking fit. All ready for the ceremony, I see."

"The world's first prostrate wedding."

"I now pronounce you man and floor."

"God help me. I'm so dizzy. Stop this room, for God's sake. Why is this happening today?"

"You don't know? It's called 'getting married.' Hang on." Rent went outside and returned with a small brown jar. "I haven't seen you in two months, you invite me to be the best man at your wedding, I come to your house, and all you can do is…prostrate yourself before me? It's flattering, Joseph, but I think you're supposed to offer me a dead sheep or something. And it would help if you weren't groaning so much. Here. Drink this."

"What is it?"

"The guaranteed cure for pre-nuptial nerves."

"Is it poisonous?"

"Absolutely." I held out my hand and Rent pulled me to a sitting position. I groaned. "There you go again. Now down this." He handed me the bottle and I slugged it.

"Ugh! It tastes like bird poop."

"There's a good reason why it does that. Feeling better?"

"No."

"You will. Now please, get me something with alcohol in it and tell me how you happened to become the luckiest man on earth."

We talked for an hour; I was feeling much better. Rent asked who else was coming—I told him I'd invited the whole team but chose Af and Amman as groomsmen. They would meet here at my place. There was a knock at the door, and it was Af. We poured him a drink, talked about the game I had missed (the Welldiggers lost, as Rent had predicted, then dropped their first tournament game to the Generals of Jericho), talked about my run, and about Anna. I had already written Rent and related to him the amazing encounter in Sidon. "And thanks to you, Joseph," Rent said between swigs of Botschler's, "Anna and I are writing again. And do you know what she's calling herself now? 'Goddess of Nazareth,' of all things."

"Mother of Lot," I said. "She did it."

There was another knock, and I announced that it was probably Amman. Af opened the door and stood there for a stupidly long time. "Well, Af? Who is it?"

"Some chick," Af said. "It might be Mary."

It was my sister Jeshra.

"Jesh!" I hadn't seen her since the last feast. We hugged and she congratulated me on finishing my run, on the wedding, on finding clothing appropriate for the occasion. "There's a first time for everything," I said.

Jeshra said, "If we don't hurry, Joseph, you're going to miss your own wedding. I was just at Mary's and everyone's asking about you."

"Mother of Mars!" Rent said. "We've got to go!" He sprang from the sofa. "Come on. I'm not sure, Joseph, but I think you're required to attend this thing."

The four of us marched up the street to Mary's. On the way, I had an incredible urge to pee. "For God's sake," Rent said, "we can see Mary's house from here. You can't make it?"

"It's that bird crap you gave me," I said. We stepped off to the side of the road and Rent told Jeshra not to look.

"The neighbors will see you!" Af whined.

Rent shielded me from the road like a giant bush. "Be quiet, Af," Rent said.

"I'm going to remember this picture," said Jeshra.

I said, "You're not supposed to be looking, Jesh."

"Hurry up, Camel-boy," said Rent. "I can't stand here all day. I'm foliating."

"Ahh! This feels so good."

"I want to get married some day," Af whined. "You look like a water fountain, Joe-Joe."

We got to the house and I was surprised at how many donkeys were there.

"You're not supposed to see the bride before the wedding," Jeshra said.

"Then somebody better run interference for me."

Rent burst in the door, "Groom, coming through!"

I heard Mary squeal, "Don't look!"

"Nobody listens to that," whined Af. "Jeshra just saw Joseph pee."

"*What?*"

"Nothing, Mary," Rent said. "How are you? It's been a long time. You look great. May I kiss your hand later? Several times? *Oops, gotta go.*"

Rent and Af and I snaked our way to the bathroom, and it seemed like a thousand hands clapped me on the back. "Joseph." "Congratulations, Joseph." "Way to go, soldier." "Lucky bastard." "Mary's a doe." Practically the whole team had shown up. Amman (better late than never) linked up with our train and followed us into an upstairs bedroom, as did several of my old classmates.

Joseph, Rent, and Joseph's sister Jeshra came in like a herd of bulls. There was a ringball player with them, but I didn't know who he was.

"That's Af Weckter," Mother said. "He misses *baqa yanach.*"

While mother adjusted my veil, I heard many conversations between Van Holdens and Jabreckis. Mostly it was Van Holdens asking Jabreckis what occupied their days, Jabreckis answering proudly and with great volume, and then Van Holdens walking slowly away under pretense of refreshing their drinks. Joseph's teammates behaved well, apart from wanting to kiss my hand. I declined each time, though Mother was slobbered upon by so many young men that I asked what Father would think. "Maybe he'll get wise," she said, and continued to receive as many lips as presented themselves.

"Remember that time in grammar school when Maaz Dan fell down in the mud puddle at recess and got his pants wet?"

"Rabbi Salahiyya brought him to the front of the class and made him take his pants off."

"Like we were really supposed to keep our heads down."

"*I* did."

"At least Salahiyya held a blanket up so Maaz could change his pants."

"Yeah, but it didn't work. He held it too high."

"How do you know?"

"I read it in the newspaper."

"So you peeked?"

"Sure I did. Didn't you?"

"Hell yes."

"Why didn't he do it in the closet or something?"

"We're talking about Salahiyya."

"Did you peek, Nathan?"

"Absolutely. Didn't you?"

"Not me. Can you believe Maaz's underwear were blue?"

"What killed me was how ratty they were."

"I think it was the only pair he owned."

"Correction. I think those little panties owned *him*."

"Salahiyya should have cut him out a new pair from the blanket."

"Yeah. Cut them out with a meat cleaver and Maaz wrapped in the blanket."

"Naw. I'd cut him out a nice little boxer set from boar hair."

"A *Persian* boar."

"A wild female in heat."

"There's some *other* kind?"

"And no door for his wanker!"

Jeshra called into the bedroom to break up our impromptu grammar school reunion. "Hey! Rabbi Rekem is ready to go."

"Who's Rabbi Rekem?" I wanted to know.

"Um, the man who's going to marry you?"

"Oh, *him*. We'll be right there."

※

The orange blossom arrangement still wasn't right—according to mother. And neither was the veil. "Mother, we don't have time to fix either thing. They're fine."

"We may have to give up on the veil, yes" she said, "but these orange blossoms simple *must* be trimmed." Mother yanked the orange blossoms from my neck so hard that she practically took my hair off with it. I winced and said something I shouldn't have. "Whoops," Mother said. "Sorry."

A steady hum of talking wafted over the living room; no one was seeming to mind the delay. I peeked out. Where was Joseph? He was supposed to be standing at the railing Father had built next to our front door where Joseph and I would wed. I tapped my hand impatiently against my leg. Mother was still not back with the garland.

"Who votes for me passing the peanut bowl while we wait?" It was Joseph's Uncle Darius.

Father's brother, Muristan, said, "Who votes that all nuts keep their seats until the ceremony is over?" Several arguments now rippled through the room. *Please hurry, Joseph.* I peeked around the archway again and saw Joseph and Rent moving up the hallway. Thank goodness. Now why wasn't Jeshra playing the song? She was supposed to be starting some *Harney Barney* song on her lute. At least the song would hold off a riot—or start one. At last, the song began. *Now, I thought, if mother can just get back with the blossoms.* Well, here she came—without them. "Screw those damn blossoms," she whispered.

The song from Harney Barney was making me cry. Jeshra had never played it with such passion. I looked over at her; she was crying, too.

I stared at the archway, waiting for Mary. My heart was beating so hard that I was sure everyone could see it. I wanted Rent to check my chest, but his eyes were glued to the archway, so my eyes went there, too. The glory of the arch, its whole glory, was to frame my wife-to-be.

The Love Song, on the arm of her father, began. It turned the rounded edge of arch, shone, floated, commanded every eye. The architecture had its fame, but now it was nothing, for Mary had passed it. Her veil covered her face, but was no match for her eyes. Black pearls, those eyes—they could penetrate brick. I, Joseph Jabrecki, was no match. The deeps and the darks found me behind that sheet of snow, melted me, made me swallow hard. Rent whispered, "Keep breathing, boy." It was all I could do.

Mary's long auburn hair fell in front of her and behind her, glorifying her. Her shoulders were bare but for a heavenly sheerness; a garment made at the right hand of God, a wisp to make strong men genuflect. *Keep breathing.* A virgin goddess, a mystery, drew near me with a feminine purpose that shook my earth. She would give me her life.

Marney told me later that she had never seen Ben so happy. Rabbi Rekem must have said something, he must have. Ben made a little joke and sat down, so they said. My vows made Af cry, according to Af. Mary and I exchanged rings, because there they were on our fingers. It all became a blur to me. All I know for certain is that I became wed to one Mary Van Holden, as the papers later reported. I can only tell you that I lifted a veil of unimaginable lightness, and gazed at the face of God. And nothing else do I recall until our lips parted, when Hassler asked if it was his turn yet.

It was customary to stay at the bride's home and celebrate for a week after the ceremony, but these were not my plans. I would leave with my bride that same day for Caesarea. I'd rented us an apartment in a villa by the sea. Ben and Marney were not too keen on it, but oh well. Mary was ecstatic. As much as she loved her parents, she couldn't wait to go somewhere. Anywhere.

We would not travel to Caesarea by donkey. My teammates had chipped in and rented us a horse-driven carriage, with our own driver. I felt embarrassingly rich as I loaded our luggage into the back of the carriage later that evening. Guests came by and ribbed me about it, about me not being man enough to drive my own bride to the coast. Others joked that I was heading off to war. Horses were generally used only for war, and the joke was that here I was going off on my honeymoon with two horses. *Funny.* But most of the Van Holdens were impressed, perceiving this extravagance as the favor of God, which it was.

As I placed the last of our belongings into the carriage, Rent approached, acting all secret-like, scanning the horizon like a spy out of *Salt Sea Intrigue*. "What's up?" I noticed him keeping one hand behind his back.

"Joseph, I have something for you, and I must say that I can't wait to be rid of it, as it burns my hand even as I hold it."

"You're giving me a lump of live coal?"

"I might as well be." He brought his hand forward, and in it was a black leather pouch, a pouch I'd seen somewhere before. "It's from our mutual friend," Rent said in a whisper reserved for religion. "She sent it to me three weeks ago and told me that I should give it to you on your wedding day. She said that the girl who married you would be the luckiest girl alive. She wanted you to have this."

I stared at the pouch. *Father Abraham. No. It couldn't be.* I took it from Rent, loosened the strings, reached inside. It was. Father Abraham, it was the ensemble from Sidon. "Great God, Rent. Do you know what this is?"

"You will forgive me, but yes, I do. It was none of my business, understand, just as the fruit on the tree in the garden was none of Adam's. I willed myself not to look, I swear to you. But what is a man's will against *this*? Again, forgive me. But when the words 'SHACHAH BEGADIM'* are embossed in gold on the top of a black leather pouch sent me by a beautiful woman, it's generally my custom to investigate." Rent turned the bag around and showed me the lettering.

"I don't believe this," I said.

"I know. The Goddess of Nazareth strikes again. I'm supposed to tell you, too, that this is the only set of its kind. Anna says she has no immediate plans to make another. This is it. You have it. You *own* it."

"This is worth a hundred silver pieces."

"More."

"It's the only one."

"Yes, and thank God it is. Joseph, if the world were filled with these, it would be the end of civilization as we know it.

---

* Hebrew, literally, *worship clothes.*

Women would take over and we would be their subjects."

"Then praise Yahweh for the end of civilization as we know it."

"I'd be the happiest taxpayer on the planet. My God. If Mary actually *wears* this…"

I grabbed rent's clothing at the neck in mock aggression. "If you *dare* to picture my wife in this…" I smiled as I tried to think of the worst thing I would do.

"It's too late, my friend. I pray that you take it as a compliment."

"I'll take it as a compliment just before running a rusty lance through your liver."

"At least I would die a happy man. You are fortunate beyond belief. How I envy you."

"What a day it is when Rent Hassler envies *me*. Just think. The ringball star."

"And just look at these arms." Rent flexed his muscle. "My day will come. In the meantime, I endure the fawning of your mother-in-law." I laughed. "But your day is here. God's favor be with you, my brother. May He prosper your trip—in every manner possible."

As the day closed and night fell upon Nazareth, I sat with my bride in Elijah's chariot. My world was on fire. We waved good-bye to the ghosts of some faraway past, bathed in nothing but moonlight, friends, and family lining a place already gone. The carriage jolted, throwing us back in our seats. I looked at Mary and smiled, our hands locked together. Her arm, soft and warm in its wisp, rested in my lap.

A shout from the driver, and we bolted toward heaven.

CHAPTER 12

THE HONEYMOON

We rode non-stop to Caesarea, making the twenty-five mile trip to the coast in three hours. I'd never been to Caesarea. It was the new capital of Samaria, a busy and worldly seaport, not especially known for the worship of Jehovah. It was famous—infamous, rather—as the residence of Herod the Great, Idumean procurator of Galilee, who had built it twenty years before. Herod was not my favorite erotomaniac. I did not want to come to his city for our honeymoon; it was Joseph's idea. I would have preferred a quiet cabin in the Judean mountains. But my husband has a bent for the cosmopolitan experience, and this was the closest thing to that south of Antioch.

※

Caesarea smelled like *shamat*. Or maybe it was only a sense of loosening mixed with ambient odors like capsicum seeds. I'd been here with the team, but only under the curse of a curfew. Even so, I'd gotten the essence of the place just standing in the agora watching people walk. Caesareans held their heads higher even than the dead chickens hanging beneath the butchers' umbrellas. How many cities boasted procreating statuary? But this was Caesarea. I'd promised myself I'd be back some day, and here I was.

Night now. Forget the agora. Shake the stupid chickens from your mind, if you can. Daylight exists in another world. The sun is the only thing gone to bed *this* night. Torch lights lined the flagstone walks in front of the Herodian Villa Complex. It was nearly midnight, yet people overspilled the sidewalks in colors and spastic chatter. Some music played far away, down the street. Shouts came and went. Across from the Herodian, people stood gawking from upper-floored apartment windows, happily fearful of missing some moment. I said to Mary, "Well, we're not in Nazareth anymore."

The sea foamed and frothed somewhere behind the villa. A wonderful hotness settled on my bare arms. I thought to myself, *this is the best night of my life*. Mary was my wife; hot air sank for a change; lutes and drums made glorious noises; torch light twisted erotically; the sidewalk was a stage; the cracks between the flagstones reeked of *shamat* (or pepper seeds); the sea foamed and frothed; Nazareth was a world away.

I had put *shachah begadim* in with my personal belongings. The porter grabbed the strap of my backpack and I almost said, "Careful, friend; you're playing with fire." I had three days to gauge the timing of the conflagration. Mary gladly took my arm and we followed the porter into the Herodian.

A heavy door of glass and gold revolved in front of us. It spun as men and women charged through it. I had never seen such a thing.

"How do we go through this, Joseph?"

He said, "I think we just go," and so we pushed our way into it, Joseph shoving me through in front of him. So much adventure already, just coming in the door!

The lobby of the Herodian was beautiful. Persian rugs of various colors and patterns lay as one, showing not a trace of bare floor beneath. Gold spittoons, sleek glass statues, and many, many exotic ferns and palms decorated the lobby. There were many richly-upholstered chairs and sofas lining the walls, and a considerable area in the corner, roped off, where people drank alcohol (I assume) from odd-looking glasses. I was amazed at all the people not in bed. Everywhere I looked, people gathered in small conclaves, engaged in exciting conversations. There seemed to be not even a thought of retiring for the night. Only a very few people sat off by themselves, reading newspapers and books. I thought it funny that the men reading, almost without exception, smoked pipes.

The porter marched us to the front desk, and Joseph fetched some coins and gave them to him. How did he know to do that? I was so glad that Joseph was with me. He knew about things like tipping porters, buying newspapers, operating strange doors, and reserving apartments in fancy, foreign places. I held onto his arm. It was so big and strong. Joseph liked it, I could tell. I felt so helpless here in Caesarea and, I had to admit, I liked the feeling. I liked the feeling when I was with Joseph, that is.

I'd never seen a revolving door in my life, but I think I did a fair job negotiating us through it. I got us into the Herodian without hobbling either of us, so our evening was off to a grand start. I had no idea what to tip the porter, so I just grabbed a handful of coins, counted them on the run, and handed them over. I tried to judge by his face how well I'd tipped him. I'd never been to a place this nice, so how would I know? The porter lauded me with such gratitude that his face turned red. *Okay,* I thought. *Next time, not so much.*

I leaned up against the front desk and rang a black-handled bell. A young woman appeared and asked for our names, giving me the opportunity, for the first time ever, to say, "Mr. and Mrs. Joseph Jabrecki." Mary and I both fondled the sound of it. The clerk acted like she knew us and hustled around the corner, returning carrying the largest basket of fruit either of us had ever seen. She set it on the counter and told us it was ours. Mary and I babbled about it like, well, fruit babblers. The clerk must have thought we'd never seen a pineapple. We were just so flattered and surprised, is all. There was a card on the basket, and I read it out loud: "To the happiest couple in God's universe. Grace and peace to you, Mom and Pops Van Holden and several neighbors, whoever we could squeeze a mite out of." We laughed because we knew that Mary's mother had written the card. The clerk asked if it was our anniversary. "It's our honeymoon," I said. "We were married not five hours ago in Nazareth."

"Gerges!" This is what the clerk shouted then, and I thought maybe I'd said something wrong; I thought maybe "Gerges!" was a Caesarean curse word. But a velvety, rust-colored man soon appeared, as noiselessly as a human could. "Gerges, escort Joseph and Mary to the honeymoon suite, Apartment 202, upstairs." *What? What's this?* I hadn't reserved a suite. "Mr. and Mrs. Jabrecki, this is a gift to you from the Herodian. And here, you will need this." She reached under the desk and hauled a log onto the counter. "For the fireplace." Mary raised her eyebrows. "Welcome to the Herodian of Caesarea," said the clerk. "If you need another log, just stop down. We have as many as you need. And here are your towels and washcloths, and two bars of scented soap, and several of the newest fashion magazines from Rome, and a package of chocolate bars..." her arm was a blur of product, "...and scented soap—oh, I see I already gave you that, but take this anyway—the honeymoon candles are in the room, in the sconces next to the dining room table. But here are your matches, and a complimentary bottle of wine—please drink responsibly—and the corkscrew is in the drawer next to the coffeemaker."

All we could do was thank and thank that woman, and say gushing things about how royal the Herodian made us feel.

"At the Herodian of Caesarea, you *are* royalty. Three days? Excellent. Gerges will now escort you to your apartment." The rust and velvet Gerges stepped forward militarily and swept our newest worldly possessions onto a cart that he pushed before him across silent carpets. Mary squeezed my arm with such delight that I pranced. I waggled. I strutted. It would all mean another tip, but I was willing to give Gerges everything.

Our apartment wasn't an apartment, it was a house. "Joseph, just look at this place!" It went on forever, room after room. There was a living room, a separate kitchen, a bedroom, a bathroom, even a walk-in closet. I opened every door in a flurry of investigation. My first thought was to check out the bathroom. It was so clean. "You can't imagine how clean the bathroom is," I said. "I've never seen a cleaner one. I'm serious. Not even Elizabeth keeps her bathroom so tidy. And what smells so good? I think it's orchids. I want orchids for our bathroom…Joseph?"

"It's perfect, isn't it? Just listen to the sea, Love. Close your eyes. It's hypnotizing." Joseph had called me out onto the veranda. "And there's something hypnotic about you, too," he said. "You're the most beautiful woman in the world."

"I bet you say that to all the girls on verandas at the Herodian," I said.

"Only to the most beautiful ones."

"Let's see if we can start something in the fireplace."

"Or next to it," said Joseph.

While Mary smelled the bathroom, I found a door that opened to a veranda. How perfect was this: our room overlooked the sea. Mary finally came out with me and we listened to the surf. I wanted to kiss her right there, but it seemed too fast. Maybe the way she stood so much facing the sea made me hesitate. I knew she liked the fireplace, so I decided on a fire. I'd kiss her by the fireplace and take it from there.

It took me forty-five minutes to light the stupid fire. The log wouldn't catch, so I rolled up some villa advertising and finally got something going. It was good to have something to do, really. Mary kept talking about the bathroom. We both talked about the fire, about how we could keep it going and how maybe we should go down and get a couple more logs now, before it got too late. Mary had settled into a chair.

We finally had the fire going, though it must have taken an hour. Joseph got upset about it, even though it was only a fire. But I guess he wanted it to be a good fire. Or any fire. Finally, it was filling the room with beautiful light. It was overly warm, but we didn't care. I loved to hear a fire crackling, always. I closed my eyes and was beginning to relax. Then I heard Joseph say, "Mary, you're so beautiful."

I moved on my knees to her. "Don't fall asleep on me," I said. "You're too beautiful for that." I enclosed her with my arms on the sides of her chair and moved toward her. She opened her eyes and the dark mystery of her overwhelmed me again, as it had behind that veil in Nazareth. Oh, what her gaze did to me. I sat lightly upon her legs, straddle fashion, then, moving my face close to hers, breathed softly and carefully onto her mouth. Then, with the tip of my tongue, I slowly began licking her lips. A deep kiss wanted to come, but it wasn't the time.

I licked her lips as gently as I could. Her breathing thickened. I licked in wider circles outside her mouth, barely touching along her chin, then up her smooth cheek. When I knew she was enjoying it, I pressed harder and made wider circles away from her mouth. Now I was licking her eyes, touching them gently with my tongue. Her eyes were closed and I tasted the delicate paints of her lids. I imbibed of her scents. I grasped Mary's head between both my hands and sniffed her, easily at first, then deeply. Nuzzling my nose into her hair, I inhaled it. A surge of pleasure came; I groaned into her ear. She rocked her hips into the chair.

I was freed now and licked her hair harder. I grasped her harder with my hands, pushing and pulling her hair into my mouth. Her head was so small in my hands. My tongue then moved down her neck. My licks elongated and I thickened them along the length of her neck. I craned my own neck in stronger strokes to taste the smoothness of hers. Then a deep sound came from her own lips, and she told me to kiss her.

※

I had never been drunk before, but it must feel like this, I thought. Joseph was doing things to me. He began licking my lips, then my eyes, then my hair. My first instinct was to stop him, but it was too much pleasure. He smelled my hair and licked it. *A man is licking my hair*, I thought. My mouth was open. All I wanted was for him to kiss me. I moved for his mouth, but he kept moving it away. How this aroused me! Joseph circled and circled me. I wanted it so much now that I grabbed fistfuls of his hair and begged for him to kiss me.

※

Finally, paradise. If only I could crawl into Mary's mouth and curl up inside her.

※

Tears trickled down my cheeks. Joseph's, too. He took his tongue from me and licked my tears. He followed them to my eyes where he kissed them again. And he kissed my eyebrows and licked my lashes. He licked each lash.

※

My face fell down into her lap then. I was back upon my knees, kneeling before a woman, my dream. I ran my face down along her thighs on top of her skirts, then down her calves and to her naked feet. I kissed each of her feet once, running my hands along the sides of her legs, beneath her skirts. She tried to push me away a little, but I pushed harder against her, moving my tongue up her legs—but this is not saying it strongly enough.

I'd draped my head over the back of the chair. Joseph laid his face in my lap, then pushed it down my legs. He moved his face now, down toward my feet. I felt his hands all over me. I felt a kiss on one foot, then on the other. His hands moved beneath me up the sides of my thighs. I tried subtly to push him away, but then *very* hard licks came up the sides of my thigh beneath my clothing, toward my hips. I squirmed. "Joseph, it's enough. Please don't."

I felt her stiffen. I had done that long ago, on the veranda. I was worshipping a woman, my dream. I worshipped Mary on her throne. Everything in me and on me that had a soul arose and begged in its extremity to adore this goddess. I think she sensed that.

"Please, Joseph. Don't." He continued licking and kissing me. But I bent my knee and gently pushed away his face.
"What's wrong?"
"I don't know," I said.
"Everything is right about it."
"We need to talk."

The fire burned brightly. We needed to talk, she said. I didn't need to talk. But Mary was right, and I knew what was coming.

"You know we cannot enter *shamat*. Gabriel said—"

"I know."

"We discussed this."

"Nothing's changed, Mary. But there are many things we can do without *shamat*, believe me."

"The kissing. Can you believe it?"

"No. I want to do it again. Now and for the eons. Do we have to talk? I want you. Your mouth is—" And I moved again toward it.

"Please. Yes, it's wonderful. I want it again, too. I do. But we have to talk. Before something happens."

"You mean before I take my clothes off?" I stood and removed my shirt. I knew I was fit, and I turned obliquely to the fire so that the shadows captured my cuts and depths.

"Your chest!"

"Do you like it?"

"Turn around."

"Like this, Majesty?"

"Yes. Now back again." Her eyes dipped low now, to regions more, um, in the center of me. I was still clothed from the waist down, but certain things were standing out—or perhaps I should say, *outstanding*. "Oh!"

"What, my love?" I feigned innocence.

"Father Abraham!"

"It's yours. See what you do to me, Mary. See what power you have." I began disrobing completely for her.

"Joseph, no."

"I want you to see me."

"We must talk."

"You mean like…now?"

"Yes!" She was laughing. I was glad she was laughing. But she was right and I knew it.

�

The fire was making us sweat. It was way too hot in the room. I suggested to Joseph that we put out the fire.

"Just tell me one thing," he said. "Are our chocolate bars melting?"

I checked them. "They're getting soft. Why?"

"They cannot match me in endurance, then" he said. Joseph always amused me. "Let's light our honeymoon candles and sip a little wine," he then said.

"*You* can sip wine," I said. "I am going to eat an apple from our fruit basket."

"You know what happened the last time Eve did that."

"Let's see if history repeats itself."

�

Mary was talking friskily, which I was glad for. She was relaxed and things were going well. I thought we would relax a little more, cool off, then have our talk. Then I'd bring out *shachah begadim* and ask her to try it on.

I doused the fire. Mary lit our candles.

Mary and I had never talked about *shamat* before—never *really* talked about it. The crunches from Mary's apple bites sounded amazingly loud. *Caesarea certainly has the market cornered on crisp apples*, I thought. I was relieved to have wine to sip. I never have liked the taste of wine, and this bottle was no exception. But it seemed much easier to talk about *shamat* with a wine glass in one's hand than to attempt the feat without one.

"What are the 'many things' we can do without *shamat*, Husband of Mine?"

The crispness of her apple was emboldening my new wife. I sipped from my glass and forced down its contents. I sipped again. *A simple question.*

"I bought something for you to wear." I said it so quietly. Crunch. "And then?"

Damn the apples of Caesarea. How could she just skip over that so quickly? I couldn't bring myself to say the word "*shachah*," not with her tearing into her apple like that. And she was very coolly staring at me. I knew it was a test. My forehead grew great beads of sweat on top of the sweat already there. She saw it and tore another small bite from the great fruit of temptation. "Well?" she asked. A smile played on her lips.

"I want to appreciate your body."

Crunch. "Understandable. What next?"

I swallowed hard. This was not the Mary of Nazareth. Coy little doe here in Caesarea. She surprised me with that. I could never be a chocolate bar, no, we had too little in common during heat. What next? *Well, honestly. I want to shachah at your womanhood, Mary, kiss the midnight leather, lick the purse strings of your temple, loosen you, lap between the temple flanks, carry you to bed, suckle you, eat you to convulsions and become the straddling rail beneath a ceiling-wetting climax that will have the villa staff running to discover who was murdered.*

Sip. "I don't know," I said. "What do *you* think?"

Crunch. "Tell me what *you* think."

Sip. *Damn.* "I thought maybe I could kiss you again. You know. More *places*…"

Crunch. "And what could I do for you?"

Sip. *Well…* "Um. Oh, *I* don't know." *Abraham and God.* "Maybe…" *Holy Moses.* "Um, maybe what you do to your cows?"

No crunch now. Staring instead. "My *cows?*"

No sip. Looking at ceiling. *Holy Moses.* "Oh, you know, not *exactly* what you do to your cows, but…" *Beelzebub.* "…the same, um…"

"You want me to *milk* you?"

"*Could* you?"

"Spill your *seed?*"

"Um, *yes?* So that it hits the *ceiling?*"

"Joseph!"

"Mary?"

"I can't. What about Onan?"

※

Long, awkward pause. (Insert long awkward pause here, along with troubled breathing.) Ah, dear reader. We must suspend the action here for a moment—as only the magic of literature or the theater play allows us. Suffer me now to turn from the coy doe to address you as though this *were* a theater play—thank you for the indulgence. Let us leave dear Mary to her apple—picture her in dim lighting now, in the background, and me in the spotlight—and I shall entrance you, soliloquy-fashion, with grand and awful mistakes from the pens of our most popular expositors, whose opinions are a matter of them making things up as they go.

Dear God and David-damned Israel. *Onan.* Why him? Why now? But of course him and now. It's the man's specialty. It's the day of Onan, whenever pleasure is near. Though the man is a thousand years to dust, he yet haunts passion-filled affairs, and only these. He ruins lives from his stinking tomb. *Onan*, of all people. I should have seen it coming. All right, I did see it. But I live in the world of *chazon*.*

---

* Hebrew, *vision*. Idiomatically, *fantasy*.

My *chazon* yanks from the stage such characters as the infamous son of Judah.

I know I have just squashed the mood of Caesarea, but welcome to my world. Look at Mary there—sweet girl, wonderful girl, adorned for sex yet arrested in the swamp of misinterpretation; see how she enjoys that ridiculous apple. How *un*fortunate—for me. This is about *me,* mind you, the young hero pining for his wife. Speaking of fortune, for those fortunate readers yet unfamiliar with this cretin named Onan who has just been resurrected here before us by my fair maiden: he haunts male happiness from the grave through our grim and miserable expositors. Here's how.

There is a law in Israel which states that if a man dies childless, one of his brothers (should the deceased have one) must come to his widow so that his brother's name may not be lacking from Israel. I know how mad this sounds to those not of my race, but so it is. I get the point, I do. To keep a name alive is important to us. And better that the brother should fulfill this duty for the widow than some foreigner. God wanted a man familiar to the bereaved mother—and He wanted him now. As in 'immediately.' But the villainous, toad-spotted nut-hook that I've been telling you about, Onan, he did a bad, bad thing. Here's what happened.

Our forefather Judah's firstborn son's name was Er. He was hitched to a woman named Thamar, but he did some evil in the eyes of Yahweh, and Yahweh put him to death while still childless. In accord with the law just referenced, Judah told his next son, Onan, to marry Thamar and come to her, keeping Er's name from extinction. It was a casual thing, as in, *Carry on in the great tradition, boy. Get in there and do your duty, son.* Judah probably gave him a healthy slap on the back, possibly a beer, and for sure a "go-get-'em, laddie" fatherly type of pep talk besides. Not to mention, it was the law. But do you know what that artless, idle-headed clotpole of a measle Onan did? He suck it in and then pulled it out. I swear on my mother's grave, that's what happened. Watch now as I demonstrate the motion. Do you see? Watch my hips, here it goes again. *There.* He mounted, withdrew, and spewed. That roguish, onion-eyed flap-dragon now threatening my Caesarean honeymoon from his fen-sucked tomb, socked that little bunny boiler, felt the thrill, didn't want a kid, and shot the spill. And guess what God did? He killed the guy. God struck Onan dead, possibly on the spot. So now venture a supposition as to what all the paunchy, flap-mouthed, dick-dead commentators *then* said—and *still* say? They said that God killed Onan for spilling his seed outside the "God-appointed receptacle of precious holiness."

Excuse me? Onan shamed his brother's *memory.* He did not merely break the law by refusing to give his brother's widow a child—that would have been bad enough, though unworthy of the death penalty—but sought the thrill of the filly without the responsibility—*that's* what did him in. He shortchanged his deceased brother Er in the most ignoble fashion possible. God killed him for *that.* The spilling of seed was incidental. Do you see it the way *I* do? The way all normal and logical people see it? Have you any notion how many marriages this wayward philosophy has wrecked? How many glorious bouts of unfettered self-eroticism it has sidetracked?

From *this* they conclude that a man's seed is *holy.* As in, you should never ever *see* it. As in, it's the equivalent of *stardust* that must be roped-off and *whispered* at. As in, if you *could* see it, let us huddle around a pool of it and *pray* to it. Some of the ninnies go *so* far as to say that the baby is in the emission, that is, in the seed of the fluid. *The baby!* Thus—in case you have not noticed—they equate masturbation with murder. If this be the case, then I have sent so many potential nurslings over the great divide that I should be imprisoned for 4,000 years.

They say, also, that people like me want to control *birth*. Or, if you want to say: I'm supposedly into "birth control." I say to that: a man who wants children puts it in and leaves it in. A man who *doesn't* want children eases his passions into the bedsheets. But what of the man who is joined to a wife and simply wants a speedy solution to the inner heat on his way to work? *Must* he intend to populate the world each time the hotness comes to call? Why? Could anyone construe this as the control of birth? Even if it could be so, then what of it? If you ask me, the world has too many people in it already. But I digress.

I should have practiced a speech in front of a mirror before I left, before the treacherous Onan could have stowed away like a leech into our baggage and drained our joy—the wrong thing has gotten drained here, if you ask me.

There was no law specifically saying, "Thou shalt not, under any circumstance, spill thy seed on the ground, or upon thy ceiling, or upon thy wife's *shaqasah*." What did *my* situation in Caesarea, on my wedding night, have to do with Onan? I was legally married, loving my wife, loving God, not shaming anyone, not breaking law. My crime? I boiled with passion for my wife—perfectly legal in every civilized nation known to man and woman. The only law in my case, spoken by Gabriel, was to abstain from *shamat* until our son was born. That, I could understand. I could live with that. But what, specifically, is *shamat?* Ah, that is the question.

To God, it is the putting of *that* in *there*—I speak delicately to you. So many other sexual offerings grace the menu besides this specific thing—unless you are an Onanite, of course. For this is what the intelligent among us call these sour grapes: Onanites. In such a case, for an Onanite, there is no fun at all; no happy expulsion, no, but only emotional repulsion. Ah—to misappropriate an obscure passage of scripture to rob my toes of the curling experience? Expedient or not, I was unwilling to tolerate it. But neither was I prepared to offend Mary. Ah, another *shamat* tightrope, stretched taut for the suffering male.

Now, let us now see if I, Joseph Jabrecki, with blinding logic and loaded passions—ordinarily mutually exclusive entities—can turn the tide in the favor of common sense—and the fulfillment of my own intemperate desires, of course. We now re-join Mary in the dimly-lit Caesarean honeymoon suite, in progress.

"Onan's case was different," I said. "He dishonored his brother. He misled Er's widow. He wanted his own rocks off."

"*Huh?*"

"We're doing neither thing. Onan's context is not ours."

Mary wasn't having it. "It seems like an awful chance to take."

"You think God will strike me dead?"

"We don't have life insurance."

At least Mary had a sense of humor about it. "Mary, I'm burning for you." I shouldn't have said that. It sounded so desperate.

"Can't you wait?"

"I don't think you know what it's like."

Crunch. "I'm just not comfortable with it."

That's it? *Crunch, I'm just not comfortable with it?* I'm dying, she's eating an apple. She's "just not comfortable with it." As if I'm lying in a hammock drinking pineapple juice. So typical. And yet, so arousing. A bite of the apple, a pout, a casual glance at the fingernails. And me, hanging naked by my seed-containers, inches from her hand, begging. The man swings and burns, the woman eats the apple, examining her fingernails. So typical. And yet I was swelled now to the size of a fishing boat.

"What if I can prove to you that it's all right?" I said.

"Then I suppose it would be fine."

Thank God.

"But a doctor of the law would be better," she said.

"*What?*"

"No offense. But if a doctor of the law could prove it, I'd feel better about it."

"Then we'll go to one. Tomorrow morning."

"You can't be serious."

"Oh, but I am."

She grinned. "It's not how I expected to spend our first whole day as man and wife."

I grinned back, first fake, then genuine. "It might be the day, but it won't be the night. It's an easy point, if you ask me. We'll find a lawyer in the morning, at the synagogue. In the meantime…I'd very much like a taste of that apple of yours." She handed it to me. "That's not what I meant." She smiled, touched her hair, then ran the tip of her tongue along her bottom lip. The candles burned down toward morning.

※

Breakfast was a romance of food. Joseph called it a *buffet*. "That's what the Romans call it, anyway," he said. I wasn't used to so much food, especially not at breakfast. And you just go up and get whatever you want, as many times as you want—at a restaurant! There were eggs on warming-plates cooked every way imaginable, wheat cakes with different colored syrups in lovely glass pouring vessels, pitas and biscuits and lamb pieces still sizzling on top of a small fire. And there was no end of fruit, arranged in such a way as to qualify as art. And juices. And fried potatoes. And coffees—

the aroma! Even the dishes were beautiful. Joseph said they were blue Hebron glass. Our waiter's name was Rabin. "If you go away hungry from the Herodian," said Rabin, "it is not the fault of our cooking staff."

Breakfast was a disaster of titanic proportions. It's not that I hated it, and certainly not that I despised Mary's company. I had other things on my mind. Mary talked appreciatively and at supernatural length about the flowers on our table, and about the staff—Rabin in particular. I tried to appreciate the flowers, I really did. I think I did well by those blossoms—ask anyone who heard me lie about them. Rabin received my unfeigned praise, ask anyone who was there. But my future tottered in the balance. It was either thumbs up or down for the young gladiator. It amazed me how Mary could be so free about it. It didn't matter to her, one way or the other. It was a thing as inconsequential to her as biscuits or pitas. Of course she would be happy for me, but she didn't live or die by it. Oh, to have that free of a mind. But then, what would I do with it?

What if we got some gnarly old lawyer whose only pleasure in life was a satisfying bowel movement? I'd be finished. Or, should I say, I'd *never* be finished. I'd go for a second opinion, that's what. If not that, then a third. I'd keep asking until a diplomaed man in robes agreed with me. Seven months without Mary-managed relief? God help me, I'd seek a fourth opinion.

At last we'd tipped our servers, folded our napkins (I wadded mine into a ball), and were walking hand-in-hand down Qana Street, toward the synagogue.

"May I help you?" A gnarly old man (blast my luck) with apparently remarkable hearing, responded to my tepid knocks.

"We're looking for the rabbi," I said. "The chief teacher. Or a lawyer, perhaps. We have a dispute in the law." I held my breath.

"Might I ask the source of your dispute, and why you do not breathe?"

I looked at Mary. "It's rather personal, rabbi. Yet we are willing to discuss it with the one—not that you are not he. Are you?"

He laughed a gnarly laugh. "I am not he. No, my son. I am not the one you seek. You request his holiness, Rabbi Ajulan ben Shaufun. Ah, but this is his day off. I am sorry."

"Please, Rabbi. It's very important."

He raised his eyebrows. "It is a matter of life and death, then?"

"It is." If Mary could have kicked me, I'd still be crutched and bleeding.

"Very well. But his holiness will not be pleased. I will have my courier tell him that you are on the way to his home. When he asks, you must tell him that Rabbi Baybar sent you."

I grasped both his gnarly hands. I could feel his veins and bones. "Thank you, Rabbi Baybar."

"Oh, but I am Rabbi Horb."

Mary and I laughed all the way to the holy man's house.

House? Strange name for bonfire fuel. An ancient typhoon must have tested the structure one fateful day, found it wanting, and regurgitated it. "This is it," Mary said. "33 Heleni Lane."

"I think thirty-three is the number of seconds this chimney has left before it topples," I joked, pointing at the pile of bricks leaning crazily on the roof.

"Or the number of nails it took to build this place." Mary laughed into her hand at her own joke.

"*Or*, the number of water buffaloes that have sharpened their horns on those freaky-looking porch posts."

Mary laughed out loud. I could tell she was thinking. "*Or*," she said, "it's the number of people who stand staring at this place each day and decide to leave."

God, I laughed. Mary could be so funny, while somehow staying so practical. "All I know," I said, "is that if this guy doesn't give me a satisfactory answer, thirty-three will be the number of times I'll have to accidentally rub myself against our bedpost."

"Joseph!"

In the face of our misgivings, we pushed at a half-open gate. It squeaked badly. The gate hated us, it was clear. Had it been human, it would have flung us from the premises by our intestines.

"I don't like this gate," Mary said.

"Neither do I," I said. "It's foul. It's an evil gate. It hates us, that much is certain." But as it was only an abortion of lumber, two nails and a hinge, it merely squeaked badly as I pushed it open.

The barest remnant of stone sidewalk allowed us passage between tufts of yard that might better be called pastures devoid of sheep. Either that or the sheep foundered within. The house itself was white, or once was. Now it was a pale imitation of dirty oysters—not to disparage oysters. Someone had rimmed the two windows flanking the door in maroon paint, then covered them from the inside with oil paper. A fine color, this maroon, were it not for the porch posts, which were sky blue. I asked Mary what color she thought the large urn was, the one sitting by itself in the middle of the yard. She guessed yellow, but she was wrong; it was the color of something I'd once seen pulled from a fish; it had no name. Why someone had nailed a green wagon wheel to the house, neither of us knew. Yet we dreaded an encounter with that individual.

I was afraid that our combined weight would collapse the porch, so I had Mary stand on the remaining crumb of sidewalk while I knocked on the door. I used extraordinary caution this time, for fear of destroying the house with the first knock. A very old woman answered. Truly, this was the witch of Endor.

"What want ye?" she squawked.

"We beg your pardon, Madame," I began. "But we seek the counsel of his holiness, the Rabbi Ajulan ben Shaufun."

"On the Rabbi's day off? Who be ye? And further, who sent ye?"

"We be Joseph and Mary Jabrecki." I gestured toward Mary, who nodded in slow deference. "We be recently married, with a question as to law. We be sent by Rabbi Baybar. Has not the courier arrived?"

"Ha! Baybar, indeed. It was probably that bastard Horb." She ran a long fingernail beneath her crater-pocked chin and looked wise. "It is the Rabbi's day off. Disturb him today and fan the flames of Hinnom. And yet, ye are married. Of a truth?"

"Of a truth, excellent woman. Just yesterday."

"This be a matter of *shamat*, then."

I was so startled by this statement that my right foot went through the porch.

"Ai! And what harm have I done ye? What crime has Horna Bpespos done to ye and yers to make ye take out yer demented destructions on an old woman's porch?"

"It was an accident, Excellency."

"Then come in, please. And wipe your feet. It is a matter of *shamat*, then. How beauteous. His holiness will be most glad to see ye, most glad. Can I fetch ye something from the distillery?"

"We're fine, thank you."

"A leg of lamb?"

"We just ate."

"Onion soup, then?"

"No, thank you."

"I shall tell the Rabbi ye have come. Joseph and...."

"Mary. Yes. Joseph and Mary. Of Nazareth."

"*Shamat*, is it. And ye tell no tales?"

"We are tellers of truth, noblewoman. It is all about *shamat—shamat* to the extreme, and may I rent in quarters by horses if it's anything else."

"Wait here by the greenery."

I could describe for you the condition of the living room and its contents, but no words exist for such extravagances. Suffice to say that "living room" was a misnomer of the vulgarest proportions. Mary looked at me as if to say, "Let's get out of here." But we had come too far to turn back now.

The witch of Endor returned. "His holiness will now see ye. Down the hallway, first door to the right. Knock seven times, then sniff loudly into the keyhole. The woman must enter first. Understand ye?"

"Yes. All thanks be yours—I mean, thank you."

We traveled cautiously down the hallway. The first door to the right was unmistakably his; it was green. I knocked seven times, then sniffed into the keyhole. "What kind of crazy code is this?" I whispered to Mary. "Knocking and sniffing? It's ridiculous."

"This is his world," Mary said.

Nothing happened.

"He didn't hear you," Mary said. "Sniff louder."

I sniffed for all I was worth. Nothing. "Come on, Joseph. You're good at this. Pretend it's my hair."

It was so easy after that.

"Come in!"

We did so, to our utter regret. I should not have used the word "gnarly" to describe Rabbi Horb, for now I've nothing left for the relic before us; he was indescribable. Yet I attempt it as an exercise in literary disappointment: a random concoction of bones and sinews, leathery to the eye, full of veins, hair white as snow growing ten decades down his face, out his ears, atop his eyes, from his nose, reaching all the way to his desk to conceal his books and a large, petrified scorpion; a blue hat shaped like the head of an octopus, a nose so sharp it could split pomegranates; the face of a rat. When he saw us he raised a bony finger to heaven, a finger so tall one could raise a standard to its summit and call soldiers to war: "I hear only from angels, and speak only from God!" said the relic in a squeal so irregular that it reminded me of…nothing. "This had better be about *shamat*. Come near and disgorge it. Why tarry ye? Death stalks, procreating tortoises. Divine force and human fences. You present the facts, I, the consequences."

I grabbed Mary's hand and we slowly approached him.

"Thank you, Rabbi ben Shaufun. It's very kind of you to see us on such short notice, and on your day off and all."

I had said something wrong, deadly wrong. For the rabbi rose from his seat by the will of his arm bones and gritted his yellow teeth. "And already you waste my time, so precious given me, by Him! I fear, friend Joseph, for your purpose tarries. Already I loathe your verbal scrolleries. I shall give you a moment to think, then pose your query. Fifty words, no more. Fifty-one, and our business is done." With that, he sank to his seat and appeared comatose.

Mary noted my severe concentration and said nothing. I stood motionless for a good minute. Rabbi ben Shaufun's closed eyes sat dead in their sockets. Finally, I felt confident enough.

"Rabbi ben Shaufun?"

"Utter, tortoise, and be rid of your purpose."

"My wife cannot *shamat* until our baby is born, seven

months. I'm burning with passion. If I can't get relief, I'll die. I want milked like a...*cow* (I was at around thirty words, by my estimate) but...I would spill...*seed*. Enemy of happiness is...*Onan*. God kill him for...seed-spill...or...law-break?"

Fifty words, I was pretty sure. Everything depended on his assessment of contractions and hyphens.

A piece of the ben Shaufun beard moved. Then, a piece of eyebrow. Then one of the large veins on the back of his left hand began wriggling like a desert asp. Apparently, he would grace us. And more. The ben Shaufun eye sockets disgorged their prisoners and the veins in the ben Shaufun forehead stalked that wrinkled country like displaced earthworms. His long fingers shook and the end of his nose turned the color of winter radishes. Our own breath fell silent as the Savant of the Petrified Scorpion drew the fuel necessary to transfer his eonian wisdoms from God, to us.

"*Onan!* I can barely utter it. To utter that name is to invite God's wrath. He who infected Earth by his semen, found death. We who have uttered it are spared by your marriage. Have you grasped this insistency, procreators?"

"Yes, Rabbi!" I said. Mary was speechless.

"You want to waste seed. To spill it on the ground and *kill* it. To dig death's pit, and then to *fill* it."

"Well, actually, no," I said. "Of a truth, Excellency, I can assure you that—"

"Silence! Your admission is tacit. And birth control destroys the souls of those that practice it."

"Ah, but, pardon, Exalted Rabbi, I should clear up this matter..."

"Birth control is sodomy. And by this, one kills progeny."

"My wife is already pregnant, Excellency. I just want a little relief."

"Ah! A man, in wrongs, is never righted. The human race, by you, is blighted."

"I already told you that my wife is pregnant. Surely your holiness does not suggest that...*persons* live in my seed."

"As you say! Torn from the maternal womb, are they. The baby is formed in miniature, in the sperm. The mother is but the garden in which children grow warm. Thus, the baby is not conceived, but *implanted*. Heed you my sayings, unrecanted."

"You have no scripture for this."

"In the words of the devout, "Dost thou not, as milk, pour me out?'"

"You speak of Job. But Excellency. Surely that is a picture of his trials, not his swimming in the—"

"Silence! The son of Judah hath despoiled his brother. And for his trouble—Yahweh, divine adjudicator."

"So you think Onan was a murderer?"

"Do not speak his name! For now, you seek the same."

"I'm not a murderer, Rabbi. How can you imply that?"

"You eliminate future people from Israel. From Jacob, a boy. From Leah, a pretty-girl."

"All I want is a little relief, a little enjoyment."

"Enjoyment! You refuse a woman's natural function. And for this, you plot to ruin a nation."

"Women are not to be enjoyed? Is that what you're saying?"

"Guard your tongue, fornicator. The law doth say, "Revere thy mother."

"I beg forgiveness, Wise One. But to say that—"

"I learned my lessons in the corridors of Harrigum. God does not give women breasts, so that men can stare at them."

"You've never stared at a woman's breasts?"

"Your tone, young sinner, I abhor! Dispensaries of nourishment are these, no more."

"But your Excellency must agree that God packages this nourishment in most attractive containers."

"Enough! The sea is teeming, as is the trough. Men's sins fill up always, the abyss beneath."

"Can't you appreciate a dual purpose here?"

"I am blind to all dualities, dead. For the hills of Mereschmat, I have tread."

"Apparently. Then the wideness of a woman's hips…"

"The same. To accommodate her offspring, and naught to inflame."

"But Rabbi. Hasn't your blood ever arisen, even in the least, at the contemplation of a woman's delicate curves, wherein—"

"Silence, fornicator! Carnality! Man's offspring doth expand, in practicality."

"Then the rabbi, I assume, eats only to exercise his jaw and to sustain his withering frame."

"Do not become personal with me, wiseass—or be lowered into Sheol, as by windlass. Or do you think that you are better than me? As to food, you have guessed correctly. By the God Who lives, it is time for my chart. And excuse me, for cometh from my depths, a fart."

Again, by the power of a bony forearm, he raised himself from his chair, at the same time disgorging a great noise of gas that threatened our lives and happiness. Our instinct was to escape, but the prospect of his chart held us.

In the course of an agonizing minute, he had journeyed to the nearest wall, taking much of his air with him, praise Yahweh. Extending his frame to its extremity and curling a fingernail around a bare metal ring, he tugged with a grunt to produce a roll of papyrus on which he had penned four listings, labeled on top in large letters: THE FOUR SEXUAL SINS.

He faced us and his aspect darkened. "Heed my words, if ye have wisdom. For herein lies the death of men, and women." A bony finger addressed the chart. "Number one, males lying with males. Stick it in *there,* and the judgment is fair. An abhorrence! And from your faces, the nod of concurrence."

"Certainly, Rabbi."

"And next, these two, as one are paired, males and females with animals, bodies bared."

"An abomination before God, no question."

"And now, young seekers, number four. Of crimes offending God, most dour. The wasting of seed, as mounting a boar. And now you know the list—beware!"

Oh, the lawlessness of it. "Your holiness, I beg to interject. For see what you have done. The first three items come from the law, and are grouped near one another in scripture. Yet the fourth, the spilling of seed, you have taken from the *first* book of Moses, as far removed from the law as Sinai is from here. Excellency—and I beg your most gracious pardon and patience—you have wrenched this last out of context, and put it where it does not belong."

"You despise my chart! And so—"

"Please, no! Not another bodily indiscretion. You grieve us, Rabbi ben Shaufun. It's unlawful, what your chart pretends to accomplish. Admit it, for I think you know."

"My chart, for this I am famous! And the man who despises it, before God is blasphemous."

My wits had been exhausted. The man loved his chart, not me. Heaven knows what he thought of Mary. I could think of nothing more to say. He took my silence as advantage.

"Puzzle, puzzle, what is your trouble? Your tongue is gone, a right, now wrong. Despise, at your risk, God's progeny, unborn. The door is my friend now; go see it—*be gone!*"

I tell you, Mary and I could not leave that room quickly enough.

The witch of Endor met us near the greenery. She was sipping something from a ladle. "Have ye found satisfaction beyond the corridor?"

"We have not," I said. "In fact, we are most dissatisfied. At least, I am."

"What stirs yer spirit so? Did he feed ye the crap about Job swimming in his father's milk?"

I thought I had run out of amazed expressions. But no—I found a new one for the enchantress of Endor. "He said the very thing. How did you know?"

She sharpened the fingernail of an index finger on her remaining tooth. "'Tis an old standard of his, like 'Kiryati Shamona' from the Hit Parade. He does not tell ye everything, this I know. He holds out on ye."

"But noblewoman. He makes as though there are no answers for us."

"And the desert appears to horde water, where naught exists." She peered down the hallway, looked about the room, then drew us into her confidence with a lowering of her voice. "If ye wish, young friends, I shall speak to ye of the sacred deliberations of Horna Bpespos, ay, the deliberations into God's own law. Those seeking truth do find it at stones unturned, and in the bending of Bpespos, perchance comes maturity sharp as a pruning hook."

I looked at Mary, who returned my glance. What did we have to lose? Stranger things had happened, though none that I could think of. I took a breath, then jumped in.

"My wife and I were married just yesterday," I began. "Due to circumstances we're forbidden to talk about, she's pregnant. Due to other circumstances that *also* must be hushed, I'm not to come to her until our baby is born;

approximately seven months from now. My problem is…" I paused. It was so hard to talk about this, especially in front of such a woman as Horna.

"Yer *problem*," said Horna Bpespos, gesturing toward Mary, "is the hotness of this sweet marmalade and the stirrings of yer nutsack."

I laughed out loud. "Yes!" I said. "That's *just* it. I can think of nothing else. I'm afraid that if I don't get relief I'll be useless for any practical business in life other than pining for my wife."

"Did he show ye his chart?"

"Oh, it's his pride and joy."

"He slapped ye with Onan soon after, this I know."

"Of a truth, he did. He hates the man."

"The doctor abandons sacred contexts to set the man, Onan, within matters of the law."

"Amazing. That is *just* what happened."

"And now, yer solution lay simple."

"How?"

"From the writings of Priests, the fifth of Moses—for your purposes, 'Leviticus'—scroll 15, lines 16 and the following: 'Now if a man has a seminal emission, he shall bathe all his body in water and be unclean until evening. As for any garment or any leather on which there is seminal emission, it shall be washed with water and be unclean until evening.…'"

My God! Sunbeams broke forth from my soul. How could it be so simple? How could I have missed it?

"A simple clean-up job," said the Noblewoman. "I prefer to use handkerchiefs, meself."

"Madam, I—"

"No more words. The leap o' yer nutsack within speaks books and volumes."

I reached into my clothes for a silver piece.

"Yer money be not Horna's wish," she said. "But a kiss on the cheek from the handsome stranger, that be the going rate of service *this* day."

I would rather have remitted the silver, to be honest. I liked Horna, but—*well*. I looked at Mary, who smiled more than necessary. There was nothing else to do, so I closed my eyes and touched my lips to Horna's cheek. Her flesh was amazingly warm. My duty done, I noticed that her face had lightened considerably. "And now," she said, "Horna Bpespos bounces through the day, and places ye, in her spirit, on the wings of God."

Horna Bpespos was the woman who greeted us at the home of the rabbi. We thought she was a bit strange at first, but she turned out to be quite normal and actually wonderful compared to Rabbi ben Shaufun. He was evil. I did not dare utter a word in his presence. He discouraged us very much, especially Joseph. I was willing to concede Joseph's point, simply on the grounds that Rabbi ben Shaufun opposed it. He had an overly pretentious speaking manner, and poor control of his functions. He showed us a chart, which was as dear to him as offspring. I thought that Joseph made a good point concerning it, but the rabbi refused to even hear Joseph out. Whenever that happens, I instantly suspect that a person is hiding something, or is committed to his course in spite of the facts.

God was with us. An amazing thing happened as we were leaving. The elderly woman, Horna Bpespos, proved to be an able expositor of the law. She directed us to a fine detail from Moses, yet so clear that one wonders how it could have eluded us. All the woman wanted for her services was a kiss from Joseph. You should have seen him! I've never let Joseph forget how he puckered up for Horna. Horna just beamed over it. Joseph told me later that it wasn't nearly as bad as he thought it would be. Then, of all things, Horna wished us Godspeed. And so she was not strange after all, she was a God-fearing woman. How quick we are to judge people by first impressions.

On the evening of the second day, I wore my grandmother's beautiful white gown for Joseph, and it pleased him greatly. What a weekend we had. All my fears and insecurities vanished in the acceptance and unconditional love of my husband. In him, my peace was restored.

If you wanted me to unveil *shachah begadim*, that makes two of us. You're disappointed—and I might have been. But God gave me wisdom, and those mystical purse strings remained untugged. There would be another opportunity. In the meantime, I'll have the unmarried among you to know that the pleasure of a man, from a bed, does not quite attain to the ceiling. But a man's soul, in the grasp of the woman who loves him, does reach the gates of heaven, and beyond.

CHAPTER 13

THE FULLNESS OF TIME

Every now and then in life, a significant thing happens that freezes you in time. It stops your blood and you forever remember where you were when the thing occurred. I was in the living room with my feet up, fanning myself, having just finished an article in the *Nazareth Enterprise Review* about a local family that had put out a fire in their home, when Joseph came in from the shop and stood in the doorway.

"What is it?" I asked.

"Ab Bodie just left. He told me that Quirinius has just issued a decree from Caesar that every citizen of the Roman Empire fifty years and younger has to register an oath of allegiance. And I mean, like, now."

"What for? Didn't they do that seven or eight years ago?"

"Not this. Augustus has just received the Pater Patriae. And it's his Silver Jubilee, or some such wonder. Now he wants something big."

The title "Pater Patriae" is the most acclaimed title a Roman emperor can receive. It means. "Father of the Country." Still, this didn't seem like a big deal to me. At the last registration, we had each simply signed our names to a document at the town hall.

"This is different," Joseph said. "It's not just a registration like last time. This is an oath of allegiance. And Herod has added his little handful of spice to the pot."

"How?"

"All 'royal claimants' have to register in Bethlehem."

"What? Why?"

"The government is afraid of us child-bearing types, if you can believe that. Herod wants an accounting of anyone belonging to the royal throne. He's using this as an excuse."

"But I'm exempt. I'm married now, and you're not a royal claimant. So I can just register here."

"No you can't. Herod says—are you ready for this?—that females could give Davidic heirship to descendants with or without a certificate of marriage. It's true, I hate to admit. But it's the premise of the thing that's so stupid."

"Well, we can just go after the baby is born." I was well into my ninth month.

"I wish we could. But we have to go now. Herod wants this done before the Day of Trumpets."

"*What?*"

"I know. Four days."

I threw down the newspaper. "You have got to be kidding me. Don't they care that people have lives? We can't just pick up and leave on their whim. What's *with* these people? Who says we have to register before the Day of Trumpets? I swear allegiance to Caesar, not Herod. When does Augustus say that we have to go?"

"The Day of Trumpets. They're all in cahoots."

"What does he care? Augustus doesn't know Trumpets from Saturnalia."

"I know. This Bethlehem thing is all Herod's idea. And so is the deadline. But apparently, he's got the sanction of Rome. Ab said everything's coming down fast. If we don't go to Bethlehem to take the oath, Rome can shut down our business. I doubt they would, but that's what they're saying. That's what Ab's saying they're saying."

"So you're dead serious. You're absolutely not kidding about this."

"I'm absolutely not kidding."

"What ever happened to 'advanced notice?' Hello? I'm about to have a baby here. I've got a midwife. Sarah won't be able to go with us. She's got too many other pregnancies now."

"I don't think Herod is much into maternity issues."

"Are you absolutely positive about this royal claimant thing? That sounds so dumb. I mean, I really look like I could take over Israel."

"You look pretty mean to me. Anyway, Ab's on the counsel. He knows. The whole town is just finding out about it. But I think we're the only ones who have to go to Bethlehem. I don't know anyone else in Nazareth who's blue-blooded and still procreating."

"This is just so stupid."

"Tell me about it. But, hey. C'mon." Joseph flexed his arm muscle. "I could take the nation barehanded, don't you think?"

Joseph could make me laugh even during an earthquake. "But you're not a royal claimant." Now he was just standing there again, looking at me. "What are you staring at?" I asked.

"*You.* I want to catch your reaction. I *am* a royal claimant."

My arms were crossed and sitting on my very round belly. "Okay, sweetheart."

"No, really. I'm David to the core."

"You don't know your lineage. Don't you remember you told my father you were related to the guy who invented the hay bale? Remember that?"

"I didn't know it then. But Gabriel thought I should know."

That got my attention. "Gabriel told you? In all truth…"

"I swear it. God's truth."

"I'm of Nathan."

"I know. I'm of Solomon."

"He told you that?"

"He said it was no trouble at all; he said I had no idea how big this whole thing was, and that me being related to Solomon was, like, the easiest thing in the world."

"Joseph! This is too wonderful! Why didn't you say anything before?"

"I didn't want anything to change between your father and me. I want to be the underdog. As for you…" Joseph raised his eyebrows. "Well, you know I was going to get around to telling you eventually. I was just kind of hanging onto it."

"Come here, Lover. This whole thing is getting scarier by the minute. What's God doing with us?"

"I don't know. But there's some reason we have to go to Bethlehem, I know that. Think of it as a second honeymoon. It'll be fun." He bent over and hugged me.

"Fun? I wasn't nine months pregnant on our honeymoon. What if I have the baby on the way?"

"I'm a ringball star, Darlin'. Nothing gets through these hands."

Augustus Caesar came through with an asinine plan that every royal claimant of childbearing age in the Roman Empire was to take an oath of allegiance. I guess that wasn't so asinine, except that Mary and I would get a no-expenses-paid trip to Bethlehem, compliments of Herod. His Royal Bombasity wanted an accounting of everyone related to David, just in case one of us kingly types got the idea of overthrowing Rome, declaring Israel's sovereignty, and tossing Herod's fat ass out the window. I was too busy in the shop to overthrow Rome, but I think Mary was mad enough to at least pitch His Royal Lardhood headfirst down our meat cellar.

I looked at the whole thing as an adventure. And since I was included in Herod's paranoid little scheme, I finally had to tell Mary about my lineage. She was surprised, but it didn't make any difference between us. I'm the same guy I've always been. It hasn't changed me. Gabriel spoke wisdom when he said how different I'd have been had I known my lineage as a child. I've thought about that ever since. I think it's so true.

From the day we moved into my house after our honeymoon, I'd looked for an opportunity to unveil *shachah begadim*. Mary forgot all about me saying in Caesarea that I'd brought something for her to wear. I was feeling sporty one night about a week after we got home. I wanted to try kneeling again at Mary's feet, to see if she'd let me. If it went well, I could bring out the ensemble.

I wish I hadn't just written the word "try." But now that it's there, I'll explain why it's wrong. I wasn't *trying* that night; I had to do it. This worship thing comes on like a power. Mary is the power, I only react. When I see her in terms of *shamat*, I want to throw myself at her feet. God, I adore that woman. It's instinct. It's nothing I have to try to do. She can rebuff me as she did in Caesarea, so I guess that's why I said "try." I follow my instincts. The rest? It's up to God and Mary.

Joseph packed everything. I left everything to him; I had no choice. I could hardly bend over to latch my sandals, let alone throw loads onto Frisk. Frisk was a good girl, the offspring of Joseph's first donkey, Imra. I told Joseph he should have named her Friskie, with the "ie" added, to make her more feminine. Joseph said she was sweet and dainty enough, and that if we added the "ie" it would make her impossible to live with. It would be Frisk who we would trust to get us to Bethlehem, me mounted, and Joseph walking beside.

Though it was early autumn and we were in the driveway finishing our packing by seven, it was already hot.

Most of our neighbors knew I was of David, and I think they assumed Joseph was merely accompanying me to Bethlehem, not registering himself. Joseph didn't tell anyone differently. He was so humble that way, so good. Father and Mother were there to see us off, Father attempting to look calm but unsucceeding, Mother wringing her hands and hugging me, then patting my belly. "The next time I see you," Mother said, "you'll be a mother yourself."

"Maybe not," I said. "God may be merciful and make the baby late." That's what I said to Mother, but the real mercy would have been a contraction right there in the driveway. It had been a long summer and I was ready to have it over with.

"God bless you, Father."

"God be with you, dear Child," Father said. We embraced for a long time.

Sarah, my midwife, had checked me a final time the day before we left. Joseph was there, kneeling beside me next to the sofa as Sarah felt my stomach. "The baby's good, Mary," she said. "Right where he should be." I asked her how long.

"Honestly," she said, "you should be ready to deliver on the way. God forbid it, but you must be ready. Have towels, blankets, and a razor on hand. Be sure to have water on board at all times, I know you will. God will be with you." Then she fetched a razor, a piece of my knitting yarn, and some fishing line, and showed Joseph, with the yarn, how to tie and cut the umbilical cord.

Sarah smiled and pet my hand. Then she put Joseph's hand on my belly and told him to feel the movement. Joseph had already done that so many times before, but for Sarah he acted as delighted and surprised as if it were the first time. But now I retract that and say that Joseph was not acting. The movements of the child always astounded him. Since early in the pregnancy, Joseph read scripture to Jesus every evening through my belly. And each time he read, Jesus would jump. To see Joseph's eyes when that happened! "How can a whole person actually be curled up inside there?" Joseph would ask. But it astounded him even more, I think, to wonder how in the world it would get out.

I can't get over how beautiful women are, Mary in particular. What does a man do when he meets a woman? He bends at the waist, takes her hand, and kisses it. It's all the tradition and perfectly normal. And when he proposes marriage? We know from all the magazines that he takes her hand and drops to one knee before her. How beautiful and proper. Such a thing comes straight from God's throne room into the male and female nervous systems. Every normal person knows what to do. It excites me even to write about it. It ought to excite women, too. They know what to do;

they stand there and take it. All is well with the world when marvels like this occur.

Bethlehem was a hard three days from Nazareth. Our first day was hot and miserable. We had to stop frequently, whenever we found trees enough for shade, to rest Frisk and get us all some water. Public wells came infrequently between towns, so we stopped at private homes where there looked to be a source of water. Joseph was our front man for this operation. I would see him in the distance talking to the homeowner. Then, in accordance with our plan, he would gesture toward Frisk and me and I would sit up straight so that my belly would show. If anyone was willing to take pity on us, I was most willing to let them.

Now here is an obscene thought, if I may vex you with it: imagine a woman taking a man's hand and kissing it. Imagine a woman kneeling before a man to ask his hand in marriage. Now that I've made this vulgar request, please do not honor it; it will send you away choking. Of the genders, women belong to the beautiful one. They are the earthly angels, the half of the equation that we all admire and bow to. God stole beauty from Adam and gave it to Eve. Old Adam must have fallen back onto the earth to his knees when first beholding the newest wonder from God's hand. And good men, ever since, have bowed, kissed, and knelt publicly in deference to the better gender.

The first contraction hit on the evening of the second day, in the wilderness of Mount Ebal. It was the worst possible place to have a baby. The contraction came so hard that I doubled over. "Honey, I just had a *really* bad cramp. I think this is it." Joseph told me not to panic. We stopped Frisk in the middle of the road and Joseph slowly brought me down. He led me to the softest place we could find beyond the ditch and laid me on my back, kneeling beside me. Several minutes passed. I had got my breath and we thought everything was all right. But then another terrible contraction came. "Oh, God, no. Not now," I said. Then Joseph said words that I still treasure. He told me that this was a beautiful place to meet our son, that it was God's nature at the foot of His mountain, with just us and Frisk and God and the angels. He spoke so convincingly. He massaged my belly then, and made a pillow for me from one of our packs. He kept giving me water, sprinkling me with it, and talking to me.

Several minutes passed and not another contraction came. We at last surmised that this was false labor. Sarah had told us it could happen. Still, we waited ten more minutes. "I guess this isn't the place," Joseph said. When he was sure I was ready, he gathered me—literally picked me up—and set me on Frisk. The strength of that man! Thank God that it was only four miles to Colchis, where we found an inn.

Now translate that to the bedroom. The bedroom is God's gift to the married couple. Here, the couple is allowed—required—to live a life of exaggerated passion. What do I mean by that? Everything a man does in public for women, in general, he does to exaggeration in the bedroom, for the wife. God gave him this. For purging?

I think so, yes. This is not exaggeration for the sake of it. Please. This is passion. This is "have to or die." This is "do the deep thing or go to the grave miserable with the adoration still inside you."

We pushed harder than I thought possible. Everything in us taxed itself to make Bethlehem by nightfall. Jerusalem, which would have been a stopping place of magnificence and a mecca to reach and rest in, was now only a place in which to have dinner before the final five miles to Bethlehem. "This is not a bad place to have a baby," Joseph said. "We still have a day and a half before Trumpets." But I told Joseph no. If I had the baby here, it would be much harder to get to Bethlehem. "How could I possibly ride a donkey after delivering a baby?" I said. Joseph said we could rent a cart and I could ride in that. I knew he was right. We could. But the spirit told me to push to Bethlehem. "It's only five miles," I told Joseph. "There's something about Bethlehem." Then he, too, remembered how he had felt about the City of David. Joseph said he thought we could make it by nightfall. "I feel fine," I said. "Let's sail."

Is a man brave enough to expose his passions? That's the thing. It's so much easier to cower behind walls where everything is safe. But is a safe life a life lived? Every layer of passion peeled from life entails risk, and *shamat* is no exception. There is a place for that risk, as there are arenas in Rome where men courting ladies might prove their physical prowess.

The 11th of Elul, on the edge of night. The stars were just appearing as we made the city limits. Frisk was barely walking. "You're a good girl, Frisk," Joseph said. He patted her rump and reached into his clothes to pull out a sugar cube for her. She munched it without stopping. A strange thing happened then. It was as if I had already seen the whole scene before: Joseph pulling the sugar cube from his pocket, and Frisk eating it. It almost made me dizzy; it felt that real to me that I had seen it all before. If I concentrate today, I can still hear Frisk, dead these many years, munching that sugar cube. That sound pierced everything and sealed the moment forever in my mind. Strangely, this is the thing I associate with arriving in Bethlehem that night: Joseph pulling out that sugar cube, and Frisk eating it.

We were surprised at the number of people in the city. "I can't believe this," Joseph said. "What's up?"

"It's the registration," I said.

"Great Moses, we'll be lucky to find a room."

The bedroom, in marriage, is for the exercise of all things exaggerated. It's the emptying place for every hidden emotion. Nothing should be left after the bedroom, nothing. It should leave you clean. If anything remains in the heart, soul, or the bottom of the toes, then God's gift has been left unopened. This is a terrible thing to let happen. We offend the Maker of Shamat to allow such disdain of His gift. He knew His business when creating magnets and the genders. Men and women are polar opposites, destined to meet hard and for long periods of time. Man needs it, woman needs it,

God provides it. Otherwise, we all go insane. This requires honesty, and a fearlessness concerning the strength and power of the poles. But this is the difficult thing.

"It's impossible," Joseph said. He came back out after the fifth place we had checked. "There isn't a room left in this city. Not one. And this is the last inn in Bethlehem. *Damn* it."

"Did you tell them I'm about to have a baby?"

"Of course I told them. But these people don't give a damn about us or our baby. Some louse of a city this has turned out to be."

I started to cry. "Please don't talk like that."

"All right, but please don't cry. It's not going to help. I'm doing the best I can."

Night had fallen. We were surrounded by people and never so lonely in our lives. Our only friend was God. "I think we should pray," I said.

"No!" Joseph said. "I mean; no. Look, we just have to start trying people's houses or something."

I would never have predicted such a reaction from my husband to my request for prayer. I did not understand it and it pained me. "You don't want to pray? Who else can help us but God…oh…*God*."

"A cramp?"

"My water has released. This is it. We've got to do something—*now*."

It's a small step from bowing and grasping the hand—and kissing the hand—to licking the hand and the wrist and then moving up the arm. It's a small step from dropping to one knee in deference—and gazing up at the woman—to dropping to both knees in deeper deference and gazing up further. If a man kisses the hand in public to demonstrate his reverence, he kisses the foot in the bedroom to show the same, in depth. Well? The bedroom is the next step in the progression of depth.

※

Joseph said, "I love you, Mary. Please, just hang on."

At that moment, a man came out of the inn that Joseph had just tried. "*You*—with the pregnant lady."

Joseph turned. "Me?"

"No, your donkey. Come here. Aber wants to see you."

My husband looked to me then. "Go," I said. "I'm all right. Maybe this is good news. But hurry."

It did not take long. "This guy has a stable behind the inn. It's warm and dry and we'll have some privacy."

Joy and relief! God had provided for us, as I knew He would. A stable seemed a luxury. Joseph led us behind the inn.

※

You must remember, this is a place designated by God for exaggeration. The innerness of this room is the inverse of the dining room, and of the dance hall, and of the wedding chamber, times ten—and without clothes.

※

A muddy alleyway separated the stable from the inn, and this is where travelers took shortcuts through town. I could never have imagined waiting for traffic in an alley just to get into a stable, but such was Bethlehem that night. Joseph finally couldn't stand it any longer and pushed us in, saying "excuse me, excuse me" and then, "get the hell out of our way, please." Some people cursed at us. One man spat.

I was thankful to see that the stable was deep. Three horses stood tied in their stalls to the left, with an open but narrow area to the right. "Over to the right, Joseph. And take us all the way back. Can we close the doors?"

"I know, I know." Joseph slid both doors shut. This shut off some of the noise of the people, but now it was dark as pitch. A horse whinnied loudly when Joseph slammed the door, and Frisk backed up—with me still on her—and ran me hard into one of the doors. I nearly fell off. Joseph was cursing again, "For God's sake, Frisk, what in *God* damned—"

"Stop that. *Please.*"

He felt over to us. "I'm going to get you down now. Put your arms around my neck." I fell onto him, and he carried me to the back of the stable and set me down. We could still not see anything.

"I'm going inside to get a lamp," said Joseph. "And I'm going to see if I can find someone who knows something about delivering babies." He groped for my hand. "I'll be back as soon as I can." Another cramp wracked me, and I cried out.

"Hang on. Don't even move," Joseph pleaded.

The contractions came more regularly now. I cried out to Frisk, to God, to the three horses. I was sure that the people outside could hear me, but I couldn't help myself. Whenever a contraction came, I put my clothes into my mouth. The contractions hurt so badly. Each one was a knife cutting me. I was scared. *Dear God, please help me. Joseph, hurry.* My clothing was soaked now, from water and sweat. "Joseph!" I cried.

Here's another thing. I've heard stories of men—it's in our literature—who drape their clothing across mud patches for women, so that the women can walk across neat and clean. It's a beautiful picture to me, though I've never seen it accomplished. I hope that someone has done it. I would love to do it, myself. And yet, for all its worthiness, it's but public honor. Transfer that honor to a place of privacy, to the bedroom, and multiply it by ten. Multiply it by a hundred, if you're a bold enough man and the depth of your soul—and your wife—can accommodate it. A man removes all his clothes and drapes himself for his lady's pleasure. Is it extremity? Yes, of course.

One of the doors finally slid open and Joseph came in holding a lamp. Another person stood behind him, also holding a lamp. "Honey," he said, "this is Bathsheba. Bathsheba, Mary."

"Just like the wife of David," I managed to say. "Are you related to David?"

A deep voice came from behind Joseph. "What *David?*"

"Bathsheba is from Ethiopia," Joseph said. "I'm sorry we took so long. Bathsheba can do this. She's delivered...how many babies, Bathsheba?"

"One."

"How about that, Mary? One baby. See? Bathsheba can do this. Praise God."

Anyway, about that evening. I had talked Mary into buying a *chaphet*. Start small, right? That's how I approached it. So she came to bed with it on that night, and—*whoa*—she looked fabulous. We had lit two lamps, and I finally got a good look at her. We had not even seen each other yet without clothes. It just hadn't worked out. We had kissed and cuddled in bed, but always in the dark. Mary always made sure it was dark. She was a bit of ashamed of her body, I think. Not of her body itself—because she had the body of a goddess, I swear to you—but of her nakedness. She was embarrassed to be naked in front of a man.

Bathsheba put the lamps on either side of me. Another contraction came, and I screamed into my handful of clothing. "Sir," Bathsheba said to Joseph, "take bales and make wall against outside sound." Bathsheba took my hand. "No one will hear now," she said to me. "And you will be free." I sank into Bathsheba's warmth and care. And I travailed. There were enough hay bales for Joseph to stack them three-quarters of the way to the top.

"And now, Child. I must reach and feel for him. You have woman-helper before, and she does this?"

"No. She never did this."

"That is fine. But now see how slow I make it. Breathe now. Hold still, please. And now, I feel him, yes. Good. He is ready. Sir. Give me lamp please, very close here."

"Don't let him," I said.

Bathsheba took my hand. "Your husband is here," she said. "And blessings of all gods is here. Do not be in the shame. The crown of woman is nothing to feel shame for. And this—this is the crown of woman."

Joseph was still in the shadows, near the doors. "It's all right," he said. "This is your glory. It's God's glory, too. I want to see, Mary. I love you. Please let me."

I closed my eyes. "Then come," I said. Another contraction then, and I bit my clothes and moaned my agony.

※

So anyway, we had two lamps lit in the bedroom that night, and in she came wearing the *chaphet*. It was off-yellow, very pretty and slightly sheer, so that I could see through the space between her breasts and her body underneath, where her breasts held the *chaphet* out and away from her body. The bottom of the *chaphet* was ruffled and very short, coming only halfway down her thighs. I was in bed when she walked into the room, and as she came around the corner of the bedpost I think she thought she was doing herself a favor by cinching the ribbon-belt of the *chaphet* tighter, as if that would somehow aid her campaign for modesty. But it only served to hike up the *chaphet* and expose another inch of thigh. That, and the belt hugged the gorgeous indent of her waist, exposing the fullness of her magnificent hips.

※

The contractions wrenched me in two. The pain was too much for me. It was a clear pain, so pure and hard and terrible. I could not escape it. It made me see bright lights behind my eyes. Then the knife would come again, to slash the soul. How could God allow so much pain? How could I stand more? There was no remedy for the onslaught except to bite my clothes and try to swallow the small screams through my teeth and pray that God would soon end the misery.

Joseph had knelt in front of me with Bathsheba, and was holding the lamp. "The baby is here now, Sir," Bathsheba said to Joseph. "Come. Here he is. This is the head of him. See?" Then to me: "Now, Child. Push."

"My Lord," Joseph said. "My Lord, that's his head. Mary, I can see his head."

More contractions came, faster and harder and closer than the ones before. "It hurts so much. Help me, Joseph!"

He rushed to kneel at my head, stroking the sweat from my hairline into my hair and sprinkling me with water. "It won't be long now. The baby's coming. He's coming. Push him out now. He's almost out. God is with you. Keep breathing. That's it. Just keep taking air. I swear to you he's coming. It's almost over."

She was just ready to get into bed and I said, "Mary. Wait." I had the strongest urge I'd ever had to kneel at her feet. It was the passion boiling up from my depths to honor Mary's womanhood. It had a lot to do with that *chaphet*, I suppose. Maybe it was selfish. I don't think it was. Instincts are instincts. As she stood there next to her side of the bed, I swung around a bedpost, dropped to my knees, and began kissing her feet. And I mean, kissing them ravenously. But, I guess she wasn't in the mood for it.

"God help me, please. God help me—oh…*God!*"

"Sir, come now," Bathsheba called. "Here he is, the whole of him. He is out."

I said, "Don't leave me," but Joseph had run and knelt between my legs with Bathsheba.

"Joseph, what are you doing?" She was always asking me that. What did it look like I was doing? I treated it as a rhetorical question, and kept falling into her womanhood. I was so deep for her. But she stepped away. Hard. *"Don't,"* she said. "My feet are dirty."

"Oh, Lord." Joseph sounded panicked.

"What's wrong?" I said. "What's wrong? *Tell* me."

"He's so white. Is he supposed to be that white? What's wrong with him? Moses, help us."

"Oh, he is fine, fine," Bathsheba said. "Oh, how beautiful is this one."

"He's fine? Oh, Moses, look at him. Thank God. Mary, he's fine. You should see this."

I was breathing in spasms now, half crying, half laughing. He was out of me. The relief is unknown, except to women. "Show him to me. Bring him here."

Good Lord. As if I cared. "It doesn't matter, Mary. God, if you only knew how much I loved you," and I fell again to her for the deliverance of my soul. And I was crying.

I was crying, *"Oh, my baby."*

And she pulled away from me again and left me there and said, "Why does everyone keep insisting on worshipping me?"

✣

Joseph and Bathsheba moved the lamps and brought him to me.

✣

Then she stepped over me and extinguished both of our lamps.

CHAPTER 14

DEEP CALLS UNTO DEEP

Shepherds came and old men came and old women arrived and famous thinkers cameled in from the east, and I just kept running to different places to find fresh coffee. The miracles and the ceremonies came and went in a flurry of miracles and ceremonies. Two weeks took us from the stable, to the synagogue, to Jerusalem for the dedication. It was all too fast to mull upon then.

Mary was annihilated in a quiet way that did not appear on the surface. The pain of the birth panicked her. She loved the baby and "precioused" him and fed him every hour or so, but an undercurrent of disturbance harrowed her spirit. The pain awakened Mary to pain; she had never felt it like that.

For what this is worth, I banged my head on a piece of wood sticking out from a woodpile once, and I literally saw stars, just like they say. I even saw some planets and several comets, and a big green thing with sparks coming out of it. I had never felt such pain in my life. But instead of cursing as I would usually do, I thanked God. Isn't that strange? I said,

"I *praise* you, Father!" because the pain was just so amazing. Only God could come up with pain like that, I thought. It was divine, magnificent, and perfect in its severity. I suppose that praising Him like that was another way of cursing, to be honest. Mary's pain was worse because it kept coming.

I explained to her about the curse of Adam, and about God increasing pain in childbearing. I may as well have slapped her, for her reaction. She said that I was too pragmatic. I still don't know what that means. I was only trying to help. She said that I didn't know and could never know. She was right about that. So I just let her brood in her unutterable joy.

The shepherds came to our little hideaway. Five of them pounded on the door in the middle of the night one night. I thought, *Oh, crap*, because I thought at first that it was someone from the inn come to kick us out. But it was five men with beards and staffs; exactly how you expect shepherds to look, only these were worse. I at first thought they might be robbers. Shepherd-robbers. Well? I went so far as to look around for something to hit the shepherd-robbers with. I would kill them if I had to. *Whack, whack, whackety-whack*, I'd use both sides of the board in a flurry of shepherd-killing—that's how sharpened my senses became when the knocks sounded and I saw the shepherd-robbers. I spoke through a crack in the hay bales only after they'd asked for the third time if anyone occupied the stable. They weren't going away and I thought they might break down the door, so I answered that, yes, someone was in the stable, but that the someone had a three-by-seven and would use it in a death-like manner on their heads.

One of them finally said that messengers of the Lord (angels, basically) had led them to our stable, telling them that the Messiah had just been born here. That little statement saved that shepherd's life, and the life of his friends. I was excited then, I can tell you. I let down three of the bales, pulled open the door a bit, and the shepherds filed in. Who could make up that story?

They had been in the field for a week, they said. You may say that this is business as usual for shepherds—and a lousy business at that—but it's not. I had never heard of a week of non-stop shepherding; shepherds usually worked in two-day shifts. I knew this because my uncle's kid is a shepherd. But these men weren't kidding, not unless they had been afield nine days.

Several angelic messengers had appeared to them in a purple light in the Wange district, telling them specifically what had happened and how they would find the Messiah wrapped and lying in a manger—isn't that amazing? "A brooding messenger," according to one, led them to our stable. The men were half-afraid of me, I could tell. I think they thought I was a prophet. They were extremely deferential to me, bowing and bowing. I finally had to tell them to stop it. They didn't. I asked them if they knew a shepherd named Dollahan. They thought hard and decided they didn't know him, and neither did I. But at least I got their minds off the bowing.

I lit a lamp.

I awoke Mary because the shepherds said they had to see her before they saw the baby. That's what they said. It couldn't have been protocol because nothing like this had ever happened. Perhaps it was a shepherd superstition, I don't know. Anyway, they insisted. Waking Mary was a tough job, let me tell you. The five of them watched in amazement as I attempted to rouse the Mother of Messiah. When she came to, she began rubbing her eyes like crazy. The men backed away. They were frightened, I could tell. "She rubs her eyes so *hard*," I heard one whisper. I had to smile at that. You bet she rubs her eyes hard. That's Mary.

Mary finally woke up enough to appreciate what was happening. Each of the shepherds held the baby. Jesus never woke up through any of it. He was passed around like a stone in a quarry line. Not really. The shepherds were very gentle. They were in awe of Jesus, though none of them really knew what to do with him. Apparently, none of them had ever held a baby before. They just looked down at him and stared, then gave him to the next guy.

Mary watched it and didn't say anything; she was lying on her side. I lit another lamp. The shepherds said they would watch for Jesus to rise to power. They wanted to know how many years before "the takeover." *Takeover? Power?* I was only hoping that the inn would keep us in coffee and that we wouldn't get thrown out. There was too much going on and I was too tired to think such grand and glorious thoughts. I would have thought such thoughts, possibly, but everything was too big for me then. Every time I tried to think a grand and glorious thought, Jesus would cry, or Mary would need repositioned. Had I spent a week in a field and been able to get some sleep, it would have been different. I'd have been primed for the grandeur and glory. As it was, I just wanted something to eat and drink, and to go back to the bale that served as my lounging place.

I tried to think of it from the shepherds' point of view so I responded politely and said that I had no idea when my son would rise to power. I think they were disappointed. They really did think I was a prophet. I disappointed them, I know. I told them how the baby came to be, that Mary was a virgin, and that I was just the caretaker, so to speak. None of them really talked to me much after that. Then I was kind of sorry I had belittled myself. It kind of hurt my feelings the way they ignored me after that.

They were disturbed at the sight of Mary, for sure. She had rubbed her eyes so much that she did look bad and not really herself. She looked bad besides that, if you've ever seen a woman after childbirth. It's no insult to women to say that, it's just how it is. A soldier looks bad after a war, but he wears his dishevelment like a badge. I see childbirth the same way. Mary did put a bit of a scare into the shepherds, though, which entertained me. I think they thought that the Mother of Messiah would be either glowing in the dark, or levitating, or both. I could understand it after what they'd seen in the field.

One of the shepherds asked me if Mary was all right. That irritated me because the shepherd said it loud enough so that Mary could have heard him. She didn't need any negativity right then. I gave the shepherd a sour look that I guess he didn't see, because he asked again. I pulled him off to the side and said, "Look, don't say that. She just had a baby. Have you ever seen a woman just after she's had a baby?" He admitted that he hadn't. "All right then. Neither have I. Anyway, you should have seen the baby. You can't believe how white they are when they come out. They're covered with blood, too. And greasy stuff—only God knows what *that* is. Have you ever seen a baby come out?" He never had, and said that he didn't want to learn any more about it. "All right then," I said. "Take that as a clue and please be more careful in the future."

A room opened up at the inn two days later, and we had our names at the top of the list, so we got it. It wasn't much, but after living in a stable for two days we thought we were at Caesar's palace. We had to stay in Bethlehem at least until the circumcision.

The law required us to take Jesus to Jerusalem for circumcision on the eighth day. We had to do it on the eighth day, not the seventh, not the ninth. In God's scheme of things, eight is the number of a new beginning. Every number has meaning for us. One is the number of God, two is the number of witness, three is the number of completeness, four the number of earth, five the number of grace, six the number of man, seven is the perfect number—don't know why, sorry—eight is the number of a new beginning, as I said; that's why we circumcise on the eighth day. It's a new beginning in God's sight. There were eight people on the ark of Noah, which I think is interesting. That sure was a new beginning. I can't remember what nine is but it isn't good—it's the only number between one and ten that's no good—and ten is the number of a complete cycle. Eleven stinks, twelve is the number of government—the twelve tribes—and thirteen is so bad that some people won't even pronounce it.

Mary couldn't go anywhere in those eight days because according to our law she was unclean. It has to do with losing blood. She was unclean for forty days after that still, because of other fluids and things that came out. The fluids cleansed her, personally, but they made her unclean as to law; I've never figured it out. You can't believe what else a woman loses during childbirth, if you've never seen it. I was moved to tremors and terrified exclamations by what came out two minutes after the baby did, but that's another story. Bathsheba said it was normal. She called it *felungi*, and said it's the thing that fed Jesus for nine months in the womb. It was all too anatomical for me. The birth, I mean. It was wonderful, but anatomical. Nothing is clean and neat in childbirth, let me tell you. You sometimes wonder why God wants everything so gooey and bloody. Everything has slime on it. You have to wonder about it. It could all be so neat if He wanted it that way—and dry. But it's not. Nothing about it is dry. I suppose it could be a protective coating. Mummies are dry, and that's generally not a good sign for the mummy. But my God.

I couldn't watch the circumcision. You know what circumcision is, if you're an Israelite. Other people might not know. The foreskin of the penis is cut off; the foreskin is the skin that hangs over the penis head. Our boys don't have any of that loose skin, so you just have the head there, if you've never seen it. I'm not going to draw a picture, I've said enough already. The priest cuts around it, like peeling an orange.

Mary was lucky that she was unclean and didn't have to attend the circumcision. I could hardly stand it, but I had to be there. I had to stand next to the priest while he prayed and fondled his knife. They really like fondling that goddamn knife—at least *this* priest did. I shouldn't judge other priests by the priest *we* had, but I will. I hate knives. I wouldn't do circumcisions for any amount of money. "What did you do today, dear?" "Oh, I cut forty-nine foreskins off." Blood is something I can live without. I could never be a priest in the temple, either. I used to wish I was a Levite, but after witnessing the birth of my son and the circumcision, I'd had all the blood I wanted. Fine, if it has to cover my sins, but let someone else slash the arteries, thanks.

I had to answer certain things to the prayers. I shouldn't say this, but I have no idea why all the prayers are necessary. I can understand the circumcision, because it's the sign God gave Abraham to demonstrate our weakness in the flesh without Him. I understand the symbolism there. It's just all the prayers that I'm questioning. You look in the law, and you don't see any of them. Where does it say that the priest is supposed to pray like a frostbitten baboon and make the father respond, the poor man who can hardly stand up to begin with and is getting weaker by the second due to all the blood? They repeat three sentences, and you're supposed to remember them. I did it, but that's not the point.

I couldn't watch the actual cutting. Here's the strange thing, though; Jesus hardly made a peep during it. I'm not kidding. I asked the priest about it later, and he said that it happens once in a while, but not very often. Usually they scream and cry like crazy. That, I could believe. I asked the priest how my son had done so well, and he couldn't explain it; said he had no idea.

We stayed in Bethlehem and Mary rested. We wrote her parents and relayed to them the uncertainty of our plans after Jerusalem. We had to go to Jerusalem forty days after the birth for the dedication at the temple. (Mary would became ceremonially clean after that.) We told Ben and Marney that everything was fine, that Jesus was healthy, and that Mary was feeling better by the day. She was, too. She was looking better, as well. I had half a mind to hike out to the Wange district and look up those shepherds and bring them back to see Mary. They hadn't seen how beautiful Mary was. It bothered me that they would go the rest of their lives thinking I was married to an eye-rubbing, not-very-attractive, bloated person who didn't talk much.

We went by donkey to the dedication in Jerusalem. It was only five miles and Mary could ride fairly well side-saddled, which is a figure of speech because we didn't have saddles, just heavy blankets.

The dedication is another formal ceremony, just as important as circumcision. The law requires that every male or female opening the matrix be presented to the Lord at the temple in Jerusalem. The firstborn is officially called holy there. Firstborns have many advantages in Israel, but this isn't one of them, in my book. Not for the parents, anyway. We're required to offer a year-old he-lamb as an ascent offering, and a dove squab or a turtledove as a sin offering to the priest. The law makes provision for the…for those of us who don't have a lot of money, and so we were able to offer a pair of dove squabs instead of the lamb. I felt sorry for the birds, but I was glad my financial status spared the lamb. I'm a little weird in this regard, I realize that.

We didn't tell either the priest back in Bethlehem who performed the circumcision or the priests in Jerusalem that Jesus was the Messiah. None of them knew. They couldn't tell by looking at him, that's for sure. No one could. There was nothing special about Jesus physically; he looked like every other baby. (Not that we didn't check for some extraordinary thing; we did. I don't know what we were looking for—a birthmark that said "Messiah?" I don't know. It's just something we did. But no. He looked normal in every way.) We didn't say anything. No one would believe us anyway. Knowing the priesthood, they probably would have stoned us for blasphemy. Gabriel didn't say anything about telling or not telling people, so we just didn't tell people. It simplified things. We loved the anonymity of it all; we loved that nobody knew. It was fun watching people holding him. *They're holding the Messiah of Israel*, we'd think, *and they don't even know it*. That tickled me. I took a special joy in it, making me all-over warm. I didn't like any of the clergy, overly.

I wasn't sure about who the sin offering was for that day, us or the baby. I never have figured that out. No one has ever specified it for me, and I've never asked. This was a point of discussion between Mary and me, because we didn't know the status of Jesus. Status is a bad word. What I mean is that we didn't know if he was sinless or not. He was the Messiah, yes. But did that mean he was sinless? We just didn't know. We argued about it, and I said I thought the sin offering was for just her and me. But Mary said that we were already covered by the yearly sacrifice on the Day of Atonement. So she must not have thought Jesus was sinless. I asked if it really mattered. It didn't matter to us enough back then to take pains to find out. We had to raise him, that's all we knew. We had to do our best by the law.

Now the amazing thing. We were standing in line at the temple to get our turtledoves when an old man came scuffing up. And I mean, scuffing. We weren't even sure he was coming to speak to us until the moment he stopped. The first thing he said was, "Praise God, I have beheld the Messiah of Israel. Please, let me hold him." I was holding Jesus at the time and, like an idiot, was ready to hand him right over. I guess the shepherds in Bethlehem had primed me for anything. But Mary grabbed my arm and wouldn't let me hand over Jesus. This was maternal wisdom raising its beautiful head. On second glance, the man did look dangerous. His eyeballs gobbled up everything, moving all over us, and his head snipped around like a bird's head. I thought there was something the matter with him. Then he told us that he had been apprised by the holy spirit in a trance that he would not see death, in his words now, "before being acquainted with the Lord's Christ." He said that his name was Simeon and that he was just and pious and anticipating the consolation of Israel. I don't think he was bragging, it was just the facts. That was enough for Mary, and she held Jesus out to Simeon. Simeon cradled Jesus so gently. I get tears in my eyes today when I think of that old man. I really misjudged him. He clasped my son to his breast, and this is what he said, to the best of my recollection:

"Now are You dismissing Your slave from this earth, O Owner, God, in accord with Your declaration made to me, for my peace. For today my eyes perceive Your salvation, which You make ready before all the people. A Light, this One, for the revelation of nations, and the Glory of Thy people Israel."

Lots of people stood around as he spoke. They didn't know what to make of it. I don't think old Simeon even saw these people, that's how enraptured he was with Jesus. Then Simeon blessed Mary and me. He said a long prayer for us, and it was the only long prayer I've ever heard that moved me. This man could pray, let me tell you. I couldn't get enough of his words. I wanted him to pray forever. I felt saved and bathed in God's spirit as long as Simeon prayed. Neither Mary nor I moved a muscle. And neither did anyone else standing there who could hear him.

But then his mood changed; I could see the change overcoming him. His joy slowly passed into concern. He looked older than his ancientness as he turned to Mary and said words that I had been tempted to speak, but couldn't. And now, this emissary from the throne room of God, come by the spirit in my stead, spoke them. I didn't know whether to be glad or to cry. He turned to Mary and said, "Lo! He is lying for the fall and rising of many in Israel, and for a sign contradicted. Yet through your own soul also shall be passing a blade, so that the reasonings of many hearts should be revealed."

At that, he handed Jesus back to me, and went away. No formal good-byes, he just left. We couldn't stay in line after that. We had to get away. People were staring at us, and Mary looked ill. We excused ourselves and went away to a corner of the Royal Porch. Mary *really* looked bad now. She sat down and leaned against the wall.

"What did he mean by that?" she said. "What did he mean by saying that a blade would pass through my soul? That already happened. That's just how it felt when he was born. It was as if a blade went through me. But why did the old man say that through my own *soul* shall be passing a blade? Isn't that what he said? I heard him right, didn't I?

But that has already happened to me. I don't like him. How do we know he has the spirit?"

What was I to tell her? During my three weeks in the mountains of Lebanon after my run to Antioch, the same holy spirit that had spoken through Simeon had also shown me some disturbing things concerning our son. The spirit showed me, in the pictures of the sacrificed lambs, an ultimate sacrifice for the sins of Israel. I didn't want to confront this. Whenever I came up against it, I walked away. I walked to town, or I cooked something, or made coffee. Sometimes I would lay down. But always, when I came back to the scrolls, there it was. What is written does not easily disappear. Our son, the Messiah, was to be the sacrifice for Israel's sins, I knew. Without the shedding of blood, so says our law, there is no remission of sins.

This was a curse of the worst kind, to know ahead of time what will befall a loved one, and be unable to stop it. The march of time *will* bring it to you, and there's nothing you can do. My son would be the ultimate sacrifice for his people. Yet how? In some optimistic corner, I saw it all as figurative. He would not actually be killed, but would be offered to God in another way, a figurative way. Abraham came to mind. I shuddered at my first contemplation of the scene with Isaac. God asked Abraham to sacrifice his own son as a test of faith and obedience. But thinking further on this, hope filled me. As Abraham drew the knife, a messenger of the Lord stopped him. And there, in the thicket, was a ram for sacrifice. So the son was spared. This buoyed me—for a while.

Until Daniel. In the book of Daniel, one of our greatest prophets, seventy sevens of years—four hundred and ninety years—are segregated for our people and for our holy city, to accomplish these goals: to detain transgression, to cause sin to end, to make a propitiatory shelter for us, to bring the righteousness of the eons to Israel, to seal the vision and the prophesy, and to anoint the holy of holies.

Daniel gives more detail further on: "And you shall know and be intelligent: from the faring forth of the word to cause a return and to rebuild Jerusalem—from then till Messiah the Governor is seven sevens, and sixty-two sevens. It will return and will be rebuilt, square and salient, even in eras of constraint."

That had already happened. Jerusalem was rebuilt under Zerubabel seventy years after Nebuchadnezzar, and his armies sacked the city and took our forefathers, including Daniel, into Babylon. From the rebuilding of the temple, then, it would be 434 years (sixty-two sevens) "till Messiah the Governor." But what exactly did that mean, "till Messiah the Governor"? I added up the years between Cyrus' decree and the birth of Jesus; four hundred years. From this I knew that Jesus' birth was not counted as "till Messiah, the Governor," for thirty-four years remained to the fulfillment of the prophecy, by my reckoning. The time must have counted toward something else, then, besides the birth. Daniel's very next prophesy, when I saw it, raised hairs on my flesh that I didn't know I had.

"After the sixty-two sevens, Messiah will be cut off, and there is no adjudication for Him."

This was something that would happen later in Messiah's life. See how I take to calling him "Messiah" whenever I speak of these things? We do this whenever we speak of such things, which is not often. We can't bear to say "our son" when discussing his sacrifice. The words "cut off" are what harrowed my soul. How would Messiah be cut off? And what did this have to do with the sacrifice for sin? I lacked specific answers, but it was enough to make me realize that a time of great sadness lay ahead for us. This was, and has been, a curse. I never dwell on it, because when I do I become morbid, and angry at God. How much better not to know. To live life in ignorance is a gift. People say they wish they could see into the future. What fools. It's the greatest curse you can imagine.

By the prophecy of Daniel, I knew that Messiah would be around thirty-four years of age when he would be "cut off."

How could I tell Mary? We were so excited then about the wedding, and the birth. Those were times of joy. Could I spoil them with my terrible scriptures? I didn't see how I could, or why I would want to. At that time, we had thirty-four years to go. Why ruin everything on Day One? As a man and a husband, I felt responsible for sheltering Mary, emotionally. And yet I felt at the same time that I was living a lie. I would have to talk to her about it sometime. *Sometime.* That was one of my favorite words, and still is. That, and the word "eventually." These two words, and the phrase "one of these days;" I love them all. These are my comfort in times of trouble. If ever there was a thing to procrastinate over, this was it.

But now—Simeon. Sooner than I wanted came Simeon, predicting sorrow, not for me, but for Mary. And he said, "a blade." As soon as he said that, the phrase "cut off" came to me. I privately winced. A blade awaited us, then. For Mary, I believed and still believe it to be a figurative blade. It isn't that I won't suffer, but that I won't suffer as Mary will. I could be dead by then, who knows? But there is no suffering like the suffering of a mother for her child. For Jesus? I think the blade will be literal, I grieve to say. But as soon as I say this, I say this as well: There is no such thing as a dead Messiah. There will be a mighty resurrection, this I know. There has to be. As he raised his own blade to sacrifice his son, Abraham knew in his heart that God would raise his son from the dead. God had promised Abraham a seed, and this boy was that seed. It was obvious to Abraham—and such was his faith that I often thank God for it, and for giving the same faith to me—-that God had to raise Isaac. Abraham knew, I think, that Moriah was a test of his faith. Our faith, too, is tested. It was tested this day at the temple, and would be tested again. And again. But pardon me for repeating this: There is no such thing as a dead Messiah. This is our comfort. There must be a sacrifice, but there also must be a living King. And so, when the blade does come, it will not be forever. Resurrection must follow. And God will turn mourning to gladness, as He always does.

Jesus is such a happy boy now, and we're all very happy. I have not talked to him about any of this, specifically. Only little hints. I'm waiting for him to come of age—two more years now, as I write—and it can't happen too slowly for me. We read scripture together; maybe he knows. I don't think he does. I get indications once in a while—from things he does and says, and from his incredible understanding of God and the scriptures—that he knows who he is. Then something else will happen and I'll think, no, he doesn't know. I've probed him in subtle ways. Personally, I don't think that he knows. But he might. I'm putting everything off; I don't want to know. It will come soon enough. I savor every moment that we have together. Every moment is a gift for us. There is not a day goes by that we are not thankful for being together as a family. I hope this helps other families that are reading. Appreciate one another while you have one another. Things may not always be so happy. I know that many reading are under the thumb of an occupying power, but things could be worse. Let's be thankful for what we have, here and now.

Speaking of here and now, how quickly God is to replace sorrow with gladness. At least He shines a glimmer of light into the deepest darks. As we sat at the Royal Porch, backs against the wall, eyes red from crying, an elderly woman approached with steady purpose, sandals flapping. It had not been an hour since Simeon's prophecy. This woman introduced herself as Anna. "I am a prophetess," she said, "a daughter of Penuel, of the tribe of Asher."

"Hello," Mary said.

"Hi," I said.

"I can't help but to see that you are distraught," Anna said, "sitting here against a wall at the Royal Porch in the great city. But why? There is a baby boy in your lap, is there not?" She pointed at Jesus. "And have you not a newborn in your arms who is appointed the Redeemer in Israel?"

She must have been in the temple when Simeon had come in.

"Did you hear what that old man said in the temple earlier?" I asked.

"No," she said, "I did not." And then, raising her voice to a level that could only have been granted her by God, she cried out, "I give to you, to all who are anticipating redemption, the Redeemer!" People all around stopped and looked over at us. Anna was pointing at us even more strongly now and raising her voice to an even louder pitch. "He comes in the name of God, this Child, to detain transgression, to cause sin to end, and to make a propitiatory shelter for us; to bring the righteousness of the eons to Israel, and to seal the vision and the prophesy; to anoint the holy of holies!" I couldn't believe it. She was quoting Daniel. I cringed in preparation for the death knell, the cutting off. But no. A miracle. God's spirit dictated Anna's words, I truly believe this. For only the spirit of God could know what Mary and I needed then, to get us to our feet and pursuing happiness again with the living. "And by His life and the resurrection to life, shall Israel live for the eons and beyond!"

Thank you, God. Oh, thank you, Holy One. Only You could have given Anna those words, so perfect. And also dictated to her what not to say. What that did for me. Mary was relieved, but not as much as I. In the very portion of scripture that spoke of the severing, Anna overlooked it and heralded resurrection. Divine inspiration! Yes, the blade would come, but also resurrection. And here within an hour of each other was both, each spoken by a prophet of the Lord. It occurred to me then that perhaps this was God's timing. Perhaps Messiah would be dead only an hour, a literal hour, until the resurrection. I still believe this. We both do. It's the only thing that brings us peace. Glory!

I jumped up and took Mary's hand, pulling her to her feet. "Mary! This is a day of gladness and celebration!" I knew that God was filling me with holy spirit. I could feel it, even as I had in the mountains of Lebanon. The gloom fell off me. "God breaks, but He heals. He kills, but He makes alive. He brings evil, only to show forth His righteousness. In the evening, lamentation may lodge, but in the morning there is jubilant song. The travail of childbirth brings forth the Chosen One. For an hour's pain, an eon of righteousness and peace. Oh Yahweh! In Your benevolence, You have made my mountain to stand in strength, so that I make melody to You, O my Glory, and shall not be still! O Yahweh, my Elohim, for the eon shall I acclaim Your works!"

I think Mary was impressed. I didn't care what anyone else thought.

We debated whether or not to return to Nazareth from Jerusalem, or go back to Bethlehem. Everything was taken care of at home. Mary was still not up to a three-day's journey.

The man at the inn said he had an apartment for rent. We looked at it, and it was a clean place, small but cheap. It was so cheap that I wondered what was wrong with it. But nothing was wrong with it, it was just small. This pushed us toward returning to Bethlehem.

The biggest factor was the market for my work. The census had brought so many people to the city, with many of them traveling a week or more. Some had been on the road for a month. Broken carts were everywhere, and this was my line of work when I wasn't playing ringball. I'd get full price, too; most of the travelers were wealthy. I knew I could make more in a month in Bethlehem than in the next six months in Nazareth. Plus, it was only a five-mile trip for Mary. Everything taken into consideration, we chose to return to Bethlehem.

And now, a very strange thing happened. We had been in Bethlehem only two weeks when a knock came at the door. Knocks on doors were really something for us in those days. It was around noon. Mary was making lunch and I was out back in my little shop, which was really only a glorified lean-to. I'll never forget that I was installing a new vice when Mary poked her head in. "There are more than a dozen people on camels with a cavalry escort out in the street in front of our house, and three of them are at the door wearing white conical hats with the tops lopped off." Well, you don't get a piece of information like that every day. They were probably selling something. "And they're carrying small bundles of divining rods," Mary said.

Salesmen! "Tell them that we're quite happy with the divining rods we have," I said.

"They're asking about the baby."

Divining rods for babies? This was something new. *For the baby who has everything: divining rods, made to order in three sizes: infant, toddler, and pre-sorcerer.* This, I had to see.

I looked around the corner before going into the house, confirming that there was indeed a circus amassed in front of our home. It was odd, I thought, that traveling salesmen should require a retinue. I shaded my eyes for a better look. None of the horsemen or camel drivers wore the hats Mary described; they all wore turbans. I had never seen a conical hat, especially not one with the top lopped off. I would never have known what to call the breed had not Mary said that the three men at the door were wearing *conical* hats.

A crowd had formed around the camel-people and the horsemen. A lemonade salesman would have done brisk business.

I wiped my hands, walked into the living room, and introduced myself. The three men at the door, who Mary had invited in, introduced themselves as Balthazar of Arabia, Melchior of Persia, and Gaspar of India. I do not joke you, these were their names. Besides the semi-conical hats, the men appeared turquoisey, wearing plain, turquoise-colored robes—as though they were all on the same team. As to their physical appearance and attendant odors, they were old, white-bearded, and tobacco addicts (I'm guessing). Two of the three wore thick black paint beneath their eyes. The one without the paint was the chief spokesman and the only one ornamented; he wore at least a dozen pearl necklaces.

Now was when we got the surprise of our lives. These men were not salesmen, but magi. The spokesman of the group, Melchior, said that magi were professional astrologers, politicians, and priests. I had heard of them, vaguely. Their religion was Zoroastrian, said Melchior, although they borrowed from other religions and writings, even from the Hebrew scriptures. They had come from the East, from the land beyond the Euphrates, the old Persian Empire. Melchior tried to explain the location to me. "Have you ever heard of Jarmo?" he asked. I had not. "Have you ever heard of Nuzi?" I had not. "Have you ever heard of Tepe Giyan?" Unfortunately, I had not. Have you ever heard of Lake Van?" I admitted my ignorance once again. Melchior was very patient. "Have you ever heard of Babylon?" Yes! I had heard of Babylon. Mary looked relieved. "We are about two-hundred and seventy miles north of there as the condor flies," Melchior said, "near M'lefaat, on the banks of the Great Zab. That is our homeland."

But here was the thing. These three men, and the entire entourage, had been on the road for thirty days—looking for *us*.

Mary asked if they wanted to sit down. They did not. Both Mary and I looked troubledly out the door to see what was happening with the circus. "Don't worry about them," said Melchior. "Don't worry about anything." Melchior looked kind, but we decided to obey him and not worry—just in case Melchior had a mean streak. Melchior asked where the baby was. Mary hesitated; Jesus was sleeping in our bedroom.

"Tell us more of why you've come," Mary said. "How did you find us?" When it came to protecting her loved ones, my wife was smart and direct.

Melchior's answer, which I'm about to give, is recorded to the best of our recollection. Melchior liked to talk. You'll think I'm exaggerating by putting so many words together at once. You'll be tempted to think I'm doing this for my own convenience sake, so that I will not have to keep track of who said what, when. You'd be wrong on both counts, because only one person said what and when, and it was Melchior. The reason I remember his words is that Mary and I both sat down for an hour after the magi left and pieced together Melchior's dialogue for Jesus' scrapbook. Melchior's soliloquy was so amazing that we felt obliged to record it. I present it now, give or take a thousand and six syllables:

"We are not charlatans, as many think. We are professional astrologers of a most serious aspect and occupation. You do not have June, but Sivan. We have June, so I begin there. On the seventeenth of that month, approximately three months ago, we beheld a rare conjunction of the planets Jupiter and Venus. These planets came within .09 degrees of one another on a longitudinal plane, to form one great star. Point-zero-nine. Besides this, seventy-two days after, there came to be an amassing of four other planets in nearly perfect longitudinal conjunction, all within small degrees. All of this in the constellation Leo." He stared at us, and we stared back.

"Your countenance does not change," he continued, "for you do not discern the importance of my words. Jupiter is reckoned as King of the heavens. Venus is Genetrix, the Mother of all. All of a figure, but with meaning most great. Concerning the other planets and their amassing, nothing since the founding of Hob has witnessed it. But still I see that the proximity matter escapes you. *Gaspar.*" One of the men with the eye paint handed Melchior a small roll of papyrus. Melchior unrolled it and read: "Jupiter, along the elliptic at 142.6 degrees; Mars at 142.64; Venus at 141.67; Mercury at 143.71. This speaks of communion of purpose; a new beginning. Thank you, Gaspar." The roll snapped shut and Melchior returned it to his friend. We were too amazed to speak.

"The astrological year begins at Leo," continued Melchior, "which constellation bespeaks power and royalty. We reckon Leo's chief star, Regulus, as the Royal Star, as do all the szahs of Calah. Today—*today*—Jupiter and Regulus juxtapose, only .33 degrees apart, with Venus in retrogression at .04. Hear this: The planet king joins the king star in the royal constellation, with Mother Venus. But now, Zoroaster.

"Do not look startled. For he, himself, taught that there would come from the loins of Abraham a king who would abolish death and inaugurate eons of peace. These celestial marvels of which I speak portend the fulfillment of this prophecy. Why the look of amazement? Our forefathers counseled Daniel. And so, we look to Israel. But now, the retrogression.

"I finally impress you, I see, yet your amazement turns to perplexity before my eyes. For how does it come that a planet and a star and a planet, conjuncted, unobserved to the eye of laity, lead a procession of man and beast across desert and mountain to this wretched place on Tickbuck Street in the nothing-burg of Bethlehem?" I tried not to feel offended. I wouldn't have looked at Mary for anything; she had just re-arranged the furniture and swept.

"They do not; they lead us to Jerusalem. For there the shadow of Venus fell, and we inquired of Herod as to where the King would be born." I shuddered to hear the name Herod. Again, I did not look at Mary, but kept my eyes glued to Melchior, who continued. "He did not know, himself, but he called his wise men together, the chief priests and scribes of your people, and they produced from your literature a passage from the prophet Micah: 'And you, Bethlehem, land of Judah, are you in any respect least among the mentors of Judah? For out of you shall come forth the Ruler who shall shepherd my people Israel.'"

My heart stopped. Where had *that* passage come from? I didn't even remember it. I must have read it; Mary and I both must have. How plain could it be? How better could it stand out? And yet God had hidden it from us—from both of us—until now. *The Messiah would be born in Bethlehem.*

Dear God. I did look at Mary this time, and she looked as amazed as I felt. Everything was of God, then. Everything. The census, the ridiculous decree of Herod, our decision to push on to Bethlehem from Jerusalem; it was all predetermined. We *had* to go to Bethlehem—to fulfill prophecy. *Prophecy, for God's sake.* Mary and Joseph Jabrecki were fulfilling prophecy. I knew we were fulfilling it on some large scale, but this was different. When I heard Melchior quote from our own scriptures the specific city of Bethlehem—I don't know. I felt the stare of a million eyes. Everything was of God. A chill ran through me.

Neither Mary nor I listened to Melchior after that. We still don't know how a conjunction of planets and a star could lead somebody to a particular doorstep. Melchior did explain it, but I can't even begin to. I personally believe it was a miracle. Consider it that, and you'll have the truth.

So Mary told the men that they could go back to the bedroom. The men said they couldn't, "as yet." They needed to retrieve gifts for Jesus, they said, and purify themselves. They went out and were gone for some time, maybe a half hour. We kept looking out the window. The crowd outside was growing. The men returned, each holding a gift, and smelling much better. Mary led them down the hallway to the bedroom. I followed.

Jesus was asleep on his stomach on our bed. Each of the magi put his gift on the bed and dropped to his knees and stared at Jesus. None of them prayed, they just stared. Then they opened their gifts one at a time. One gift was gold, another was frankincense, another was myrrh—very expensive gifts. The men announced each gift as they opened it. We stood at the doorway, but we may as well have been on one of the juxtaposed planets. The magi did not speak a word to us, they spoke only to Jesus. Each of them spoke of his gift for at least five minutes to our sleeping son.

Then the men arose, left the room, and exuded a relief that comes with the fulfillment of duty. This isn't to say that they were not happy. They may have been happy, and probably were. To me, they just looked tired. Finally, they made to leave. I asked if they were going directly home, but they did not tell me. They ignored me, actually. They were acting very mysterious as they prepared their departure. Melchior wasn't talking any more, except to say that he was getting a headache. I asked him if he wanted an aspirin, but he said he did not. Mary stayed inside while I followed the men to their entourage. I walked next to Melchior with my hands in my pockets. If I'd had pocket change, I'd have been fondling it.

"Thanks for coming, Melchior," I said. He didn't even look at me. "I mean, you guys went to a lot of trouble." He adjusted the straps on his camel as I spoke, ignoring my presence all the while. Finally, I just spit it out. "Excuse me. Melchior?"

"What do you want?"

"Why does a man's, um, baby-making thing, um, *grow*, you know, when he sees a beautiful woman?"

Melchior looked as if I'd thrown a watermelon at his feet. "*What?*"

"You know," I said. "The *organ*. *The* organ. Why does it get big?" There was obviously some kind of language barrier thing going on between us. "The *member*," I said, and I pointed between my legs.

"Oh," Melchior said, "*dombo*." And he smiled. Was I seeing things? Had Melchior actually bared his discolored teeth?

"Yes!" I said. "Dombo! Why does it get hard? I mean, what is it about women that makes dombo do that? Do you know? I'm talking about the deep-down beginnings of it. When did it all start; the attraction? Something must have happened between the first couple, is what I think. You seem pretty wise, so I can't even believe I'm even telling you what I think. But I'm asking you. You read our literature, which is great. Have you read the first book of Moses?'"

"Many times."

"Really? Oh, that's great. Then maybe you know. Did you ever wonder about—*why* it happens? About the source of the energy? It's so strong. I hope I'm not being too forward here. I just feel like maybe this is my big chance to ask. Maybe you already know. Maybe I should just shut up and let you talk. Do you…do you…*want* to talk?"

Melchior's whole countenance changed. In the midst of my fumbling question, his face transformed from that of a wise man far above me to a schoolmate standing with me before a difficult problem on the blackboard.

"I don't know," Melchior said. "But yes, I have wondered. Yes, they fascinate me, even still. *Women*." He slowly shook his head. "But I have never thought to bring it back to the garden." He combed his fingers through his beard and looked blankly to the sky. "To the garden," he repeated. "To the source."

Then, just as suddenly as he had become my chum, he returned again to his magian state, found a stirrup, and swung himself onto his camel. "It is good. I will look. I will speak of it to others, and see. You have inspired me to a long-forgotten cause. I have wondered. I will go to Moses. We will speak again on this."

"That's great! Thanks, Melchior. So…you'll write to me, or—?"

"I will write."

"That's great. The name is Joseph Jabrecki. You can reach me at 29 Hen Street, Nazareth. I don't know how long we'll be here."

"Joseph Jabrecki. 29 Hen Street, Nazareth."

"Yes, sir. How's your headache?"

"Terrible. I have never had a headache before."

"Gosh, I'm sorry to hear that. I mean, I'm sorry that you have one *now*. Will you remember my name and address? Should I write it down for you?"

"Joseph Jabrecki. 29 Hen Street, Nazareth. My memory is famous. I will remember it seventy-five years from now."

"That's super."

The entourage moved out of the neighborhood, and Melchior was going to look into it. The entourage moved, and Melchior was going to look.

It was all anyone could ask for.

CHAPTER 15

INTO THE DESERT

If you wonder what being the mother and father of one who is destined to die before he's forty years old—possibly by murder—does for your sex life, the answer is that it does not exactly inspire poetry. I tried to live in the moment, but the moment kept changing. Joseph seemed steady, and that steadied *me*. For my ultimate comfort I looked to God, Who for whatever reason often chose not to comfort me. But He did do it on occasion, and these were times of respite and sunshine.

I finally saw the thing Joseph had been hinting at for weeks. He said he wasn't hiding it, but that he was planning on giving it to me when the moment was right. (Then why couldn't he look me in the eye when he talked about it? That was a sign of dishonesty to me. What was Joseph so nervous about, if this thing were as right as he said it was?) It was called *shechah begadim*, which in the Hebrew tongue is construed, "worship clothes."

I'd have been better off had I not seen the name. The name was embossed in gold on the black bag that contained the iniquitous "garments." I said I would have been better off. But no. Seeing the so-called clothing-designed-to-turn-me-into-a-prostitute-for-the-leering-and-lust-of-my-husband was enough to repel me. Besides, the things were black, a color strongly associated with evil. But then I saw the name. How terrible! Worship belonged only to God.

Joseph became defensive about it, and we had an argument. Some of my friends say that arguing increases the passions, but these friends have never argued, I don't think, about a strange new kind of *qum* with a knitting needle for a heel.

I tried to be patient with Joseph because I saw how much my refusal to wear the ensemble hurt him. I hurt him as well because I continually rejected his advances to kneel before me. Ever since our wedding day he had attempted to literally thrown himself at my feet. Elizabeth had done it—though at my belly—with the same eerie reverence, and I never wanted it to happen again. Joseph told me that it was two entirely different things between Elizabeth and him, but the common thing was seeing people kneeling in front of me, losing their sense, and babbling things about me that were entirely untrue and ridiculous. If you have never had it done to you, you would not know how uncomfortable a thing it is.

I asked Joseph where in the world he had gotten such a thing as *shechah begadim*. This is when his eyeballs would come undone. Even when he looked at me, he could not maintain his gaze. This made me suspect his story, or what was missing from it. He said he got the ensemble from Rent Hassler. That was embarrassing enough, knowing that Rent knew we had it. For all I knew, Rent thought I would actually wear it. I did suspect that Joseph got his wrong ideas about *shamat* from Rent, who I considered to be a fast-living person and not especially keen on the Law of Moses. But I thought that Joseph knew where Rent had gotten it, and wasn't telling me. The so-called clothing had probably come from one of those underground Samarian shops. Rent could have gone into such a shop, but I knew Joseph could not have. Joseph knew I would not like how Rent had come upon such a thing, and so here was another roadblock to intimacy: your husband not telling you everything about something that he knows is wrong.

To change the subject now, can four days become a routine? In our fast-changing world of that time, they could. Four days of domesticity was, for us, a lifetime of happiness. And so our lives were almost normal in Bethlehem—until about four days after the magi returned East. Joseph awakened me in a panic. Gabriel had appeared to him in a dream, he said, and told him that Herod wanted to kill our son. He insisted that Gabriel said we were to flee to Egypt. I did not take Joseph seriously. I took it seriously that he'd had a bad dream, but I wasn't sure it was of God. It was only a dream, I thought. "But the dream was so real," Joseph said, and he jumped out of bed and paced our bedroom.

It was the middle of the night. I lit a lamp and sat on the edge of the bed. My husband was acting strangely, pacing and sweating. I took the dream seriously then. Joseph finally sat down with me, and we prayed. We prayed that what my husband had heard was of God. There were no voices from heaven then, no Gabriel in the room, just Joseph and me holding onto one another and talking and praying. I thought we should try to go back to sleep. I wanted to talk about it in the morning, when we would be more alert and better able to make decisions. It was so hard for me to talk about frightening things at night, and it still is. "It will be too late in the morning," Joseph said. "Jesus may be dead by then." I knew then that this was serious, and that the dream was of God. My husband would never have said anything like that to me, not ever. It was not outrageous to think that Herod could do such a thing. But how had Herod found out about our son? Then I remembered the magi; they had been to Herod. "We have to be out of this house before dawn," Joseph said. "That's what I'm telling you. I know it in my spirit." Joseph's conviction and strength, in those dark hours of the morning, became God Himself pulling me from bed and setting me on my feet, making me hurry to gather our belongings, to wake Jesus, to prepare a load for Frisk that would sustain us—for how long?

I consider this now from your point of view. *A holy night*, you say. *They hear from God Himself. The drama is physically discernible in a room thick with holy messengers. The mysteries of candlelight play upon the holy couple as they prepare to whisk the future Redeemer of Israel from the grasp of evil. It shall be recorded for the ages*, you say, *this night when Israel's future lay in the balance.* But you do not know what Joseph said to me when we had finished our pre-dawn breakfast and had left the note on the kitchen table for the neighbors to find. Joseph had gathered himself to load Frisk when he stopped at the door, turned back to me in the kitchen and said, "Did you pack *shachah begadim?*" Imagine! We are fleeing for our lives, rushing in the middle of the night to save Israel, and my husband cannot think of anything but his misguided fantasies. Nothing Joseph could have said or done could have been more out of keeping with our circumstance. Nothing more outrageous or ridiculous could have come from his lips.

"Of course I didn't pack it!" I said. "Do you realize what's happening here? Can you see from some higher perspective what we're up against? In an hour, we'll be in the middle of the desert on a donkey headed for...God-knows-where. We're fleeing for our lives. Look out the window and discern the times, man. I see how careful you are now with my life and the life of our son. And we're entrusting our lives to you?" Oh, how I shamed him. "Do you honestly believe that God will prosper us with your...your...*thing* on board? I see now what's important to you. How you can even think of your strange fantasies at a time like this, I'll never know. We are not taking that thing to Egypt, and that's final!"

"I'll go get it then," he said. "You never know."

The cool night air came into the kitchen through the open door and engulfed me.

"What did you say?"

Joseph said something about me changing my mind. I wanted to say that God had a better chance of changing the stars, but I didn't even want to grace the conversation with an apt comparison. Our situation was already absurd. To add *this* conversation to what was already happening was to push absurdity to insanity.

"Anyway, I'm the head of the household," Joseph said, "and we're taking it." He turned and walked down the hall to the bedroom.

When they say that men can compartmentalize—believe them! Fleeing into the unknown for one's life one moment, then contemplating one's soulish fantasies the next—I couldn't fathom it. I could have screamed then, but why expend the energy? Joseph was the head of our home, it was true. If he wanted to take it, then our blood be upon his head. *Let him take it*, I thought. *Let him board an asp with us. Let him put a cobra in our packs at the moment we were committing our way to God.* There was as much a chance of me wearing *shachah begadim* as there was of me eating an asp, or tying a cobra around my waist. Our lives were in God's hands. *Maybe we'll all die.* I actually thought that. *Maybe we'll all perish in the desert. That will show Joseph!*

The sun was not yet over the horizon when we eased through Bethlehem. No one was on the streets. It was appropriately lonely. I didn't want to hear the pealing of a bell or the click of a horse hoof on the cobblestones. No one must announce us or bid us either well or ill. No one must appear in our path to inquire of us. My dream was so silent. There was no background sound in my dream at all. There was only a voice. It was exactly like that now, except for the voice. Now, in the infancy of this special morning, even speaking was disallowed; neither Mary nor I said anything.

The air was chilly and we had wrapped ourselves; I speak literally as well as the self-preservation of our souls. The marketplaces were eerily empty. Scales hung still in the absence of breeze. Boxes sat motionless upon tables. Only the hundreds of silent human footprints in the sand behind these tables suggested a thriving humanity, recently afoot. That was yesterday. In an hour, the hordes would return. In an hour, the human ants would again swarm the marketplaces, and Earth would groan and creak in the latest starting of her course. But at five-thirty in the morning, the world is pure. What exactly happens between five-thirty and six, I don't know. At six o'clock, I knew, nothing would speak of our passage. Everything about us—about what we had been then—would be gone. Not even an echo of Frisk's gentle clicks on the cobbles would bear witness of our passage.

That echo belonged to now, not then. What would belong to then? I had no idea.

I thought I could see my breath. I breathed out heavily and tried to imagine that I could see it. But I didn't see anything; it was not that cool. The breath-cloud was in my mind, not in the air. Never could I remember living so much in the moment, not even on the run to Antioch.

No one cares how you feel in the midday heat. Men in a hurry go by on their horses, to war or wherever, and they don't even stop to ask if you want water. You start to say something to them and make a polite gesture—begging, if you will—but they're already gone in their cavalcades, insulated from the desert and its lower inhabitants by their numbers and grim purpose. I hated the cavalcades.

I despised their sufficiency and lack of care for us. Shouldn't every passing person care for our plight? Shouldn't they know that we were on a mission from God?

It was a miracle to find an oasis. We thanked God whenever we saw palms ahead. The land was so flat between Keila and Lachish, however, that it was a good hour after seeing a cluster of trees that we actually arrived at them. By then, we were ready to dive into the pools. Joseph actually would. He would strip to his undershorts and dive in. Frisk and I would drink. I drank until I felt my stomach would burst. We had no idea when we'd run across water again. I would see Joseph's head pop up from the middle of the pool, and in my new and better mood I would joke to him that he should swim while he could, because the pool would soon be drained from Frisk and me drinking. He would flick his wet hair back and laugh, then go back down again into the water.

We had a terrible night in the desert after the oasis at Beth-gurbin, so an inland route was now out of the question. Gabriel was specific that we should go to Egypt, but he didn't say how. So I steered us for the coast, where travel would be easier and we'd have more shade. Neither did Gabriel say where in Egypt we should go, so as far as I was concerned we could place one foot over the "Welcome to Egypt, Land of the Pharaohs" sign, set up our tent, and wait for the next communication. The dream gave me no clue as to how long we'd have to stay. It could be days, maybe months. I wished Gabriel had said. I only thought seriously about the tent for a minute. Since I didn't know how long it would be, I had to assume it would be for a while. So I fixed it in my mind that I had to find us a decent dwelling. But these were all considerations for the future. Right then, I was headed only for Gaza and the coast. If we had to travel, we might as well have the Great Sea for company. That way, we could catch fish and cool off any time we wanted.

A funny thing happened in Beth-Medeba, between Lachish and Gaza. Another cavalcade passed at a hundred miles per hour, leaving more than the usual amount of horse droppings for our stepping pleasure. The Gaza Road was so narrow that we couldn't avoid stepping in the horse crap. Mary was mounted; I was on foot next to her, holding Frisk's reins. It was a dodgy situation for me, if I may once again speak both figuratively and literally. I said to Mary, "This horse-hooey is driving me crazy. I can't get around it." And she said, "Maybe we should leave some extra donkey dung behind us for the next batch of horsemen." I laughed at that—at Mary actually saying it. That's what started the game. From horse hooey to donkey dung and beyond, Mary and I each tried to outdo one another in the alliterating waste-fields of God's bestial creation. Our first efforts were conservative and sensible, things like "pig poop," "weasel waste," and "tiger turds." But things turned exotic and, losing the game, I decided to offer up "skunk scat" for Mary's consideration. She rewarded me with her blessed peals of mirth, reminded me that I was still losing, then paused to think.

"Porcupine pellets!" she finally burst, and I must say she amused herself with it, and me. Had my wife actually said "porcupine pellets"? It was a hard thing to outdo, yet one must try.

"Monkey moss," I said, and Mary groaned.

"Monkey *moss?* You have got to be kidding me. *Moss?*"

"You know. Stringy and green. They eat leaves and stuff."

"Man, you are *way* off."

"Well? Porcupine pellets was taken."

"As if you were going to use it."

"I might have. Your turn."

"Cat crap," said Mary.

"Ho! Don't stop to think or anything. How long has *that* been brewing?"

"A whole fifteen seconds. It's a lot better than monkey moss." She was dead serious. That's what was so funny about it; she was dead serious. "Cat crap actually makes sense," she said.

"Yes, but is it as good as—beaver biscuits?"

"Beaver—?!" The sheer stupidity of it struck Mary just right, I guess, and she reared back on Frisk, seeming to be in danger of falling off. When she stopped laughing, she said, "That is so *stupid!*"

"Thank you," I said, and I took a little bow. We walked on a little more. All was quiet then, and I could almost hear

Mary concentrating. Then she started to laugh. I knew she had a doozie. She tried three or four times to say it. "Come on," I said. "The world awaits."

Finally, she exploded with, "Fish fritters!"

Well, we both broke up over that, and it put her squarely into the lead.

"Okay," I said. "I've got one. Are you ready?"

"I doubt it," Mary said, wiping her eyes.

"'Leopard loafs.'"

Silence.

"*Leopard* loafs," I said again.

"Good one."

"No, you hated it. I can tell. I thought it was hilarious."

"It *was* hilarious. Really, Joseph."

"I mean, it's clever..."

"Yes, it is that. But have we said 'sheep shit' yet?"

I informed my bride that, no, we had not said it yet, but that it was now duly noted and entered into the log.

"Llama logs!" said Mary.

"You're out of turn," I said.

"But it was a good one, wasn't it? Why didn't you laugh? I think that was really creative. I came up with it spontaneously when you said 'log.'"

"It was a masterpiece of spontaneity, yes. I couldn't have done better myself." I looked up at my wife, and she was smiling.

"Okay, Joseph. It's your turn. But you're way behind in this game. *Loser.*"

I knew I had to come up with the dumbest, stupidest, most idiotic thing ever to infect human conversation. There was no better man for the job, I knew. It was the fourth quarter, with two-minutes remaining. I needed a big score. And so, after much deliberation, I expelled "jackal jam" from my system, carrying away my second-place trophy to a cacophony of screams and howls, hisses and boos, nevertheless quite proud of my accomplishment.

It was a relief to get to Gaza. But then we stopped at the synagogue. It was the afternoon before the Sabbath.

We came upon the synagogue at Gaza, hoping to spend the night there, as it was common courtesy at such places to lodge visitors. Joseph introduced us to the rabbi, whose name was Hyrax. Or Hyreax. He was very nice to us at first—overly and artificially nice, I thought—and we sat at his table for lunch. He asked where we were from and where we were going. He chucked Jesus once under the chin. So much for us, then. After that, we ceased to exist. The rabbi spent the remaining afternoon telling us all about himself, about how he had grown up in such a religious family, about how he had come to be a rabbi, about all the money he had raised for the synagogue, about all the wonderful changes he had made and how God had blessed his efforts. If he said, "God has blessed my efforts here" once, he said it a hundred times. It was making me sick. I felt like I could regurgitate, really. I looked at Joseph, who was trying very hard to pay attention and be nice. I tried to make Joseph laugh. I snuck a face at him, and he saw it. I saw him wince. I almost had him, but he forced himself to stare at the rabbi. I tried playing with his ankles under the table. Again, I saw him flinch, but he never took his eyes from Rabbi Hyreax. It occurred to me to ask Joseph where *shachah begadim* was packed, so that I could wear it to dinner. That would have wrecked his little cart.

The rabbi interrupted himself only to get up occasionally and make tea, or fetch raisins. Other than that, the afternoon was a non-stop marathon of Rabbi Hyena's (that became Joseph's nickname for him) accomplishments.

Again, we assumed we would get a room in the synagogue, especially since we had the baby. Were we ever wrong. When evening arrived, the rabbi handed Joseph a rolled-up wad of canvas, informing my husband that the wad was a tent, and that there was a "wonderful patch of grass" adjoining the synagogue, which turned out to be a small square of dry and brittle field grass. I was quite put off. It rained hard during the night, and the tent leaked. I hardly slept a wink. Joseph made light of it, saying that he would kill Rabbi Hyena in the morning.

※

We spent the Sabbath enjoying the rich accommodations of a whacko rabbi whom I dubbed Rabbi Hyena. This was in Gaza. The accommodation I speak of was a canvas tent that had surely accompanied Joshua across the Jordan. The tent looked bigger than ours, so for the sake of adventure, I pitched it. Did that ever turn out to be a mistake. The tent leaked twelve hundred years ago, and it leaks yet today, I am supposing. We rediscovered the leaks compliments of a rare rainstorm that crashed down on us during the night. I had flashbacks of Tyre.

Synagogue services the next day included long-winded reveries by Rabbi Hyena. It seemed that our host had wrought more marvels for the Gaza Synagogue than God Himself. It is the custom in synagogues to ask visitors for a testimony, and I was ready. When it came my time to speak, I stood and said, "The people of the Gaza Synagogue are rejoicing today because of the blessing of rain that fell in torrents through the night, watering the herbage of earth. I do not know how many in this city were praying for that rain, but I was not among them." There were little gasps from the assemblage, precisely the reaction I had bargained for. "In fact, gathered faithful, I was among those heathen entities praying for the drought to proceed in its devastations." Mary hit me hard in the thigh with her fist. It hurt enough for me to pause for a moment—which I was planning to do anyway, for dramatic effect—but not enough to alter my pre-determined course.

"You do not mistake me, friends, and I bare my heart before you this day, hoping that honesty counts for currency in this hallowed house of worship. Yes, I prayed for the clouds of evening to withhold their watery fruit. Why? Because my wife and my newborn son and I were pitched in a tent beside the synagogue; pitched, yea, in a tent of dubious reliability, a tent owned by your own Rabbi Hyreax."

Several heads turned to look at the synagogue leader.

"Friends and faithful! Do not gaze at your rabbi in this way, as if he has done us, or you, a disservice. And do not think that I am ungrateful for even the least of this man's ministrations. For see the lesson with which God has graced us on the subject of prayer. See what a window is offered us into His omnipotent mind. *You* were praying for it to rain, *I* was praying for it not to. Truly, God was beside Himself last night, knowing not which way to turn." There came hearty laughter now from the congregation—all except from Rabbi Hyena. "And so God decided to bless both you *and* us." I left my audience baited, at the same time absorbing another fist from my beloved wife. "Ah! I sense that the faithful here today are mystified by my words. And so consider what I say next, brethren and sistren." I had heard the "brethren and sistren" thing from a stand-up comic in Nazareth, and it worked beautifully; more laughter. Mary had given up on me. She knew I was lost in my newfound celebrity. "For you, my friends, the herbage is watered. And for me, I've the satisfaction of a service provided. Yes, I said, a service provided. For the rain has allowed me to mark all the leaks in the rabbi's withering domicile, that he may now repair it in the wake of our absence and offer it again, whole and unblemished, to his next honored guests."

The laughter at least did not blow the roof off the place, though it threatened to, and it subsided—by conservative estimate—in less than six or seven minutes.

Joseph made fools of us at the synagogue service. He completely embarrassed me, not to mention what he did to Rabbi Hyena. But a most amazing thing did happen during Joseph's "testimony." I looked down at Jesus, and for the first time in his young life—*for the first time!*—our baby son grinned from ear to ear.

CHAPTER 16

DRAMA NEAR THE PANEAS CRATER

by Mary Jabrecki

(**Originally published in the** *Nazareth Enterprise Review*)

In the Judean Desert, there is a road that skirts the Badley mountain range, then bisects Haffida Lake. Haffida Lake has been dry since triceratops.

My husband Joseph and I were on that road in the month of Elul, four years ago, on our way to Egypt. Neither Joseph nor I had ever seen the Badley range, neither had we ever attempted a journey west into the land that tested our fathers.

We first viewed the emptiness upon leaving Bethgurbin, fresh from an encampment in the last fertileness of the Kanatha Valley, drinking grape juice and enjoying a breeze. As we neared the edge of comfort, we beheld a land composed of nothing. One of us commented upon the depth of the nothing, the other blithely agreed, and we held hands in a pact of ignorance, setting happily away toward the unknown.

Reality struck as early as ten o'clock that morning atop the earth's outer crust, on a knobby road paved with stones beat into the crust by heat. We picked our way through the wilderness without a map, without the holding of hands, with nothing but hot water to drink from our four canteens.

That night, we pitched our tent somewhere east of Bersabee. We did not know where we slept because the blackness of the desert night does not allow such information. We thought it might have been an abandoned rest stop. There was a hitching pole there, and a lantern long rusted and dry. Had we been able to light it, the lantern would have illumined a dozen wooden crates nailed hastily together by men who had long ago turned to skeletons.

In spite of stars, the desert is dark. Before finding our resting spot, we had walked the unmarked road, navigating only by the noise of our steps. When our sandals crushed sand, we knew we had stepped off the road. "Whoa!" we would say, and step back on. Such is the darkness of the Judean Desert.

It was midnight by then, and you should see the stars of the desert. They beam like gems from a celestial treasury. The stars illumined the heavens, but certainly not that road. So we followed the sound of our steps, and these led us to our hitching pole and our crates of wood. My husband and I stopped there, unable to see one another. But the tension between us was palpable.

Joseph wanted to push on, to travel on in the cool of the night. I wanted to camp.

"I'm staying here for the night," I said. "You go on if you want to, but Jesus and I are staying." (Jesus is our son, an infant then.)

This was panic. You may not have detected it, so I'll show it to you. The panic abides in the words: "You go on if you want to." My husband had not challenged me. He had not threatened to leave. I had drawn my own battle line out of my fear, and molded the panic with my voice into a pleasing shape that I thought might have disguised it. It didn't.

"Don't talk like that," Joseph said. "I'm a reasonable man."

"You're *not* reasonable," I shot back. "You don't care if we live or die."

The panic lay all over me; it was the fear of the unknown. Something about Joseph must have suggested to me a tint of selfishness; a callousness toward my feelings—though I could never have said it so nakedly. But the Judean Desert strips everything bare and shows you what you are.

"Look at the stars," Joseph said. "See how beautiful they are."

"All you care about is the stars?"

"No one knows we're here," he said. "No one can find us." To him, that was a blessing. He spoke not to me, but to his own well-being.

"We could die out here," I said.

"So what if we die? This is a good place for it. If you want to camp here, we'll camp. I'd go on, but we'll do what you want."

"You're crazy," I said to him. "You have always been this way. You have never cared about anything. I'm staying here."

"I want to stay here," he said. "I just said I did. You're right. It would be stupid to go on."

I respected the night and its terrors. Joseph did not care at all for the night, only for the stars. But that's not altogether true. He cared for the scrub-brush that flanked us beyond our powers of detection, and for the virginity of the ground. Joseph at last respected my fear, but once he decided to camp, he cared more about where we would put our tent, and how the earth would receive our stakes.

The stakes went into the crust only with a large, round rock, and by the strong arm of my husband.

I was surprised to wake up the following morning.

We quickly packed, then set out again down that road. In the sweetness of daylight, the road became relatively friendly. After fifteen minutes of walking, however, the road took an elbow-turn north (we had been walking due west the night before), surprising us. In the night, we would have missed the elbow and walked into the desert.

The low morning light made that road look knobbier still.

Sun lotion indelibly presses the desert into a traveler's mind because the traveler uses a common brand and will smell it often in the years to come. When the traveler smells it in the years to come, he or she will always think of the sun and the loneliness, and of the hot road, and of the scrub of the desert, and perhaps even of the feeling of walking through it with one's best friend, a friend kind enough and strong enough to drive stakes for your sake into millennia-old crust.

According to what people in Beth-gurbin told us, our road would take us to a small village called Paneas, on the old Marisa Road, and a place to eat. Before getting to Paneas, however, we would see the Paneas crater to the west. We should look for the Paneas crater, they all said.

The Paneas crater, if that's what we saw, is not a crater at all, but a weird cone, or a mountain, or a mound of waste-matter from the Old Earth, rising from the desert at will. I do not know how it came to be, but it beguiles and mystifies. The Paneas crater moved on us, I could have sworn it. It moved through the desert heat, becoming surreal. With every step, it evaded us and dared us to find our way.

To navigate by the Paneas crater (if that is indeed what we saw) is an exercise in futility. No one should attempt it. Neither should we have attempted it, but we did, so much so that the Paneas crater discouraged us, and by its shimmery deceits made us think that we'd never, ever, get to Paneas. And the sun was making me mean again.

Three travelers approached on horseback around noon, and they stopped to talk with us and give us water. We asked them if Paneas was ahead, and whether or not we were on the right road. One of the men said, "Yes, you're on the right road," but I could tell by his expression that he wondered what a man with his wife was doing on this road, in this desert. He did not notice our baby under my clothes, thank God.

The sign said, "Paneas, Population 12." There was only one thing there, and it was Isca-Issen, a small and broken-down café. There was a small inn, also.

Paneas sat at the intersection of our highway and the old Marisa Road, the famous road laid between Marisa and Elusador over a hundred years ago. Except for people like us looking for the shortest distance between two points, the Marisa Road died when the pavements came. When pavements like the Gaza Highway appeared, Marisa towns like Paneas, Obs, and Nisir were left to bake in the sun. Now, the road that used to be Marisa did not have a name that we knew of, but Isca-Issen was a pleasant place, with raisin cakes, coffee, and water from a spring.

When we came out of Isca-Issen, we sat down on the packed dirt outside and leaned against the café. That's when Joseph drew the sketch of me.

Joseph is not a professional artist, and yet he somehow captures the essence of things with even his crudest lines. He carried a charcoal pencil and small drawing cards on

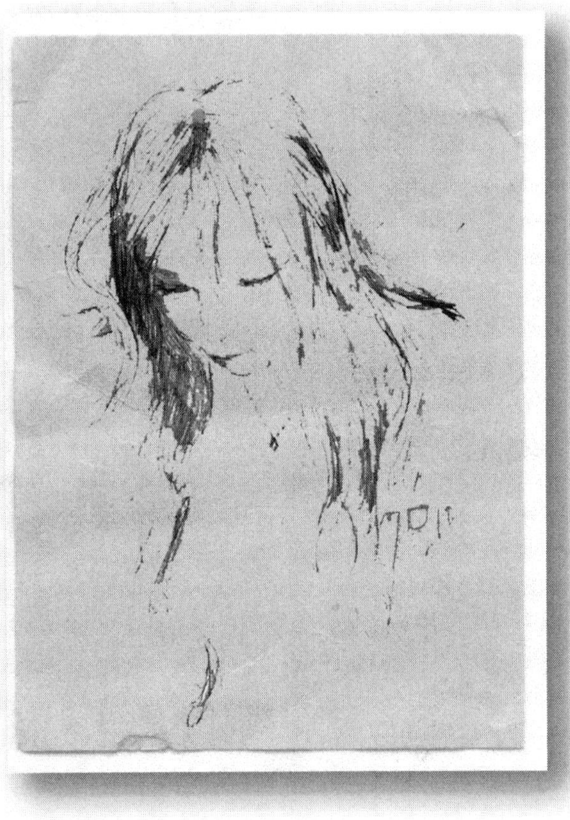

our trip, and he sketched me leaned back against the wall of Isca-Issen. I did not even know he was doing it. I still have that sketch. It's a somber still-life, a portrait of depression, fatigue, and doubt. In the hardness of the desert, I doubted God's love for me. I should have known that the circumstance would test me, but I was surprised, once again, by my weakness.

I'm physically able in the sketch; I'm always physically able. But ability comes from heart and spirit, and in the sketch I have neither. My chin is touching my chest, and my long brown hair is mussed. My clothes are dirty. Joseph filled the card with nothing but the very top of my clothes and my head. A gold chain hangs around my neck, a decoration. At the end of the chain is a diamond, the hard-won fruit of the earth I suffered upon.

A mind sketch is a portrait you draw with your mind. You stare at something and commit it to memory for life. Joseph suggested a mind sketch to me later that evening. The sketch was of the dying evening sky, from the comfort of a good camping place. I stared at it and I found it: the light, the darkness, the happiness, the despair. Between the earth and the blackness of space were straight bands of colors—all of the rainbow—from a sun already set. What colors the gone sun made! I saw the colors. And it has pleased my God to this day that I have never forgotten them, or those things which bordered them.

CHAPTER 17

THE PARTY

Gaza was our jumping-off point for the coastal road. The coastal road took us through Raphia, our last city in Israel. The aqueduct crossing the River of Egypt reminded me of the aqueduct at Antioch, except that it was dirty-white instead of white-white, and the water beneath us was siltier. We celebrated the change in country with a brief sit-down under the first palm tree we came to, and two large bags of trail mix. Mary nursed Jesus while I took a nap. Where would we go next? I'd figure that out after my nap.

"Figure that out" doesn't sound very spiritual, I realize. It's much easier to know what to do next when God gives you dreams. It's even better when God sends a heavenly emissary to your bathroom and tells you, say, that you're going to have a baby and, oh, his name will be Jesus. But dreams such as the one in Ancyra and the one that brought us to Egypt happened infrequently. In fact, that was it. Gabriel came once. We made most of our decisions, then, based on common sense and on what felt right at the time.

I invented a saying then that Mary didn't like much. Once I explained it to her, she liked it even less. The saying was: "If it feels good, do it." Mary thought it was dangerous because, according to her, it "promoted licentiousness." I told her she was dead wrong, and that there was no way it would promote licentiousness. "The probability of licentiousness is *extremely* low," I told her. Then I looked up licentiousness in the dictionary. Glory to God, I still thought she was wrong.

We humans ever tend toward the selfish thing, so why not state this honestly? I've put this theory before friends and relatives, who unanimously doubt it. They give examples ("noble examples") of self-sacrificing people (individuals such as themselves) who choose to forgo the pleasures of self for the sake of others. This is my cue to laugh. Every case is, without exception, a matter of the "selfless" person finding more satisfaction in the "sacrifice" than he or she would from the selfish act. For instance, if I tell Mary that I'll quit the shop early on Tuesday so I can watch Jesus and she can go to bed, am I a hero? I'd like to be, but it's self-deception. I've still chosen the path of least resistance, that is, the path that pampers my flesh. Think about it. I know that getting "my way" and upsetting Mary will go harder on me in the long run than giving in to her, so giving in to Mary and quitting early is still the best thing for *me*.

"Men go to war," my detractors say, "even when they don't want to. They go because they care more for God and Israel than they do for themselves." A noble theory, but wrong. Men go to war because the social stigma of dodging it hurts worse than fighting. People always do what feels best to them, whether they're indulging their flesh, avoiding guilt, or saving face. In the first case, the pleasure is direct; in the other two it's the lesser (always the lesser) of two personal evils. In either case, self is catered to. Oh, the ingenuity of God. By enslaving humanity to its own desires, God paints humanity into corners they claim sovereignty over. It's like my cat Reuben. He follows me everywhere, then struts around the vicinity and ignores me, like, *Hey, I was planning on coming out here anyway*. Sure, Rubie.

So while we didn't hear from God directly, our desire for better traveling conditions (that is: *God*) took us along the seashore and led us to the city of Pelusium, on the west side of the little land strip between the sea and Lake Sirbonis, on the Sinai peninsula. Why here? Mary liked the spelling. I'm serious. That's why. The little town before that was Splecht, which I thought was a great little town. There was a house for rent right next to the market, and the town had a library and a restaurant. I wanted to check on the house right away. But no. Splecht wouldn't do. "It has too many consonants," Mary said. Again, please? "It has too many consonants. It sounds funny. Say it, Joseph. How can I tell people back home that we live in…*Splecht*? It sounds like something you get, not someplace you live." The queen had spoken.

So we walked another five miles and came upon Pelusium. I thanked God that the consonants and vowels were at least evenly distributed because I was getting tired. I looked hopefully at Mary. She loved the name.

"Say it, Joseph. It rolls off the tongue." So I said it, and, yes, it did roll, somewhat, as long as one emphasized the second syllable. So we pitched a tent at the public camping ground until I could find a job and a house, or at least an apartment. I would obviously not be starting up a business since I didn't know how long we'd be in Pelusium, so I got a part-time job delivering mail for the Evil Institution. The mailbag was only slightly heavier than Goliath's breastplate, and after two weeks it aggravated the shoulder problem I'd contracted with the Welldiggers. So delivering mail was a totally selfless act on my part, believe me.

I worked for about three weeks, saved most my money, and we found a house in the country: "A beautiful little place on the corner of Mons and Serabit Roads, in Pelusium," Mary loved to write in her postcards. She hoped that no one would ever decide to visit us because in reality the house was a dump.

Now, it seems to me that you can pray and pray for a thing, and the thing might never happen. You can starve yourself (piously called "fasting"), cut yourself (some deities are impressed), and promise to love your neighbor *as* yourself—and still there are no guarantees (that I know of) that the rare thing you seek will occur. On the other hand (the better hand), you can meander through life like an idiot, taking things as they come, keeping your nose decently clean, and one day God will lay in your path something so stupendous, so outrageous, so odds-damningly rare and fine that not in six millennia would you ever have dreamed to request it. This happened, for my benefit, in the magical land of Egypt two weeks after we moved in.

Even though we officially lived in the rurals, we weren't far from town—about a mile. One glorious Wednesday morning, a group of four women walked into our driveway. I was off that day, sitting on the porch with my coffee, the Official Greeter of Anyone Wishing to Happen Upon Our Tabernacle. I got up quickly enough, holding my mug jauntily at my waist while trying not to trip on a paving stone. The women were by no means ugly.

"Good morning," I said cleverly. "What can I do for you ladies this morning?"

One of the women extended her hand. It was Antina. "Hello," she said, "I'm Antina." She turned to introduce the others. "This is Milda, and Tanise, and Sophie. We heard that a young family had moved into the old Hillgen place, so we just wanted to come over and welcome you to Pelusium."

I thanked them. I think I said, "wow." I'm sure I mentioned how impressed I was at how far the women had walked, which was—

"Two miles so far," said Antina. "We walk four miles every day. We go past here all the time."

I used one flowery adjective to describe the women's effort, another their dedication. I went on and on about the value of exercise. I believe I heralded walking in particular.

"The walking is wonderful around here," said Antina, "as long as you do it early."

"We were glad to hear that you were a young couple," said Sophie. "Mostly old people live in this town."

"You're kidding," I said sagaciously.

Tanise spoke up. "You haven't noticed? There are more white heads here than at the beer joint."

I laughed in an ingenious and enlightened way. "I haven't noticed too much. I just started working for the mail service a couple weeks ago."

"Oh," said Antina. "Was that you I saw on Fig Street yesterday, walking around that house?"

"No, that was my identical twin. He's an idiot. He has trouble finding mailboxes, the moron. You really can't believe the stupid places people put mailboxes these days. Even so—"

"Your *twin* must have walked around that house a dozen times," Antina said with a cute and knowing grin.

"I know," I said. "He really is an dodo. But he gets paid by the hour, so he doesn't care." Everyone seemed to like my legs, stealing glances at them. "So why don't you come in and meet my wife?"

They'd hoped to find her at home, they said, and so I led my harem kitchenward.

"This kitchen is lovely," said Antina.

"You should have seen it when we moved in," I said. "My wife has a touch for decorating."

"Everything's so *cute*," said Milda.

"If it's cute, Mary did it. If it looks like crap…" I took a little bow. Mary walked in just then. "Ah! Behold, the author of cute. Mary, this is Antina, Sophie, Tanise, and…I'm sorry—"

"Milda."

"And Milda. Honey, these girls walked out from town to see us."

"How nice."

"I was telling your husband how glad we were that a young couple moved in here," said Sophie. "Welcome to Pelusium."

"Thank you. Can I get you some coffee? I don't want to ruin your walk or anything. I know how it is, once you get rolling."

"Oh, that's not an issue," Sophie said. "Our goal on this walk was to meet you. Yes. We'd love to visit for a while."

Mary made coffee and we all sat at the kitchen table. I didn't feel intrudish, so I hung out. Besides—and I mean, really—the girls were not in any way repulsive.

They asked where we were from, and we explained almost the whole situation. We told them that we were from Nazareth, in Israel, and that we had a baby but that he was sleeping, and that we had come to Egypt because…because the mail service had transferred me to one of their Egyptian branches to help out temporarily—which was a ridiculous story because it was two different countries. It wasn't that we were lying, it was just that we were…lying.

The girls seemed disappointed. "You mean you're not moving here permanently?" said Milda.

"We're not sure," Mary said. "It's open-ended. But I do like it here. Who knows? And yet it will be difficult for us to practice our religion—I mean, long-term."

"You're faithful Jews, then," said Antina.

"Yes," Mary answered.

Tanise looked surprised. "You're not supposed to have us in your house, are you? Aren't Jews supposed to keep away from sinners like us?" Milda and Sophie giggled. Antina did not.

"My wife told you wrong," I said. "We're *not* faithful Jews." Mary's head jerked in my direction. "We're faithful human beings before we're faithful Jews. It's true that our law forbids intimate fraternization with peoples of other nations, but I'm such a sinner myself that I relate better to sinners than I do to saints." Milda and Sophie giggled again. Tanise looked amused. Antina looked down at the table, but was smiling. "Besides," I continued, "I don't see how a little coffee and conversation will hurt you too badly. It usually takes an Israelite several weeks to corrupt somebody." Well, that was the icebreaker. All the girls laughed—even Mary, sort of—and we were buddies.

Finally, Antina got down to business. "Mary, how would you like to get to know some of the ladies from town? Tanise has a small business and needs someone to host a party. What I was thinking was, we could have the party here and see how many girls we could get to come."

"A business party?" Mary said.

"A women's nightwear party," said Tanise. "You know. Sleepwear and things."

See what I was saying about prayer? Mary squirmed slightly in her seat. My seat squirmed of its own volition.

"I've never heard of such a thing," Mary said.

"It's the latest thing here," said Sophie. "Women have all kinds of parties to sell stuff. If you buy something at the party, you get a discount. You try to get other people to sell for you. Have you heard of Cutlery for the Kitchen?"

"I think they have wine parties now," said Milda.

"Some girl in town sells candles," Sophie said.

"Just like Elizabeth, honey," said the ever-helpful husband. "It's like what Elizabeth is doing in Ramah. Didn't you say Elizabeth was starting some kind of cosmetics business?" I smiled brightly at everyone.

"She wants to get women together to sell cosmetics for her," Mary said dully.

"Yes. Kind of like that," said Tanise. "Only I get women together and we look at nightwear. Very fine garments. But really, it's just an excuse to get together and have a good time."

"Oh, no. You're not in it for the money," Antina joked.

Mary wanted to know what kind of nightwear it was. I knew the subject made her uncomfortable. "I don't really need any nightwear."

"Oh, that's okay," Tanise said. "You don't have to buy anything. This is just a way to introduce you to other women. Since you're hosting the party, you'll get a free gift. And you'll get a discount if you do decide to order. You can't lose."

Mary scrunched her face. "Well…"

"Oh, c'mon, Mary," I said. "It'll be fun." I looked at Tanise with my perky little chipmunk look. "Can I come?"

Tanise slapped me playfully on the hand. "No men allowed!" she said.

"Awww. C'mon. I'm an expert in women's nightwear." Mary was going to kill me, I knew, but I couldn't help myself.

"Oh, I'm sure you'd like to see the girls model *this* stuff," said Antina, laughing.

Mary did not laugh. "Model? Someone actually models the nightwear?"

"Yes," Tanise said. "I like to show how great the products look on live women."

Pelusium, my glorious Desert Pearl.

Antina had seen Mary's reaction. "Oh, don't worry. You won't have to model anything. You're just hosting the party, is all."

I commented that I thought it would be a great time. "I think it will be a great time," I said, putting the feelings of others *way* before my own. Who knew what great free gift Mary could get. Maybe another *chaphat*. I was tempted to ask if there would be *chaphat*s for sale, but thought better of it. Then I changed my mind.

"Will there be *chaphat*s for sale?" I asked.

"That and more," Tanise said. "That and more, Joseph."

I would die anyway—some day—so I said, "C'mon Mary. It'll be a great way for you to meet some other women. I'll get out of here, I promise. I'll go to the café uptown. I'll go to Jake's. I've been wanting to try that place. You'll get me out of your hair for a while. This is just what you need."

Mary perfectly ignored me and concentrated on Tanise. "Will it be late? I have to think of the baby."

"Oh, don't worry about that," Tanise said. "There will be plenty of girls here to help with the baby."

Mary knew it would hurt the girls' feelings to refuse. And she couldn't think of a good excuse not to host the party.

This is what I was saying about how God paints people into corners. This was Mary's lovely little corner. Once Mary made up her mind, though, she gave into it and was back to her usual, social self. "Yes," she said. "I think it will be fun. I'd be glad to host the party. Thanks for asking. When is it?"

"Let's do it tomorrow night," said Tanise. "Does seven o'clock sound okay?"

Fabulous!

"That will be fine," Mary said. "Oh, but my house is a mess."

"I'll take care of that," I said. "I'll help out with the housework, no problem."

"Oh, okay, Joseph. I'll let you." That's what Mary *said*, but between the lines it was, *I've never known you to volunteer for housework so quickly, Penis-head. Why now?*

The women began arriving at six forty-five. There were some dark ravens aflight that night, crossing our threshold. And the smell! Daniella, Orlander, Prixim of Egypt; I recognized them all. The air was laden with othersexly scents. I had never been encased by so many womanly aromas.

I introduced myself to everyone. *Hello, I'm Joseph, glad you could come, my house is yours, I'll be walking to Jake's— Lekker Street, isn't it?* The four women we had met earlier arrived, three of them helping Tanise carry a dozen or so red and pink boxes (with gold ribbons and bows tied on everything and stuck everywhere) into the house. Oh, how I wanted to look into those boxes!

The house looked great. Mary had lit lamps and scented candles and I had poured mixed nuts into the glass bowls we found in one of the cupboards. I had bought wine and juice and three different non-alcoholic elixirs (or so I thought; more on this in a moment), and Mary bought a dozen new drinking glasses from the uptown pottery mart.

Everything was set except that I had to leave. I had to go now. The hour of my departure had arrived, when I would leave and not be home. So I found Mary's hair in the jungle of hair, kissed her goodbye, told her to have fun, to not worry about me, that I was leaving now and would have a great time at Jake's with coffee and maybe a pot pie and a paper.

Mary was already enjoying herself—tremendously so. She flitted and chatted with all the women in a gloriously un-Mary-like fashion. But when she answered my announced departure with an enthusiastic, "Sensational!" I knew something was up.

"'Sensational?'"

"Yes! This is *tons* of fun!"

I stared at her. "It is?"

"Don't *you* think so?"

"Well, yes, but—"

"I can't believe how many new *friends* I'm making. This is *so* exciting! Thanks for getting those elixirs, buddy. They're *sensational!*"

"'Buddy?'"

"Oh, especially the kiwi and strawberry ones."

"How many did you drink?"

She was fussing with her hair. "Oh, I don't know. At least six. Maybe seven. They're so small; I drank them while I cleaned the house. They were really refreshing and gave me energy. Where have these things been all our lives? You can't get elixirs like this in Israel, I can tell you *that*. For-*get*-about-it. I've never tasted *anything* so good. Let's thank our lucky stars that they're non-alcoholic!"

"Um, yeah. Good thing. Kiss me good-bye, you crazy woman."

She slathered me with at least a half dozen wet kisses. "Get a pot pie for me!" she said.

"Oh, I will."

I asked some of the women on my way out when they thought the party would be over. They said that one could never guess about these things, and that I shouldn't even *try* to guess because *they* could not guess, ever. I said I was going to Jake's and that I thought it was on Lekker Street—*was it?* Everyone acknowledged that Jake's was on Lekker Street; yes, everyone I asked acknowledged it, which was everyone. I wondered if it was a nice café. Everyone said that Jake's was so-so ("it's a *pee* hole," said one), but would it be *hard* (I wanted to know), on a *Tuesday* (I wished to discover), to find a *seat* (I longed to be apprised), at Jake's? It would *not*, said the women I asked, and those women just arriving inquired of by me, and the ones who would yet arrive in the process of my leaving, to whom I posed the question. I would not have a problem on a Tuesday night, agreed every woman inquired of, peripherally stared at, and listened to by me.

So I said good-bye, wished everyone a good party, told everyone I'd be out of their hair and definitely not *in* their hair—a spontaneous joke told approximately twelve times, eight of those times earning laughter and sweet-smelling comments about how funny and charming I was. I was the life of a party that would not begin until I left.

Speaking of leaving, on my way out the door I looked at the bottoms of the empty kiwi and strawberry elixir bottles, saw the astounding figure "7.5%" there, said *shit!* to myself, followed that with, *oh well, I didn't do it on purpose*, and then vanished into the sin-warm evening.

But how can you read the same paragraph about the new jockey from Sais taking Delta Reed to the wire at the Rjaru track the previous Saturday and sit next to a man who smokes cigars and reads his menu out loud *to* his menu while a gaggle of gorgeous women at your home model *chaphats* at the same hour you sit alone sipping too-strong coffee and choking on cigar smoke and overblown descriptions of blackened shrimp, trying to ignore a teenager attempting *Let the Trumpet Blow For Me and Jesmondine* on a garage-sale ziggophone tuned by the devil?

I looked outside; it was already dusk. I'd been at Jake's for a miraculously long and historically notable hour. "To hell with this," I finally said to the jockey from Sais. "I can't stand it anymore," I said to the fire-breathing shrimp seer. "Yes," I said to Jake, who asked if the pot pie tasted fresh to me. "Thank you," I said to God, Who had broomed the last webs of guilt from the happy corners of what I was about to do.

I tested them all on my hands and knees, and the east window proved perfect. A bush grew outside it in a shabby mess of leaves extending halfway up the house. I hadn't gotten around to trimming it, and now I appreciated why. What had I missed? Nothing, hopefully.

They were all sitting in the living room, with Tanise standing in the middle saying that Goshen Clothiers started the reverse stitching craze and "imported silk from the Orient on the longest boats imaginable." I could hear and see everything. I would remain perfectly immobile for five hours, or six, or twelve, or seven days, including the Sabbath and the Day of Atonement, if need be. I could be a statue of invisibility in a bush with eyes, perpetually awake. The modeling had not yet begun in a perfect world, if this was that world.

The darkness, the leaves, the height of the window, the speed of sound, and the way the sound arrived at my kneeling place; well, I shuddered. I do that when everything lays so perfectly that I have to pee. I had to pee very badly at this time. I always have to do that when a perfection of this nature ushers in shudders. I get colder and shake, and that is not even mentioning what happens to my scalp and spine, even if it's warm. So I shook with cold and had to pee during shudders that I would not trade for a throne of gold in the upper tiers of God's kingdom.

I had drank too much coffee, I knew. And so the taste in my mouth was also transcendent every time I exhaled to taste parts of the coffee in my nose. I was on my knees, actually *inside* the bush, my eyes at the bottom of the window sill, my pee perched directly between masses of perfectly-messed leaves and a stone wall; perfect.

I removed my pee-port and relaxed the muscles of it just as a tanned woman in layers of belt-metal came from around the corner where the bathroom was, dressed like the Queen of Egypt in a moral downslide with lipstick whipped and scooped onto a stick from the coal mines of Nubia. I let the pee go perfectly at the mincing of this model, refusing to interpret her divine interpretations before the fullness of my portal hit that wall in keeping with deferred pleasure and a wall still somehow radiantly warm in spite of the sunlight's end and my steady wettings, which included a splash or two.

I put my hands on my hips to unencumber everything unassociated with myself, and to smell the heat from the wall, which was not a mild mocha. We are born to be free and to let it go on occasion, even if some of it rejects hard walls and returns to its source, dropleted. I shuddered again at the perfection of my accumulated poisons abandoning me *with* the grain—not against it—and the redness accompanying my watercourses as the Goddess of Pyramids surrendered what few remaining morals lodged behind her breathing just beyond the heat of a wall slightly burning my urethra.

She jangled in the cold-link metals of the effects surrounding her almondness, then assumed a pose that could kill a man, kneeling, as the last of me delivered itself and I felt lightened. She accompanied these authentic Egyptian soul-horrors with fawns over the very sheerness of the garment that teased her legs and at last delivered the tongue of a hiding man's mindset into naked panic-licks. She paused only to drag her nails down an imaginary post of sharpening to damn a man brought from her dungeons for a proper night's damning.

This one sat, then, and a New One—an Undulating One—rounded the miraculous corner, already in a frenzy of pulling hip-wisps from the Orient lower and lower and lower down the thickest parts of her, beneath her fanning bones, then snapping those bones.

She was a blur of silks, all lithe until the cleavage of her almondness swept past and below that cobra waist and the sheathes draped upon breasts beneath her chokers.

Then she sat, and on came a sort of Fable Girl, a Pouting Female Deity breathing through my window in a pink *chaphat*, including the anklets and the glovelets in pink-colored candy. She carried what looked to be a long hard cinnamon stick in the right pink glovelet, thrusting it in and out of her lip-effects, past teeth scraping it up and down and down over the sides and the top of her tongue which darted in dives to take all the sugar off. The stick, metaphorically, is a man's whole body grasped by the feet in the glovelet, traveling through the wetness from darkness to light to darkness to light to darkness to light with the speed of the glovelet, dooming all but the man's feet to pretty indecisions of how she wants him: caved and wetted or uncaved and naked, to be thrust again and again tightly, or to never see light again, or to see it again, or to see the cave-and-light so quickly that groans from his stupidly male lips betray his breathing and embarrass his face and his forced-open eyes thrust over and over and over this woman's wet portal, sugared, as his eyelids flap over the painted and large disappointments that are this young girl's pressed lips, then back again to her throat past those sharpened teeth, or out there naked again and cooling, hardening, that she might lick, or not, being bored, her disappointments in all things male making sighs emerge from her dark-moist throat—while nothing comes from *him*—as she plunges him back across his eyes and face to contemplate—still—his undecided fate.

And then came what I could not have expected or seen in my tunnel, or in all my tumblings, and what blinding passions my body betrayed me into behind this terrible wall. But I soon was to know how much I had missed and what things were to come that had happened without my coming.

"She is the host of our party," Tanise said in the moment pre-destined for it. "She did not know, when I came, what our products fully meant, or did. The conservative wear at the beginning, she praised for its lines and lays, for she is an artist, I know this; just look at her home. Her glass sits empty before you, for what has happened between that time and this is not the result of drink (*you got that one wrong, lady*) but of art, and an appreciation of art newly appreciated: her own body.

"We all witnessed her reaction to the *chaphats*, and we helped her. We saw her relax and see God, so that she commented, recall, on Moon's *chaphat*, and how a thicker silk belt could serve as a bodice; it was brilliant and we flushed with the pleasure of it, of how she transformed. Then she spoke of her husband, a full-blooded male who adores the form, longing to exercise the worship-passions, knowing how his wife slaps down the outer crusts of *that* art. We know what Mary thinks of *that*.

"She cried for a moment, so I went to the room with her, together with her—you saw me—to speak with her woman-to-woman. I went with Moon and Sheila and Mareva, and we all spoke together as women, as heart-to-heart as any women have spoken. You waited for us. We spoke of the deepest things of our gender, and of the male gender that once, long ago, escaped us. Mary did not despise the decorations of our models, but appreciated them at the last and came to say, 'They are good, because God has made the female form and it is right to decorate it, just as I have decorated this house.' I marvel, too. You are not the only ones. This transformation is goddess-like. But there is more.

"Where is she? You will know. For she spoke to me, and to the others, of an ensemble given her by her husband Joseph, a collection called—hear this—*shachah begadim*—the likes of which—I promise you—you have not seen. The ensemble—lying limp in my hand—mystified even me. It was too strong for Mary; she said it was too dangerous for her. I can see why. It is that and more. You do not know; you have not seen it. I am unaware of what genius produced it. It is too strong and dangerous for any of us. But for Mary, no. I dissuaded her from thinking that way. Mary is art, and honesty. She is worthy of it. She cried again.

"We dried her tears and hugged her. She said that no one had ever worn it. We knew that. Then she found herself. We saw a strength come into her, a conviction. I would call it an awareness of destiny, nothing less. *Destiny*. And she felt a camaraderie with us—a connection—though she exceeds us in everything. *Everything*. So teachable and true, this woman, and she can express that shamelessly—I wish we could all be thus.

"I yet held the ensemble—its bare weight shining like God—and looked at Mary. We all looked—Moon, Sheila, and Mareva—the four of us. We all knew what would happen then. She seemed to glow, Mary did. And now, prepare yourselves, for you are about to witness something that you have never witnessed, that no one in the world has ever beheld. I can't prepare you. Nothing can, for nothing like this has ever existed in the history of the world. There is not a goddess in Egypt, or in Israel, or on the inhabited earth, equal to the vision you are about to behold—*right now.*"

Tanise called her, and she walked into that room.

And I was finished. *Done.* Awake, finally awake. Fully open-eyed, at last.

I have betrayed you in my heart, my Wife. My thoughts have often strayed far from you. I am swift to make ruin and misery my mark, and there has been, for you, no fear. I am corrupt and abhorrent, a man of stubbornness and an unrepentant heart. You conceal yourself from me in terrors, my Savioress. There is none other beside you, no, not one; former of light, creator of darkness, maker of good, creator of evil. You do all these things.

"You gaze down from your heavens on the sons of humanity, to see if there is one doing good, even one. I have withdrawn aside with the rest, and there is no one righteous, no, not one. Yet you; your throne has been established from long ago. The streams shall lift up their crushing waves. *Lift yourself up, O judge!* Turn back a requital upon the proud. To whom else can I turn? Unless you were my help, soon my soul would tabernacle in stillness. If I say, 'My foot slips!' your benignity, it is already bracing me. When my disquieting thoughts within me are many, your consolations, they hearten my soul. You are my impregnable retreat, the rock of my refuge. Heal me!"

The women sat, stunned. I leaned into my wall, spent. Mary stood in a prism of light, radiant. The universe revolved, around her.

"And tomorrow night," said Tanise, "she will wear it for her husband. I have heard it from her own lips. Tomorrow, Joseph will see and taste its powers, the first of his gender to be granted the privilege."

Then she was…gone.

CHAPTER 18

THE DAY AFTER

I awoke early the next morning, but not before I'd crawled—most typically—from my hiding place the night before and walked back to town, shaken. I returned to Jake's, to the same corner table I'd occupied earlier and ordered pumpkin pie. It was not yet midnight; I sat marveling at a world where pumpkin pie coexisted with goddesses, minutes apart.

I repeatedly got up to look at the paintings on the walls at Jakes. How could people paint that well? There were even paint chips on green boats moored in a harbor along the sea. Jake was closing and he told me so. "But look at these paint chips, Jake," I said. "Who painted *this* one? Appreciate the decay." It wasn't coated in grease, so Jake didn't get it. He could have grabbed me by my scruff and thrown me into the street; it wouldn't have mattered. I was insulated by the protective sheen of having something that not one other human had.

"What's the matter with you?" Jake wanted to know.

"Nothing, Jake. There's something the matter with your pie, though. Check what you're doing with the crust—and study that boat."

I paid my bill and left.

The wind blew, and the air smelled like rain. I had forgotten this was Egypt, and that it could not rain.

I walked a three-block circuit near Jake's, pitying the people in their homes with their dim-witted lights. People turned the pages of their newspapers to read about what had happened to their world while they slept. I would die if I had to be them. Some of their lights went out; a face would be illumined for a moment, then I was once again alone. How could they sleep? It hit me that I had to work in the morning, and this realization fell upon me like a cold stone. How could Bane care if people got their mail? How could the people themselves give the faintest damn? I lusted for unconsciousness, until the time when all the mail would be discarded and the Goddess of Women would smooth the last wrinkles before me, in front of me, for the lacings of my tongue.

I thought that some of the women might linger so I began the circuit again. I would not return home just yet. The cool had begun settling into the sidewalk cracks. Had I been able to see these cracks, I'd have avoided them. I would not interfere with anything now, or ask a question, or even brood. I could think but not brood. The night had to be abandoned. My dirty paws had already moved too many things. One more pawing from me and everything could crumble. Happiness is too finely balanced, is my conclusion. You never land in a broad place where you can see your reflection to a distant tree. Instead, you're in a forest with a hundred trees staggered everywhere between you and the broad place. It's always the opposite of what you want and need. Trees can hide anything, and they've been here longer than pastures.

I would be naked, that I knew. For a man, it is his penance. The woman must see him from the safety of her clothing. Safety and danger, heart and stone. Skin and leather. Living things, and those things from which life has passed.

I headed home.

The cold sat heavily down now and occupied the low places. Hitting these spots on Serabit Road felt like rousing disembodied spirits. Jackrabbits ran from the ditch grass, scaring me. Or maybe I was the jackrabbit. I would wait for her in a corner, near her chair. She was so much a woman beneath her long hair. The dim outline of the house appeared. There were no lights on, so I hoped that Mary and Jesus were asleep.

They were.

I crept into bed and not one of my bones cracked. Mary breathed in sleep, I could tell. I tried to roll into my sleeping position, but Mary moaned and moved. I stopped to let her go through that cycle until her breathing became deep again.

I laid awake for two hours, my mind an endlessly burning wick, inextinguishable. I'd read once that, to fall asleep, you relax the tongue. A tense tongue means that you're ready to contribute verbally to something urgent in your mind. So I thought about relaxing my tongue and it worked—except for sleep. I knew then how ready I'd been to confess everything. She would lift my chin with the toe-tip of her *qum*.

My tongue returned at the thought of this, and I was ready to explain the dynamics of it to Rent, to Mary, to Tanise, even to Jake. So I relaxed my tongue again and thought that I would note the moment of sleep. But just when that line came, I jerked awake. That's when she entered the room again, so tall. Another vision. I consciously relaxed my tongue again, and the next thing I knew, I thought it was morning, and it was.

I accidentally touched my foot to Mary's calf. She did not move. I slipped out from under the covers, out into the hallway, then into the bathroom. I stepped into my clothes. A perfume bottle on the counter said, "Destiny by Qunatir." I wondered where it had come from. Then I appreciated the thin gold ribbon and I thought that it must have been Mary's free gift. I was disappointed. I thought that maybe it would have been a *chaphet*.

Out in the living room, two bows lay on the floor. Other than those, nothing in the room bore witness to goddess-hood. In the kitchen, all the drinking glasses and the nut bowls lay tumbled in the sink.

Perfume, bows, bowls and glasses attested to the happenings. So it had not been a dream.

Work went on and on. I resented my patrons. I kept seeing Mary. In-between houses, her heels clicked ominously on a dark stone floor we didn't have. Her long hair hung darkly, and paints flashed upon her eyelids. I surmised at day's end that my patrons got their mail because when I got back to the office my cart was empty and nothing remained in my bag.

When I got home, I smelled something burning. I was so happy to see Mary. It was not raining, but it was overcast.

"Hi, honey," I said.

"Hi. How was your day?"

"Terrible. All I could think about was coming home and seeing you. I missed you so badly."

I went behind her and pushed my body against hers. I rubbed my hands up and down the sides of her thighs and hips, and kissed her on the neck.

"I appreciate that, Joseph, but I'm trying to get these muffins out. They're ruined."

"What's burning?"

"These stupid muffins. I was painting the lattice and I left them in too long." A muffin finally surrendered to the prying of Mary's knife. "Oh, look at that. *Dang.* They're ruined."

"I like burned muffins."

"I'm making them for Tanise. I wanted to walk them into town this evening. I haven't done my walking yet."

"How was the party?"

"Fine."

"Did you have a good time?"

"Yes. I met a lot of nice women."

"The ones I met seemed nice. The party went okay, then?"

"It was pretty fun. But it went so late. I didn't get to sleep until midnight. I woke up with a terrible headache, and I still have it. How did your evening go?"

"Okay. I went to Jake's."

"Did you get your pot pie?"

"Yep."

"What else did you do? When did you get home?"

"I got home around twelve thirty, I think. I basically just read the newspaper. I hung around and talked to Jake, basically. What's with the perfume in the bathroom?"

"That was my door prize."

"You mean your free gift?"

"Whatever."

"How is it?"

"What do you mean?"

"Have you tried it? I don't smell anything."

"Are you kidding? I haven't had time."

"What's been going on?"

"Jesus had a hard time waking up today. He usually wakes right up, but he was groggy this morning. I didn't like it at all. I'm still worried about him."

"He just got to bed late, is all."

"No. I put him down on time. I've been worried about him all day."

"Is he okay now? Where is he?"

"He's taking his nap."

"Well, he's okay then. He's fine."

"He's usually awake by now. Will you go check on him?"

He was awake and staring at the ceiling. I laid down next to him and kissed his forehead. "What's the big idea worrying your mother, huh?" He just looked at me. "Huh, big boy? You shouldn't be worrying your mother like that. How come you didn't wake up so good this morning? Huh? Did you have a bad dream last night? Too much perfume? Poor little guy."

He looked into my eyes, and I kissed him on the lips. "You're so soft. Mm. I love you. You've got to stop worrying your poor mother like that. Mamas get so upset about things. How come you didn't wake up so good? You okay?"

I kissed him on the lips again. "I love you, Jesus. Ready to get up?" I picked Jesus up beneath his armpits and held him against my chest. I wish I'd been naked, because of how good his skin always felt against my chest. Jesus was naked except for his diaper. His skin was soft peach. His hair was fuzzy so I buzzed his hair with the bottom of my fingers, just on top of the fuzz. "You're pretty fuzzy up there, big boy. We're going to have to get you a haircut. Let's go see Mom and tell her about how much better you are."

I brought Jesus into the kitchen. "Here comes baby," I said. I zoomed him up to Mary, then away, like he was flying.

"Don't get him near this burny smell!" Mary said.

"He's fine," I said. "Don't be so paranoid. Why don't you go relax. Give Jesus a little snack, and I'll take care of these muffins."

"What are *you* going to do?"

"I'll save the good parts and scrape out the rest. I'll go uptown and buy you some muffins. How's that?"

"I can't give Tanise store-bought muffins."

"Why not?"

"I just can't."

"Then I'll help you make some more. We'll do it together."

"I don't think I'm up to it."

"Why not?"

"I didn't sleep well last night. I kept having bad dreams."

"What about?"

"About you and Tanise."

"*What?* What happened?"

"You liked her."

"That's ridiculous. What did I do?"

"I really don't want to talk about it."

"You're the one who brought it up."

"You really liked Tanise."

"But it was a dream. Dreams aren't real."

"I *know* dreams aren't real. It just bothered me. Okay?"

"Don't get so uptight. I can't help it that I showed up in your dream. Why didn't you take a nap today?"

"You have no idea what I've done around here. You didn't even notice the furniture."

"What about it?"

"I re-arranged it."

"Oh. That's nice."

"How could you not have noticed?"

"I don't know. I just didn't." I looked. "Okay. Hey, that looks great."

"Right."

"Why do you re-arrange the furniture every other day?"

"I don't re-arrange it every other day. I've re-arranged it twice."

"I'm sorry I didn't notice it. So…you're…painting the lattice?"

"Whoever put up that lattice was crazy."

"So let's get rid of it."

"We can't. We're renting."

"Why don't I help you paint it on Thursday? I'm off."

"Really?"

"Sure. We'll do it together. It'll be fun."

"Since when do you want to help me fix up this place?"

"Since today."

"Why the big change?"

"Do I have to have a reason? Why do I have to have a reason? Can't I just be nice?"

"You don't have to get defensive."

"I'm not. I'm just trying to help."

"I know. I'm sorry. I'm just tired. I don't feel well."

"Then go sit down."

"I can't. What are we going to eat?"

"We'll go out."

"How will we pay for it?"

"I've got enough. I get paid on Friday."

"I know how much we have, and this is Tuesday. We can't afford it tonight."

"If that damn post office would give me more hours…"

"I didn't mean to bring up money."

"Let's change the subject."

"Was Jesus already awake?"

"Yes. Everything is fine."

"You didn't see him this morning. I'm worried."

"What for? He's fine."

"You didn't hear him coughing."

"You didn't tell me he was coughing."

"Just a little. But he usually doesn't do it."

"He's not coughing now. You're not coughing now, are you, Jesus? Huh? See? He hasn't coughed once since I got home."

"Did you get off early today?"

"No. Why?"

"What time is it?"

"Three forty-five."

"You're kidding!"

"Why?"

"I wanted to get that letter out to my parents. My mother's birthday is next week. Shoot! I meant to get uptown before four."

"You've got fifteen minutes."

"But I think they pick up early."

"Who picks up early?"

"Those stupid people you work with. Dan, or whoever."

"Dan does not pick up early."

"I was uptown the day before yesterday, and I saw him tapping the box at ten 'til."

"You're kidding. He's not supposed to do that."

"Well, he does."

"He's not supposed to. I'll talk to him. Look, the mail doesn't leave until about twenty after. Do you have the letter?"

"Everything but the address."

"Address it and give it to me. I'll run it uptown. I can make it in ten minutes."

"You're a sweetheart, Joseph."

"Joseph Jabrecki, at your cervix. Go get the letter. I'll stretch."

Mary addressed the letter while I stretched. She handed it to me and I ran uptown and gave it to Bane out on the dock. "I think Dan might be tapping the box early," I said. Bane said he didn't think so. "Check on him," I said, but I knew there wasn't a chance in hell that Bane would check.

"Did your mother ever get over it?"

I had just gotten into the door.

"Did my mother ever get over what?"

"Did she ever get over you not sending her birthday cards?"

"I sent my mother birthday cards."

"Maybe two. After you moved out."

"That's card*s*."

"Did my letter make it okay?"

"Fine. Why are you bringing that up about my mother?"

"Just curious. How could you have forgotten?"

"I don't know. I got busy, I guess."

"Do you think Jesus will ever forget to send me a birthday card?"

"Probably."

"*What?*"

"You asked. Can we eat soon? I'm starving."

"How could Jesus ever forget to send me a birthday card?"

"Because he's a guy. Seriously. That's why."

"Guys are so insensitive. All I have is salad."

"Salad is great."

"Could you chop some onions?"

"Sure."

I chopped onions and Mary tore lettuce. For a long time, the only noise in the kitchen was chopping and tearing. Jesus lay on his back on his blanket on the floor, staring at us.

"What do you want to do tonight?" I asked.

"What do you mean?"

"You know. I mean, I thought maybe we could be romantic tonight. Get to bed early."

"What do you have in mind?"

"I just want to be with you."

"I think that would be nice."

"You have an unbelievable body, Mary. You really turn me on."

"You think about sex a lot, don't you."

"Yeah."

"Why do guys think about sex so much?"

"I don't know. We're guys. It's women's fault. If you women weren't so beautiful, we wouldn't think about it so much."

"What about me turns you on?"

"Lots. Your hair. Your figure. Your face. Everything."

"Do you love me for just being me?"

"Of course."

"Would you love me if I was ugly?"

"What kind of question is that?"

"Would you?"

"But you're not ugly. You're beautiful."

"But would you love me if I weren't beautiful?"

"Of course I would."

"Good answer."

"It's not a good answer, it's the right answer."

"But it helps that I'm pretty."

"It helps. Sure, it helps."

"What if I were crippled and couldn't walk?"

"Why are you asking these crazy questions?"

"I don't know. I'm just curious."

"Women think too much. See, guys don't think. That's the thing about guys. We don't ask so many questions. We take everything at face value."

"Maybe you should look deeper."

"I *do* look deeper. But things are how they are. Why imagine that they're some other way?"

"You like to play games."

"No I don't."

"Yes, you do. You've told me. You like to play *shamat* games."

"They're not games."

"I'm not really a Princess, am I?"

"To me you are."

"Do you think my breasts are too small?"

"No. Your breasts are perfect."

"I noticed you looking at Tanise's breasts."

"*What?* I was not looking at Tanise's breasts."

"They're huge."

"Are they? I wouldn't know."

"Why do some women get all the breasts? It's not fair. You don't have to lie. You can tell me if you like them."

"Okay. Tanise has great tits. Are you happy?"

"So you like big tits?"

"No! I like *your* tits."

"Do you think mine are too small?"

"I just told you. They're perfect. Do we have green peppers?"

"No. Do other women turn you on? Be honest."

"What does it matter? You're the one I love. What's with all the questions? You're way sexier than Tanise."

"Why?"

"You just are."

"But why?"

"You've just got the whole package. I mean, like, your hair. Take your hair, for instance. Tanise's hair is too short. Your hair is the best. Nobody has better hair than you."

"That's all? Just my hair?"

"For God's sake, I said the whole package. You're *way* more beautiful than Tanise. You've got the eyes. Tanise's face is too fat. Cripe, already."

"We've got to get to bed early tonight."

"Believe me, I want to. I'm looking forward to it. Are you?"

"Yes. I'm just worried about Jesus, though. I'm sorry. I'm distracted."

"We'll put him to bed early, and then we'll have the evening to ourselves."

"Sometimes I wish he weren't in the room with us."

"So let's put him in another room."

"I won't be able to hear him if he starts coughing."

"We'll leave the door open. He's not even coughing now."

"I can't do *shamat* with the door open."

"Who's going to see?"

"It's just the idea of it."

"Oh, for God's sake…"

"It's important to me."

"Okay. So we'll close the door. We'll put him right outside in the hallway. How about that?"

"On the floor?"

"We'll drag his mattress out there."

"It'll be too drafty in the hallway."

"Where's the bassinet we got at that sale?"

"You put it in the attic."

"Fine. I'll go up and get it after supper."

"The attic is a mess. The people who lived here were pack rats."

"They didn't know they'd be going off to a nursing home."

"We've got to clean that attic someday."

"*Some*day. Let's forget about it for now, how about."

"You're getting upset."

"No, I'm not. Do we have any aspirin?"

"Are *you* getting a headache now?"

"Something like that."

The truth was, my nuts were aching.

We ate dinner.

"I really don't feel well," Mary said.

Here it came.

"Why not? What's wrong?" I already knew.

"Where did we get that lettuce?"

"Bleuses."

"Who got it at Bleuses?"

"*I* got it at Bleuses."

"Why did you get it at Bleuses?"

"We always get it at Bleuses."

"No we don't. We get it at Sid's. We get our bread at Bleuses."

"Why can't we just get everything at Bleuses?"

"Because their produce is terrible. I thought you knew that."

"You never told me."

"I *did* tell you. I remember I told you right before you left."

"You must not have said it loud enough."

"I *did* say it loud enough. I said, 'Make sure you get our bread at Bleuses, but don't get the produce there. Get the produce at Sid's.' And you said, 'Okay.'"

"I did? Well, I'm sorry. I don't remember. I've never even heard of Sid's."

"You've never heard of Sid's? We went to Sid's the first day we got here."

"If you say so. Sorry I can't remember."

"You never listen to me."

"No. Never. I never listen to you."

"You listen, but you don't hear me."

"I'll never get produce at Bleuses again. I promise."

"That's not the point."

"It's not? What *is* the point?"

"I told you. I think I'm feeling sick because of this lettuce."

"You never told me that, specifically."

"They put something on it at Bleuses. The women uptown told me."

"I doubt it's the lettuce. Why don't you lie down?"

Jesus started to cry.

"What's the matter with him?" I asked.

"God, Joseph. It's not his fault he doesn't feel well." She knelt over Jesus. "Aww, the poor baby. Whazza matter, honey? You have a tummy ache?"

"I'm going for a walk."

"I thought we were going to bed early."

"You're right. Let's go to bed early."

"I'm sorry, Joseph. I'll feed Jesus. You go up to the attic and get that bassinet. I'll wash up. We'll have some time together."

"*Some* time?"

"It's better than no time."

"I just thought maybe we could have a significant amount of time together tonight."

"We will."

"It's not looking that way."

"We will."

Mary was smiling, so I smiled. "Okay. I'll go get the bassinet."

I went upstairs and got the bassinet. It was dirty and cobwebby. I dragged it down the steps.

"Don't bring that thing through the living room, honey."

"I'm trying to take it outside. It needs cleaned."

"I just swept today."

"Do you want me to throw it out the window?"

"That's better than dragging it through the living room."

I threw the bassinet out the window, went outside, dragged it to the pond, and washed it off. But now it was all wet. I went back inside, got a towel off the bathroom doorknob, then went back out and dried off the bassinet. Then I brought the bassinet back in the house and dragged it upstairs and down the hallway outside the bedroom. Jesus was crying like crazy. Mary called out from the bathroom: "Can't you do something to make him stop crying?"

I got one of Jesus' toys and dangled it in front of him. It was Mr. Jingles. "Hey, Jesus. Look at Mr. Jingles." Jesus' face was red and he wouldn't stop crying. "Look at Mr. Jingles," I said. "Mr. Jingles is happy, and he wants you to stop crying. See?" I wiggled Mr. Jingles and made him talk to Jesus. "C'mon, little boy. This is your friend, Mr. Jingles. Stop crying for Mr. Jingles. Okay? Mr. Jingles says, 'Stop crying!'"

"Joseph!" Mary called from the bathroom. "Are you yelling at the baby?"

"No. Mr. Jingles is yelling at him."

"I thought you were going to make him stop crying."

"I'm trying. He won't stop. What the hell is wrong with this kid?"

"I think his stomach is upset from his last feeding."

"Oh, for God's sake…"

"It's not his fault."

"Did I say it was his fault? Why don't you come in here and quiet him down? You're the damn expert at it."

"I'll be out in a minute."

Mary came out a minute later. Her hair was soaked.

"Why did you wash your hair?"

"What?"

"It wasn't that dirty."

"I haven't washed it since yesterday."

"That's only one day."

"What have you got against me washing my hair?"

"It's just…all…*wet* now."

"Uh…*yeah*. I just washed it."

"How long do you think it will take to dry? Can't you towel it or something? I was hoping I could see your hair."

"Yeah, well, I *would* dry it, except somebody stole the towel off the doorknob."

"Oh, for God's sake. I used it to dry the bassinet. That's the only towel we have?"

"It's the only one that was clean. And you don't need to curse over it."

"I'm not cursing. All I said was, 'For God's sake.'"

"You said 'damn' earlier. I don't think you should be saying 'damn' around the baby."

"It's not going to ruin his life."

"It might. You never know."

"Oh, so if he ever says 'damn' in his life, it's my fault?"

"Doctor Telglotten says—"

"Please, Mary. I'm not in the mood to hear what Doctor Telglotten says. Let's just try to relax. Can we? Do you think we can do that? Let's just lay down, get Jesus to sleep, and be together."

We got ready for bed.

"Did you put out the lamps downstairs?" Mary asked.

"Crap. You lay down with Jesus, I'll go put out the lamps."

I went downstairs and put out the lamps. When I got back upstairs, Mary was in bed with Jesus. Everything was dark and quiet. I crawled into bed.

"You awake?" I asked.

"Yes. Shhh! He's just falling asleep."

"Good."

It was quiet for several minutes.

"Joseph?"

"Yes, my love?"

"Will you go see if I put out the lamp in the bathroom?"

"You put it out."

"Are you sure?"

"You always do."

"Would you go check? I just don't remember doing it. Please?"

"Cripe."

I went into the bathroom. The lamp was out. I went back to bed.

"Was it out?"

"No. It was lit and the bathroom was burning down."

"*Shh.* I think he's going to sleep."

Again, in my mind, I heard the click of Mary's heels on a stone floor we didn't have. I saw her gorgeous brown hair, hanging down. Her eyes were large and dark, searching me in the lamplight. I opened myself to her. My tongue was tense. A tense tongue means that you're ready to contribute verbally to something urgent in your mind. But if there are whispers in the subconscious world that make one alive, there are also those that, breaking into the consciousness, kill one.

Mary's breathing became the deep and regular breathing of sleep.

I accidentally touched my foot to Mary's calf. She didn't move. I slipped out from under the covers, out into the hallway, and into the bathroom. I put on my clothes. There sat "Destiny by Qunatir" again.

It had not been a dream.

I went outside into the dark, alone except for the stars and every celestial eye. The cold sat down heavily now and occupied the low places. Hitting these spots on Serabit Road was like rousing disembodied spirits.

I removed all my clothes. Everyone set? Fine. God damn you, then. *Piss-fucks.*

I laid down on my back in the road, naked. From soil I had come, and to soil I would return. I opened myself for the throng.

You are bad, Joseph.

Watch this, fuckers. *Piss-fucks!* I'll fuck it myself, motherfucks.

Look at you.

See what you've made me.

How can you do this to yourself?

You made me this way!

(Silence. Then...

...guttural, graphic noises.)

This is what it's all about, Joseph?

God!

Does it make you cry?

No! (animal noises, weeping, rubbing, rubbing up...)

Say it.

My God!

I love you, Joseph.

CHAPTER 19

BACK TO NAZARETH

"Herod is dead."

This is what Joseph said to me one morning as I rolled over in bed. He said it that matter-of-factly. "God gave me another dream," he said. What did it portend for us? "We're going back to Bethlehem. After that, I don't know."

The news upset me. I was glad the danger was past; I shed no tears over Herod. But I resented yet another disturbance in our lives. We had not been in Egypt for even three months, and already we were leaving. I always knew deep down that we would return to Israel, but I didn't know it would be so soon. I was just feeling comfortable in our house, and I had made friends. But this was not to be the era for friends.

Our sexual relationship deteriorated in Egypt. I actually tried on Joseph's "thing" there, not in front of him, but at a so-called sleepwear party. (It was quite more than sleepwear.) The party was put on at our house by some of the town girls.

These were the first girls I met in Pelusium. They visited about two weeks after we'd moved in and told me about the little get-together. They said it would be a good way for me to meet other women.

I could not have imagined modeling such a thing in front of other people, but the women made me feel comfortable. Everyone else was doing it, so it seemed like what I should do at the time. I don't know what came over me, really. I got caught up in the excitement. I was not myself. I felt so crazy that night. So I walked out in front of a dozen women (if you can believe that) and modeled the ensemble. (Bizarre *qum*, something called *yad kasah*, stretching up the arms—all of leather—and a leather *gara*—if I haven't mentioned it before.)

We made Joseph go to town during the party. This was not a party for men. One of the women, Tanise, said that I should wear the ensemble for Joseph the next night. For some reason I said I would, but in the end could not bring myself to do it. I had felt somewhat comfortable around the women, but I knew that the outfit would make Joseph crazy.

As soon as I was standing in front of everyone in the middle of the living room, I thought to myself, *Mary, what are you doing?* Once I came out, I wished I hadn't. I suddenly felt extremely embarrassed. I came to myself, went back to the bathroom and locked myself in. I changed my clothes as quickly as I could; I felt just awful. I cried and prayed for God to forgive me for what I had done. For the rest of the evening, I tried to hide my feelings from the girls. I could hardly face them. I never mentioned this first-time modeling adventure to anyone. Joseph will find out about it for the first time when he reads this, and I'm sure he will be amused. Surprise!

Joseph became moody during what turned out to be our last three weeks in Egypt. He did not want to talk much about anything, not even *shamat*. It seems that when men get upset, they go inside themselves and refuse to communicate. Some of our psychologists now are comparing this to going into a cave. It's an apt comparison. Women refuse to enter caves, either physically or metaphorically. We don't like it where it is dark, wet, and cold. We like to talk about things and be open about our feelings. Sharing our feelings with others is what heals us. This is what makes me wonder whether men really want to be healed. I kept asking Joseph what was wrong. He said nothing was wrong, but of course that was not true. He burrowed deeper into his hole in the rocks, where I assumed he had his little campfire lit to warm himself. How was I supposed to draw him out? Was I supposed to crawl into the cave and sit by the campfire with him? I didn't think so. If he wanted to starve himself of my affections, let him be starved. This is what I thought at the time. It was his choice.

Our departure from Egypt was unceremonious, though not unfriendly. I said good-bye to the house many times. I still think fondly of that house. I made it livable in a short time with simple things like paint, flowers, and putty. I left part of my personality there.

One of Joseph's workmates from the mail service brought in a box of fried and frosted "dough circles" on his last day. (We Jews call them "donuts.") Joseph said they joked that it was a shame he was leaving just when he was figuring out where the mailboxes were. My girlfriends came over to watch us load Frisk and see us down the road. Besides leaving the house, that was the hardest part for me, leaving my friends. We shed tears and embraced in the early morning of our departure. Five of them walked with us to the village limits. Joseph stopped in at Jake's one more time (he became a fan the night of my impromptu modeling gig), to say good-bye and to get one more cup of Jidda-walnut. I knew Jake's would miss him; Joseph's absence would leave a dent in the coffee and muffin sales.

We retraced our route back to Bethlehem, coming eastward across the seacoast this time, and heading south at Gaza. It was not nearly as hot in the desert as when we had come, so that was a blessing. The road through Paneas did not seem like the same road; what a difference temperature makes. We traveled all day without discomfort.

When we got to Bethlehem, it was as if we had never left. But then we talked to the townspeople, and, dear God, what an unimaginable nightmare they related.

The very day we left Bethlehem—the very day—Herod ordered all the baby boys two years of age and younger to be slain by the sword. These words cannot now reflect how I felt then. I knew it was the magi who related Jesus' birth to Herod, and I came to despise them because of it. Herod's motives were evilly self-centered. He feared that one of the babies, the Messiah, would one day usurp his throne. How right he was. But the Messiah—by an act of God—was in Egypt.

I knew many of the mothers, and I grieved with them. I could not imagine the horror of that day. And yet I had to imagine it, and to feel it, because story after harrowing story was told me. Each woman's grief touched me. I knew that it could have been Jesus. It could just as easily have been us. But it could not have been Jesus, and it could not have been us, because of the prophecies. That's when the guilt set in. The guilt just tortured me after that. I felt ashamed that my son was spared while their sons were lost. They were innocents. What had they done to deserve so awful a fate? Nothing. And so I became angry at God again, angry at being chosen and spared by Him. I would want nothing else but to be spared, yet I could not bear the sorrow of the other mothers. They told me how lucky I was that we left just before. How could I tell them that God had chosen to warn us but not them, no, not even when He could easily have done so? I could not say it, nor could I even bear to think it myself. All I could do was cry, and I did, and not even Joseph could comfort me. How I hated our destiny in those dark days.

Joseph took heavily to the study of scripture at this time. When he wasn't working, he was burrowed away in his scrolls. I was glad for this, even if it made me jealous. I confess my honest feelings to you. He was paying more mind to the scrolls than to me. I should not have resented it, but such is my constitution, and now you see how it opposes itself. It had always been my dream to have a husband zealous for the things of the spirit, and now that I had one I resented it.

I wrote my parents as often as I could. I was beginning to miss Nazareth. Joseph's business had had its boom, and now the work had dried up. By force of circumstance, God made us look north again. We both agreed that Nazareth was the better place to raise Jesus. Besides, my parents and all my family were anxious to meet him for the first time.

Frisk was used to the vagabond lifestyle by now, and once again bore our meager belongings with sturdy resignation. Frisk was blessed among beasts, said Joseph, in that her owners were light in the way of possessions.

On our way out of town, we decided on a detour to see once more the little stable where Jesus was born. For all I knew, it would be the last time we would ever see it. We got to the inn, went back behind it to look—and it wasn't there! Oh, the shock of it. Workmen were on the site, building—of all things—a gambling house for the inn. I cried. Joseph was stunned as well, but was more detached and philosophical about it. "God doesn't want us looking back, I guess," he said sadly. "We have our memories of it, and no one can take those away." And yet I saw him look back more than once as we turned east, and then north out of Bethlehem.

I had not told my parents the exact date of our departure (we hadn't known it ourselves), so they got the surprise of their lives when Joseph and I pulled up at 19 Hen Street on a Wednesday afternoon. Mother showered us with kisses (even kisses for Frisk, for getting us home safely), and danced a jig in the front yard, her robes and hair flying like an unpegged tent in a whirlwind. Father went straight for Jesus, holding him in the manner of Simeon, muttering to himself and quite unable to take his eyes off him.

We were so close to our house, hardly a stone's throw away, and yet we spent the night at my parents' and never went to our house at all that night. Pharaoh was so glad to see us. He jumped onto our bed that evening and lay between us. He nuzzled us each in turn, as if begging to be apprised of all that had happened. Funny thing was, we told him. And he listened! We know he did.

Pharaoh got his first good look at Jesus the following morning when Mother had Jesus on the floor to change his nappy. Pharaoh sat at Jesus' head, studying his expressions. Jesus was well aware of him. Pharaoh touched his nose to Jesus' forehead once, and a small, blue spark jumped between them. It made an audible little snap. Amazing! They had communicated in that little spark, I just knew.

Our neighbor Wallace Khawalida did a good job keeping our house up while we were away. Reuben was his usual self, and did not seem to care which side of the road claimed him. He simply wandered across the road from Wallace's to our place as if to say, *So I'm staying here again? All right. Whatever.*

We humans never take change as lightly as that. The ensuing two years changed Joseph and me for better and for worse, depending on the day. God did not grace us with the ambivalence of a cat, so whatever Joseph and I experienced, we felt. We rose and fell with each day's joys and pains—and not always into each other's arms.

Our second child, James, came just after Jesus' first birthday. Simeon came, similarly, before James learned to walk. I assumed, with every other ignorant parent, that two children was merely one child, times two. If I can spare anyone my naivety, I will. The draw, with James, upon our minds and nervous systems, was fourfold that with Jesus. And how I often wished I had four hands. Simeon (named after the prophet at the temple) was much easier. My theory is, once you have two children, you can have twenty-two. This is not to say I mean to test the theory.

Joseph and I enjoyed *shamat*, but only sporadically. The bedroom was not our refuge, but only a place to rest our baggage before we each hurried off to our own destinations. I could not give him *shamat* how he wanted it, I knew. Joseph was polite and loving about it, but unfulfilled in that way. But then, so was I. Unfulfilled, I mean. My joy depended on Joseph's. I held the key to our happiness, it seemed, but had neither the strength nor the desire to turn it in the lock—a strange situation. Joseph took more and more to his studies and to the children, I, to the house.

Joseph was wonderful with the children, the best father I could imagine. If there was some kind of ruckus out of doors, I knew Joseph was swinging Jesus on our little swing set. He had a game called Boot Game, which I was not fond of, but which Joseph and Jesus loved dearly. Joseph would get Jesus swinging high on the swing, and then he would throw an old flaxoline boot straight up in the air—high in the air, mind you—to see if it would land on Jesus. Imagine! But Jesus loved it, squealing in the swing as the boot came down, wondering if the timing of his swing would spare him or set him up for a clobbering. *Boys.* I couldn't even watch the game. Joseph said the thrill was that maybe you might get hit, maybe you might not. I would have called that the problem. I said, "Maybe that's the thrill for you, but what about Jesus?"

"I like it, Mama," Jesus would say. "Daddy no stop."

As for me, I found solace turning our house into a home. If I was mystified by Boot Game, Joseph was at a loss to grasp my passion for home improvement. "How can you take refuge in plaster?" he would ask. "How can shaping a bunch of old weeds into a wreath satisfy you?" It was a world I could control. I could not control my son's destiny. I could not control my husband's sexual disposition. I could not control the fate of our nation. But, by God, I could turn a bunch of dry sticks into a beautiful decoration. The walls needed me. The furniture was in want of my hands. I could take an ugly stone partition and turn it into a wall worthy of the temple. Paint and plaster, wood and wax, dried cumin and camphor shoots, these became the working tools of my well-being. The house became my salvation. As frustrated as it often made me, I found more peace in it than pain.

That's what I had come to.

I remember the remarkable day.

Joseph wanted to spend the evening studying; I wanted the screen door fixed. This was the clashing of the Titans. Scripture was the furthest thing from my mind, and the screen door, to Joseph, might as well have occupied some other universe.

"It's off the hinge, Joseph. How long do you think it will be until it falls off the frame completely? Perhaps you are conducting an experiment to find out?"

"It still works," he said. "It still opens and shuts, doesn't it?"

"It wobbles," I said. "And it looks terrible. The screen is peeling up at one end. Can't you see that? Are you blind?"

I had pushed him too far.

"What about *me*?" he shot back. "Can't you see that *I* might be peeling up at one end? Can't you see that maybe *I'm* about to fall off the frame? God, Mary. You care more about the screen door than you do about me."

"Oh. Sorry. Off to your books, then. If you'd spend half the time living the truth as you do studying it, maybe I would actually get something done around here."

"Is that it? I'm required by God to provide you food, shelter, and clothing. And I do that—and more. I support you emotionally. I never forget our anniversary. I work hard for you. Do you think I like sweating in the shop every day? Do you really think I like fixing carts? Don't you stop to think that maybe being stuck in the grand metropolis of Nazareth and taking care of you and the kids isn't exactly my idea of a dream life?"

"Oh. Now it's coming out."

"Nothing's coming out. Do you know why the screen door isn't fixed? Because I'm out playing with the kids. Or I'm studying. Or I'm working my *ass* off. I told you I'd fix it when the cart orders slow down. I told you. But no. That's not good enough for you. You have to have it fixed yesterday. I think your priorities are in sorry shape."

I was becoming teary. "I just want you to respect what I want, that's all. Is that too much to ask? Can't you care about what I care about for one second? I'm sorry I depend on you so much, I really am. If you made more money, I'd hire the job done."

"Okay. Here we go again with the money."

"It's not about the money."

"It's not? It sounds like it's about the money to me. I think that's what would really make you happy. That's the answer, isn't it? It's the answer to all your little troubles.

Go ahead and deny it like you always do, but that's what's important to you. If I could just make more money, then you could have a house like Wallace's. Or your parents'. Or the Dels'."

"Do you really think I'm that shallow?"

"Oh, absolutely."

"*Fuck* you, Joseph!"

"Oh, that's nice. Good one, Miss Spiritual. Sorry I study God's Word so much. How about this screen door? Why don't we just fuck *it?* Is that what God wants us to do?" And Joseph walked over to the door, grabbed it calmly on either side with both hands, wrenched it from the frame, held it over his head, and threw it into the yard.

I ran up to the bedroom, wailing. Joseph ran after me. I tried to slam the door but I caught Joseph's wrist in it.

"Ow! I will not let you lock yourself in here."

"Go away!" I cried. "I hate you!"

"But I don't hate *you*," he said.

I threw myself onto the bed, face down. Joseph tried to lay next to me and put his arm around me, but I pushed him away. Hard. "Get your hands off me!"

"No, Mary. I want my hands *on* you." He got off the bed and the next thing I knew, he had grabbed me by my waist and turned me onto my back. I was looking up at Joseph's face through my tears. He was straddling me and had my shoulders pinned to the bed. "Let me go!" I shouted at him again. He released me. As soon as he did, I reared back and slapped him. He did not move, nor did he turn. I slapped him again on the same side of his face, harder, rolling my hips beneath me to hit him flat-on. Still, he did not turn away. Again, I rolled my hips and slapped him. I would flay him alive. But his eyes only glazed, as if he had not felt the blows at all.

He was breathing harder now, and he pinned me with his hands again, only this time by my wrists, which were now above my head. I did not even try to push him away; I could not have. I was trembling in my stomach, and then, strangely, down in my sex. I felt my nostrils flare, and my chest heaved vainly at the air.

Joseph lowered his body onto mine and started biting my neck. Before I could cry out, his tongue came up the side of my face and entered my mouth. I heard myself make a small noise, like a hurt bird, but then felt myself sucking his tongue desperately, as if trying to draw milk from it. I felt myself spreading apart against my will. Joseph reached down and shoved my skirts to my waist, leaning hard against me as if desperate to impregnate me. I pressed against this violation and strangled it with my hips—but then drew it deeper. I heard a small voice I had never heard before, coming from my own throat: "*fuck*, my little baby; oh, *fuck*, my little baby…" I could not stop saying it.

Then, it was as if a needle began pricking my inner flesh-folds. Again I cried, because there was a terror behind the needle, a terror I did not know. I pinched down hard on it, trying to stop it. But I could not stop it. A demon opened my mouth then, or a god, or a demon-god, and sounds came forth that seemed not to be human. I shook the demon-god with all my being. I tried to force it away with my hips, but the more I shook it, the more it came. The room began spinning then, and disappeared in shades of red. I was dimly aware of a multitude of violations. The violations widened me, then pushed my skin and mouth through the opening of my throat.

Something happened then. A honeysweet pleasure, unendurable in its sweetness and its waves, washed over me. My throat and tongue cried out against it to God, to man, to the devils. A handful of worlds began spinning, like globes in a pristine glass, making sounds like glass and then more glasses, spinning upon cut glass.

I did not know where I was.

Eventually, the spinning slowed. One by one, the worlds decelerated. I waited in a half-world; it happened so magnificently, dying, as from a dream coming out of the sky. The worlds dissolved and returned me to my bed. Joseph was still on top of me. The sun shone in our room. It was a Friday. The boys were at Mother's. My husband's back was dripping wet. I was dripping wet. The world I knew was still returning to my consciousness at a dream-like pace. "Am I back?" I asked. "Oh, my God. What happened?"

"I don't know," Joseph said. He was kissing my neck so gently. "Where did you go?"

"I went away," I said. "Far away."

And Joseph said, "It's a good place."

At that moment, I wanted desperately to believe him.

CHAPTER 20

DEDICATIONS

Three significant things happened late in Jesus' second year, around the time of Dedications. Melchior's report arrived in the mail on a Thursday afternoon, while Mary was at her parents' with the boys. I had stopped waiting for it; it had been nearly three years.

The pages—nearly twenty pages of thick papyri in the faultless script of the Magus's hand—came in and out of my own hands. I knew I was reading a miracle. The miracle was that this was my heart and soul, recorded on papyri with the weight of scholarship. I stopped only to pace the room and cry.

A storm approached Nazareth that afternoon, and the wind blew remarkably. When I had finished the report and verified its findings (more on this later), I went up the road against the wind to see Mary. I had to go to El-Bekkers with her; I *had* to. I posed the "question" as soon as I saw her ("Let's go to El-Bekkers"), and she wanted to go. So we left the boys with her parents and walked there.

Because of the wind, we could barely talk on the way. Then it started to rain. We ran in a dash of mad laughter to escape it, the weather intensifying everything beautiful about Mary.

El-Bekkers was especially a haven for us that day, and it did what it always did to us, with its green and stucco protections.

"God did not take a rib from Adam to make Eve," I said. "I know it's what we always thought, but it's dead wrong. I realize now how ridiculous it is. Coffee?"

Mary smoothed her napkin into her lap and told me to slow down. She didn't know what I was talking about. I told her what I had asked Melchior in Bethlehem. She said, "Who's Melchior?" and I reminded her he was one of the magi. As soon as I said "magi," her mood changed. I'd forgotten how much she hated the magi, because of Herod. And yet we were here, now, because of them.

"Anyway," I said, "his report arrived today." She shrugged.

I decided to order us wine instead of coffee, but neither of us drank it.

"Our common translations are wrong," I persisted. "Nothing new about that, eh?"

She nodded no. Or she may have nodded yes. Or someone may have placed menus in front of us.

"What did you say about a rib?" she finally asked. "You say it wasn't a rib?"

"Right. The word Moses used there was *tsela*. If it had been an anatomical rib, he would have used the word *ala*. But he used *tsela*."

A waiter came—a waiter I didn't know—and I ordered baked fish. Mary ordered a T-bone and mushroom soup. She chose her potato topping and did manage to ask, when the waiter had left, "What about it?"

"Well get this. This word—*tsela*—it's the same word Ezekiel used for the sidewalls of the temple. But these were actually rooms, not walls. Right? They were hollow walls, technically. They stored stuff there. Remember seeing your father's cutaways? The temple was three stories, but the stories were not consistently wide. The rooms at the top story were eight cubits wide, the middle story was seven, and the bottom six. So the rooms tapered from the top story to the bottom. Like this," and I put down the fork I'd been fidgeting with and made a spade-like shape with my thumbs and index fingers, then turned it upside down to show the shape of the rooms.

Mary touched her wine glass and stroked the narrow neck, as if she would drink. But she did not drink. She did stare at the shape, however.

"The translators saw *tsela* and because of Ezekiel they thought of 'sidewalls'. They couldn't get over 'side.' So they took *tsela* to be the location of the thing; they made it 'rib;' they thought it was a thing on Adam's side. The problem is, *tsela* has to do with the nature of the thing—the shape—not the location. Watch out, here's our salads."

The waiter set our salads down and Mary squeezed a lemon slice onto hers. Then she picked through the greens.

"Anyway, this thing wasn't a thing on Adam's side. It was a hollow and angular-shaped thing *in* him. It was shaped like the tapering walls of the temple described in Ezekiel."

Now she looked up. "What was it?"

"It was the womb." I sipped my wine and looked around at the cedar lattice, at all the plants hanging down, green little tendrils from the gods of love. For romance, this was where you wanted to be.

"The *womb?*" she said.

I made the shape again. Again, Mary stared at it. "'And falling is a stupor on the human, caused by Yahweh Elohim, and he is sleeping. And taking is He one of his angular organs and is closing the flesh under it. And Yahweh Elohim is building the angular organ, which he takes from the human, into a woman.'"

"Lines two, ten, and eleven."

"Right. The first book of Moses. But that's how Melchior says the text *should* read. And he's got tons of proof."

"I've never heard it that way."

"But it's dead on. And it makes so much sense. Listen. God closed the flesh *under* it, not on the side. It's perfect. That's where God took out the womb from Adam, from underneath. Think back to the last time you changed any of the boys. Haven't you noticed that dark line running underneath there? It kind of looks like a scar, right? Well guess what? Every male has it. I checked it on myself, an hour ago."

"You checked?"

"I did it in the bathroom with your hand mirror."

Mary looked at me funny.

"Don't worry, I locked the door. But listen, it was so there. Melchior said it was transmitted to every male because it preceded the initial reproduction. Every man has it, he said. Women don't have it. What else can explain it being there? This...*scar*...is a remnant of the most sublime operation ever performed on humankind. It's proof that Melchior's translation is right."

Mary looked intrigued, but said nothing. Our food came. Stab, devour, stab, devour; my wife's steak diminished quickly. Whenever she paused to rest, she fondled the neck of her wine glass. One time, I thought she would pick up the glass and drink, but she didn't. I wanted my words to sink in, so I left her to the meat. I knew she had to be thinking.

Neither of us spoke. She looked at me occasionally, but could not sustain the look. Her meat and the thin neck of her wine glass comforted her. I understood this. But then the rain stopped (the dull tapping on the roof) and a warmth seemed to radiate from the stucco. I had paused long enough.

"Do you see how much this answers? In the marriage embrace, what does a man long for? Not his wife's rib, for heaven's sake. He longs for what he lost in Eden. So does his anatomy; *it* knows what's missing. It instinctively knows, Mary. Think about it. When Adam saw Eve, he craved her. Right? He's the one who moved, not her. Why? Because Eve didn't lack. Adam lacked. Can you picture it? Adam moved toward her. Something had been taken from him, and God built it into this marvelous creature—his wife. Eve wondered, I'm sure, why the man was coming to her. All she knew was that this hairy being that somewhat resembled her was staring between her legs and breathing heavy. It was Adam who moved, not her. Here's why: Nothing was taken from her. She didn't lack. Men have been chasing women ever since. Haven't they? Men go crazy after women, not vice-versa. We need you more than you need us, you have to admit that. Why don't women chase men, can you explain that? I can—now. This is the answer. God pulled you away from us. He took our beauty, our brains, our compassion, our honesty—He gave it all to you. He took our most refined qualities and gave them to you. He took the organ essential to life and gave it to you. I tell you, this explains everything. Especially worship."

She actually did pick up her wine glass then, and put it to her lips. I watched as the red liquid moved to the edge of the glass.

Sun replacing night—it's so obvious to me now. The sun rising every day is God's picture of resurrection following death. No one needs an advanced education to appreciate it. The whole world sees it, but how many truly read it? Few, but it doesn't matter. It testifies. Somewhere deep in the liver or the heart, humanity suspects truth because of it. And God repeats the picture every single day of our lives. *Sunrise.* Get it? *Sunrise.* Get it? *Sunrise.* Get it?

Shamat rules our world like the sun rules heaven. This moment, everywhere on Earth, passions run. Breasts are wetted, sweating bodies rise and fall, biles ascend into mouths to ecstasies of *Oh, God!* There! Did you hear it? Why do people call upon their Maker at the height of sexual ecstasy? Because deep down, humanity knows. Somewhere deep down, it knows. Man moving to woman is a picture of humanity and God—of how humanity moves as a race toward Him.

The sexual climax is a parable of arriving home, of how it will feel when we finally leave this earth to rejoin Him. *It will feel so good.* The sexual climax is so dim a picture, I know. It goes away so fast, but it's still a picture. How else do you explain it? God didn't have to do it this way. He could have made it emotionless. He could have made *shamat* a soulless transaction. He could have grown babies up from the ground like potatoes. But He put men and women together and made it feel like heaven. Why? Because God has not left us bereft. He has given us a parable of what oneness with Him will feel like. *Oh, God!* Get it? *Oh, God!* Get it? *Oh, God!* Get it?

The energy of the sexes is lack in sight of fullness—just like us and God. The male anatomy responds to the aching contrast. Through woman, God returns man to his completed humanity. In the marriage embrace, humanity is whole again. The two puzzle pieces—separated at the genesis of humanity, if you will—rejoin to form the full picture. When man is fulfilled in woman, then woman is fulfilled. When that happens, both man and woman move together toward mutual fulfillment in God. But sexual energy is the picture.

The parable.

I said all this. Mary looked different now. A little calmer. The wine touched her lips. Our eyes came closer together.

"That's why there are two sexes now," I said. "To make the picture. It won't be this way in the resurrection because we won't need the picture then. But for now, one gender has to worship, the other must receive. It has to be this way, for the parable. Even the anatomy is correct; the male goes outward toward the woman, but the woman goes inward, toward herself. See how perfect it is? Everything goes toward the woman."

This is what I had been subtly suggesting to her for years about worship. I acted on instinct then, but now I had the science. And the Scripture. God is invisible, so He gives a visible picture of how it will be for humanity to find fulfillment in Him. It's an earthly illustration of divine worship. It's physical, but not sinful. It's so full of health. It's of God. It's the acceptable parable.

"Consider it practice." I said to her. "Practice for becoming one in God. God has given you to me for this purpose. It delights Him. The celestial world looks on and marvels. The whole thing is to prepare us both for our return to Him."

Our booth at El-Bekkers was a tunnel now.

"Mary. You have what I don't. Tenderness, compassion, mercy, beauty. I adore these things." I looked at her deeply. "I've lost so much. You're my restoration. You complete me. Please. Do you believe me? Please say that you believe me."

Mary lowered the glass, her lips glistening. Had she drank? She touched my hand. "I don't know," she said. "I just don't know; not yet."

The second significant thing will be explained to you in Ben's article, which appeared around this time in the *Nazareth Enterprise Review*:

> And now, if I may divert your attention to consider the cat, that marvelous creature of God, a visible embodiment of our own quirks and curiosities.
>
> Animals have souls, our scriptures say, and these connect with ours in mysterious ways. All is of God! And thus with Pharaoh, my four-legged companion.
>
> He had simply wandered onto our property one day, and where he came from, I do not know. I asked, but he did not tell me. He would not reveal it. So I did not push him, but only fed him goat's milk and let him read the newspaper with me whenever he perched on top of my chair. Cats must never be manipulated, you see. They will tell you things when they wish to, when the time is right and something needs said. Otherwise, you must not insist upon it. Theirs is an independent way, the way of spirit. It rests on the timing of God, not man.
>
> His gentle manners, by the way, made me name him Pharaoh. So now you know something of my sense of humor.
>
> My daughter, Mary, took an especial liking to him. She is fond of all animals, but especially cats. I do think that Pharaoh withheld from me to give to her. Well, she is the better listener.
>
> The thing I wish to know, today, is: Where does God make His plans for us? When is that dreadful moment when His decisions speed from celestial altars to Earth?
>
> I was walking with Mary up the hill from her home this Tuesday last, the day of the storms. Dark storm clouds hid the setting sun. Jagged flashes of lightning lit the sky. Because of this, we were hurried home from our walk.

And there stood Pharaoh in our yard, as though waiting for us. He *was* waiting for us! But then (*God, why?*) the blue light came, from the angels I pray, but I do not know. It encircled him perfectly and terribly, whatever it was, and it glowed like a specter, this light from above. There was a loud snap then, like a spark, and then the light disappeared—but the booming noise common to lightning did not come. Oh, but look! What had happened to Pharaoh, to my precious companion? How could *light* have struck him so? He lay still in the yard. "Oh, *no!*" Mary cried, and she let go of my hand and ran to him.

The sun should not rise while death exists in the world. And yet it does rise. Pharaoh was so light that you barely knew you had him on your lap. In death, his lightness was even more profound and terrible, for now it was heavy. My wife and I, and Mary and her husband Joseph, were soon in the yard together stroking Pharaoh for the last time; long and loving strokes for our friend, the friend of God.

Joseph wrapped him in a blanket and lowered him into the grave he had dug in our back yard. I padded the dirt around my Pharaoh; I did it so carefully. My tears mixed with the soil and fell onto Pharaoh's yellow blanket. I talked to him, as did Joseph. My son-in-law told him that we were no greater than he, that we, too, would follow him to the earth, that he had only gone first. Joseph crushed small clods of soil between his fingers as he cried. In this, Pharaoh was greater than all of us because he had understood these things. Mary told him how much we would all miss him.

And so now you know something deeper about cats. Something more.

At the end of Kislev, we all decided to go to Jerusalem for the weeklong festival of Dedications. Our law does not prescribe this, but we felt led of the spirit to go. The very thought of it brought us peace. It was a time for new beginnings. Dedications pictured this for us, and I think the nature of the festival made us want to experience the lighting of the candles in Jerusalem.

Mary and Marney packed us for the trip.

Our camps at night, on the way to Jerusalem, were happy. Ben and I would make the campfire, Mary and Marney cooked, Jesus entertained his brothers. We all sang hymns at the close of each day and spoke of the future as well as the past. But especially of the future.

The third significant thing happened in Jerusalem, during Dedications. Ben and Marney had reserved a luxury suite for Mary and me at the best inn in Jerusalem where they were also lodged, "the only one with real stone floors," Ben said, "not to mention built-in babysitters down the hall." Cherry tomatoes flourished in the sill boxes beneath our windows (a parable of God laughing), and these we plucked and tossed, catching them in our open mouths near the Mount of Olives the morning after one of the most significant things I had ever witnessed in my life. I had witnessed it once, through a glass darkly, but nothing properly prepares one for the towering reality.

All is still at the moment. (I am still recovering!) But when the spirit blows again, it will be God granting me wisdom to apprise you more deeply of *such* a significant thing. When that happens, it will serve the purpose of helping you through this life, of course. Until then, let the discouraged and disheartened among you know that the darkest evil precedes the greatest good, that night births dawn, and that the female form rises gloriously, indeed, from the leather *begadim* of beasts long dead.

The Macabees delivered our holy places from Syria nearly two hundred years ago. Today, we celebrate this time when the temple was rededicated and the worship restored. Dedications is a time of renewal. It is also called the Festival of Lights. We light one candle each day of this joyous celebration, eight candles in all.

God has delivered us from many enemies, the greatest of which is fear. We fear death, change, the future. It is hard, sometimes, to worship an invisible Deity. God knows this, and in His mercy He has given us each other. In human relationships, I believe, we see a picture of humanity's ultimate relationship to God. This is especially so in the relationship of the sexes. In the sacred union between man and woman abides much power and truth. This power, I believe, is a parable of how God draws all of us to Himself.

This is a deep truth, and I pray that God makes it yours. It is not a truth without pain, but one where the joys and surprises overwhelm and erase the pain. Joseph and I believe it this way. We live it. We imbibe of it. And the surprises have only begun.

About the Author

Sheila Leeds

Martin Zender is known as The World's Most Outspoken Bible Scholar. He is an essayist, conference speaker, radio personality, humorist, and the author of several books on spiritual freedom. His essays have appeared in the *Chicago Tribune*, the *Atlanta Journal-Constitution*, the *Cleveland Plain Dealer*, and other newspapers. He has hosted the Grace Café radio program at WCCD in Cleveland, and the syndicated Zender/Sheridan Show at flagship station WBRI in Indianapolis.
www.martinzender.com

In the popular Christian bestseller, *Every Man's Battle*, Stephen Arterburn and Fred Stoeker warn men they should repress their natural appreciation of feminine beauty for fear of creating a "wall of separation" between them and the Lord. Now, in this outspoken response, Martin Zender and co-author Heidi Colpo break down the dangers of actually heeding that cautionary advice. Using Scripture, common sense, and real-life examples, they challenge you to dig deeper in order to find out what God *really* wants you to know about sexuality.

Even if you haven't read the original book, *The Lie of Every Man's Battle* can free you from guilt and spiritual bondage, as well as help you accept your own sexuality and better understand your partner.

The LIE of Every Man's Battle

How to undo the spiritual damage wreaked upon the sexes by the Christian bestseller.

Martin Zender
Heidi Colpo

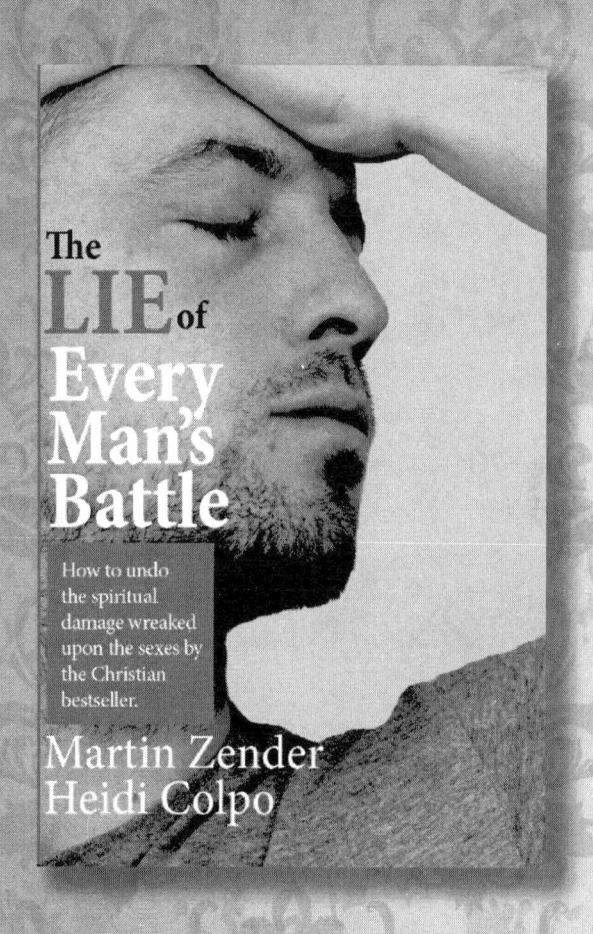

"Let healing between the sexes begin. Zender & Colpo lay spiritual and common-sensical waste to the Christian lie that makes male appreciation of feminine beauty a sin."

—Clyde Pilkington
Author, *Due Benevolence*

464 pages. Published by Starke & Hartmann, Inc. Available at www.martinzender.com

Let the *real* sexual revolution begin.

Read the book that puts the sexual truths discovered by Joseph and Mary into a practical, how-to guide for the modern reader.

www.martinzender.com

"A social, sexual, and spiritual masterpiece. It's the answer."

—Frank Whalen
Republic Broadcasting Network

MARTIN ZENDER

shä·gah

King Solomon's 3000 year-old secret to successful relationships